The ENIGMA GAME

ELIZABETH WEIN

BLOOMSBURY YA
Bloomsbury Publishing Plc
50 Bedford Square, London WC1B 3DP, UK

BLOOMSBURY, BLOOMSBURY YA and the Diana logo
are trademarks of Bloomsbury Publishing Plc

First published in Great Britain in 2020 by Bloomsbury Publishing Plc

A catalogue record for this book is available from the British Library

ISBN: PB: 978-1-5266-0165-0; eBook: 978-1-5266-0166-7

2 4 6 8 10 9 7 5 3 1

Typeset by RefineCatch Limited, Bungay, Suffolk

Printed and bound in Great Britain by CPI Group (UK) Ltd, Croydon CR0 4YY

FSC www.fsc.org MIX Paper from responsible sources FSC® C020471

To find out more about our authors and books visit www.bloomsbury.com
and sign up for our newsletters

For Tina,
my travelling companion

Part One

Odysseus

--- -.. -.-- ... ...- ...

Flight Lieutenant
James G. Beaufort-Stuart:

The night of 6/7 November 1940 – how many of us dead in that raid?

I don't know.

I know nine men in 648 Squadron's A-Flight were killed that night just because of *weather*. Two planes collided in fog just before landing, and one came down heavy with ice. But I don't know how many in A-Flight fell to enemy fire.

How many in B-Flight, then? My own lads … I ought to know that, at least.

But I don't. Not offhand. I'd have to sit and count. I probably made a note in my logbook. That night wasn't the first time we took a heavy loss, and it wasn't the last time. *Buckets of blood*. It wasn't as many as last time. Anyway it's hard to remember all the losses, which for Bristol Blenheim bomber crews was just about every mission, and I get some of the dead men muddled when I try to count. The Royal Air Force isn't going to win the war flying Bristol Blenheims.

I'd argued with Wing Commander Talbot Cromwell before we took off on that mission. That wasn't the first time, either. I knew he didn't like me, and I risked an official reprimand, or worse, a demotion, every time I challenged him. We didn't see eye to eye on *anything*.

'We'll never find German warships if we're flying at twenty thousand feet!' I told my commanding officer. I didn't even try to hide my anger. 'There's no hope in hell of a Blenheim hitting anything from that height anyway. The bomb doors don't always open when you want them to, and up there you can't tell whether a speck out the window is an enemy destroyer or a bit of runway mud stuck on the Perspex!'

'Are you quite finished, Flight Lieutenant Beaufort-Stuart?' said Cromwell, lowering his eyebrows like barrier gates. 'You'll fly at twenty thousand feet, and so will all your men. Orders are orders. That's where Coastal Command wants you to fly. I take my instructions from headquarters and you take yours from me.'

Cromwell and I had been at each other since the day we first came together about two weeks earlier.

He got transferred to us in October when we moved to Shetland as the Battle of Britain came to an end. Our squadron patrolled the North Sea for the Royal Air Force, the RAF, just as we'd done at other bases all through the summer of 1940. But Cromwell's role with 648 Squadron was new. Before he got lumbered with us, he'd commanded a squadron of speedy new Spitfire fighters. In August and September, while we were flying Blenheims under cover of cloud on low-level bombing raids targeting German ships, he'd been sending fighter pilots into soaring dogfights in the sun.

None of our experiences matched up. He couldn't manage twin engines and didn't join us when we flew. And he didn't like it that at nineteen years old I was half his age, shorter and slighter than most of the other lads and barely needing a shave, yet I talked back. He didn't like that all of B-Flight were on my side because they were Blenheim airmen too; maybe I looked like a schoolboy, but they knew I wasn't. I'd been their flight leader since August.

And sending us on a bombing raid with only a half-moon to light us, above cloud at twenty thousand feet? I was reckless with frustration.

'It's stupid, *stupid* – everyone knows it. The men are complaining. *You* know it's stupid. *Above the cloud?* We won't be able to see the sea, let alone ships in the dark! And the air's too thin up there for a Blenheim to operate efficiently. It's not like flying a Spitfire! We cruise best at fifteen thousand feet, and when we're in combat we take it as low as we can, it helps camouflage us. And the Jerries – the German fighters all *know* they can go higher and faster, and they circle like vultures, *waiting*—'

'None of my Spitfire pilots complained about danger,' Cromwell said coldly. 'I expect more of a young man of your calibre, *Beaufort-Stuart*. This sounds like lack of moral fibre.'

Lack of moral fibre – that wonderful euphemism for cowardice.

I couldn't let him accuse me, or worse, my 648 Squadron airmen, of being cowards.

I said stiffly, 'Sir. I'm leading B-Flight on a mission tonight. I want the best for them.'

'When you go in at low level, you get shot up by enemy anti-aircraft guns,' Cromwell told me, as if I didn't know. 'We need to change our tactics.'

It was true that most of our losses came from guns on the ground or at sea level. I couldn't argue with that. But I felt sure that a raid at twenty thousand feet would end in the same tears for different reasons, or at best, be completely pointless because we wouldn't hit anything. It wasn't the first time Coastal Command had tried it.

However, with no winning counterargument, off we went, hoping a few of us would make it back safely in five hours or so. Following orders.

The Blenheims were like a herd of shadowy brontosauri waiting on the airfield in the dark beneath the high cloud.

'Come on, Scotty, buck up,' said David Silvermont, my navigator, as we lowered ourselves in our bulky flight suits through the forward hatch of that night's plane. Being the only Scot in the squadron meant that I mostly hadn't been called Jamie for the past year or so, except on leave. 'We can't have you in a funk, it brings everybody down. The lads take your moods very seriously.'

'Wing Commander Cromwell bloody well doesn't,' I retorted. 'I wish he'd have a go at you sometime instead of me.'

'No chance, as you're the officer in charge. Anyway I am much bigger and older than you, and better looking too and probably smarter, so he doesn't dare.'

'And you have a bigger head than me!' I laughed.

Most of those things were true, as David Silvermont was two years my senior and had been halfway through a medical degree when the war started. But he was also my best friend. He was easy to like and smooth with girls, with the brooding dark looks of a film star, and was good at breaking up fights and at making me laugh. Silver read poetry before he went to bed; he played Mozart on the cracked fiddle he'd found in the officers' lounge when we were off duty; but those highbrow occupations didn't stop him plotting a course by dead reckoning, or spotting enemy convoys, or having a sense of humour.

He was a wizard navigator.

'What's up?' called our air gunner and wireless operator, Colin Oldham, from his place in the back of the Blenheim.

'Just the usual scrapping with Cromwell,' I grumbled. 'Accused me of "lack of moral fibre".'

'Rubbish! He's not flying tonight, is he!' Colin exclaimed.

'I expect he doesn't like your poncey double-barrelled surname,' Silver teased me. 'It reminds the old Roundhead that your dad's the Earl of Craigie, and then he wants to start the Civil War over again. Can't have teenage toffs telling him what to do.'

Colin howled. '"The Old Roundhead"! Suits him!'

'I don't tell him what to do,' I protested, checking the instruments and controls while Silver and Colin belted their harnesses in place. 'I make polite suggestions about what *not* to do. And being the youngest of five sons doesn't mean a thing. They ran out of titles before they got to me.'

'It's your classical education he doesn't like,' put in Colin.

'I'll make a list, shall I? Perhaps if I were taller or bigger or grew a moustache—'

'He doesn't like me much, either,' Silver said with sympathy.

'You both make him feel inferior,' said Colin. 'All that heady talk in the officers' lounge comparing hydraulics to blood pressure. He can't keep up.'

'Hydraulics and blood pressure are endlessly fascinating,' said Silver. He spread his chart on his knees, holding his electric torch ready in his gauntleted hand. He declared with satisfaction, 'From tonight I shall always think of him as the Old Roundhead.'

My B-Flight aircrews knew what we were doing that night – three planes in my own Pimms Section and three in Madeira Section, with three men in each plane. In a few minutes I'd be in the sky in the dark in charge of eighteen men, counting myself, and in a few hours half of them would be dead.

I didn't know then what the full toll of that night would be, and I tried to lighten the tone as we set out. I called over the radio to Pimms and Madeira as we took off. 'Setting course for target and climbing to twenty thousand feet, as per orders from the Old Roundhead.'

Over the intercom I heard Colin behind me laughing again.

'The Old Roundhead might be keeping a listening watch,' Silver warned me.

'I don't mind. I'll get another damned reprimand. He already knows what I think of him.'

We flew obediently high, heading for a flotilla of German warships that was supposed to be cruising fifty miles off the Norwegian coast. After about an hour and a half, maybe we were over the ships we were supposed to hit and maybe we weren't. The sky was clear and blue-black, but the half-moon lit the thin cloud below us like a sheet of milky Chinese silk. I could see the other B-Flight planes standing out in black silhouette like decals against that cloud.

So, too, could the German Messerschmitt 110 night fighters on patrol.

We didn't have lights and neither did they, and we didn't see them coming. They can fly a hundred miles an hour faster than we can. But Silver and I both saw the streaks of green flame as the tracers flew from the first rounds of their thundering guns. And we saw the explosion of golden fire as the bullets struck an engine on another Blenheim in our formation.

Silver opened the observer's panel in the window next to his head and twisted around to stick his nose out so he could see behind us. 'There's one on our tail!' he cried. '*Dive, dive—*'

'Down, *everybody get down*!' I called to my lads over the radio. 'Use the cloud! Get into it or below it where they can't see you! Drop your bombs if you have to, lose the weight—'

I pushed my own plane into a nosedive. Our only hope against an Me-110 was to get away from it. Hide in cloud, camouflage yourself against the earth's surface. For a moment, behind me, I could hear Colin's gun rattling back at our attackers.

In a Blenheim, the air gunner has to sit with his head up out of the plane in a bubble of Perspex like a goldfish bowl on a window sill. The gunner's turret is often the first thing that goes when the Jerries are after you. And that's exactly what happened that night, with a deafening bang that I felt more than heard. *God*. The wind in the cockpit, after our turret exploded, howling around us as we sped towards the black sea below. The mess of blood and bone that had been Colin, all over the inside of the plane and the back of Silver's leather helmet.

That missed me, anyway – I was protected from Colin by the bulkhead between the pilot's seat and the radio equipment.

The sky went small and grey. I was diving too fast – in another few seconds the increased gravity would knock us out.

I must have levelled up somehow.

I skimmed so low over the sea, when I reached it, that the poor Blenheim's tail wheel snagged in a swell and snapped off.

In front of us, seawater erupted like a geyser as someone overhead got rid of their explosives, and I was too close to the surface to turn away from the pluming waterspout. I had to fly through it. We lost windowpanes in the front cockpit and Silver's charts were soaked, but we were still flying on the other side.

We were being bombed by our *own planes*.

We saw two Blenheims go plummeting in flames into the water around us while we struggled away from the waves.

It was the morning of 7 November 1940, and I was so stunned and spent after I landed back at our base in Shetland that I couldn't think. I shut down the engines, and Silver and I sat in silence. We didn't even try to get out.

Then a couple of mechanics climbed on the wing to open the hatches, and Silver looked up. He put a hand on my shoulder and said softly, 'Nice flying, Scotty, as per usual. Thanks for getting us home.'

He'd taken off his gloves to rescue the charts and to use the pencils and flight calculator on the way back. His hands must have been freezing. But he made the same cheesy joke every time we landed safely – he'd be able to play the violin again. He pulled the little box of rosin from his knee pocket, the lucky charm that went with him on every op, and held it between thumb and forefinger with both hands in front of his face.

'Look, everything still in one piece.'

He couldn't *not* say it. He couldn't *not* take the rosin with him. I had a charm too, in the breast pocket of my uniform beneath my flight suit, a perfectly round quartz pebble from the Iron Age hill fort on my father's grouse moor.

'You're welcome,' I croaked.

Our clothes were soaked with seawater and Colin Oldham's blood. It was all over the cockpit, and we had to climb through it to get out the hatch.

Half an hour later I sat down in front of Flight Officer Phyllis Pennyworth, our brisk, chirpy robin of a Women's Auxiliary Air Force interrogator who was in charge of grilling us after a mission – and I got so choked up I couldn't talk. I sat for a while with my elbows on my knees and my head in my hands, and she just let me do that, didn't say anything, knew what was coming – or guessed, anyway.

When I looked up, the pretty pink had faded a bit from her rosy cheeks. She loved us all very much. But in the debriefing room Pennyworth took care to be all business, and this time I was too broken and beat to do my job politely.

'Too many German planes to count,' I told her. 'Bloody Jerries in their bloody Messerschmitt 110s. Those Luftwaffe night fighters. Like a swarm of hornets – they know where we're coming from and what we're after, and they're a million miles an hour faster than us—'

'Not a million, Scotty,' Phyllis corrected me gently. Using my nickname instead of my rank title the way most of my lads did, so that I knew she cared, but reminding me to be precise so she could make an accurate report. She was a stickler for rules herself, and she was scared of the Old Roundhead.

'Might as well be a million.' It came out as a sort of sob. 'These old Blenheims we fly, these airborne buckets of bolts we're in, these crates don't have a chance against a Messerschmitt 110 night fighter!'

And I gave a real sob then, because of Colin.

I didn't tell Phyllis Pennyworth about the mess. She'd seen our busted-up plane – half the glass in the front cockpit punched out, a furrow ploughed in the airfield behind us by our tail because we'd lost the tail wheel, the gaping hole where the gunner's turret used to be. She wasn't stupid; she knew what had happened to Colin. She waited while I tried to pull myself together, and when I still didn't say anything, she sighed and put down her pen and lit a cigarette for me.

I took it and my hands didn't shake. I hadn't lost my nerve – I was angry. Not just at the Germans, our enemy. I was angry at my commanding officer, at Wing Commander

Talbot Cromwell, for being so blind to what we were up against, and at Coastal Command itself, whoever they were, making impossible rules in some comfortable headquarters in England while we bled our lives out in unforgiving sky and sea.

I tried to smoke. Phyllis passed me her ashtray. I was nearly angry at her, too, behaving herself and reporting to them. But she was good at her job, unlike Cromwell; she'd been with us since June and she knew us well.

'When we fly that high the mission is absolutely pointless, but when we come in at a low level to bomb the German ships, we get shot up by their anti-aircraft guns,' I said bitterly. 'I just want an advantage, you know? I want to know where their submarines are, or if there are night fighters about, before they're on top of us. Some wee thing. *One thing* that we can do better than the Germans. One surprising smack in their faces.'

'We stopped the invasion,' Phyllis said. 'You helped too, two months ago when we were fighting the Battle of Britain. We made them back off. That was a smack in their faces.'

'Now they're bombing our cities to blazes – that's not backing off!'

'We all want revenge,' Phyllis said softly.

That surprised me a little. I didn't think of earnest, diligent Flight Officer Pennyworth as someone who had unwholesome emotions that might involve a thirst for blood. I glanced up at her, thinking she might be offering mechanical sympathy to another shot-down airman – or I suppose I should say *shot up*, not *shot down*, as I'd managed to bring the crate back and land it in one piece.

Her eyes were red and her mouth was set in a stubborn, steely pout. I guess Flight Officer Pennyworth got the job partly because she didn't cry easily. Maybe she did want revenge.

'We'll win,' Phyllis said firmly. 'We'll keep fighting, and someday we'll win fair and square.'

I'd let my cigarette go out. I dumped it in the ashtray. What had Cromwell told me?

We need to change our tactics.

'I don't want to win fair and square any more,' I said through my teeth. '*I want to cheat.*'

Louisa Adair:

Daddy said I lost my Jamaican accent in one year. *One year* at the rather posh London school where my mother taught music, and I had a polite accent I'd picked up from my schoolteachers. I didn't even know it was happening. There wasn't any other obvious way to blend in, with my light brown skin and springing dark brown hair, tamed into plaits by Mummy and then into tight rolls by me when I got older. 'Me boonoonoonoos country gal is turning into a little English lady,' Daddy teased. But it stopped the other girls from teasing.

In November 1940, my polite English accent came in useful.

I was fifteen years old and both my parents were killed in a single month by German explosives, Mummy in an air raid and Daddy in a sea battle, thousands of miles apart. My school closed because of the Blitz even before Mummy was killed, but I was old enough that I didn't need to stay in school anyway. Now I was stuck by myself in Mummy's rented attic room surrounded by falling bombs. Our elderly landladies looked in on me and made sure I didn't starve, but all I did in the first shocked horrible weeks after Mummy's death was bury my nose in books whose orphaned heroines got happy endings.

I reread *A Little Princess*, *Jane Eyre*, and *Anne of Green Gables*, but my literary friends began to feel disappointing. They didn't have to cope with air raids. Nobody was rude to them for being foreign. Sara Crewe was born in India and spoke Hindustani, but she still *looked* English. When people shooed her away it wasn't because she was brown.

I had a bit more money than Sara Crewe or Jane Eyre or Anne Shirley, that was true. There was twenty-five pounds in Mummy's post office account. But it wouldn't last forever. I had to have something to do when it ran out, or I would end up living in an air-raid shelter on an Underground platform. The only person I could go to was Granny Adair, Daddy's mother in Jamaica, and how was I going to get back to Jamaica, past the U-boats and destroyers? The *City of Benares*, full of evacuated children, was torpedoed by a German submarine in September!

I knew I couldn't go back. We'd moved to England when I was twelve, and I knew, because of the dustbin of rubbish true facts in the back of my head, that I could not live with Granny Adair. I'd have to earn my keep there by picking up stones in her tiny field of sugarcane, or herding her goats.

At best, taking in washing, which in the Jamaica bush means scrubbing sheets in the river and walking six miles with a laundry basket on your head. Three years in London had ruined me for such a life. No, if I am honest, it was Mummy's fault, with music lessons and library books and her pretty tailored suits. Even in our Jamaican bungalow we'd had a piano and a veranda and a little garden of English roses. And we *left* Kingston because Mummy was afraid of the workers' strikes and the Caribbean riots. Daddy grew up in the bush, but he went to sea when he was fifteen.

At *fifteen*! My age in November 1940. You can do that if you're a boy – even a West Indian boy can do that. The rules won't let any kind of girl do that. And I was a West Indian girl.

What can a West Indian girl do at fifteen?

A girl whose parents are both killed by enemy action and who burns, *burns* to fight back? A schoolgirl with no skills who stands in the street watching the vapour trails of the fighter planes and wants to be up there with them so badly that it *hurts*?

Some of those children on the *City of Benares* were rescued from the sea. They were the ones who hung on, who fought to stay awake in the cold water and who wouldn't let go of the wreckage that kept them afloat.

I am like those children. Not the ones who sank. The ones who *fought*.

Rules are made to be broken, Mummy always told me. She believed that you can get away with breaking rules if you are polite about it, and underneath her cultured British charm my mother was the boldest of rule-breakers, a white

Englishwoman who married a black Jamaican. But she was carefully polite. That's how she got around our landladies in London, with harp music and flute music and smart, stylish hats. Mummy had always been there to protect me from the rules. Now I was going to have to break them on my own.

I had to find work. At my age it wasn't going to be war work, but I had to pay rent and buy food. Sensible positions such as 'salesgirl in record shop' and 'music teacher's assistant' weren't the answer because time and again people made it clear they didn't want to hire someone with a tropical complexion, even a pale one – light brown, dark brown, it was all the same to the English. 'The Caribbean sun makes people lazy,' explained one well-meaning person as she turned me away.

And Mummy had trained me so carefully to be polite that I *thanked her* as I left.

Afterwards I sat on a bench by the Serpentine and cried.

But then I found Nancy Campbell's notice in the newspaper. Her old aunt Jane needed someone to look after her; I had to ring a number in Scotland to ask about it. And that was perfect, because over the telephone I was able to get around the rules by invisibly using my most practical, useful skill – my polite English accent.

I was surprised at how quickly my plan worked. Nancy Campbell, whoever she was, seemed ready to snap me up straightaway.

'You must be tidy, and able to make travel arrangements by yourself,' she told me. 'I'll send the rail fare if you're willing.'

It seemed too good to be true.

'But haven't you other people applying as well?' I asked.

'I'll accept the first suitable candidate who wants the position. I've lost count how many lasses have rung me, then changed their minds – oh, twenty, at least. No one wants to be seen with Aunt Jane, and that's the truth.'

'Is she West Indian?' I blurted, before I could stop myself.

'No,' said the Scotswoman. 'She's German.'

German!

'She's suspected of being a risk to national security,' the woman on the phone continued grimly. 'She has to be collected from an alien detainment camp on the Isle of Man.'

A risk to national security in an alien detainment camp!

Worrying I'd hang up on her, Mrs Campbell rushed to give me more information. 'My aunt's what they call "category C", a low-risk prisoner. She broke her hip last summer, hillwalking at eighty-two, silly woman! She needs help getting about. Not heavy lifting, just minding … and keeping her out of my way, to be honest. I have the pub to manage, and I can't look after an invalid. Aunt Jane is far too old to be locked up like a criminal anyway, though that's her own fault for lying about her age – she told the policemen who arrested her that she was sixty! And how she pulled off such a devilish falsehood, I can't tell you. I've a mind she *wanted* to be arrested – attention-seeking Jezebel! But the government's releasing quite a few folk they detained earlier this year. Most of them are Jewish and not Nazis at all, and people aren't happy about imprisoning folk the way the Germans do.'

Mrs Campbell paused for breath.

'Why did they arrest her?' I asked cautiously. 'Besides her being German?'

'She was a telegraphist. She worked five years in a wireless exchange in Berlin when she was a girl, sending Morse code, before she became an opera singer.' Mrs Campbell added hastily, 'But that was more than sixty years ago, in the *1870s*. Before the telephone – plenty of young ladies did the same! It's not as if she was Mata Hari, taking messages and spying in the Great War!'

A telegraphist and an opera singer! Morse code! I thought the old woman might turn out to be quite interesting. And I wasn't scared of an old woman, even if she was German. I *liked* old women. I liked our landladies, who were kind to me when Mummy and Daddy were killed. I liked Granny Adair.

Mrs Campbell elaborated, 'Aunt Jane's no blood relation, you understand. She's my father's brother's wife. They lived a wicked bohemian life, Uncle John and Aunt Jane, in the last century – Berlin, Vienna, Paris. She was famous the world over, to hear her tell it. Her real name is Johanna von Arnim, though she's Jane Warner now.'

'How is she? Can she walk?' I tried to think of any information I needed before the money for the phone call ran out. 'Did she live alone before she broke her hip?'

'Yes, she had a flat in London,' said Mrs Campbell. 'Uncle John had a long lease on it which expired ten years ago, and afterwards the landowner rented it to them year to year. But Uncle John's dead now, and Aunt Jane's let the flat go and has no place to live. At *eighty-two*! What am I to do with an eighty-two-year-old invalid who's made her living in music halls – put her behind the bar? Oh – and you must be quiet about her being German. The pub is next to a Royal Air Force base, and the bomber lads often come here when they're not in the air.'

'Does your aunt speak English?' I asked.

Nancy Campbell huffed at the other end of the telephone line. 'Aye, did I not say? She married a Scotsman – they kept a London flat for fifty years! Of course she speaks English.'

I took the job over the telephone without the desperate Nancy Campbell seeing me. She was easily persuaded when I told her that Mummy had been a music teacher, and that I could play the flute and the piano. Mrs Campbell thought her operatic auntie would like to have a musical companion.

So I filled a pasteboard suitcase with books and sheet music, and a larger one with all the winter clothes I could cram into it. I said goodbye to the landladies at Number 88, Gibraltar Road, in Tooting. Then I started on my first journey all alone across the British Isles.

That journey passed in a swirl of November leaves and rain outside moving windows: train to Liverpool, overnight ferry to the Isle of Man, and another train to Rushen Camp, grey and wet, in a seaside town surrounded by barbed wire. I kept my nose in a book or pressed against the window the whole way, being polite to everyone, ignoring the stares, avoiding looking at anybody – just the way Mummy had always done when we went out together.

The prison guards were social workers, Society of Friends

volunteers, they said. A young woman wearing a patched cardigan, with her hair tied back in a school ribbon, led me up the stairs in a Victorian guest house converted into barracks. 'Are you from East Africa, perhaps? You do speak English very well. Was it difficult to pick up?'

She was as nice as possible, but annoyed me by asking the same old stupid questions, which I answered politely as usual.

'I'm from Jamaica. My mother was English.'

'Oh, Jamaica, even further! Don't you mind the cold? Here we are.'

She didn't give me a moment to answer about whether I minded the cold or not. She knocked and opened a door.

'On you go.' She waved me ahead of her.

I stepped into the room and came face to face with Johanna von Arnim.

The old woman sat swaddled in a mothy wool blanket. There were no curtains in her small room, which was filled entirely by the chair and bed and wardrobe. The window glass was slabbed with dark blue paint and tape because of the blackout, so that German bombers wouldn't see a light on the ground at night. The window was open to let in daylight, and the air inside was as cold and damp as outside.

Johanna von Arnim stared at the Friends volunteer with cool, pale blue eyes. Then she turned those eyes on me, and they widened in surprise.

I held my breath, ridiculously expecting her to say something in German.

Instead, she sang an English singing game.

'"*Who shall we send to take her away?*"'

Her voice was *amazing*. It was a rich, fruity mezzo-soprano, perhaps a little quavery with age, but not at all weak or thin. The song filled the room. When she stopped singing, the air seemed to hum with the memory of it.

I used to play 'Nuts in May' too, outside my primary school in Jamaica, holding hands with my friends in a circle beneath the Bombay mango tree. So I sang to her in reply.

'"*You'll have Miss to take you away!*"'

My own voice embarrassed me. It sounded like a tin whistle following a golden flute.

The old woman's parchment skin crinkled around those pale blue eyes into a silent laugh.

'Here I am,' I said. I held out my hand for her to shake.

'Which corner of the British Empire do you come from, my dusky maid?' she asked, shaking hands politely.

'Jamaica. I grew up in Kingston,' I said. 'My mother was English.'

I waited for her to compliment my English or ask me if I was cold, but she surprised me.

'Is that a flute you're carrying?' she asked. 'Do you play?'

I'd left my cases at the camp headquarters, but I had the flute on its strap over my shoulder. 'A bit,' I said cautiously.

Mummy would have told her I didn't like to practise. I didn't want to admit this right away to a professional opera singer. Or to the only person who'd started out by showing as much interest in my flute as in the colour of my skin.

'Frau von Arnim, this is Louisa Adair.' The woman from the camp office introduced us. 'Louisa can help you pack.'

'I don't want help packing,' said Frau von Arnim. 'My things are my own business. But I shall need assistance to get to the bank to collect my furs.'

'Your furs are at the bank?' I echoed.

'Yes, of course, we're not allowed locks. I don't trust that damned Nazi Ella Fiesler across the passage, and there are three children downstairs who stain everything they touch. They're not Nazis – they're just children. I cannot keep their sticky paws off my gramophone. If that martinet of a commander would allow us to listen to the radio they might be less trouble, but as it stands, my gramophone is the only entertainment in the house. Open the wardrobe – you'll see. Go on, girl, don't stand there staring.'

Not only could she speak English, but her English was flawlessly proper. She sounded like a radio announcer. Like a duchess. Like the Queen.

She watched me as a cat watches a bird, hungrily. I opened the wardrobe.

There was the gramophone, and next to it was a stack of records higher than my knees. Gowns bloomed like hibiscus and oleander on the rail, pushed to the back so she could reach the gramophone.

'Well, Louisa, now you've met Johanna von Arnim, help her to her feet,' said the young woman from the camp headquarters. I thought she must be evaluating me.

I clasped Frau von Arnim by the forearms and braced my heels while she pulled herself up. She was a good deal heavier than she looked.

'The coat, and then the sticks – ugh, dreadful things, I look like an old spider,' said Frau von Arnim. 'And my bag beneath the pillow. The passbooks are behind the notes for one of the Django Reinhardts, I forget which.'

'Pardon?'

'In the record album,' she explained impatiently. 'At the bottom, beneath the frocks. That damned Nazi Ella Fiesler would never pick up a jazz record.'

Frau von Arnim got down the stairs by herself. I was relieved that she could manage stairs, but goodness, they seemed to take *forever* – she did them one at a time. The volunteer and I came down behind her. I carried her walking sticks, wondering if I should have gone first to break her fall if she went plummeting forward.

'You must have very strong arms,' I said.

'I have, girl,' she agreed.

And then a long plod to the bank, where we collected a mountain of furs. The Society of Friends woman came with us, watching how I got on. Frau von Arnim, frowning with hostility, examined each piece of fur and signed for it.

'I shall be withdrawing my savings, as well,' she announced with queenly pomp.

That was more complicated, and the bank manager took her into a private room to sort it out.

This left me alone with the detainment camp volunteer.

She grasped my arm and pulled me away from the bank manager's office. She glanced about to be sure none of the clerks were listening, and then she spoke to me quickly, with her voice carefully lowered.

'Thank you for coming for Frau von Arnim,' she said. 'She should have been released over a month ago, and frankly she ought never to have been sent here in the first place. It really is too bad! She's well aware of why it's taken so long for her niece to find someone to help her travel. There's nothing worse than knowing nobody wants you.'

I nodded. I thought I understood that.

'Do keep a careful eye on her, won't you?' said the social worker. 'That fall she had on the cliffs was providential, if you ask me. We think she was planning to throw herself over the top when she made it to the edge.'

It took me a moment to realise she was serious.

Oh, heavens, did Nancy Campbell know *that* about her aunt? If she did, she'd been a bit secretive about it.

'Frau von Arnim has always been very unhappy here,' the camp volunteer explained, seeing my wary expression. 'The Rushen Camp women are allowed to go about the town freely, to the shops and the cinema and such, but Frau von Arnim would keep doing things we had to put a stop to. Bathing in the sea naked – at her age! Playing records at three o'clock in the morning, purposefully hiding library books when they were due to be returned. Tossing out other people's post! She'd say it was an accident, but she always picked out the ones belonging to people she didn't like. And then there would have to be consequences, so she wasn't allowed on the beach, or to the library, or to speak to the postman, and we had to move her three times in four months, and her gramophone got taken away for a bit … just constant scrapping with *everybody*. And it always ended in us having to treat her more and more like – like—'

I was sure she was going to say *more like a prisoner*, but she surprised me.

'More and more like a very elderly woman indeed.'

The social worker paused. She had me by the arm, as if she expected me to try to escape. She searched my face, no doubt wondering if I understood her.

I thought of Frau von Arnim's whacking great lie about her age. I put that together with what I'd seen of her in the past hour: stubborn, independent, regal and elegant, with a voice like a nightingale and a cupboard full of jazz records. She was still looking for adventure. Perhaps when she was arrested she imagined a few nights in prison before someone discovered how old she was – perhaps she imagined she would charm her guards with song, and then there might be outraged news headlines about her brave spirit and the injustice of her arrest, and people would remember her operatic past. Retired, perhaps, but not *old*.

A rule-breaker, just like Mummy.

Just like me.

'And now that she can't walk properly, of course she *does* have to be treated like an old woman,' the social worker finished.

'I expect she'll cheer up once she's off the island,' I said.

'I expect she'll cheer up now she has you to order about,' replied the social worker, at last letting go of my arm.

She smiled at me. Then she ruined it by adding ominously: 'Do take care that Frau von Arnim isn't allowed to hurt herself again.'

We had one last visit to the camp office. I was to be the Official Keeper of Documents, and there was a brief argument over my suitability for the job.

'Miss Adair is perhaps rather, um, perhaps too *young*?' said someone. 'To be entrusted with such responsibility, I mean.'

'I don't believe the commander would approve,' said another. 'Not if she saw the girl herself.'

'But she *hasn't* seen the girl,' protested Frau von Arnim, who was ready to leave.

What a stupid argument! I was sure it had nothing to do with my youth and everything to do with my skin colour.

I said, in my best English accent, 'I should think it will be rather difficult for Frau von Arnim to manage her walking sticks and her papers at the same time.'

In the end I was put properly in charge, with sheepish excuses as the Society of Friends people avoided looking me in the eye. But they apologised by making a bit of a fuss over Frau von Arnim before she left, and me as well, feasting us with scones slathered in jam and butter. 'There's no rationing here!' somebody told me. 'People on the mainland are envious when they find out how well the detainees eat. But we can't let it go to waste, can we? And we're not allowed to send any foodstuffs off the island. You must guzzle as much as you can before you go!'

I studied the documents they'd given me so grudgingly. It said *Johanna von Arnim* on the old woman's passport and her ration books and release papers. Hadn't Nancy Campbell told me her aunt was called Jane Warner now? But everyone in Rushen Camp called her Frau von Arnim. I wasn't sure how to keep her Germanness quiet, as Mrs Campbell said I should; or even what to call her.

*

The mainland ferry set sail for Liverpool, and I sighed with relief as I unwrapped the sandwiches I'd bought at a kiosk on the pier in Douglas. (*Roast beef!* I hadn't tasted beef that wasn't out of a tin since the war started.) Taxi, rail station, taxi, ferry, loading and unloading everything at each stop, helping Frau von Arnim in and out of vehicles and up and down from platforms – hauling all the travelling cases along with us again, hers full of record albums and mine full of books. There was the gramophone, too. We had to wear the furs; I felt like a trapper. Had Nancy Campbell suspected the fuss? She must have.

But at last I had a chance to breathe, with a long night at sea ahead. We weren't in a cabin, but the ferry lounge was more comfortable than the train, and Frau von Arnim's furs were incredibly warm and surprisingly light. I had never worn anything so soft. Johanna von Arnim sat straight and elegant in her own beaver coat and fox stole, with her back to the Isle of Man as we steamed away from it. Her thin powder-white hair peeped out beneath her fur hat, and her watery blue eyes gleamed as if they were wet.

'Good riddance to that godforsaken place,' she said abruptly. 'Tell me, my dear, how does a Jamaican schoolgirl end up traipsing across Britain with a released German detainee?'

I swallowed. I hadn't yet had to *tell* anyone about Mummy and Daddy being killed – my landladies were there when it happened, and it was nobody else's business. Mrs Campbell hadn't even asked.

'I needed work,' I said evasively.

'No people of your own to go to?'

'Not here,' I said.

I bent over my cup of tea.

'You're dreadfully young not to have any people,' said Johanna von Arnim.

I didn't want to talk about it.

But I'd just make it worse for later if I was mysterious. It wouldn't be the last time I'd have to tell someone, even if it was the first.

'My parents were killed by bombs last month,' I said. 'In the same week. Not in the same place. My mother, she was called Carrie, Caroline Adair – she – she was riding in the front of a bus that fell into a crater when Balham tube station was bombed. You might have seen the pictures in the papers.'

'No, we aren't allowed newspapers,' the old woman said gently. She cocked her head to favour her left ear, listening carefully over the ferry's engines. 'How terrible, and how unhappy you must be! Were you in the accident?'

I shook my head. This I *couldn't* talk about – that I hadn't been along. I hadn't been there when it happened, I hadn't been there when Mummy was taken away in the ambulance, I hadn't been there when she died all alone in the hospital four days later. No one needed to know that. No one could fix that, and I didn't want anyone to pretend to try.

'My father, Lenford Adair, was a merchant seaman on a ship that was torpedoed three days after my mother died,' I said carefully. 'I didn't find out until about two weeks later. Poor Daddy! I don't know if he knew what happened to Mummy. I sent a telegram, but it might not have reached him. I can't decide if I hope he did know, or if I hope he didn't.' I swallowed again. 'Hundreds of men drowned. He hadn't been let in the Royal Navy because he wasn't born in Europe, but the German U-boats don't seem to care whether it's a navy or civilian ship they're sinking—'

I choked on my words, my face and eyes burning.

'I'm sorry!' I gasped. 'I didn't mean it to sound like anyone who's German—'

'It didn't,' she said. 'And the U-boats don't. Well done, Lenford Adair! Those merchant seamen are just as heroic as the military seamen, even if they're not in battle. I'm sorry they wouldn't let your father in the navy. There's nothing more frustrating than having an open door slammed in your face.'

It reminded me of what the social worker said: *There's nothing worse than knowing nobody wants you.*

'And grief is a burden you can never put down,' said the old woman. 'Though it gets easier to hide. I've been alone for three years. It doesn't feel very long.' She suddenly sounded stubborn. 'It *isn't* very long. It never stops hurting. You learn to bear the pain.'

'Do you?' I asked longingly, caught off guard by her intimacy and kindness.

She shrugged her thin shoulders. 'It depends on where you are and what you're doing.'

The social worker's warning nagged in my head. *Do keep a careful eye on her, won't you? Do take care that Frau von Arnim isn't allowed to hurt herself again.*

We'd finished our sandwiches. The old woman drooped and was instantly asleep, snoring lightly against my shoulder.

I didn't blame her. I couldn't remember ever being so tired in my life. Johanna von Arnim's sleek head pressed against me like a sandbag full of concrete. It hadn't been easy, talking about Mummy and Daddy. I let the tears come quietly and didn't make a noise. It was comforting to have the old woman's head lolling heavy and trusting against my shoulder.

I thought it would be impossible for her to steal off and throw herself into the Irish Sea without waking me up, so I gave up trying to keep my own eyes open.

I recognised the drone of German planes even in my sleep. I dreamed I was standing in Balham High Road back in London, staring at the sky. It was blue and empty, and I wasn't worried about being attacked. I was happy and excited, as if I were going to a party. I could hear the thudding engines all around and I held my breath, longing for the air battle to begin. I couldn't wait to cheer on the Spitfires and Hurricanes as they cut up the sky with their vapour trails.

Then I remembered what the bombers would do to Mummy, and woke myself with a sob.

The engines were real. The German air force, the Luftwaffe, was bombing the Liverpool docks. The ferry lounge lights had been switched off, but the ship steamed onward, with a kind of grim determination that reminded me of Mrs Campbell on the phone.

I jumped up and peeked beneath the blackout curtains. We hadn't far to go, but fire lit the low black land. The ship rocked, and I thought of U-boats and torpedoes. We were helpless. Had Daddy felt this way, waiting for his ship to sink? I couldn't believe it. He must have had a job to do, right up to the instant he was killed.

I thought I would choke to death with wanting to fight back, to join in, to make a difference, to *do something*.

Johanna von Arnim slept peacefully, snoring gently.

Well, *she* was my responsibility. Looking after her was my wartime job right now, and it was too bad if it wasn't very exciting or even very patriotic. I sat down beside her again and sighed. It wouldn't matter anyway if our ship sank on the way to Liverpool.

But mercifully it didn't, and by the time we docked the raid was over. I hauled the cases and gramophone on to land as the all-clear sirens hooted. My wartime job was going to keep me fit, whatever else happened.

We spent hours in the city police station getting her registered, and then in the railway station at Liverpool Lime Street queuing to buy our tickets.

'Identity documents, miss?' the ticket seller asked, eyeing me suspiciously, when I finally got to the front of the line. I felt conspicuous in the fur coat.

Be polite, Lula, warned Mummy's calm, comforting voice in my head.

I gave a false, bright smile. 'Oh – yes, sorry! I haven't had to show ID to buy a rail ticket before.' Of course I hadn't. No one has to. But I dug in my school satchel for my National Registration card anyway.

'Please step aside so you don't hold up the queue,' said the ticket seller coolly.

My heart plummeted as I bit back rising anger. It is hard to stand your ground and politely break rules at the same time. Why hadn't I parked Frau von Arnim with the luggage instead of shuffling everything along in the queue with us? If we lost our place I'd have to shift it all again—

The old woman reached over me with an official-looking booklet open to a smiling photograph of her own face. The ticket seller nodded and pushed the passport back.

'Apologies, madam, I didn't realise you were together.' He smiled at her over my shoulder.

'Well, we are,' said Frau von Arnim. 'Two singles for Stonehaven.' She added in a friendly way, 'We are visiting my niece in Scotland.'

My face burned as the horrid man thumped our tickets with the date stamp. I paid without saying anything.

'Thank you,' said the old woman as we turned away. But she might have been talking to me.

Afterwards we sat in the ladies' waiting room, surrounded by our piles of luggage, until it was time for our train.

'What did you show that man?' I asked. I was supposed to help her with her papers, and here was something she'd kept to herself.

The old woman gave a slow, shy smile, as if she were the one who was a bit embarrassed this time. She handed over the booklet and let me look at it.

It was an ordinary British passport, more ordinary than mine, even, because mine says JAMAICA across the front below BRITISH PASSPORT. The smiling photograph pasted inside was definitely a recent picture of the person sitting next to me – at least, it wasn't taken so long ago you couldn't tell who it was. But the name read clearly, *Jane Warner, British subject by birth.*

It also said she was a musician. And it said she was born in Aberdeen, in Scotland, in 1868, ten years later than the date on Johanna von Arnim's alien registration card.

'You can call me Jane,' said the old woman. 'It's what I call myself.'

I stared at the lying document, then looked up at the person who called herself Jane. The shy smile was gone. She watched me seriously, trusting me with a secret.

'*How did you get this?*' I demanded. It came out sounding very stern, and her thin shoulders cringed a little. Perhaps she was expecting me to take it away from her. That's what they'd have done at Rushen Camp if they'd known about it.

'It was my husband's,' she said defiantly. 'I kept it when he died. It wasn't until I was already locked up in that miserable place that I started fiddling with it. Of course they knew who I was, but I've called myself Jane Warner since the early thirties … And who doesn't look forward to a better life ahead? I thought I should be ready if the chance arose. It was simple to fix – a razor and ink is all it took. Rubbing the raised stamp on to the photograph was the difficult bit.'

She was more of a rule-breaker than I'd realised.

'You really ought not to use it,' I scolded. 'You could get into terrible trouble.'

She laughed. 'What do you think they would do? Put me in prison? At my age? Imagine!'

'It would be worse than the camp,' I argued.

'I was in prison for three weeks before I went to the camp, so I know what it would be like,' she told me.

I gazed at the glamorous smiling face of the elderly, but younger, woman in the fake passport.

'You don't need to show identification papers to buy a rail ticket,' said Jane Warner. 'That man was a bully. He was bullying *you*.'

'I know he was bullying me,' I said. 'People often do.'

I'd been saved by an old German woman! Suddenly I laughed too. 'Stupid bossy official! Aren't there enough rules already? I wish we could report him for making up extra ones.'

'Never mind,' said Jane. 'There's no danger to national security, and we have our rail tickets. If he goes on making up extra rules, the stupid bossy official may get himself in trouble without our assistance.'

I gave her back her husband's doctored passport.

'This is going to expire next year,' I pointed out.

'I'll worry about that next year,' said Jane.

I rang Mrs Campbell from the red telephone kiosk by the bus shelter on the Aberdeen road. That was as far as we could get to the village of Windyedge without having to walk, and Mrs Campbell said she'd arranged for someone to come in a car to collect us.

It felt like the end of the earth. I remembered, in a flash, a time when I'd been very small, following a path in the bush behind Granny Adair's tiny ramshackle house, and suddenly everything seemed strange. I was alone among the giant ferns and banana trees and huge Anansi spiderwebs, and I panicked. I wasn't lost – I shouldn't have been afraid. But I was terrified. I turned around and ran screeching back down the path to Granny Adair's familiar shack and henhouses.

I felt a bit like that now. Only the bus shelter, the telephone kiosk, and a small postbox sunk in a stone wall showed it was the twentieth century. All around were brown winter fields dotted with sheep, a brown hillside wreathed in low clouds, and unhappy blackthorns stooped by sea wind. There weren't even any *signposts*. They'd all been taken down to confuse the Germans if they invaded. Smoke rose from the invisible village down the lane, almost a smell of tobacco, because they were burning peat, not coal – just as they'd done for thousands of years. Beyond the smoke stretched the sea, the cold North Sea.

But Mrs Campbell had said there was an aerodrome nearby, for a Royal Air Force bomber squadron. The airmen came to her pub. Perhaps I'd see some of them there, young British men returning from combat over the North Sea.

The longing I felt when I watched an air battle swelled up in my throat again until it was drowning me. What in the world was I going to do here, or learn to do here, to help win the war? Looking after Jane Warner would keep me from starving, but it wasn't going to lead to anything else, was it?

My chest grew tight with the same kind of panic I'd felt in the green strangeness of the Jamaica bush.

But I couldn't turn around and run screeching home this time.

Neither one of us could.

Volunteer Ellen McEwen:

There's always someone telling you to move on if you're a Traveller. There's always someone calling you dirty or sly, or slamming a door in your face. *Filthy sleekit tinker.* That's what I live with, and not just me, but all my family too. Then the war came along and gave me a chance to be someone different.

It wasn't that folk changed the way they felt about us, mind. It wasn't some la-di-da virtuous 'fighting a common enemy' rubbish. It was just that once I was in uniform, folk couldn't tell where I'd come from.

The war began when I was eighteen, and my twin brother and I joined up at the same time early in 1940. Euan went for a soldier and was sent to France, but a lass like me wasn't going to have to shoot at people. I became a driver for the ATS, the Auxiliary Territorial Service. I was proud to do it, and I had steady wages I could share with my mam and dad if they told me a post office to send it to.

When I finished the training course and was assigned to be the driver for an RAF aerodrome, no one at my new RAF base had the least idea where I'd come from. Scotland, aye, that was clear, but the English erks and airmen didn't know I was a Traveller. I became a gadgy dilly like the other girls, living under a roof and wearing a uniform, and no one but me kent I'd rather be sleeping in a camp tent.

And I kept quiet about it.

At first it wasn't on purpose. But when I realised folk weren't bothered about me, I was careful not to let them know. A fresh start. No need to stir up trouble, aye? There was no women's barracks at RAF Windyedge so I was billeted at the Limehouse, Nancy Campbell's pub in the village, and she didn't bat an eyelash over me staying there. She was just the crabbit sort who wouldn't take well to a fiery-haired, long-legged Scots Traveller lass staying under her roof, but she tolerated me well enough. It was grand being tolerated instead of shunned.

Better than that, at the airfield and in the pub, it was grand being liked by the RAF lads and trusted by their commanders. It's true that Jamie Stuart knew who I was. We were both at RAF Windyedge late in the summer of 1940. But he was an old friend and didn't give my game away. He had his own posh family that he tried to keep quiet about, being the laird's son educated at Eton and all that. My mam and dad used to camp on his grandad's land.

We were lucky to be close by, and I missed him when 648 Squadron went up to Shetland – I worried about him the way I worried about my own twin brother.

But apart from the worry, if I'm honest, the war so far made me grow a mite comfortable in ways I'd never expected. I didn't think about the future – how did anyone? Should I go back to my own folk, would I marry, could I make a living? No one needed to decide any of that now, not when we might all be speaking German in another year! I might as well enjoy myself in my wartime job, enjoy being just the same as other folk.

And then in November 1940, it all turned over. After November 1940, I couldn't be so comfortable.

It started with Nan Campbell asking me to do her a favour on my way back from delivering a load of engine parts to Deeside near Aberdeen. She had two guests arriving to stay at the Limehouse and needed help getting them there. One was Jane Warner, Nan Campbell's ancient auntie, who had broken her hip and had to walk with two sticks. She'd just come out of hospital and had no other place in the world to go. The other was the girl Nan hired to help her auntie make the journey, and to look after her a time. Could I collect them in the Tilly from the nearest bus stop, Nan asked – the Tilly was the Hillman Minx van I had charge of, converted for carrying bags of stuff or a troop of men, with wooden benches in the back under a canvas top. Nan's old auntie had brought piles of luggage and couldn't possibly walk two miles to the Limehouse.

I said I didn't mind, and when I got back from Deeside, there was the old woman waiting with her young assistant at the bus shelter on the Aberdeen road. They did make me laugh, all among their furs and their cases, when I pulled up! They looked like a pair of imperial Russian princesses running away from the Red Revolution.

The hired lassie gave me a surprise, for her smooth skin was the pale brown of milky tea or the inside of a fiddle. I wondered if crabbit Nan Campbell knew she'd hired a black girl. It had all been done over the telephone and in the post, and if this lass was anything like me, she might not have said. It's easiest not to say, if you're trying to get work. Unlike me, she wasn't going to be able to hide her secret for much longer.

She was a pretty young thing, neat and small, with a heart-shaped face that looked a mite fed up at the minute. She wore a sleek black mink coat that shone more glossy than her dark hair, and she had a flute case on a long strap carried over her shoulder. The poor old lady, also bundled in a pile of fur, had fallen fast asleep waiting for me to turn up. She sat perched on one of her cases, bent with her hands clasped together over her sticks, her forehead resting on her knuckles.

I parked the Tilly at the bus stop and got out to help with the luggage. The old lady jerked awake as I slammed my door shut behind me.

I'd only ever spoken to one other black person in my life, and it had been a most uncomfortable conversation. But I was going to have to live under the same roof with this one. I swallowed hard and reminded myself she was just hired help and I was an ATS volunteer. She wasn't going to start by calling me a dirty tinker, and I'd better not start by making her feel like a British Colonies outcast.

'I'm Volunteer Ellen McEwen,' I said, taking great care with it. 'I'm the ATS driver for RAF Windyedge. I also stay at the Limehouse.'

'I'm Louisa Adair,' said the lassie, sharply holding out her hand, like a challenge to fight.

I shook hands with her. Her grip was very firm for somebody so slight and so polite. I made an effort. 'What a bonny coat!' I told her.

'The furs belong to Mrs Warner,' Louisa said, waving the other hand towards the old woman. 'The only way we could get them here was to wear them!'

'How do you do, Mrs Warner?' I said.

'You may call me Jane,' said the old woman, with a look at Louisa that made Louisa smile, as if they were leaving me out of a joke between them.

'Jane it is, then,' I said.

I took a breath and went round the back of the Tilly to drop the tailboard so I could load up the pile of cases. It could have gone worse. Ah well!

'Och, a *gramophone*!' I sang out when I found it.

Piled on top of the biggest leather valise, to keep it off the damp ground, was a portable wind-up record player – a very good one, too, with its own loudspeaker built into a beautiful wooden case. Louisa helped me to lift it into the Tilly.

'That'll liven things up at Mrs Campbell's,' I said. 'You'll be popular with the airmen when the next squadron gets here!'

I was most curious about Louisa's dark skin, but I didn't like to ask. I didn't let people poke their nebs into my business, and I wasn't going to poke into hers. What must it be like, I wondered, never to be able to hide?

I tossed all our gas masks, my one as well, and Louisa's satchel and flute and her own two cardboard suitcases, on top of the luggage in the back, and slammed the door. God pity her, how had Louisa ever managed that lot on her own? She must have hidden pools of strength. I could guess where the fed-up look came from.

It was no easy task getting Jane into the Tilly, either. Her old arthritic knees didn't do any bending, and the seat in the cab was high. She couldn't manage to stand on the running board. Louisa and I had to lift her in feet first – with our arms full of fur, it was like lifting a bear.

At last we managed it, and Louisa climbed in on my side to ride in the middle, and I climbed in behind the steering wheel. Louisa sat right up on the edge of the seat like a tiny tot so she could see over the dashboard.

'And now you are high enough to get a braw view of Windyedge as we come down the lane,' I said to them as I started up the van.

Windyedge Aerodrome sits on top of the moor above the fishing village it is named for, just south of Aberdeen. It has sat there some time, built before the Great War, in the early days of flying. About it runs a proud stone wall, with its good looks all ruined by a high wire fence topped off with barbs. The road follows the wall for a mile and a half, past lookout towers and bunkers for anti-aircraft cannons. The other side of the road is all wind-bent hedge and fields and wild woodland.

I drove through this drearysome landscape as I'd done a hundred times before, one hand resting on the gear stick and the other lightly steering as we passed along the narrow lane. The road was dry, and the clouds seemed far away, high and rippling, a sky like a wide sheet of grey river pearls.

One black spot floated low over the North Sea like a fly on my windscreen.

I blinked.

Not a spot: an aeroplane. Such a totsy wee speck before it became frightening: before I knew how close it was going to get to me.

'That's a German plane,' said Louisa.

'Don't be daft!' I said. 'It's coming in to land.'

'I don't know what kind it is,' she told me. 'But I can tell them apart. I was in London all through the Battle of Britain and the Blitz.'

The plane had wings like blunt butcher's knives, not the tapered wings of our Hurricanes and Spitfires. It screamed in low over our heads.

'That's a German plane,' the lass Louisa insisted. 'It's a *German fighter*.'

'They'd be shooting at it if it was a German plane,' I said uneasily. 'See the watchtower? There are guards there, with machine guns. There's an anti-aircraft battery just below them that you can't see from here, and another at the edge of the cliffs.'

The old woman, Jane Warner, didn't say anything. She and Louisa craned their necks away off their shoulders and swivelled their heads around, trying to see in back of them to watch as the plane landed. But I had to keep my eyes on the road.

We passed the aerodrome entrance and its guards' shed. The lane gives a sharp turn there, heading downhill. Below us now, Windyedge village lowered itself cottage by cottage into its dark and narrow harbour. Down there was a post office playing at being a shop, a handful of cold-looking stone dwelling places whose thatched roofs were tied down with rope so they couldn't blow away, and a Presbyterian chapel behind a shut door, all with small, deep-set windows to keep their inhabitants in a state of eternal darkness. Beyond the harbour lurked a little beach, but you couldn't get to it through bales of barbed wire and concrete blocks that were supposed to keep German tanks and troops from unloading there. It felt like the most unwelcoming place on God's earth in 1940.

You had to go into the village a ways and back up another

narrow lane to get to Nancy Campbell's pub. The pub was perched above a row of four stone arches built right into the hillside, like underground lairs. Heavy oak and iron doors fitted into the archways, and these were soundly locked and bolted to keep folk out.

'Those are limekilns,' I told Louisa. 'Where they used to make lime, for concrete and plaster, back in the day. That's why the pub is called the Limehouse. Then they got used as a prison, for deserters in the Great War, and—'

I shut up my blethering. She didn't need to know that my two uncles had been locked up in those limekilns for a week after they got caught 'trespassing' on the airfield ten years ago, in peacetime – snaring rabbits. That's my family connection to Windyedge. It doesn't fash me – it made my mam split her sides laughing when I told her I was getting paid to work there now. But I wouldn't want anyone to know.

The Tilly whinged and complained as it slowly climbed the steep lane past the old limekilns. Waiting for us at the top of the hill was the hotchpotch of granite walls and blue slate roofs of the Limehouse, like an old laird's castle collapsed into the moor. A few tall Scotch pines tossed their limbs restlessly about above it in the wet wind.

The pub sign was a painting of the four limekiln arches. Louisa gave a shudder as we pulled up in front.

'I expect you'll find Scotland a great deal colder than where you come from,' I said. 'But you'll be warm enough inside. There are gas fires in the bedrooms.'

'I'll be fine,' Louisa answered through tight lips. 'I've only come from London just now.'

I helped to unload the old woman's things, but I couldn't

stop to move them in. I was meant to be on my way back to the airfield, not wasting Air Ministry petrol running errands for Nancy Campbell. As I turned the Tilly to face about so I didn't have to reverse down the lane, I saw Louisa holding the door open for the old woman. I wondered how the brown-skinned lass would cope with Nan when they met for the first time.

Not my lookout, I thought with relief, as I headed back to RAF Windyedge.

I didn't have any idea who was in the plane that had just landed, but I didn't take Louisa's warning very seriously. It was likely some bigwig, or prisoner even, who needed to be shuttled someplace. The airfield staff would miss me right away if they needed me.

Sergeant Norbert Fergusson was standing outside his guard's hut in front of the barrier to the aerodrome drive, watching the sky through field glasses.

I cranked down the window of the Tilly and leaned out. 'What is it, Nobby?'

'Bloody Jerry just landed on our airfield,' he said through his teeth.

Shaness. The oath in Traveller cant hissed in my head, though I'd taught myself not to speak it aloud. Louisa had been right. It was a German plane.

'Why didn't we shoot him on his way in?' I exclaimed.

'The ack-ack lads on the north side gave him a burst, didn't you hear? But then they stopped. He had his cockpit open, waving a big white sheet behind him, and his Luftwaffe markings are all covered up, too. Looks like he means to surrender, or something.'

'Get the barrier up,' I told him. 'They might need me to drive somebody somewhere.'

'Better you than me if there's a bloody Jerry involved,' said Nobby, and raised the barrier.

I went along the gravel drive as fast as I dared. I was in two minds as to whether I ought to hurry in case I got in trouble for not being about when I was supposed to, or to go slowly so I didn't have to meet any German airmen. The Tilly's tyres spat up pebbles behind me. I passed the concrete barracks and the aircraft hangar with its faded green paint, and pulled up in front of the operations building.

There was one plane on the airfield, a great grey ugly thing, wings like knife blades and high Perspex cockpit bulging on top like a giant one-eyed insect.

I could see what it was, up close on the ground. It was a Messerschmitt 109 fighter.

The Luftwaffe markings, German black cross and Nazi swastika, were covered up with white canvas sheets, bound tight and flat with strips of webbing. Two lads from Windyedge's short-staffed ground crew were standing stiffly on guard in front of each wing, holding rifles. There wasn't anyone else about – they'd all trooped into the radio room to talk to the wireless op.

I waved to the guards, but they were taking their job seriously and didn't wave back.

So then I made a great howling mistake.

When I think on it, I don't see how I could have known it was a mistake. I went into the operations building. It had been put up before the last lot, the Great War, one of the oldest ops buildings in the nation, and everywhere was a mite mazy and crumbly inside. I went looking for everybody.

The door to the radio room was open. I heard a low voice talking. When it stopped, I heard the high-pitched nagging bleep and click of a Morse code key.

Standing in the open doorway, where he could see who might be coming down the passage as well as all the folk gathered in the room, was the German pilot.

I foolishly didn't take on who he was.

I thought he was a good-looking lad – tall and clean-shaven, with close-cut, mouse-blond hair. He wasn't in uniform, maybe that's why I didn't guess. He wore a dark blue roll-necked sweater, like a sailor, and a knitted scarf, underneath a long leather coat. He didn't have anything on his head. A leather bag, darker and more worn than his coat, hung on a strap over his shoulder. He stood with his booted feet parked on either side of a small wooden case, like a gramophone.

There wasn't anything about him to tell me he was a pilot, still less an enemy one.

So I came bold as brass to poke my neb in at the door, and he just took hold of my arm – carefully, like a gentleman at a ball – and when I turned to look at his face in surprise, he raised his other hand.

He was holding a narrow black pistol.

He pulled me close against his squeaking leather coat and pressed the muzzle of the pistol firmly against the side of my head.

I could not have been more easily caught if I had been a rabbit in a poacher's snare.

That was the moment when I learned *hate*.

Even more than I feared him, I hated him. I hated all Germans. I was blind with it. I couldn't move nor think, not even to fight.

And I *couldn't* fight, because now I was his hostage.

Jamie:

'Hey, Cap'n, I'm getting another of those bastard Kraut messages in Morse code.'

Chip's voice crackled through my headset over the roar of the Blenheim's engines.

Silver and I had a new wireless op, Chester P. Wingate – Chip for short, or sometimes Tex because he was a full-blooded American from Texas. The USA wasn't at war, but our Tex had come over as a sparks on a cargo liner just as the Atlantic grew dangerous: merchant vessels escorted by destroyers, civilians drowned alongside navy men, passenger lines cancelled. Chip was going home on a ship that was dive-bombed by the Luftwaffe off the South Foreland Light and it went down right under his feet. Chip was one of the lucky ones pulled out of the water, and when he'd dried off, he marched straight to the nearest RAF recruitment office.

He was fluent in Morse code from his radio days at sea, and he was happy to be given a gun, too, so they made him a wireless op/rear gunner. He and I came to 648 Squadron on the very same day in July 1940, but it wasn't until November that we flew together. He'd lost the rest of his crew on that same terrible hop when Silver and I lost Colin. Chip's damaged Blenheim had stalled and nosedived on landing back in Shetland, and his pilot and navigator were both killed instantly. Chip, in the back, had been lucky again.

In fact Chip and Silver and I were all that was left of last summer's Pimms Section. We'd all been lucky before, so we reckoned we'd be lucky together. God knows we needed luck.

On 18 November we were flying reconnaissance. My other two Pimms Section crews were new to me and one of them was completely new to 648 Squadron, and though we were in freshly maintenanced Blenheims, we needed practice at formation flying. We'd been sent out over the North Sea in broad daylight, without a fighter escort. I wasn't happy about that, and of course I'd said so and got told off by the Old Roundhead again for arguing with my superiors.

We had guns ready front and rear, but were generally loaded up with cameras instead of bombs. Now we were overhearing these German transmissions in Morse code from somewhere. The last thing I wanted for my new flight section was to run into German planes.

'How many does that make?' I asked Chip. Behind me in the cramped gloom of the aircraft's body, perched in his bulky flight suit at the radio set, Chip had been reporting them for the last hour.

'Fourteen. Got five of 'em all at once last time.'

'In code?'

'No, in *Kraut*. If it was in code I wouldn't know it was Kraut, would I?'

'Tex is physically incapable of saying the word *German*,' Silver suggested. He crouched in the glassed-in nose of the plane where there was a ledge for him to lay out his charts.

'I *can* say it. I just think it's bad luck to say it in the air.'

'Let me see,' Silver said to Chip.

I'd told Chip to write everything down. Silver crawled out of the nose to sit beside me and reached behind the bulkhead to the radio set, and Chip passed him a sheet of paper. Silver frowned at Chip's scrawled columns of letters.

'What is this, are you trying your hand at nursery rhymes? *Fun kistka putt, ichho ere nichts – funkist kaput, tich* ... ?'

'And Humpty Dumpty sat on a wall!' I laughed. 'That's not German.'

'He's written it like code, in five-letter blocks,' Silver said. 'Maybe you can figure it out.'

With one hand on the flight controls and the other balancing the throttles, I glanced at the page and looked away again. I thought about it as I stared at the high grey cirrus cloud, five thousand feet above us even though we were flying at ten thousand feet. The sky looked like a sheet of silk spilt all over with grey river pearls, serene and beautiful. Even after five months of operational flying I still couldn't marry the pure sky with the menacing enemy radio messages coming out of it from who knows where. It felt like evil magic.

'*Funk ist kaputt*, maybe?' I guessed. 'I think that means *radio is broken*.'

'You speak Kraut, Cap'n?' Tex sounded more shocked than outraged.

'I don't *speak* it,' I protested. 'I understand a little. My wee sister went to finishing school in Switzerland, and she's always wittering away in German. Reads German novels and all. *O mein liebster Bruder!* Thinks it's cute. Does my head in.'

I couldn't fly the plane, keep an eye on the new pilots just off my wingtips, and interpret German radio messages all at once. Silver helped me think. Chip was good at Morse, but not a brilliant detective.

'"Radio is broken",' Silver mused. 'It's two planes communicating. Reconnaissance, maybe. The first message has the word *Morse* in it – I think one plane can't give or receive radio calls, and he's telling the other to transmit in code.'

The last flurry of messages Chip intercepted seemed to be someone in a second plane trying, more and more frantically, to contact the first.

There didn't seem to be any reply.

'What do you think these Germans are flying?' I asked uneasily. 'Clapped-out old Blenheims?'

'Ha-ha,' said Silver.

'We don't want to tangle with a Luftwaffe fighter. We're close enough to Norway they could be Messerschmitt 109s.'

'Let's find the guy sending the messages and call a Spitfire from Deeside to put him out of his misery,' said Chip.

There was no question of tackling him ourselves – that would be suicidal, and we knew it. Our guns only fired half the distance of a Messerschmitt's.

But we could figure out where he was. With the Jerry's wireless making so much noise, we might get lucky. It would be good practice for the new Pimms Section.

One of the crews in formation with me was completely wet behind the ears, a trio of fresh-faced Australian classmates who'd come straight here from some posh school in

Sydney. They were even younger than me. In our third plane were two survivors of 7 November: Ignacy Mazur, the Polish pilot who'd walked across Eastern Europe so he could get to Britain, and Derfel Cledwyn, his Welsh navigator. They'd moved to Pimms from A-Flight. I wasn't used to flying with Ignacy. He was hell-bent on shooting down Nazis and had a habit of tearing out ahead of everybody; I had to keep yelling at him to watch for the rest of us. After the shake-up, like me and Silver, Ignacy and Derfel had a new wireless op: Bill Yorke had transferred from another squadron, and we didn't know how good he was.

So getting a position fix on a German plane would test our new wireless operators, Bill Yorke and the Australian lad, Dougie Kerr. And if it worked it would give Ignacy Mazur the satisfaction of sending someone to chase down a Nazi fighter without putting my youthful Aussie lads in too much danger – the perfect practice op. Although it was real enough, even if we were practising.

Funny how it's easier to remember who was *alive* and flying with you on a hop than to count the ones who died in the air around you.

So we hatched a plan to snare this German plane.

Ignacy and Derfel raced off towards Norway to try to receive the transmission from a different place. I told Harry Morrow, the new pilot, to stay with me – the Australians had not a whiff of combat experience between them, and if it came to an air battle I meant to get them out alive or die trying. Our two planes circled beneath the pearly sky until we'd had three more German radio transmissions, stronger and stronger each time.

Bill Yorke, in Ignacy's plane, heard it too. When his navigator, Derfel, told us where they were and where the noise was coming from, clever old David Silvermont plotted a web of lines and gave us coordinates for where he thought the Luftwaffe plane might be.

But bloody Ignacy wasn't satisfied with calling up Spitfires from Aberdeen to finish off the German.

'Pimms Leader, hello, I am going to meet him,' said Ignacy's voice over my headset.

'You damn well won't!' I told him. 'Get back here with the rest of us.'

'He'll be surprised,' said Ignacy.

This was mutiny and suicide rolled into one, and of course I couldn't let him go alone.

So with my wet-behind-the-ears Australian sprogs on my port wing, we set off after Ignacy.

I was sure he would get there before us. But I flew full throttles anyway. Chip was up in his gun turret now; no point in sitting in the belly of the plane at the radio where he couldn't see anything, listening to dah-dit beeping in German, when he could be firing guns. The Luftwaffe plane wasn't saying anything new anyway. Silver showed me the last sequence Chip had taken down:

WOBIS
TDUKA
NNSTD
UMICH
HOERE
N

Wobis, wobist? Wo bist … Wo bist du, like Old English, like Chaucer. Where beest thou?

Wo bist du, kannst du mich hoeren?

I gnawed at it as I flew, trying not to think about Ignacy and his underpowered guns.

Where are you … canst thou me hear?

Can you hear me?

Ich hoere nichts.

I hear nothing.

It sort of got me in the stomach. I wondered what had happened to the other plane. Poor lonely Jerry, losing his wingman. I knew how that felt.

We found the pilot who was transmitting, though. We even got there before Ignacy.

The Luftwaffe pilot was alone, as we'd guessed, flying a Messerschmitt 109 fighter dangerously low over the sea, skimming the whitecaps. He circled and climbed and descended again, which was why his messages faded in and out. He was looking for something, a wreck, or a trace of his companion's crash, maybe.

It wasn't even a fortnight since 7 November. And here in front of me, getting nearer, were iron-grey wings like knife blades, emblazoned with black Luftwaffe crosses, and with the ugly whirl of a black swastika on the tail.

He saw us and began to climb to meet us.

Silver and I both spotted him – but I was the one with the guns in front.

There wasn't enough cloud to hide in. The only thing we could do was get down, but you can't hedge-hop over waves and expect the sea to camouflage you the way valleys and woodland and riverbanks do.

Well, this was probably it, then …

I rammed the controls forward under full power, turning and diving. I'd out-turned a Messerschmitt 109 once before, even if I couldn't outfly or outshoot them – the Jerry probably didn't know that, and if he went after me he might leave the Australian lads alone …

The blasted Australians thought this was a game, their first dogfight. I could hear their pilot, tall Harry Morrow, whooping with excitement as they fired away at the German pilot. They didn't hit him, though. He swooped up over us, made a wide turn, and came back in over the Australians from behind. I could see tracers flaming from the Luftwaffe cannons and from Dougie Kerr's gun turret. I threw the Blenheim around and leaned into my own guns.

It sometimes doesn't feel real when you're there. You're so focused on flying and firing. Afterwards, you feel choked up or frightened – especially if it's gone badly, and you have miles of empty sea to cross in a broken plane, and your mates are dead. But in battle, there's nothing else to think about.

Suddenly the Messer just stopped playing. He shot off east as if he couldn't be bothered to waste time with us. I don't think he was out of ammunition; he must have been low on fuel. He'd probably already been pushing his luck, with all that haring about after his missing wingman, and now he couldn't risk the toll an air battle would take on whatever was left in his tanks.

Thank God – *thank God*. Thank God I hadn't lost these kids on their first operational mission.

By the time Ignacy found us we were alone and heading home under the pearly grey sheet of sky.

'You blooming great fool, Mazur, you're on report,' I snarled at Ignacy over the radio.

'Save it, Scotty,' said Silver gently through the intercom, which Ignacy couldn't hear. 'Wait till we're on the ground.'

I was seething. I took a deep breath.

'Get back in formation, Pimms Section.'

That was the only order they paid attention to all afternoon.

I wondered briefly if the lost Messerschmitt pilot had been disobeying orders too. But only briefly; that was someone else's problem, and Pimms was mine.

Louisa:

Look at that lion kill. That's what I thought Daddy said to me, pointing out the bus window along the road to Granny Adair's, on the edge of St Andrew Parish back in Jamaica. I was only little, sitting on one of his knees and wedged against the window by his canvas duffel bag on the other. Around us were people with luggage and groceries and chickens, and the smell of sweat and tobacco. Daddy pointed to the limekiln every time we passed it and I always thought he said, *That's an old lion kill.* I thought that abandoned stone-and-brick building, half-buried in ferns, was a place where brave and terrible people took lions to be slaughtered. Whenever we went to Granny Adair's and passed that place it gave me a queer, nervous thrill of fear and mystery.

The limekilns at Windyedge village made it all come back. Just when Ellen said that – *Those are limekilns.* And again when she left us, as I looked up at the pub sign with its painted limekilns. The back of my neck prickled chilly, even beneath Jane Warner's warm fur coat.

I wasn't a fool-fool country gal and I knew they were just limekilns. But maybe it was the German plane that gave me the shivers.

The Limehouse had a small porch made of black-painted tree trunks framing the front door. Through that was a vestibule with a coat rack and two more doors leading into the hotel hall if you turned right, or into the public bar if you turned left. Nancy Campbell stood inside the left-hand door, waiting for us to arrive.

She was a thin woman in a drably flowered pinny apron over a brown dress; her grey-streaked black hair was pulled back with diamante clips, except for a few wisps escaping in frizzled curls around her face. When I opened the door for Jane, Mrs Campbell held out her arms stiffly and put them around her old auntie in a quick, awkward hug.

'Aunt Jane!'

Jane planted frosty kisses on her niece's cheeks, and Mrs Campbell looked as if she were trying to dodge them.

'Welcome to Windyedge, Aunt Jane,' Mrs Campbell said, with that same grim determination I'd heard on the phone. 'And to the Limehouse. Was the journey all right? How is your hip? Can you manage stairs?' The landlady frowned.

'I'm not sure where to put you if you can't manage stairs. There aren't any ground-floor bedrooms. I suppose I could convert the dining room, as I haven't served there since the war started …'

'I can manage perfectly, Nancy. I just need someone to carry my things.'

I was doing that now, bringing in suitcases. I struggled through the vestibule and realised Mrs Campbell was staring with her mouth open. I felt the blood rise flaming in my cheeks. I wasn't going to pretend it was all right for *her* to stare. I was used to being stared at, but she was going to be my employer.

I put down the cases with a thump, straightened, and held out my open hand to the landlady.

For another moment the thin woman's face looked baffled. Then her mouth tightened as she realised who I was. 'Oh!'

She took my hand, though. She gave it one light shake and let go. She looked me up and down with her thin lips pressed shut, assessing me. I was wearing one of Mummy's neat tailored suits beneath Jane's mink coat, my hair was rolled tight against my head, and I knew I looked all right.

'Where have you come from?' she asked me.

'London,' I answered again without thinking.

Her thin mouth tightened even more.

'I mean – that's where I've been living,' I added hastily. It's true I was annoyed about the staring, but I hadn't meant to be cheeky. 'I've been in London for three years. That's where I saw your advertisement. I grew up in the West Indies.'

The prickly woman's voice was cold. 'You might have said. On the telephone.'

'My father is from Jamaica,' I confessed now, as if it weren't ruddy obvious.

'Ah, that explains it,' said that miserable landlady. 'I don't like surprises.'

'I can go, if you like,' I told her. 'Now that I've brought your aunt here.'

I did not want to be rude or have a fight. I did not want to go back to London and start looking for work all over again. But I was tired of the messing about. We might as well be clear.

'You can find someone else to help you if I won't do,' I added.

Jane put a stop to this conversation.

'Of course you will do.' She laid her hand on my arm, as if she were hanging on to me for support. 'Louisa and I understand each other. I shouldn't want a new companion after we've had such a nice time travelling together.'

A nice time travelling together! I nearly smiled.

Mrs Campbell *did* laugh, a dry snort that told me she wasn't fooled about what kind of a journey we'd had. But she didn't ask me to leave.

So I brought in the rest of the luggage. Then I got to look at the inside of the Limehouse. I'd never set foot in a pub before. Even Mummy and Daddy wouldn't have gone into a pub together, and certainly not with me tagging along.

The floor of the public bar was grey flagstones and the walls were whitewashed, with deep-set windows like the ones in the Windyedge village cottages. The bar had a brass countertop. Oak beams, black with age, held up the low ceiling above the bar. There was a scatter of tables, wooden benches and stools, and one or two proper chairs with armrests and cushions on the seats. On one side of the room, between two windows, was a battered upright piano; across from it, beside the bar, rose a chimney over a big fireplace. There was no fire burning in the grate.

The place wasn't welcoming just now. But it wasn't unfriendly. It was empty and waiting. It might be nice, if there were people drinking at the bar, and the fire were lit, and there were music.

I wondered where a girl like me would fit into that picture.

Mrs Campbell's eyes widened again when she saw Jane's luggage.

'I thought you were only allowed one case at – at *that place*. There's no surface for the gramophone in Room Number Five, and anyway I've put the wireless in there for you.'

'Oh, surely the gramophone can stay down here?' Jane suggested winningly. 'And the records? I understand the lads from the aerodrome spend time here – perhaps they'd enjoy hearing some music.'

Jane put down her sticks and dropped herself quite suddenly on to a chair.

'You said there were stairs,' she said. 'I'm just having a rest before I tackle them. Louisa, open that smaller case. I've brought a gift for Nancy.'

Inside it, wrapped in silk underwear like a pass-the-parcel, were five cheeses and six blocks of butter. Jane had smuggled dairy products off the Isle of Man in her knickers! I definitely did not see her packing them.

'There wasn't any rationing in That Place, darling, and I know you struggle because of the blockades, so I brought some contraband.'

Mrs Campbell let out another burst of dry laughter. 'My word. All that butter! You haven't changed a bit, Aunt Jane.'

She hadn't exactly said thank you.

'Nor have you, Nancy,' said Jane gently, as if it couldn't be helped.

Room Number Five was at the end of the upstairs passage. Mrs Campbell called it the 'second-best double room'.

'I've put my own wireless radio in there,' she told us again grudgingly, 'but you'll both have to share the bathroom with the lasses. There's only Volunteer Ellen McEwen just now, the driver for RAF Windyedge. When there's a squadron based at the aerodrome there are sometimes others. You'll have to take a torch or a candle when you use the stairs at night, as it's impossible to fix blackout over that tall window in the hall. I've taken out the bulbs from the electric fittings to stop anyone switching on the lights by accident.'

It was all cold. The stair was covered with faded coconut matting. This brown dull stuff underfoot had been green and alive once, palm trees blowing in a tropical sky. Far from home like me. Except that nobody stared at coconut matting. It was ordinary.

But Room Number Five was all right. It had three of the

deep-set windows, one small one like an arrow slit facing north-east towards the airfield, and two facing south-east. With great relief I set down the case of Jane's that I was carrying. I didn't think it would be too bad being here, even if it was cold and dark, because I liked Jane despite her being German, and there was a piano downstairs, and the gramophone. I leaned across one of the bigger window sills in the room, and I could see the North Sea like a strip of Christmas tinsel on the horizon. Far off in the distance, somewhere on the way to Norway, the sun was shining.

If the aerodrome gets busy, I thought, perhaps there will be other young people about.

There was already Ellen McEwen. She couldn't be much older than me. But she seemed it, in her crisp khaki uniform and tie, driving the Royal Air Force van so casually. It made me quite envious, remembering. Also, she was a tall and rather striking beauty, with shining coppery hair coiled beneath her uniform cap. She could have been on a recruitment poster. She'd made me feel mousy and shy, which wasn't helped by her being a bit stiff.

Or was she shy as well, and the uniform let her hide? She'd been perfectly welcoming. I'd have to make an effort to be friendly. I could ask what happened to the German plane after it landed. Perhaps she could take me to see the airfield sometime.

Mrs Campbell waved towards the armchair, and Jane sat with one of her thunderous backwards plunges, letting gravity drop her.

'How cosy this shall be when the fire's lit,' Jane said.

The open hearth was plugged up and fitted with a gas

fire exactly like the one Mummy and I had in the attic at Number 88, Gibraltar Road.

'We're lucky to have town gas and electricity,' Mrs Campbell said. 'They brought it to the village the same time as the aerodrome, five years ago, when they stepped up Royal Air Force training here. I don't allow the rooms heated before three p.m. and there's no hot water before six. You've got your own gas meter for the fire – it only takes shilling coins.'

'We had one like it in London,' I said.

'Well, then you'll know to treat it respectfully. If you don't top up the money, the gas cuts off, and the fire will go out. Then if you forget to turn off the gas tap, next time you put a coin in, the room will fill with gas until you turn off the tap or light the fire again. I don't want any explosions! It takes another shilling every two or three days if you're careful. And don't stuff it full of coins before the collection man comes to reset the meter – once the coin box is full you can't get more gas until he empties it.'

'Yes, that's how ours at home worked,' I said.

'Well, be careful.' She slipped a silver shilling into the meter. 'Here's a bob to start you off. Don't turn it on until three o'clock. If you want a fire before then, you'll have to sit in the bar.'

Oh, what a grouch.

But Jane caught my eye like a naughty child. I was sure she was trying to make me laugh. I looked away quickly.

I *did* like Jane.

How lucky I am to like her, I thought, as we unpacked. We each got a window sill to stack our books in; she had as many as I did.

'I shall look forward to reading yours,' she said. 'I'm tired to death of my own.'

Room Number Five, the Limehouse, I realised, wasn't a big change from her room in the alien detainment camp. Apart from the radio, of course. There was a bit more space, but now there were two of us. She'd had a bed to herself before. Now she had to share with me.

Would she mind? Would it be *worse* than the camp – would she feel she was being guarded all the time, with not even any privacy?

'I could sleep in the chair,' I said, hesitating to set Mummy's Bakelite alarm clock next to the bed in case Jane didn't want me to sleep with her.

'Nonsense, what a ridiculous idea,' said Jane. 'The bed is large enough for a family of four. You will have to sleep by the window, as I often get up in the night.'

I hesitated. 'Won't you want me to help you?' That would be the worst thing about always being watched.

'I can manage the toilet perfectly well on my own, as you know,' Jane answered.

In London I'd got used to sharing a bed with Mummy, except when Daddy was home, when I would gladly move to the settee for two nights or a fortnight or whatever it was. All through the last horrid weeks of 1940 I'd felt very alone in Mummy's bed all by myself. I was glad Jane didn't mind.

She wanted me to see to her gramophone downstairs.

After we unpacked we went down to the public bar, where Mrs Campbell said it would be warmer, and where I was hopeful of toast. Sure enough, the peat fire in the big hearth was alight, and there was a small table and a comfortable chair pulled close to it. Mrs Campbell didn't *say* it was meant for her old aunt, but I thought it probably was. Jane hovered near my shoulder, leaning on her sticks as I found a place for the gramophone on top of the piano.

'The loudspeaker needs to face the room,' she directed.

Of course it did, silly me. I shifted the case around.

'And the records over here …' There was a low, narrow cupboard beside the piano with a mostly empty shelf holding a few glossy magazines.

Jane was particular about how she wanted the records arranged. I didn't mind – it gave me a chance to look through them. There was a lot of jazz from the early 1930s, a bit of classical. A few pieces made my throat close up, thinking of Mummy playing them: Mozart's 21st Piano Concerto in C, Debussy's 'Clair de Lune'.

At last Jane settled into the chair by the fire. After I'd tucked her woolly blanket in around her legs and laid her sticks out of the way, I stood back and got my first good look at the old fireplace.

Thick black beams held up the mantel, and more thick beams braced the chimney where it went through the ceiling. The black wood was split and cracked, and in the cracks, thin pieces of metal were wedged like studs. Most were black with soot or green with age. But a few still gleamed silvery and coppery, and I could see they were coins: the ones in the front of the mantel looked like pennies and tuppences. Others were wedged so far into the wood and so discoloured that you couldn't tell what they were, or how old.

It was a bit unsettling. It gave me the same chill as the limekilns, and I don't know why.

The knobbly, uneven column holding up the low ceiling at the corner of the bar was another tree trunk, painted black, like the tree trunks holding up the porch outside. It was also studded with coins, though not as many. And there were more coins in the black beam that crossed above the bar. All those gleamed, as if someone buffed them regularly with vinegar and salt. They looked like modern sixpences and shillings.

I ran my fingertips over the pennies in the mantel. That's what I was doing when Nancy Campbell came out through a door behind the bar.

'That's dead men's money,' she snapped. 'Leave it.'

'Of course no one's altering your decorations, Nancy,' said Jane tartly.

I took my hand away and, though I was probably more annoyed than Jane at the idea I might be mining for gold in the mantelpiece, I gritted my teeth and bit my tongue again, determined not to create a stir on my first day. Also, I was curious about the coins.

'Dead men's money?' I repeated.

In fact Mrs Campbell was busting to talk about it. She was just so tight-lipped she didn't know how to start a conversation politely.

'The wood in here is all from a wishing tree. It's older than the Limehouse,' she said. 'Folk made wishes on it for hundreds of years before it fell. There were pennies in the tree when this place was built, two hundred and fifty years ago. Then the airmen from the last war put their coppers in the mantel for safekeeping before they went on a mission.'

She gestured towards the pennies I'd touched.

'Those lads would put in a tuppenny bit and after a flight they'd take it out and buy a pint. All these still in the wood are airmen who never came back. Dead men's money,' repeated Nancy Campbell. 'Wishes that didn't come true. My lads. Same age as me in the last lot.'

She pointed.

'That one was Cammy McBride. Cheeky daredevil with green eyes. I pulled his last pint. It was a reconnaissance flight – he got caught in clouds. And that was Ben Knox. His engine failed on a training flight. Just up there—'

She pulled her hand back, but not before I saw her fingers trembling. 'Alan Anderson. Cannon fire from a German warship. They think. At any rate he didn't come back either.'

She pointed to the coin nearest the bar, by itself at the edge of the mantel. 'Mr Campbell,' she said softly. 'My Duncan. His dad ran the place before I took over. I worked behind the bar for them.'

Jane gave a soft little sigh. 'Oh, Nancy!'

Then an unearthly shriek tore that moment apart. The hair on my spine stood on end – but of course it was just the kettle coming to a boil.

'Tea?' Jane added. 'You are kind!'

Mrs Campbell wiped her hands on her pinny and took the kettle off the hob. 'I was going to have a cup anyway,' she said grudgingly. 'But I'll make enough for three.'

She clattered about with a teapot and china behind the

bar. As she left the tea to stew she turned to me and demanded, 'Ration coupons.'

She made it feel as if she wouldn't give us the tea without them, though I knew she just needed our tickets to get extra supplies for our meals when she did her shopping. I had to run upstairs to get them. Over the coconut matting, down the dark passage – strange to think this was my home now.

Back downstairs again, out of breath as I handed over our booklets, I looked up at the modern coins shining in the beam over the bar.

'Those belong to the 648 Squadron lads,' said Mrs Campbell, following my eyes. 'From when they were based at Windyedge.' Her hard face softened, as it had when she'd talked about the airmen from the last war. 'They always prepaid their drinks. Their squadron is up in Shetland now.'

'Will they come back?' I asked.

'Let's hope so,' said Nancy Campbell. 'RAF Windyedge doesn't feel right without a squadron at the aerodrome. Those lads at the anti-aircraft guns on the perimeter haven't a thing to do other than smoke and play bridge and read the papers all day. Coastal Command is just asking for trouble, in my opinion.'

Ellen:

When he pressed the gun against my head, I moaned with fear, and everybody in the radio room clapped eyes on me. They all gasped together. How could one German pilot so handily get the better of a dozen Royal Air Force ground crewmen?

'What's he doing here?' I cried out. He hadn't told me to belt up. 'Why did you let him land?'

The radio operator, whom we called Old Flash because he was about ten years older than everybody else, was the only one who seemed to ken what was going on.

'We had to,' he told me. 'Orders. He has a code name on our list. He transmitted it correctly. Someone in Intelligence expected him.'

'What are you all doing in here, then?' I gasped.

'He's got some message he wants me to transmit to an Intel bigwig in England. Hard to understand him – nobody speaks his lingo, and he doesn't have much English. Everybody kind of piled in to help – and to make sure he didn't cause any bother …'

'Aye, you did that well!' I sobbed. 'He's no bother at all.'

The German pilot let his gun drop away so it wasn't touching my face, and his fingers stopped digging into my arm. 'Shh,' he whispered soft at my ear.

I gulped air and stood tall. I didn't think he was telling me I couldn't speak – more hoping I would stop panicking.

'Did you get an answer?' I asked the radio operator. 'From the bloke in England?'

'We're to refuel the plane and let him go! But we're waiting—'

And then our Flash had to take down a message that was coming in. Everybody stood frozen, listening, no one but the radio operator being able to understand the string of bleeps and blips, even though we could all hear it and it wasn't in code. Well, it was in Morse code. But in English.

When the transmission stopped, there was a long silence while we waited for more. I could hear the German pilot breathing.

Old Flash cleared his throat.

'They're saying Robert Ethan, that Intelligence chap from the War Office, is behind it. Remember him, all in tweed like Sherlock Holmes, with the thick specs that make his eyes look like billiard balls? He was snooping around the perimeter with binoculars last month. Maybe his tame Jerry's giving him a lift to Norway. He left Intelligence a message in German for the pilot that they're going to send.'

So we kept on waiting.

The German pilot never let me go. Every soul in that room believed he'd shoot me if we didn't do as he wanted.

At last the German message arrived, and the pilot pushed me across to the communications desk so he could read it, nudging his wooden case along with his foot. He eyed the page, then sighed. Whatever it said, it wasn't what he was hoping for.

For the first time since I turned up, he said something in English.

'A room?'

He pointed to me, using his gun.

'With the girls.'

Everybody gasped, and, oh, how fear swelled up in my chest! A room with *girls*? Who else was there but me, and what did he need with a *room*?

He added, 'The Limehouse? A room is there.'

Old Flash said, 'The Limehouse was mentioned in the German message. I think it said he should stay there tonight. Robert Ethan's stuck in England on a stopped train. This is his alternate plan – he wants his man to wait for him.'

'Oh!' I gave a skrike of a laugh, fear and relief bundled together. 'The Limehouse – with the girls. He means "Take a room in the hotel where the lassies stay". Not that he wants – that he – *not that*.'

I couldn't speak what we all thought he'd meant.

With his mate from Intelligence stranded, maybe the German pilot truly did just want a place to stop the night.

Everybody muttered. Then some cleversticks suggested, 'Volunteer McEwen can drive him to Mrs Campbell's for the night and bring him back tomorrow.'

'You double-crossing bastards!' I cried.

'Don't make a fuss, you'll make it worse,' said Old Flash. 'We don't want to scare him into pulling the ruddy trigger, do we? I'll check with Intelligence before you go. If it's orders it ought to be all right.'

Of course I was the driver for RAF Windyedge; this *was* my job. But – they were all so flipping helpless! 'Some heroes you turn out to be,' I sobbed. 'You bloody *bastards*.'

I wriggled my arm up beneath the Jerry pilot's and gingerly pushed his gun further away from my head. I sucked in a breath. I hated him like I'd never hated any man before in my life.

'I'll drive you there,' I told him. My voice quaked. Then, because I knew he didn't understand, I said very loudly, 'A ROOM. THE LIMEHOUSE.' I pointed to myself and mimed driving.

No one tried to keep us from leaving – they were still in a flap worrying he might shoot me.

We waited for the last message. Old Flash nodded as he listened to the beeping stream of dots and dashes. 'He's to give it till tomorrow morning. If Ethan doesn't turn up, he's to take off when it gets light, or he'll be missed back at his own base.'

Flash took off his headset and turned to me. 'Your Jerry's got a code name,' he said. 'We're supposed to call him Odysseus. He's here for a reason, whatever it is, and I don't think he's likely to wreck things for himself by hurting you.' The radio operator gave me a grim wee smile, trying to be encouraging. 'You'll be all right, lass.'

'I'll take him straight over the cliff if I'm not,' I said through my teeth.

Jamie:

'Well done, still in one piece as always,' Silver said, holding up his ratty box of rosin.

'You're welcome,' I said.

We were back on the windblown Shetland aerodrome where we'd been based whilst fighting our losing battles for the past two months. My two other crews pulled up safely alongside our Blenheim, and Silver pushed open the hatch above us.

I climbed through the canopy and jumped off the wing. Silver followed, and Chip came behind, climbing out of his own hatch forward of the rear gun turret. He stood on the wing, gazing critically at the Australian lads getting out of their plane. Then he exclaimed in his Texan drawl, 'Aw, fer cryin' out loud.'

About an inch off the top of their tail fin was shot away.

'They took a hit,' Silver exclaimed. 'We shouldn't have chanced it with a Messerschmitt!'

'We didn't have a choice,' I pointed out.

Chip laughed. 'The Kraut pilot didn't do that. I'll bet that new Australian gunner did it himself. Rookie mistake. You can't fire straight behind you without hitting yourself in the rear end!'

'Look at the turret,' said Silver grimly, pointing.

One of the Perspex sheets in the dome was missing. The panel was completely blown away.

'Dougie Kerr didn't do that himself. They took a hit,' Silver repeated.

One of the other turret panels had a small jagged hole in it. It was no rookie mistake. A German bullet had gone through one side of the dome and come out the other.

I'd nearly lost another kid.

I squeezed my eyes shut and steadied myself with one hand against the cold hull of the plane. When I opened my eyes, breathing again, I could feel the blood burning in my legs.

'Steady on, mate,' Silver said, grabbing my elbow. 'Not enough porridge this morning?'

But Dougie Kerr, the Australian wireless op and gunner with the gingery hair like a bottle brush, was alive and well on the ground, and so were his tall pilot, Harry Morrow, and his baby-faced navigator, Gavin Hamilton. All three were chattering like excited sparrows to the ground crew who came to take care of the planes.

'They're all right,' Silver said to me quietly. 'Stop acting like an old woman or everyone will notice.'

Chip leaped off the wing of our plane and scrambled on to the one next to us to get a look at the damage to the turret dome. He let out a long whistle.

'Must have made a hell of a bang going through! That Aussie gunner had a close shave! You know what? I'll bet he didn't even notice. Probably too busy kicking himself for shooting up his own plane. If he knew he nearly had his crazy hair trimmed by a German bullet, the whole crew would be up here poking at the hole and patting him on the back!'

We pointed out the damage to maintenance, but they couldn't sort it, and told me my new lads would have to fly with holes in the tail and turret – or a quick fix of cardboard and sticky tape – until the Air Transport Auxiliary could ferry another plane to us and take this one away to be mended properly.

Now I was hopping mad at the Jerries again, seeing red as I took off the bulky bits of my gear – Mae West, I mean life vest, and helmet – and fished cooled-down Ever-Hot bags out of my flight suit. I had to go be grilled by Flight Officer Pennyworth.

There wasn't anything special about that interrogation. As the rest of Pimms Section filed out to get baths and sandwiches and cups of tea, Phyllis told me apologetically,

'Wing Commander Talbot Cromwell wants you in his office.'

So I had to face the Old Roundhead by myself again.

He'd had a hell of a go at me after 7 November. This time I didn't blame him for wanting to have a go at me, because I knew we shouldn't have gone after a German fighter, and my new Australian flight crew had survived on blind luck, and Ignacy had essentially ignored everything I'd told him to do.

'Going to have to put another reprimand stamp in your logbook, Flight Lieutenant Beaufort-Stuart,' he told me. 'You'll have to get a better grip on your crews than this or I'll replace you as B-Flight's commander. Adam Stedman in Madeira's a capable chap.'

I stood in front of his desk as he defaced my logbook, clenching my teeth so hard I started to give myself jaw ache, watching his hands moving. His head was lowered, so I couldn't see any part of his face but his frowning forehead and wiry eyebrows. Of course he wanted to replace me, and this was the perfect excuse. Stedman was an easy-going, capable fellow, transferred last week from another Blenheim squadron, but he didn't have any more experience than I did, or know the new crews any better.

'Sir, with respect—' I made myself say it, polite words, without choking. '*With respect*, it'll take a couple of flights for these new pilots to learn to fly together. Mazur is a bit of a daredevil, and Morrow's just inexperienced.'

'It's not their flying that's getting them in trouble,' Cromwell said, deep-set eyes making his craggy face grimmer than it had any business being. 'It's their big mouths. "Careless talk costs lives" and all that. But you're their commander, so you'll have to be held responsible.'

Now I was confused.

'"Careless talk costs lives"?' I repeated.

'Your young Australians were chattering like magpies about receiving Morse code in German! It's all over the aerodrome – the whole squadron knows what Pimms Section did out there today. Half of 'em are jealous and want to go shooting at Messers themselves. The other half want to know what kind of secret ops you're on. I can't have such undisciplined behaviour, Beaufort-Stuart. There's a delicate operation going on, and you may have thrown a wrench in it by chasing off that Jerry.'

Wing Commander Cromwell pushed my logbook across the table and leaned back. I gaped at him.

'Isn't that what we're supposed to do, chase off Jerries?' I exclaimed.

Buckets of blood! What the hell was he talking about?

'Too bad you of all men ran into this,' Cromwell said. 'You weren't to know. This was the one German plane we weren't supposed to shoot down. Intelligence was expecting him – hoping to collar him alive.'

'Well, he's still alive, sir,' I said. 'We didn't shoot him down.'

But an idea hit me. If there was a rogue Messerschmitt pilot on the loose, maybe he'd used the broken radio as a smokescreen. Maybe our Luftwaffe fighter hadn't been trying to contact a friend at all. Maybe he'd been hunting down a traitor who'd given him the slip.

In that case, Pimms Section hadn't ruined some special

operation – we'd *helped* by distracting the enemy.

I sucked in air, wondering whether Wing Commander Talbot Cromwell was capable of understanding this. It was guesswork, and he never took me seriously. As I hesitated, the radio operator tore in, out of breath and waving a sheet of notepaper.

He slammed the page down on Cromwell's desk by my logbook and said explosively, 'It's all right, sir. We've got a message from Windyedge in Aberdeenshire: *Odysseus in port*.'

He stood panting.

I stepped forward and picked up my logbook.

'Flight Lieutenant Beaufort-Stuart, you didn't hear that,' the Old Roundhead barked.

'No, sir,' I said.

'Tell your men to keep their mouths shut.'

'Yes, sir.'

'Dismissed. Close that door on your way out.'

I stood in the corridor with my back against the wall, trying to relax the muscles of my face before the jaw ache turned into a headache. It was like being in school, like failing a test on Latin verbs because I'd studied noun declensions all night. How could I possibly have guessed any of this? No one had briefed me about 'Odysseus' in a special Messerschmitt 109 – and how were my lads to guess that today's op was a secret when yesterday's wasn't?

I was a hundred per cent on my men's side, but I wasn't sure how to get them on mine.

I steeled myself to give them a talking-to.

Louisa:

Jane and I sat by the peat fire in the public room of the Limehouse, just next to the mantel made out of the wishing tree, making the most of our first night there. I had a glass of Rose's lime because it reminded me of Mummy and Daddy, who used to drink it with rum on the veranda of our bungalow in Kingston; Jane very slowly nursed a tumbler of whisky and water.

'Ah,' she sighed. 'This is almost what I missed the most in That Place.' She closed her eyes with a blissful smile. 'Except it is really the BBC Home Service on the radio I missed the most.'

I spent the evening on edge. Every old man who came into the Limehouse eyed me curiously, and I leaped to my feet every time the door opened, as if this would somehow show people that I was there on business and not as a paying customer. It made me feel doubly out of place that not a single woman came in that night. But perhaps that was because it wasn't very busy. When the last two customers from the village said goodnight, it was only half past nine – half an hour before closing – but Mrs Campbell began to stack chairs on tables anyway. I suppose it didn't seem likely anyone else would come in so late on a weekday.

'Shall I lend a hand?' I offered.

Mrs Campbell looked at me with suspicion again. I felt my face beginning to burn and braced myself. I hoped hard she too wasn't going to make some nasty remark about the Caribbean sun making people lazy.

Instead she said, 'What age are you?'

I hadn't even thought about that. Was I old enough to be in the bar? I knew Scotland's laws were different from England's, but I didn't know how that affected me.

Rules are made to be broken.

'I am just about sixteen,' I told her.

She sniffed and raised her eyebrows.

'"Just about"! Well, you're willing, I'll give you that,' she said in her grudging way. 'Come on behind the bar then, you can do the washing-up. There's a girl from the village who helps me, Morag Torrie, but she's part-time since the squadron is away. I'm just going to sweep under these tables and then I'll lock the door.'

'What about Ellen?' I asked her.

'She has her own key,' grunted Mrs Campbell.

Of course she has her own key, I thought jealously. *Important*.

'They keep odd hours at RAF Windyedge,' Mrs Campbell added. 'The squadron that was here before mostly flew at night. Ellen's got to be on hand if someone needs her.'

When the fire was low and the chairs were hung upside down, it didn't feel as cosy. But Jane was still bright-eyed and wide awake – I don't know how, after two nights and a day and a half of travelling. There weren't many glasses to wash up, and when I finished my little job I hung about at Jane's shoulder, staying on my feet to encourage her on to hers. Mrs Campbell went into the entryway to lock the outside door.

As she opened the inner door leading into the vestibule, we heard the harsh noise of a motor engine straining up the steep hill past the limekilns.

'That'll be Ellen now,' said Mrs Campbell, and stepped back to wait for her to come in.

The engine stopped. There was a long pause. Then a van door slammed. Another slam followed a second later – like gunshots, the two slams cracking whiplash quick on top of each other. I knew it must be two people getting out at the same time, one on each side of the van. So Ellen had brought someone home.

She came in slowly, tall and graceful as a goddess in her khaki ATS trousers and tunic. Her hair was still coiled in its neat bun below her peaked cap, but I could see it gleaming like a copper whisky still as she turned to hold open the inner door for her guest. He walked in past her, and Ellen closed the door.

She'd brought home a young man! I wondered for a moment if she did it often, and what old Nancy Campbell had to say about *that*.

Then I saw that Ellen's face was as pale as a dead fish's belly. She hugged her ribs as if her body would fly into pieces if she let go, and suddenly I no longer envied her.

She was very, very scared.

The man who came in with her seemed perfectly ordinary. He wasn't in uniform; he wore a scarf and sweater like a seaman. He carried a wooden case under one arm, with the other hand hidden deep in the pocket of his heavy coat.

'I'm sorry, Mrs Campbell,' Ellen choked out. 'He needs a room.'

'A room,' the man repeated, striding to the bar.

He was strongly built and much taller than me. He gazed

up curiously at the coins in the oak beam over the bar for a few seconds. But he didn't touch them.

'A room,' he repeated. 'And –' he hesitated – 'drink.' He put his wooden case on the brass counter and mimed drinking, with his cupped hand going to his mouth.

He didn't speak much English. I held my breath, guessing what that must mean.

'He's flown from Norway,' Ellen whispered.

'Norwegian?' asked Mrs Campbell, frowning. She seemed to distrust all foreigners, but Norwegians probably ought to be made welcome. They would be refugees, escaping the iron rule of the Nazis in their invaded country.

'He's not Norwegian,' Ellen whispered. 'I think he's German.'

She raised her voice, and asked me, 'You remember the plane we saw this afternoon? You said …'

She trailed off.

'It *was* a German plane?' I asked.

Ellen nodded.

I stared at the stranger in alarm. If this was a German pilot, this wasn't someone who'd chosen to live in England for decades, like Jane. This was a military man, fighting for Hitler, like the German soldiers who killed my parents. This was the enemy, the real enemy, right here in the room with me.

My heart lurched in fear. When that passed, it lurched again, in fascination.

He was also a pilot. *A real pilot.*

The enemy pilot swept his curious glance around the room. He paused to look at Jane. Then he looked at me, standing beside her.

My cheeks began burning again. What did Nazis think of West Indians? Not much, I imagined. They wanted everybody to be just like them. They didn't like Jews, or Gypsies, or jazz.

The stranger patted the brass bar and pointed to the glasses.

Jane spoke up.

'Come now, the young man would like a drink,' she said from her seat by the now-dead fire. 'Perhaps he's come to Scotland for the whisky.'

Ellen let out a nervous squeak of a laugh.

'He'd be better off in America, then, where there's no rationing,' said Mrs Campbell, putting on a defiant brave face like a Londoner in the Blitz.

The German pilot pulled his left hand from his pocket, and the hand was closed around a sleek and sturdy black pistol.

He'd been holding it all the time, a nasty secret.

I didn't dare to move.

Jane and Mrs Campbell froze too.

But Ellen's expression didn't change. She'd known all along. She drove him here from the aerodrome, knowing that if she didn't do as he told her, he'd shoot her.

The pilot beckoned Ellen, using the pistol. She crossed the room like a whipped dog. He pointed to the beer with the gun.

'I don't ken how to draw the ale,' Ellen whimpered. 'Mrs Campbell, please get him a drink.'

Nancy Campbell shook herself to life and quietly let herself in behind the bar. She'd already covered the taps for the night, but she lifted the towel, screwed a nozzle back on, and picked up a clean glass. As she filled it, she made a fierce offer through clenched teeth: 'Would you like a sandwich?'

The German pilot didn't understand. He rested both elbows on the counter, making his hold on the gun seem terrifyingly casual.

'What does he want?' Mrs Campbell hissed. 'I don't mean the room. He can have the room. Ellen! What else does he want?'

Ellen shook her head. A wisp of fiery hair escaped her bun, like a flame flicking her cheek. She hissed back, 'How do I know? His English isn't very good, and I don't speak Jerry myself!'

Mrs Campbell said helplessly, 'Aunt Jane?'

The old woman stared at her niece with blank, pale blue eyes. She said stiffly, 'I don't speak Norwegian.'

'You know he's not Norwegian,' Mrs Campbell said through still-gritted teeth.

She handed the full glass to the grim young man. He took it, held it up in a salute, and drank half the pint in one gulp.

'Please, Aunt Jane,' begged Mrs Campbell.

'What do you want to know?'

'Ask him if he'd like a sandwich.'

Ellen exploded in fizzing nervous laughter.

The man drank off the rest of the pint. Ellen backed up and collapsed into my empty chair, at the table across from Jane. She told us, 'He's waiting for a toff from Intelligence to meet him here. If his contact doesn't turn up, he has to fly off at the crack of dawn tomorrow, and we're to let him.

He's a spy, or a double agent or some such. He has a code name, they said. "Odysseus".'

I read a lot, I read all the time, and I knew who that was. I thought of the Trojan Horse.

So did Jane.

'"Odysseus, man of many wiles,"' she said. 'From Homer's *Odyssey*.'

He must have known we were talking about him, because 'Odysseus' sounds much the same in English and German and I expect Norwegian too. He pointed his gun at Ellen again.

'You bloody Nazi bastard,' she spat, her voice catching in a sob. 'What can I do? You're the one with the gun.'

He glared at her and handed his glass back to the landlady.

While Mrs Campbell refilled his glass with beer and resentment, the German pilot crossed the room to the piano.

He took his wooden case with him. The polished blond box looked like a small gramophone, much like Jane's, but without the loudspeaker. The pilot placed his box on the piano next to Jane's gramophone and laid his gun on top of the box. The two cases looked like a mother and child gramophone sitting side by side.

With his hands free, the German opened the piano lid. His left hand pulled out a hesitant arpeggio of low notes from the keyboard.

Almost as if he were surprised to find the piano in tune, he coaxed out a few more handfuls of sound, repetitive and dark and insistent. Then he added a high, sustained trill in the right hand. It was Mendelssohn – the *Hebrides Overture*.

His fingers moved like wind over the keys, and the music was heartbreaking, heart-stopping, filling the damp walls of the old house with beauty and longing and a crashing of waves.

It was not a piece I usually think of when I think of Mummy. It is an orchestral piece. But the last time I heard it, Mummy was playing it on the school piano.

I don't remember crossing the room.

I stood next to him at the piano, tears streaming down my face, and watched his hands, long, bony, strong fingers and a plain gold ring with a bear engraved on it, flying over the keys.

The German pilot suddenly realised I was there beside him.

He broke off playing to snatch up his pistol so I couldn't pick it up myself. The music stopped abruptly, and as he grabbed at the gun he knocked it against his wooden case.

The front of the box was a narrow, hinged flap held in place by a hasp on the flat lid, and when the gun hit the catch – it must have been loose – the front flap fell open to lay bare a panel full of holes and wires, each labelled with numbers and letters of the alphabet, like a telephone switchboard.

The inside of the wooden flap was stamped with a brand name: ENIGMA.

The German pilot flipped the front flap back up. He had to raise the lid on top of the case a little bit to fit the catch back into place, and beneath the lid I saw a keyboard of ordinary typewriter keys.

It looked like a portable electrical typewriter.

He used the gun to make me step back.

Jane spoke suddenly, sharp and scolding, in a language I didn't understand.

But the pilot did.

He put the gun back into his coat pocket and stepped away from me, holding up his empty hands to show he wasn't going to threaten me any more.

'I do speak a little German,' Jane admitted grudgingly.

'I know you do,' said Mrs Campbell.

Ellen:

That brave young lassie – I'd not spent an hour in her company, and knew not a thing about her but that she had brown skin and was in London during the Blitz. But seeing her in tears at the music, and him stopping to point his gun at her, made me hate him all over again.

Nan's old auntie was calm as could be. She asked the young man a question in his own tongue. He bowed his head to Mrs Warner and I heard the name he gave her: Felix Baer.

What was he up to, sly devil? Trying to make friends, just because a body speaks your lingo? Expecting us to behave ourselves just because he was polite? I was fuming.

But the old girl, Jane Warner, just cracked on and gave him an English lesson.

When she finished, he faced Louisa standing there

with her brown eyes full of tears. His voice when he spoke was gentle and polite as a lady's maid. 'I am sorry I frightened you.'

'I told him about your parents,' Jane said softly. 'So he knows it was German bombs and torpedoes that killed them.'

Her parents were killed in the Blitz? She must have hated the Nazis even more than I did.

'Oh.' Louisa gave a great gulp of a swallow, and just about whispered, 'Thank you.'

I could see she didn't like to talk about it, and I was glad I hadn't asked.

'My mother played the piano,' she added, getting control of herself. 'You can tell him that, I suppose.'

'Ask him if he wants a sandwich,' Mrs Campbell insisted, and then I roundly lost my temper with her. *Shaness*, could she not see Louisa's tears for herself, and all she could think of was food? I jumped up and barked, 'Hold your whisht, Nan Campbell, and stop going on about sandwiches! Hitler himself could walk in here and if he was a young pilot you'd pull him a pint and stuff him full of grub! I'll get the ruddy Jerry a ruddy sandwich for you.'

I barged past her into the kitchen at the back.

The kitchen was full of weapons. Everywhere I looked I saw things I could use to hurt the bastard with. Cast-iron pans! A butcher's knife! Toasting forks! Blimey, I could break a milk bottle over his head if I were brave enough, couldn't I!

I could hear Jane cracking away in quiet German with the pilot, and Mrs Campbell dithering behind the bar. 'Tea, that's what we need,' she said, and I heard the skritch of a match as she lit the gas burner to boil the kettle.

Aye, cups of tea – that will stop the invasion!

Stupid woman, I thought, and bit my lip. I was too frighted of the strapping tall young man and his gun to get around Nan with a frying pan and try to hit him in the head. I'd never manage it fast enough or hard enough. And anyway, I'd been told to let him get on with his mission, not to knock him out.

So I yanked open the icebox and found a big slab of butter. Where did Nan Campbell get so much butter, I wondered, did she have friends in the black market? No matter, there was cheese and bread, and I slapped a sandwich together.

When I came out of the kitchen, the lass Louisa was sitting silent and small on the piano stool. She was watching the Jerry pilot with the faintest frown. *Interested*. Not frightened. Or, if she did fear him, not showing it.

He was back at the bar, with the wooden box that he never let out of his reach, answering Jane's quiet questions.

I pushed the sandwich across the bar. The Jerry pilot wolfed it down so quickly I began to make him another without thinking.

'Oi, leave off, that's not for hotel guests!' Mrs Campbell cried. 'That's Isle of Man butter!'

I froze and gave her the worst kind of cold and fearsome glare. 'And it's Scottish bread, aye? He doesn't care.' I went back to buttering.

Jane held up her empty tumbler. 'How very exciting this is!'

The Jerry took her glass and gave it to Nan to fill again. I wondered who would have to pay for that wee dram; whisky wasn't cheap. He passed the glass back to the old woman and they jawed some more. Then he took a silver cigarette case from inside his coat and held it out. She took a cigarette and leaned forward, and he struck a match.

Oh, the look on Nan's face when the German pilot gave her old auntie a cigarette!

Jane called to the lass.

'He says to tell you, Louisa, that he has great respect for the American Negro. He saw Jesse Owens run in the 1936 Olympics.'

'I'm not American,' Louisa said, her head high.

'I told him you are a British subject.' Jane smiled, her eyes wrinkling so you couldn't see the colour in them. 'From an island in the West Indies.'

The pilot took fresh interest in the lass, his brows knotted. He asked a question, and Jane translated in a soft voice. 'Do you know the music he played, the piece that made you cry?'

Louisa nodded, and glanced again curiously at the German pilot. 'The *Hebrides Overture*,' she said. 'Scottish music by a German composer. Mendelssohn is German, isn't he?'

'Yes, but he was born Jewish,' Jane explained for the benefit of us musical ignoramuses, me and Nan. 'Not a Nazi favourite. Mendelssohn's work is banned in Germany. They pretend he's not one of theirs.'

I wondered what the pilot would think of me, neither black nor Jewish, but a Traveller. What would he think of my people, who moved from place to place selling horses and willow baskets, collecting old clothes and mending pans, working in the tattie fields and at the berrying? Most *British* people don't like us. Surely the Nazis are worse.

I cringed into my uniform, as if it were a costume that didn't fit.

The outrageous Jerry asked another casual question.

'He wants to know,' said Jane to Louisa, 'if you are familiar with the music called Calypso.'

The lass nodded. She threw back her shoulders and stood straighter. 'But it's from Trinidad. I'm from Jamaica.'

The Jerry pilot breathed a long, raggedy breath. Then he held a hand towards Louisa. She flinched at first, but at last she reached to shake his offered hand. He looked her straight in the eye, solemn and serious, and repeated, 'Calypso.'

'I'm Louisa,' she said.

Nan Campbell spoke up, wiping her hands on her pinny. 'He can have Room Number Four, the best double room, at the single-room rate. Ask him how he means to pay.'

Jane asked him.

His eyes flicked up to 648 Squadron's wishing coins studding the beam above the bar. But he put his hand inside the breast of his leather coat and pulled out a wodge of limp English pound notes in a silver clip.

'I'll show him upstairs,' said Nan. 'Ellen, perhaps you'll come along so I don't have to go alone.'

The Jerry picked up his wooden box. He asked Jane another question.

'What did he say?' said Nan.

'He wants to take my gramophone to his room.'

'*You let him*,' said Nan, shaking a finger at her old auntie to make her mind. 'I've given him a bed, and I've given you another whisky, and Ellen has to drive him about. You let him choose some records.'

Everybody paraded up the pitchy stairs together as if we were about to have a party. Louisa carted the gramophone, and I brought the record albums and the torch. Jane, who couldn't do stairs quickly, jigged about trying to catch hold of things, finally anxious about something – her precious music. Louisa jigged about trying to catch hold of Jane. Mrs Campbell jigged about anxiously as well, but she was worried about something else. She needed Jane to translate as she showed the Jerry how to work the gas fire in his bedroom.

He did not at all seem to understand about putting the money in the meter. In any case he hadn't any small change. He turned the gas tap on and off about five times, which frighted me all over again, wondering if he might forget it was on and fill the house with gas.

He was only going to be here for one night, God pity us – couldn't Nan Campbell just turn the fire on herself this one time without having to teach him all the fine points of the meter?

Louisa finally ran back to Room Number Five and donated a shilling of her own, which was a very dear donation. But it got the fire going without a gas leak, and it meant we could all go to bed.

As Louisa dropped her shilling into the meter like a wishing coin itself, I wished that the enemy airman staying under our roof would not shoot any of us before he left.

Louisa:

Felix Baer looked exhausted, but he didn't go to sleep right away. I know, because I heard him playing records for half the night.

Beside me in Room Five's mysteriously lumpy bed with its musty mattress – you could smell damp in it through the clean bedclothes – Jane was asleep, I think, the moment her head hit the pillow. Not me. It was the second-longest day of my life, after the day when the bomb dropped in Balham and Mummy was killed. I dozed off, in the unfamiliar bed next to this unfamiliar old woman, but I kept waking and hearing the music in Room Four. Record after record. I'd fall asleep listening to Mozart, and wake up and hear Ravel. Or Cole Porter. Or some German song I didn't recognise.

Felix Baer couldn't have slept at all, because he kept changing records and winding the gramophone. Perhaps he was keeping himself awake on purpose, waiting for his contact from Intelligence.

The music was only a lullaby lilt through the closed doors and the passage between us, but it must have been jolly loud in the room where he was playing it. By and by I noticed that most of what he played – most of Jane's records, actually – were all forbidden in Germany now.

So he was treating himself to a feast of beautiful music from before the war, from before the Nazis, when people could listen to whatever they liked.

I wanted to hate him. But the music made my heart sore, and I remembered the warm touch of his palm against mine, and his bony fingers flying over the piano keys. What was it like to be a musician and not be able to play music you love? I thought of my flute and all it meant to me, lessons with Mummy, duets with Daddy, sitting on the roof of the flat in London trying to imitate the starlings at dusk when I should have been practising.

I drifted off once more, and this time when I woke I heard nothing but the wind in the Scotch pines on the knoll above the Limehouse, and Jane gently snoring beside me. Felix Baer was finished playing records.

I knew there wasn't a thing Jane could do if that German decided to shoot us in our sleep. But I didn't think he would, not after she let him share her music. Lying next to her, I felt like I was in the safest place in the house.

So finally I went to sleep properly.

Hours before it grew light, I opened my eyes and stared into a wholly unknown dark. I had absolutely no idea where I was. On a train? Or a boat? In an air-raid shelter? England, Jamaica, the Isle of Man? I wasn't scared – I just had no idea where I was. I'd been going so hard for so long that I'd lost my place in the world.

But I knew the sleeping person beside me was not Mummy but Johanna von Arnim, otherwise known as Jane Warner. This reminded me I'd come to Scotland to look after her, and I was in the Limehouse, and down the passage was a music-loving German pilot.

My stomach lurched with fear and fascination. It was hopeless trying to go back to sleep. I lay stiffly.

Before long there came a tapping at the door, soft but insistent. Jane slept on as if she were completely deaf. What if I opened the door and it was Felix Baer, with his pianist's hands and tired eyes? What would I say? We didn't share any language but music.

I found myself whistling the opening bars of the *Hebrides Overture* under my breath.

'Louisa!' The voice was high-pitched and urgent and definitely didn't belong to the German pilot. '*Louisa*, wake up!'

I crawled out of bed and clunked around in the dark, feeling my way. Jane and I had locked ourselves in; I'd shoved a chair under the door handle to brace it. It took me a moment to undo all this extra security.

'*Louisa!*'

'I'm coming!'

I got the door open. Ellen McEwen stood in the shadowy passage in her ATS uniform, less crisp than it was the day before, holding an electric torch.

'I have to take the pilot back to RAF Windyedge,' she said. 'His contact isn't here, but he wants to go. You can tell he's a mess of nerves. Will you come with me? Please come with me.'

'Oh—' I protested. 'But I'm supposed to help Jane – it's her first day here!'

'I asked Mrs Campbell, and she'll take over till you're back. Please, *please*, Louisa.'

Didn't I want to do something to win the war? To be in the sky? To fly into combat against German pilots?

Well, here was a German pilot.

It wasn't flying into combat, but it mattered. I could go with Ellen, and do a little thing for our side.

And I wanted to see him again.

'Yes, all right.' It came out like the croak of a tree frog. I cleared my throat and tried again. 'Let me get dressed.'

'Thank you, *thank you*. He's downstairs having coffee. We can have some too.'

Mrs Campbell had also made a great pot of porridge. We all stood at the bar strengthening ourselves, Ellen and I at one end and Felix Baer at the other. The 'coffee' was made from chicory syrup, and it was terrible. I decided I would not drink coffee again until rationing ended or I went back to Jamaica, whichever came first. But that pilot-pianist drank it greedily.

When he'd finished he looked up at the sixpences and shillings left behind by 648 Squadron, gleaming silver in the yellow light of the lamp Mrs Campbell had switched on behind the bar.

He reached into a pocket and pulled out something that shone like a silver sixpence. I couldn't tell what kind of coin it was between his thumb and forefinger. It wouldn't have fit in the gas meter, but he reached up and pressed it firmly into a crack in the black oak beam over our heads.

'You see, Louisa?'

I jumped. I didn't expect him to call me by name.

'How you say – ?' He faltered. 'For luck.'

'Aye, right,' said Mrs Campbell darkly. 'Good luck, then.'

He pushed away his coffee cup and went through to the hall. His boots clattered as he took the stairs two at a time. I worried he'd break his neck in the unfamiliar dark. A minute later we heard him come back down.

He whisked through the vestibule with his wooden box, and there was a lot of slamming of doors as he loaded his things in the Tilly. He ran up to Room Number Four again, and this time came down carrying Jane's gramophone in one arm and the armful of records in the other. He set these politely on the piano and the shelf in the cupboard beside it.

'*Danke* – thank you,' Felix Baer told us, smiling. He pointed upstairs, mimed sleep, and said, 'Thank you, ladies.'

'Aye, right,' Nancy Campbell repeated bitterly.

'Come,' he commanded Ellen.

She flinched. Her pale face was fish-belly white again, as if she expected her head to be chopped off.

Now was my chance to help her.

I swallowed hard, linked my elbow with Ellen's, and said to the airman, 'I'm coming too.'

Ellen squeezed my arm and turned her head to give me the faintest hint of a grateful smile. We stood side by side as if we were the best of friends determined to do a job together, not two strangers who'd only just met for a few minutes the day before.

The German pilot seemed perplexed. Then he figured out what I meant. He shrugged and jerked his head towards the door, beckoning us both. 'Come, two girls. It is good.'

He was going to let me go along without a fight.

I stepped away from Ellen so I could pull on my mother's winter coat.

Then we followed the German pilot into the windy dark.

Ellen:

Gripping that black pistol, the Jerry pilot chivvied Louisa to get into the Tilly ahead of him.

'You all right?' she whispered as I climbed in on my side.

'Aye, no bother,' I muttered. 'Better not chat.'

She sat squashed between me in my woollen overcoat and himself in his shiny leather one. 'He thinks we're friends,' she said. 'We *should* chat. We should act like we're not scared. He'll tell us to stop if he minds.'

I tried to get a keek at her face as I started the engine, but it was too dark. She seemed a quiet thing. But she was bolder than she looked, and clever with it.

The Jerry pilot kept his pistol pointed at me, his arm across the dashboard.

'Don't wave your hands or look as if you're going to fight him,' Louisa said sensibly. 'Just chat about the road and how long it takes to get there and things like that.'

'Well then,' I said, and swallowed. 'Um. Bit cold for the time of year, aye?'

'Is it? This is my first time in Scotland. Everyone always asks me if I'm cold! I'm used to being cold. I lived in London for three years, but I grew up in Jamaica.'

I couldn't remember if Jane had said it was in the East or West Indies, and I didn't like to ask. Was this how folk felt when they found I was a Traveller, so full of ignorance they couldn't talk sense?

Of course most folk don't ask those questions whilst driving an RAF utility vehicle, havering from hedge to hedge because they are trying to keep an eye on the German's gun on the dashboard and hoping it doesn't go off by accident when you hit a bump in the lane.

The pilot didn't tell us to hush, though, so Louisa kept going, like a terrier with a bone. 'Could you drive before the war?' she asked.

'Only – only a wee bit,' I said through gritted teeth. 'I trained when I joined up.'

'Do you like it?'

Had I ever thought whether I liked it or not? It was a fair question.

'Aye,' I whispered. 'I do like it. Makes me feel powerful, managing a big machine like this.'

'All that noise and speed!' she said as we rattled up to the airfield barrier.

'And the smell of petrol,' I agreed. 'Sharp and fumy. Exciting.'

I stopped to wait for the guards to come out.

Louisa said fiercely, 'An important job to do.'

I thought she sounded envious.

Sergeants Nobby Fergusson and Jack Hinton came up to the van, and Jack pointed his rifle at us.

Louisa:

It was still dark. Ellen cranked down her window to talk to the guards.

'All right there, Volunteer McEwen?' one of them asked

anxiously. He poked an electric torch through the window and swept it over us.

'I am still alive,' Ellen answered bitterly. 'The Jerry's heading home now. Get your light away, Nobby, you're blinding me.'

'Who's the coloured girl?'

I tightened my hands on the dashboard. Why didn't he ask *me* that question?

The light moved, and Ellen answered. 'She's called Louisa Adair. She's new at the Limehouse. I asked her to come along with me.'

'Has she got ID?'

'Nobby Fergusson, I will give you ID at the end of my arm with my fist in your teeth. Or will you take over my job?' Ellen snarled. 'Because I have got a ruddy Jerry's gun pointed at my face the day, as you can see—'

The torch's beam fell still, lighting up Felix Baer's hand on the dashboard holding the pistol. The curves of shining black metal gleamed softly in the dark.

Suddenly the barrel of the other guard's rifle cut the light as he pushed it through the window past Ellen's head, pointing it at Felix Baer. The end of the long gun was in front of my nose.

In a flash, as I flung up my hands to protect my face, a lot of terrifying things happened. Ellen cried, 'You idiot, Jack, away wi' you!' Felix Baer pulled me against his chest, which meant that if the rifle went off in that closed space in the dark, I'd be the first to die. Baer raised his pistol, reached across Ellen, and with a sharp crack, fired a shot out her window that must have missed the guard's head by a quarter of an inch.

'*Don't shoot! Don't shoot at him!*' Ellen screeched. '*You cannae see! You're too close, you'll hit us!*'

She grabbed the rifle. She couldn't push it away, but she stopped the guard from aiming it. Everything went still. Felix Baer had his arm across my shoulders, not choking me, but gripping me firm against him.

'Shh, shh,' he said softly in my ear. 'Louisa. *Stille.*'

I held still, cold against his stiff leather coat.

'Lift the barrier, will you, Nobby?' Ellen gasped. 'So we can get him to his plane and get rid of him.'

'We fly now,' agreed Felix Baer with authority. He urged Ellen to start forward. 'This girl. We fly.'

The defeated guards raised the barrier.

Ellen:

My hands on the steering wheel and the gear stick quaked like birch leaves in a wind. I couldn't drive in such a state.

I whispered, 'Crack on with your chat, will you, Louisa?'

She looked up over her shoulder at the Jerry pilot. 'I need to help her,' she said. 'Is that all right?'

He let go of her throat, but not the pistol.

Louisa pressed cold hands over mine and squeezed. 'He won't hurt us. He won't. I think it would kill him. It's all for show. We've only to get him to his plane, and he'll go back to wherever he came from—'

'He said I have to go along,' I whispered. '*This girl. We fly.*'

'He might have meant me,' Louisa said. 'But I think he meant only to the airfield, not – not to *Germany*.'

She rabbited on hopefully, and I realised her accent wasn't just London – it was actually quite posh, too. Not proper posh, not like Jamie Stuart when he was putting it on, but like someone who reads a lot – like someone whose mum was a schoolteacher. Her calm voice worked on me like a granny coaxing a sobbing bairn with promises. At last I took a deep breath and shook off her hands. Die here, or fly to Germany? We had to move, at any rate.

I put the Hillman Minx in gear. It stalled as I moved forward. I took another breath and started the motor again carefully. I didn't dare steal another keek at Nobby and his mate as we left them.

My passengers were quiet as we sped along the narrow drive. I wondered what the Jerry pilot was thinking about. What would happen at the airfield when he tried to get me, or Louisa, into his plane? Would the RAF Windyedge lads let him take off? What would happen to me, or to Louisa, if they didn't?

God pity us.

Louisa:

It wasn't as dark now. Felix Baer would have daylight to fly in.

I was crammed between him and Ellen and couldn't possibly try to escape until one of them got out. I squinted into the gloom over the gun on the dashboard, trying to ignore it, and stared out at the aerodrome.

I am on a Royal Air Force aerodrome.

I thought I'd suffocate with fear and excitement. It was like having my own private Blitz in my head and my stomach.

I saw a cluster of sheds and barracks, concrete and boards and weathered brick. The drive was rutted gravel and the runway was grass. It all looked the same colour in the grey dawn. There was one plane parked on the grass.

It was the German pilot's Luftwaffe fighter, like some giant stinging insect with broad blades for wings. Its markings were covered, but it was as sleek and dangerous as a sword, a battle weapon and armour rolled into one.

I thought of Ellen saying that driving made her feel powerful. What must it be like to *fly*?

It may have been nerves or petrol fumes going to my head, but for a moment I envied Felix Baer even more than I envied Ellen McEwen.

Ellen:

I pulled up by operations. But the Jerry wouldn't walk across the airfield with folk such as Nobby and Jack chasing him. 'Go, *go*.' He pointed angrily to his plane, on the grass outside the hangar, and rapped his pistol against the windscreen for emphasis.

I didn't ken how many shots he had in that pistol, and I didn't want to find out. Never have I felt so sick with fright.

I drove as slowly as I dared, bumping over clats of turf, trying to give our lads a chance to come after us without giving the Jerry another fright.

I stopped alongside the plane and opened my door and climbed out. So did he. He wasn't going to give us any chance to make a run for it.

Louisa:

I jumped out after both of them. In the gloom, I could see the shadows of men running, and it looked like every one of them held a rifle. It was like watching a cinema newsreel, all black and grey, soldiers rushing into battle.

Weren't we supposed to let the German pilot go? Didn't he have a code name in some secret Intelligence plan? The guards at the gate nearly killed us trying to take command of him. But there wasn't supposed to be a battle.

I shouted, 'Don't shoot! Don't shoot!'

A few of the men skipped to a stop, as if the film reel wasn't spooling properly.

'Is that Volunteer McEwen? Who's with you?'

None of them knew who I was.

'The lassie works for Mrs Campbell at the pub,' Ellen cried. 'God pity us, never mind just now – don't fright the Jerry! Keep your guns down unless he tries to take us along!'

If they threatened him, he might panic and use his pistol again. I didn't believe he'd hurt me or Ellen, but we weren't armed men. Maybe he wouldn't aim to miss this time.

Ellen:

He herded us like a pair of ewe lambs, pointing our way with his gun. He stood us on the other side of his Messerschmitt, where no one could keek any part of us but our feet beneath the carcass of the plane. Our heads were right next to where the machine guns stuck out of the wing.

'What's he doing?' Louisa whispered. She only came up to my shoulder, and we both craned to spy on him.

'Sorting his gear,' I guessed. The nose of the plane pointed over my head and I couldn't see anything, either.

She hooked her elbow through mine again.

'If we both fight him …' that brave lass whispered. But she didn't finish her idea. He was out of our sight just now, but he still had that gun.

We heard the Jerry slam the doors of the Tilly. Then he got up on the wing we couldn't see, and pulled back the cockpit canopy. He took out a parachute and life jacket and chucked them on the ground.

'What's he doing now?' Louisa asked.

'Making room for his precious box,' I said.

Louisa:

I glimpsed the top of one narrow seat in the cockpit, with nothing behind it, and only the controls in front. He must have had to fly with the wooden case in his lap. Even his long coat must have been awkward in that cramped space.

He couldn't possibly have room to take a hostage, could he?

If he did, I would be a better fit than tall, long-legged Ellen.

Could he? Cram me in between his shoulder and the metal hull, and take off into the rising sun on those knife-blade wings?

For one thousandth of a second, just before it plummeted in fear, my heart *flew*.

Ellen:

He stood on the wing opposite. His left arm was straight out with the gun once again aimed at my head.

I spat to tell him how much I hated him.

He heaved a sigh. He kept his arm out with that ugly pistol cocked, and turned to shout towards the lads lined up on the edge of the airfield, pointing at him with their rifles.

'Starter!'

Louisa, braver than me, ducked to keek underneath the Messerschmitt and see what was going on.

Louisa:

The pilot was ready to leave. I couldn't take my eyes off him. Being interested numbed my fear, like ice numbing a twisted ankle, the way reading numbed grief.

He untied the fabric covering the plane's Luftwaffe markings so he wouldn't look suspicious when he landed back in Norway or wherever he was going. He checked the engine and wheels, he checked hinges on the wings and tail, and he checked the propeller. I longed to know what he was looking for, where the fuel went, what the hinges on the wings did.

At last he strapped on his life jacket and parachute and pulled on a leather flying helmet.

He yelled again in English to the soldiers with the guns, repeating what he'd said before.

'Starter!'

He waved a crankshaft at them, just like you'd use to start an old car, and mimed winding it.

Ellen:

'He needs a mechanic to turn over the engine,' I told Louisa in a whisper. 'Perhaps when the other lad comes near we'll be able to run …'

'But he'll need both hands to drive the plane,' Louisa whispered back. 'Like you do in the van, I'm sure of it. Wait till the engine starts. And *then* we'll run.'

The Jerry had to wait along with us for the starter. He climbed in and sat there with his left arm slung out of the cockpit and his filthy old pistol *still* pointing at my head.

At least neither one of us was in the plane with him. A bonny green sprig of hope unfolded in my heart.

Louisa:

The mechanic stood on the other side of the plane to crank the engine, so we couldn't see what he was doing. But we jolly well heard and felt when it started. The roar exploded around us like a tube train pulling into an Underground station. The German pilot pulled his arm back into the cockpit as the plane jumped forward an inch or two; the wing nearly knocked us over.

Before he slid the canopy shut over his head, Felix Baer leaned out and waved at us.

The gun was gone. I was right – he needed both hands for the plane. We were in his way now, and he was trying to shoo us off like chickens.

I waved back, to let him know I understood.

Ellen:

'Go!' Louisa cried.

She grabbed my arm and harled me along beside her. We raced away across the mowed strip of runway with the noise of the Messerschmitt howling around us. Then we were stumbling over longer, slippery grass. The Luftwaffe engine screamed like a pack of devils and if anyone was shooting at anyone, I couldn't hear it.

All at once that strange lassie stopped running.

She turned about to watch him go.

Louisa:

The sky was dark blue and grey with clouds, but it was light enough that the sun must have been up somewhere, somewhere not so gloomy as northern Scotland in November. The German plane lifted off the runway into the east wind.

Felix Baer was black wings against the grey sky, and then he was a black dot over the North Sea, and then he was gone.

Jamie:

Overnight, Shetland came under a bombardment of howling wind and pouring rain, battering down from the north-east, and nobody could take off. A-Flight was in bed, exhausted after slogging through the storm, but B-Flight sat in the officers' lounge consuming shortbread and watery tea when Cromwell came in and barked, 'Pack up, you lot: 648 Squadron's posted to the mainland. A-Flight's joining the Spitfires at RAF Deeside, and B-Flight's going to fly from RAF Windyedge for the rest of the winter. The Spits have their own commanding officer, so I'll be at Windyedge with B-Flight, but as there's only ten miles between bases I'll keep tabs on all of 648 Squadron.'

This was the best news I'd had in a long time. Cromwell was going to have to commute, and I'd be back at RAF Windyedge where my friend Ellen McEwen was the ATS driver. And it was less than an hour on the train to get home if I ever had a day's leave.

'What'll we be doing there?' asked Pilot Officer Adam Stedman hopefully. He was the new leader of Madeira Section, the other half of B-Flight – the fellow Cromwell had threatened to replace me with. 'Hunting U-boats?'

Up in Shetland, our assignment was to bomb German shipping. The anti-aircraft guns on their destroyers were our worst enemy. We longed to have a go at their submarines, which would be less able to fire back at us, but we never knew where to find them.

'You'll be on warship escort and reconnaissance. And protecting coastal fishing and supply fleets. RAF Windyedge needs a squadron stationed there until a spot of bother with Intelligence blows over. Get ready to leave.'

Cromwell stormed out again, slamming the door behind him, to go wake up A-Flight and rattle them with his urgent news to start packing. But none of B-Flight jumped up to get moving.

'Bloody North Sea mist,' somebody muttered. 'We're not flying anywhere in weather like this, are we?'

Silver nudged me with his elbow. He lit a cigarette and murmured, 'Sounds like they're sending us somewhere a bit less hot. I think the lads need rallying.'

I wondered if the move was punishment for Dougie and his crew not keeping their mouths shut, or for Ignacy's overconfidence, or for my struggle to get B-Flight's new aircrews to work together.

Then I remembered the radio operator with his urgent message from Windyedge.

'Maybe it's hotter than Cromwell's letting on,' I said. 'Maybe the spot of bother with Intelligence and that Jerry we ran into were part of the same op. Maybe they're sending us as a guard force.'

'You sound very clued up.'

I stubbed out my own cigarette. 'Something's going on,' I said. 'We're supposed to play along without knowing what.' I nodded towards Dougie Kerr, leaning his wiry ginger head forward to catch what I was muttering. 'Careless talk costs lives,' I said. 'Or perhaps Dougie's going a bit deaf from all that rear gunnery, and we should invest in an ear trumpet for him.'

Silver laughed. 'I think a megaphone for you would be a better investment.' He drew on his cigarette. 'Now's your chance. Take the podium.'

He was right, as usual. I stood up, grabbed a spoon, and clinked my teacup for attention.

'All right, lads!'

They looked at me like expectant puppies. They *were* like puppies – untrained, disobedient, but anxious for praise and action, and maybe, if I worked at it, I'd win their loyalty. I'd had it before, to the death. Starting over was hard on us all.

'I'll bet every one of you began the war thinking you'd be a fighter pilot in a Spitfire or a Hurricane,' I said.

Every one of them nodded, grumbling in agreement. 'Too bloody right!' said the new Australian pilot, Harry Morrow.

'Well, we're not flying the most glamorous kites, but we're just as important and just as dead when our luck runs out. I'm not going to quote poetry, but if you like, Flying

Officer Silvermont, my navigator here, can recite John Donne's "No man is an island"—'

Laughter and hoots of 'No thank you very much!'

'What about action?' asked Dougie Kerr, the big-mouthed gingery Australian air gunner. 'I want another go, and I won't blow our own tail off this time.'

His pilot, tall Harry Morrow, and their navigator, baby-faced Gavin Hamilton, shared a laugh.

I glanced over at Ignacy, Pimms Section's bloodthirsty Polish pilot.

'We all want another go,' I said. 'Only next time we'll coordinate the action, all right? No heroics with Messerschmitts. There's only one Blenheim pilot who's an official ace, Reginald Peacock over in 235 Squadron, and he's dead now. You can't dogfight in a Blenheim; it's not built for single combat. If we want to count as aces, we have to do it as a team. German battleships and U-boats count for us as much as fighter planes. Let's aim to get five while we're at Windyedge, and we'll all be aces.'

'All right, I will drink to that,' said Ignacy.

'I'm in,' said Adam Stedman from Madeira Section.

The Welsh navigator, Derfel Cledwyn, held up his teacup to Ignacy. They both knocked back their tea as if they were sharing a toast with whisky or vodka. The only one who didn't crack a smile was their new gunner, Bill Yorke. But he was always a bit quiet. Tough job being thrown in with Ignacy and Derfel, who jawed away at each other in the air in Polish and Welsh as if they were playing at League of Nations.

'You'll all like being at Windyedge,' I added. 'It's close enough to Stonehaven and Aberdeen that you can go to the cinema or a dance hall in bad weather, and there's a jolly good village pub within walking distance—'

'I remember that pub!' Chip put in enthusiastically. 'With the wishing coins and the piano. Nancy Campbell always had the fire burning for us. That'll be fine.'

'Something to look forward to,' I agreed, deciding not to tell him off for interrupting since I wasn't being formal anyway. 'We'll polish up formation flying on our way to Windyedge. And I'll keep my ear to the ground so we don't get in trouble with Old Cromwell again.'

I looked around the room at these few friends and strangers. And Silver, my best friend, always watching my back. Pimms and Madeira, B-Flight's lads. My lads.

I raised my own teacup. 'To Windyedge!'

'To Windyedge!'

The applause was polite rather than thundering, but at least they applauded.

'Nice speech, Scotty,' said Silver, grinning at me. 'That's got everybody ready for a fight. I look forward to us all being official aces.'

Part Two

Storm Front

... - --- .-. -- ..-. .-. --- -. -

Ellen:

That Intelligence toff, Robert Ethan, turned up at the Limehouse late that morning for about three hours. He was rail thin and dressed in dapper tweeds, with huge eyes behind specs thick as bottle glass. His magnified eyes made you feel like a midgie pinned against a piece of card when he looked at you.

Nan fixed up her best double room for him – Number Four, the same one she'd let to the Jerry pilot – but Ethan didn't stay. He was in a hurry and hopping mad that he'd missed the ado. He'd spent most of the day before stuck on a train waiting for a troops transport to pass. When he got off at last – with special permission to climb down on to the railway track and walk away before the train moved! – he legged it to an RAF aerodrome and tried to fly to Windyedge to make up the lost time. But the weather down south closed in on them, so then he ended up stuck somewhere else in England overnight. Now another storm was rolling in, and he didn't want to waste his precious time being stuck here.

He hung about long enough to grill us all, and then he poked around in the Jerry pilot's room, like a terrier sniffing out rats. After his wee nosy he came downstairs and went straight to the gramophone case and tested its working parts. Finally he pawed through Jane's records, emptying all the album sleeves and checking with Louisa about which ones the Jerry had played. He didn't say what he was looking for, and as far as I could tell, he didn't find anything.

Last thing before he went, he turned his sticking-pin gaze on Louisa, standing quiet as a mouse at Jane's shoulder by the big old mantelpiece.

'That is quite the collection of wishing coins,' he said. 'Aren't airmen a superstitious lot! Well, perhaps the hoodoo will help you to feel at home, Louisa. Thank you, my dear Mrs Campbell, for being so patient while I shifted the furniture about upstairs. And you, Mrs Warner, for allowing me to disturb your recordings. You have a very youthful taste in music! I apologise if I haven't put everything back in its proper place – mustn't leave any stone unturned. I shall dash now before the weather closes in. I am damnably disappointed. Volunteer McEwen, is your utility vehicle at my service?'

As if I had a choice. At least he wouldn't pull a gun.

It wasn't until later, back at the Limehouse, that I realised how unpopular he'd made himself.

'All right, Louisa?' I asked her. She was rinsing crockery behind the bar, her pretty heart-shaped face pinched and frowning. I added, 'Where is everybody?'

'Mrs Campbell is putting things right in Room Four, and Jane is supposed to be having a rest. She spent *ages* fussing over her records, and she made me go with her to the village shop to try to find sticky tape for a torn album sleeve. Now her bad hip is hurting. She won't *say*, but I'm learning to guess.'

'Does it make you cross?'

Her frowning brows went smooth. 'I'm not cross.'

I said gently, 'But I can see that you are.'

She pressed her lips together and shook her head.

We'd only met the day before, but we'd shared a great trial that morning and it made us closer than we would be otherwise. I knew she wasn't happy. 'Was it something Nan said? Don't let her fash you,' I told her. 'She's not too old to change her ways, but she's slow to learn.'

I lived in fear Nan would twig what I was and we'd have a bitter fight over whether I should leave her house. I didn't think she'd prefer me to raise a tent in her garden, but I wasn't ready to find out.

'If she said something rude, it was ignorance,' I said. 'She's crabbit, but she doesn't mean to be hurtful.'

'Oh!' Louisa gasped, and I saw I'd hit close to truth. 'It wasn't Nan. It was that awful Intelligence officer going on about hoodoo! *Why?* Do I *look* like a fool-fool country gal? Is that because I'm only fifteen? Or because I've left school without finishing? Because I'm not doing a skilled job? *Or is it just because I'm from Jamaica?*'

She rattled the cups like a rebel. 'My mum taught music in an English school. She played the harp at weddings, and the church organ for two different congregations. I hardly know what he *meant*, and anyway it's Mrs Campbell who's superstitious, not me!' She waved at the coins over her head.

'Have you heard her going on about these? "That's dead men's money. Leave it where it is." She knows the name of every airman every penny belonged to. She talks as if they're her own children!'

'I'll wager she didn't like that filthy Jerry leaving his wish up there with the rest,' I said. 'Let's take his penny out and see if she misses it.'

Louisa raised her eyes to the wooden beam.

She might not be superstitious, but she knew exactly which one of those silver wishes belonged to that Jerry pilot.

I saw where she was looking, and reached up to pick it between my fingernails. It had a raised rim and came out easily when I pulled on it.

I held it on my open palm so Louisa could see, and we stared.

It was no coin.

'That's a typewriter key,' said Louisa.

It was a wee black enamel disc, just big enough to set your fingertip on, with a shiny, smooth nickel edge. The edge made a sort of lip around the key, like a pot lid. The letter on it was an *L*: *L* for *Louisa*.

And aye, yes, I am sure he chose it on purpose.

Louisa blinked up at the ceiling again, and I remembered Nan in the room above. We stood quiet as mice, listening, but she didn't come down.

'It's off that thing in the box,' Louisa whispered. 'It was a sort of electrical typewriter. I saw inside it when he put it on the piano and the lid fell open. The keys were just like that.'

I rolled the disc between my fingers. I wondered why he'd left it.

Louisa held out her hand, and I could see she wanted it for herself.

I dropped it into her palm. She closed her fingers like a gamekeeper's iron trap snapping shut, and caught me frowning.

She said, 'He played so beautifully.'

'You weren't at all afraid,' I said, remembering how sick I'd felt. 'You came along brave as a king going into battle.'

'No, I was terribly afraid,' she contradicted. 'But I wanted to help you! I want so much to do something useful. I didn't believe he'd hurt us – he hated bullying us. He did it because he had to. Like airmen dropping bombs.'

'I worried he'd take one of us with him,' I admitted.

'So did I, until I saw how tight a fit it would be!'

We shared a shaky laugh. It felt good to have it behind us.

'We won!' I said. 'Our first battle together! Keep that wee charm for luck.'

'What did I say about superstition?' Louisa exclaimed, and I laughed again.

'Och then, keep it as a trophy! Don't let Nan spy you, though.'

'I won't,' Louisa said.

Louisa:

Mrs Campbell flounced downstairs, carrying a heather broom in one hand and a feather duster in the other. Her wispy hair coiled in sweaty frills around her face. She looked like she'd just finished one battle and was ready for the next.

Though she didn't see what we'd been up to, my cheeks heated up. I slipped Felix Baer's typewriter key into my skirt pocket. Tea, I was supposed to be making tea for Jane. I'd lit the burner for the kettle ages ago, and it still hadn't boiled.

'The flame needs to be higher,' Mrs Campbell said, turning it up. 'Goodness, Louisa, you were in London three years already, did no one teach you how to make tea? Leaving the gas low just wastes it!'

'Don't have a go at her for not knowing her way about your kitchen, Mrs C.,' said Ellen, straightening her cap in a way that told you she was enlisted. 'She's not been here a day, and we've all had a fright.'

Mrs Campbell harrumphed and made the tea herself. She loaded a tray for me to carry up to Jane.

Then it came out why she was cross about the wasted gas. She was just blaming it on me because the real culprit had already left.

'That Robert Ethan left the fire on in Room Four, despite all I said to him, and it's been roaring away all day with no one in there,' she grumbled as she poured boiling water. 'And he got the last of the milk as well; there isn't any more till tomorrow. Aunt Jane'll have to have her tea black.'

Nan gave me the tray and turned around to check she'd turned off the burner. Then she lifted the wooden gate for me to get out from behind the bar.

'When you go upstairs, Louisa, would you run into Room Four and close the window? It was much too warm in there by the time I'd swept and put everything back.' She added, I think to herself, 'I must get the collection man to check that gas-fire fitting when he fetches the money from the meters. It has come loose. That can't be safe, and it's my best room.'

Away I went upstairs feeling assaulted by frustration. I was angry at Nancy Campbell, who was paying me but who was clearly going to be difficult to get along with – and I was angry at myself, too, for not standing up to her. I didn't understand why I was so moved by the strange German pilot I should by rights have hated, and why I so disliked the British officer who was supposed to be on my side.

It was after three o'clock. In another hour, this far north, it would start to get dark. I lit the fire in our room and left Jane with the tea tray while I went to close the window in the room down the passage.

Number Four wasn't like ours at all – I could see why Nan said it was her best. It faced south-east, like ours, but had a big Victorian bay window. The room was tidy but freezing, because the middle sash was open wide, and wind made the curtains float and stir like ghosts. I had to hang my weight on the window frame, giving a jump that got my feet off the ground, before I could shift it to close it.

I stood looking out for a moment at the beautiful, bleak brown-and-grey view of the moor and village rooftops and North Sea. It wasn't raining, but the wind made the Scotch pines bow on the ridge above the old house. Somewhere in the far sky a storm was blowing over, bad weather rushing west from Norway, across Scotland, out to the Atlantic.

My mind followed the wind west to the blue Caribbean Sea and back five years to Mummy's thirty-fifth birthday. Daddy borrowed a rowboat and took all three of us across the water from Port Royal for a picnic on the coral beach at Lime Cay, and a storm rolled in late in the afternoon when we were on our way back. Daddy rowed for ages and couldn't get any closer to the mainland, so he and Mummy each took an oar. I was at their feet bundled in the picnic blanket. We were all soaked to the skin, and I had to bang the aluminium coffee pot with a spoon and sing 'Land of Hope and Glory' to set the rhythm for their rowing.

It should have been terrifying – thinking about it, I saw that it might really have been terrifying, especially for Mummy. But for me, it was wonderful, a big adventure, helping them to fight our way home together.

So proud of my girl, Daddy had said. *A real voyager, not a bit scared*.

I turned back to the cold room. I stood there for a moment – not long, only two or three seconds – and thought about Felix Baer playing records in here for half the night. What was in his mind all that time? Was he a professional musician, like my mother, before the war? What was his family like? Did he have a sweetheart? What would happen to him if the Luftwaffe found out he'd sneaked off to Windyedge when he was supposed to be shooting down British planes?

And why had he pulled a key off his typewriter, an *L* for *Louisa*, and stuck it in the ceiling of the Limehouse?

I shook my head to clear it. Then, just before I went back to Jane, I checked to make sure the gas tap was off. The gas fires in Mrs Campbell's rooms were just like the one Mummy and I had in our London flat, and Mummy had dinned it into my head to make sure the gas was always off when I left the room.

Mrs Campbell was right – one of the Victorian panels around the new fire was loose. I rattled the fixture under my hand, worrying. What if the pipes came disconnected? Town gas was deadly when it leaked. I looked more closely, and saw there were fresh dents on both the new fire and the old frame, as if someone had forced a wedge between them and tried to pry the fire out of its setting.

I stared at the gas fire, small and neat, not as secure as it should have been. In the old fireplace behind the Victorian panels, there would be a dark, hollow space where you could hide *anything*. Secret plans. Vials of poison. A *bomb*, perhaps.

Surely Felix Baer would have made noise getting the panels off.

But no one would have heard anything over the music.

I picked at that shaky cast iron panel with my fingernails. I couldn't get enough grip on it to pry it loose.

I ran back to Room Five. Jane sat calmly drinking tea. She looked at me in surprise; I was fizzing with excitement.

'What in the world, Louisa?'

'I'll be back in a moment, just a moment,' I panted. 'I need—'

I opened my flute case and grabbed the thin steel rod for cleaning the flute.

'What's Nancy want with you now, girl?' Jane enquired. 'You're not to run her errands; you're here for me.

You mustn't let her order you about. I'll have a word if you like.'

'It's not her. It might not be anything. I'll tell you in a minute. Wish me luck!'

'What in the world?' she said again, and laughed. Now she was curious. She saluted me with her teacup. 'Off you go and hurry up! Good luck!'

I was not sure what I'd do if Nancy Campbell discovered me taking her fireplace apart, the day after I arrived in her house. What was the worst that could happen – might she fire me with no pay? I knew how desperate she was for someone to look after Jane. I could talk my way out of this.

I went back to Room Four, wedged the steel rod into the fireplace, and pulled. The panel came off easily, falling into the tiled hearth with a crash. I caught my breath, but no one seemed to hear.

I peered inside the hole I'd made in the wall of the Limehouse.

In the back of the fireplace was an old deep-set stone hearth that went right into the full thickness of the wall. The gas line came up through a pipe in the floor and ran behind the grate to connect to the new fire. It wasn't at all disturbed by the panel being out. In the dark, sitting in the two-hundred-and-fifty-year-old hearth, was Felix Baer's wooden case.

At first I was confused. I was sure I'd seen him carry it out of the house and put it in Ellen's van yesterday morning. How could it be here behind the fireplace in Room Four?

I tried to remember what I'd seen, and realised I'd seen *nothing*. He'd used the gramophone as a decoy, and by some wizardly sleight of hand he made us think he'd put his own case in the Tilly ready to fly back to Norway with him. It was dark, and nobody checked in the back of the van to see if he'd put anything there or not, and he'd made sure Ellen and I were standing on the side of the plane where we couldn't see him unloading before he took off again.

So clever. And so desperate! What exactly was this thing he'd taken such risks to deliver and leave here?

There was a small cardboard box in front of the case, not much bigger than my fist. I reached in and grabbed the box and the case, and then, as fast as I could, I fit the iron panel back in place. It was easy to take apart and put back together, because Felix Baer had done the hard work of prying the panel loose in the first place. He must have broken it free of its fixture.

I closed up Room Four behind me and went back to Jane with Felix Baer's wooden box.

The old woman's pale blue eyes flew wide when she saw what I was carrying. She didn't tell me off.

'I suppose you'd better lock the door,' she said.

I don't think Nancy Campbell would have ever allowed us near each other if she'd guessed what collaborators we'd become.

Jane rubbed her hands together. I sat the wooden case and cardboard box on the bed and, remembering Felix Baer and his records, turned on the wireless. It took half a minute to warm up. It felt like the longest thirty seconds of my life, longer than waiting for bombs to explode during the Blitz.

But at last we were in the middle of a lovely swing tune, and I turned up the radio – not too much, as I didn't want to arouse suspicion, and our operation ought to be a quiet one. I opened the case.

I had thought it was some kind of typewriter when I caught my glimpse of it on the piano. But it wasn't. There was no place to fit paper. Instead, above the keyboard was a plate of letters that exactly matched the keyboard itself. Above the letter plate were three dials and a switch.

Jane was out of her chair, hanging on to the headboard of the bed so she could get closer. The front flap of the box came unlatched and fell open as she sat. We both saw the brand name printed on the inside: ENIGMA.

Jane bent to read the metal card, all in German, that was screwed into the inside of the top lid.

'It says it is a cipher machine,' she breathed. 'It must be for creating code. Or translating code.'

'Are those *instructions*?' I gasped.

'Not *useful* instructions,' Jane answered. 'Just cleaning instructions! But it tells a bit about the moving parts …'

She kept reading, and I bent alongside her to get a closer look at the machine.

The last keypad in the bottom right corner of the keyboard was missing.

I took the *L* key out of my pocket and tried to place it over the empty peg. It didn't fit, but as I pressed the peg down, a *Q* suddenly lit up in the letter plate above the keyboard.

'It's battery-powered,' Jane said. She straightened up and tapped at other keys. Random letters lit in the display plate. Each time they lit, one of the dials moved along a notch. 'It's in perfect working order.'

'The letters don't match!' I exclaimed.

'It mixes them,' she said. 'Then they're in code. The lid says to refer to instructions we don't have.'

'Maybe we can figure it out,' I said.

Jane opened the cardboard box. Inside it, wrapped in a flannel cloth, were two notched steel gears each about the size of a tin of shoe polish.

'I think these are extra dials,' Jane said. 'You turn the dials to change the way you scramble the letters. If you put different dials in, you get even more ways to mix them up. This will keep us busy!'

I saw that you could set up the machine to turn your message into nonsense, and then someone with the same machine, or one like it, could decode your nonsense by using the same setting.

A German coding machine was sitting on my bed. Did Robert Ethan know what Felix Baer had brought with him? He hadn't said anything about it.

But he'd definitely been looking for *something*.

I knew we'd have to tell someone, but I didn't know where to start. It must be terribly, terribly secret. We couldn't telephone anybody – the people at the exchange might hear anything we said.

'What's that you've got?' Jane asked me.

'I think it is the key that goes in the corner. The pilot must have taken it off on purpose – he left it with the wishing coins this morning. He said my name. I think he *wanted* me to find it, but I don't know why.'

I showed her.

I poked the nail of my little finger into the hollow back

of the key, wondering why it didn't fit over its peg. Something was jammed in there, but even my little fingernail was too big to tease it out.

'Use a hairpin,' suggested Jane. So I did.

The jammed-in thing was a curled-up strip of paper. I unrolled it carefully and smoothed it out against the tea tray. It had a name written on it in pencil: *Django Reinhardt*.

We stared.

Jane turned one of the dials slowly. I looked over her shoulder and tried to do the maths in my head to work out how many combinations you could use to set the dials. Thousands of millions. No, I must be calculating wrong. *Millions of millions* of different ways to set the code.

It would be *so easy* to do with the machine and just about impossible to *undo* without it.

'Go fetch the Django Reinhardt records,' said Jane. 'Bring both albums.'

'But that Intelligence officer emptied all the record sleeves,' I reminded her.

'Get them anyway.'

Mrs Campbell did no more than glance at me as I came racing back downstairs for an armful of Jane's records. I felt like I'd been running up and down the dark stairs of the Limehouse carrying record albums all my life.

I got back to Room Five, breathless, and dumped the records on the bed. Jane opened the first album. 'There's a separate pocket in here for album notes,' she explained. 'That's where I used to hide my bank passbook.' She checked, found nothing, and picked up the other record.

And behind the notes in that one she found three small leaflets, each one of them made of two folded pieces of paper, a plain white sheet with a red cover. The cover was printed in German.

Jane turned the pages of one of the booklets with trembling hands. The inside of the cover was scrawled with neat, pencilled text. The printed sheet in the middle was a grid of numbers and letters.

'Instructions and dial settings,' Jane whispered.

I hardly dared to breathe.

'The dials are called rotors. I was right: the key plate comes up and you can change them.' Jane studied Felix Baer's written instructions. 'Go on, try it!'

'I'll break it!' I exclaimed.

'It's quite robust. Let's see how it works.'

It really was like having a wonderful new toy. Jane pored over Felix Baer's pencilled instructions and the printed charts, commenting aloud as she read, while I took the machine apart and fit it back together like a puzzle box. The mechanics of it were rather beautifully simple for such a complicated piece of machinery.

'These charts tell you the code settings for each day of the month for one group of the Luftwaffe,' Jane explained. 'They change *every day.* He's given us three months' worth, but November is nearly finished. Phew! What a production military communication must be!'

We forgot everything else. We played with the German cipher machine until long after it got dark.

'All we need now is a message to decode,' I said wistfully.

The old woman laughed. 'Better pack it up,' she said. 'Then hide it all in the back of the wardrobe, under the furs.'

'But we ought to tell someone!'

'We need the right person to tell, and the right way to tell them,' Jane said. Her pale blue eyes were excited in her wrinkled face. 'Perhaps the radio operator at the aerodrome? You needn't say what you've found – just that you have information for the War Office. Ellen can arrange it, perhaps.'

I nodded. That made sense.

I placed the *L* key over the empty peg. Now it fitted perfectly.

I hid the incredible machine under Jane's furs in the back of the wardrobe. Jane watched me open my flute case to put the cleaning rod back. She picked up her teacup, took a sip, and put it down again. It had gone stone cold hours ago.

'I would love to hear you play your flute, Louisa,' Jane said.

Tears stabbed at my eyes, and I squeezed them shut.

A man and a woman were crooning together on the radio, just as Mummy and Daddy used to do the minute he came into the house – even in England, where we had to use the piano in our landladies' sitting room. First thing always when he got home from sea, they'd throw themselves down on the piano bench, and play and sing together.

I realised I hadn't taken my flute out of its case since Mummy's death.

'I'm rubbish,' I said. 'I've had to do exams, and perform in school, but really I only like to play for fun. I only play for *me*. Same with the piano. Or singing. I'll never be a professional like my mother – or you! I don't like to practise. My favourite thing is just to copy tunes I hear on the radio.'

'Play what you like, then,' Jane said.

Despite the sudden wallop of grief, I was still jitterbugging with excitement – playing my flute would be a good way to get rid of the nerves, I knew, before I had to face Nan Campbell again.

But I wanted to play *well* for Jane – a thing I'd never thought about much before. I didn't mind being a mediocre piano player. But I suddenly wished I was better at the flute. How wonderful if she would sing with me! I imagined a new record album: 'The Ballads of Jane and Louisa' …

'Jane and Louisa …' Perfect! It was another game we sang under the Bombay mango tree at my first school in Jamaica, and with my cousins under the breadfruit and ackee trees on Granny Adair's land in St Andrew Parish. And the first time we'd met, Jane and I had sung a singing-game tune to each other.

All right, I'd play my flute for her.

I switched off the radio. Then I screwed the pieces of my flute together, ran up and down an F-major scale, and began to play.

The easy, lilting, cheerful tune was the sound of before the war. It was so short that I played it again, adding trills. In my head, I sang the verses along with the flute, and it warmed up with me. The music reminded me again of Mummy, who was always humming whatever piece she was working on, and of Daddy, who whistled when he wasn't singing, and my heart was full of pain and love.

'What is that?' Jane asked, when I'd finished.

I swallowed the ache in my throat and sang it for her. Because it wasn't about Mummy and Daddy. It was about *us*.

'Jane and Louisa will soon come home,
They will soon come home,
They will soon come home;
Jane and Louisa will soon come home,
Into this beautiful garden.'

She laughed softly. 'This beautiful garden indeed! I wonder if anything but heather grows out there in the gloom. I suppose Scotland must be beautiful in the summer.'

She hummed the tune. It was wonderful how fast she could learn a song.

'Have you brought any sheet music with you?' she asked. 'We could play duets. We'll have to pass the time somehow. Surely it's not going to be German spies every day.'

And of course it wasn't. The next day it was 648 Squadron, B-Flight.

Jamie:

The Old Roundhead split up B-Flight for our journey to RAF Windyedge. It was hard to believe he wasn't purposefully trying to get me in trouble. Adam Stedman took Madeira Section straight there, with Phyllis as a passenger. Meanwhile I had to lead Pimms to escort a patrol of British destroyers down the coast of Scotland on our way to our new post.

'Without bombs!' I cursed as we took off. 'Loaded with tinned beef and spare parts, but no bombs. Just ridiculous. Heavy for an air battle, not properly armed for a scrape with the German navy.'

'Beautiful night, though,' said Silver.

'Yes.'

'Look around!'

The moon was waning but silvery bright, in a bottle-blue sky, shining on a tossing black sea. It was bumpy flying, a fresh wind blowing behind the storm.

'It always kind of gets me,' Silver said.

'Me too.' I took a breath, calming down. 'Maybe there won't be a battle.'

The turbulence made it hard work for Ignacy and Harry to stay on my wingtips.

'Can you not take us higher and find some smooth air?' Ignacy called over the radio. 'Yorkie's just been sick. I never had a sparks get sick before.'

Yorkie had been in the Royal Air Force for ten years – I couldn't believe it. I resisted poking fun.

'Give him a mint imperial,' I said. 'Any higher and we'll attract attention.'

I didn't want to meet any Messerschmitts before we'd even found our convoy.

Next it was Harry Morrow reporting that Dougie was feeling sick too.

'It's his own fault,' Harry added. 'He's back there with his head down, picking up German code again.'

'Yorkie hears it too,' Ignacy reported.

'Oi, Tex!' Silver turned around to get Chip's attention. 'Can you hear it?'

'Yep,' Chip said. 'It's not German, though. Just strings of letters.'

'It's in code, you twit,' said Silver.

'I'm copying it anyway,' Chip said. 'I can read and fly and copy code and not get airsick. I should get a medal!'

'All we'll get is another telling-off,' I warned. 'Be ready to transmit when we reach the convoy.'

Silver got down in the nose of the plane, peering through the Perspex panels at the sea. He was the best observer in the RAF, he could see in the dark, I swear. He spotted the patrol, ships inky black against a sea I thought couldn't be any blacker. We kept our distance while Chip radioed and signalled to them with a few flashes in Morse. Sometimes our own lads below mistook us for the Luftwaffe and tried to kill us.

But these were glad to see us. I flew low, and there were dark silhouettes waving from the decks, tiny figures, working as hard and in as much danger as we were.

As I climbed skyward again, Silver started spluttering obscenities.

'*There's a goddam U-boat down there!*' Trust Silver to spot a submarine in the dark below the surface of the black water. 'Right beneath us! Turn to port – *turn one-twenty to port and fire at him, Jamie!* He's on the cruiser – he—'

I spiralled back in a screaming and dangerous dive, sending a volley of gunfire blindly into the black nothingness of the sea.

What I saw, what we all saw, was the explosion as the torpedo from the U-boat hit the Royal Navy ship and its engines blew up. There was a fireball of orange light in the silver and black, and we were so low that the shock rocked our wings.

'Can you still see it?' I cried, levelling the Blenheim, checking my wingtips for Ignacy and Harry. They were there, steady on me.

'Can't see anything,' Silver gasped. 'Bloody explosion blinded me.' He'd been staring right at it. 'U-boat's at two o'clock to the formation, a tenth of a mile out, moving to three, must be travelling at six or seven knots. He can't have moved far—'

'Get on the radio and warn the destroyers, Tex,' I ordered. 'Tell 'em the coordinates and get 'em to drop a depth charge.' Then, to my pilots and gunners: 'Stay low in case he surfaces.'

There wasn't a damn thing we could do unless he surfaced; we weren't bombed up to sink him, and we couldn't fire guns at him underwater.

But if he did surface, he could shoot at us, too.

The sky and sea had seemed so calm a moment ago. Now everything was on fire. Below us, a frantic rescue was going on. The sea was alight with oil and fuel and flame – the men on the sinking ship might burn before they drowned.

'They got a lifeboat away! Two of 'em!' Silver yelled. 'Eleven o'clock to the cruiser. Pass the word, Tex, send someone to pick 'em up!'

I circled over the frantic sea and fired a flare to light the surface, looking for survivors.

'Think that U-boat's gone?' I muttered.

'If he has any sense!' Silver answered.

We dogged the sinking ship until the rescuers gave up.

There wasn't anything else any of us could do. They'd beaten us again.

'Cheer up, Scotty,' Silver said as we headed to Windyedge. 'The lads behaved for you this time.'

Ellen:

I heard 648 Squadron roar in before daylight, and in a flash I was out of bed and leaning from the bathroom window. The planes were lining up over Kingsleap Light, lit specially for our lads, blazing green beneath the waning moon. The Blenheims raged past and I skriked out into the dark, 'Hurrah! *Hurrah!*'

I went downstairs with my shawl over my night things to boil a kettle. I'd have to rush to the airfield as soon as I dressed. Mrs Campbell was pottering about, pink-cheeked and excited.

'The lads are back!' she cried. 'Did you count the planes?'

'Four of 'em! A section and a transport!'

'Maybe they'll visit today!' Nan said.

Madeira had landed when I got to the airfield. Pimms turned up in full daylight, about ten o'clock in the morning on Wednesday, 20 November 1940.

And there was my old friend Jamie, bonny Jamie Stuart, hoisting himself through the hatch to get out of the Blenheim.

He looked about ten years older than when he'd left Windyedge six weeks ago.

It gave me a shock. His narrow face was thinner, those bright hazel eyes ringed with shadow. I knew 648 Squadron had taken a few knocks since I'd seen them. The Blenheims always did, and the airmen were always shattered after a night in the sky. But Jamie had a whipped-dog air about him, angry and desperate, that I didn't recognise.

He looked around at the moors to the west. The heather had been in a blaze of purple bloom when he was here at summer's end, and now it was dull with winter's coming and a thin layer of frost. The same thing had happened to him.

The other Pimms airmen were climbing out of their Blenheims.

Jamie watched them and his face relaxed a mite. He was counting them in just the way we did. He jumped down off the wing.

'*Whoo!*' Jamie gave a yell. 'We're home!'

I was hanging around his neck almost before his feet touched the ground.

'*Jamie Stuart!* Alive and whole! Hurrah, *hurrah*!' I kissed him for old times, though we'd never been true sweethearts.

He gave me a warm squeeze but gently pushed my face away. 'Not in front of the lads, Volunteer McEwen.'

When did Jamie Stuart ever worry about good form? Not himself *at all*.

'You all right?' I asked.

He nodded. 'Just damned if I'll fly another escort mission without armament. This *bloody* new commander – you'll meet him tomorrow, he's at Deeside just now – we don't see eye to eye on *anything*.'

I didn't like the sound of that. He'd be my commander, too.

'You need a warm Windyedge welcome,' I said. 'Down the pub!'

The Pimms lads who knew Windyedge were piling into the Tilly and rocking it to make the rest join them.

'Debriefing!' wailed Flight Officer Phyllis Pennyworth.

'Och, debriefing can wait,' I exclaimed. She was too good sometimes. 'Debrief 'em in the Limehouse! Come on, Phyllis …'

She gave up, and climbed in front next to me.

All nine Pimms lads sang their hearts out for the short ride, and Phyllis seemed tired and happy. How she managed to keep her air-force blue so smart after flying from Shetland in the back of someone's Blenheim I do not know.

'Oh, Ellen, it's good to be back here,' Phyllis said to me. 'Are we still room-mates?'

'Mrs Campbell's already made up your bed!' Nan loved that English robin of a WAAF officer almost as much as she loved the lads. And Nan must have heard the Tilly straining up the hill, because the door was open and she was waiting when we pulled up out front.

She wasn't the only one waiting for us. Jane was in the big chair by the fire, leaning forward to spy as we came in. Louisa was at the piano and spun around on the stool to get a keek.

We came in belting 'Goodnight, Sweetheart'. I was arm in arm with Jamie-lad, and behind us came Phyllis with *two* lads, Ignacy on one side and Derfel on the other. She was pinker-cheeked even than Nancy Campbell. Pimms Section, 648 Squadron, stamped muck off their boots in the vestibule and threw their greatcoats over chairs. They tossed caps on to tabletops and scraped furniture out of the way, warbling like a flock of off-pitch nightingales.

They wore air-force blue woollen trousers and fleece-lined leather jackets, and a few of them were still in their coverall flight suits with isinglass map holders strapped to their thighs. They made the low ceiling seem lower, the whole wide room a mite more tight. They brought with them the whiff of salt wind and oil and sweat, a reek of men and machinery.

Louisa spun back to the piano and found the right notes on its ivory keys, and she started playing along to 'Goodnight, Sweetheart'. Now that the lads had a tune to follow, they pulled their voices together. Then Jane joined in singing too, and it was – well – that woman's voice!

It was astonishing.

For one whole chorus we all just stood as we were, still, to listen to her sing.

Then the lads joined in, shouting their goodnights, though none of us was anyone's sweetheart, and it was broad daylight.

There was no holy pause at the end. They started jawing at once, carrying on for drink, and thumping on the bar.

'Mrs Campbell, that fire's not nearly hot enough! I told these new kids you always have a fire going!'

That was Chip Wingate, the American, the one they called Tex.

Derfel Cledwyn, the Welsh navigator who used to be in another flight section, snatched peat logs from the stack. He pushed them into the grate below the wishing-tree mantel. Flames roared and sparks soared, and the lads joined their voices into one big bawl of a chant.

'Nan-cy! *Nan-cy!*'

'Come on, Nan Campbell, get behind that bar, we've missed you—'

'*Nan-cy!*'

Our Nan was a new woman! She shone like the morning star, twenty years falling off her face in a moment. She glowed as if every one of these loud, foul, jaggy, bristly lads was her true love come home from a year at sea.

'My darlins, you know it's not permitted hours yet. Opening time is half eleven.'

They all moaned with disappointment, even the ones who'd never seen her before in their lives.

'Just like a Scotswoman!'

'Only a month till Christmas, Nancy Scrooge!'

'And we've been in the air all night—'

'And Flight Officer Pennyworth needs something to fortify her so she can make her report—'

Old Nan's eyes shone as if they were full of tears. 'Not a drop will be served until half past eleven,' she said in a high voice.

'It's already gone noon in Norway,' said Jamie.

'Too right!' Silver agreed. 'Only three hundred miles away, an hour and a half in a Blenheim, closer than London!'

Everyone went back to drumming on the shining brass countertop, and Nan lifted the wooden yett to let herself behind the bar. There was a great howl and a thunder of applause.

'No, no, no!'

Awash with pleasure, wisps of hair escaping their glittery grips and getting in her eyes, Nan Campbell smacked someone's hands away from the ale taps and primly began screwing on the nozzles. 'Now Chip, you know better!'

'Huh!'

Our Chip was a short and sturdy lad, with stubbled hair that made his head look like a worn-out scrubbing brush. He set to complaining. 'Aw, there's no policemen in sight, and that hill's so steep y'all can hear anything pulling up a mile away. Just one of your "wee drams", ma'am – no one will know!'

'Not until eleven thirty!' said Nan firmly. 'I keep lawful hours.'

Chip jerked his thumb over his shoulder, towards Louisa at the piano across the room.

'If you're so law-abiding, what's the little darkie doing in here?'

I flinched and froze with hate.

In my head I heard 'filthy tinker' in place of 'little darkie'. As if I *expected* it. It took a moment to realise he was being rude about Louisa and not about me.

And the stupid thing was that, being American, Chip wouldn't have known me for a Traveller if I'd pitched a tent in his granny's garden.

But the others would, the Scots and English and Welsh.

I knew how Louisa felt. Everybody turned to clap eyes on her, as if she'd been caught trying to nick something.

She leaped to her feet suddenly, pushing herself up with one hand on the piano keyboard so that it let out a crashing angry groan. She looked as if she were choosing whether to fight or to run.

She was holding it in. She was *good* at holding it in. But I could see she was afire with anger. I'd hidden my secret from these lads so well that now I was too feartie to open my gob and speak up for Louisa. As if she'd never sat between me and an enemy pilot with a gun, whispering warmth into my ear and holding my cold hands until they stopped shaking. She was brave enough to do all that, and I couldn't say one word among friends for her!

My own mammy would be ashamed of me. *Ashamed*.

Louisa kept one hand on the piano keys as if that steadied her. She wore the wee frown that turned her bonny face into a pinched heart. Then Jamie's friend Silver, all dark eyes and film-star good looks, spoke up for her. 'You're maybe thinking of the law in Texas, Chippo. The law here is different.'

They sometimes took the mick with Silver, too, because of him being Jewish. That didn't stop *him* speaking up; I suppose it is easier if you are an officer and a gentleman.

'Here it's a free country,' added Derfel, the Welsh lad. 'We even let filthy English in the place.'

Everybody laughed.

'Louisa is here to assist my aunt Jane,' said Nan. 'That's Mrs Warner to you lads.'

'Lay off Nancy's guests, Tex,' said Jamie.

You know, he is a wisp of a man, so short and slight and fair. And that boys' school accent, as toffee-nosed as Robert

Ethan's. But Jamie is no coward. I have seen him fight with the steely purpose of a gamekeeper going after a poacher. His face closed up as he turned to Chip – lost the sunny smile, as if the effort of giving a command exhausted him, so different to his usual self before he'd gone up to Shetland.

But he added in a friendly way, 'Nice to meet you, Louisa.'

'Nice to have someone at the piano, too!' Silver put in.

I pulled up a chair by Jane. 'Come along, lasses, safety in numbers,' I said, and I beckoned to Louisa. I still felt guilty for not saying anything myself, but at least I could make her welcome.

So me and Phyllis and Louisa and Jane settled in around the table by the fire. As I tucked in my chair I gave Louisa a quick pat on the knee. She was trembling with holding in her anger.

'*Don't let it fash you*,' I whispered. '*You're British and he isn't.*'

Phyllis leaned over to shake her hand. 'Hello, Louisa. Hello, Mrs Warner! I'm Phyllis Pennyworth – I'll be staying here as well.'

Jane was like an excited kiddie at a pantomime, leaning forward, her pale blue eyes wide and alight. 'Tell us who's who,' she said to me.

'Aye, well! I don't ken them all myself. Some of the lads are new.' I tried not to think about the old ones, the missing ones. 'The young man I came in with, fair hair and fox's face, that's Jamie Stuart. He's got a heart of gold. You have any trouble with the others, Louisa, you take it straight to Jamie and he'll put it right. He's a pilot, the commander for

B-Flight. Two sections, Pimms and Madeira, six aircraft, eighteen men. They take him pretty seriously.'

Did they? They used to. Silver still seemed to take him seriously.

'His best mate is his navigator, the Prince Charming with the good manners,' I added. 'David Silvermont. He plays the fiddle, proper classical stuff – you'll like him too. They get called Silver and Scotty.'

'Aren't they all Scotty?' Louisa asked.

'Jamie's the only Scot in the squadron,' I said, keeping my voice down. 'The RAF squadrons come from all over. Aw, look at them. They're like Nan's bairns, her own babies. She doesn't even ken half of them – those Aussie lads are all new.'

'Chip Wingate, the American, he's her favourite,' Phyllis said. 'He doesn't need to be here: the USA is neutral, they haven't entered the war. But he came anyway. She thinks he's the most heroic of the bunch.'

Jane rapped her fingernails against her teacup.

'I don't understand,' she said, 'how anyone fighting the principles of Nazism, which envisions a master race that does not include the Negro, can articulate a complaint against a coloured person visiting a free establishment and not choke on his own hypocrisy.'

I shrugged. 'Everybody thinks the world belongs to them. The Scots and the English aren't any better. Just different. Chip's a bit of a lad, never shuts up, always looking for a fight. But *look*. See why Nan loves him?'

He had his silvery toothbrush head down on the bar with his chin resting on his hands, and he was blinking up at Mrs Campbell like a loving pup. She swiped at him with a dishcloth. He was minding her rules, but he was making her sorry.

Louisa gave a wee superior sniff and looked away.

'Chip's the gunner for Jamie and Silver now,' Phyllis said. 'They've all swapped round. They had a rough time this month.' She yawned, and added anxiously, 'We ought to introduce them by their proper ranks, you know. Scotty's got a name a mile long, the Honourable James Gordon Erskine Murray Beaufort-Stuart. Volunteer McEwen is much too familiar with him.'

'Och, he's no' fussed about his name!' I protested. 'And I've known him longer than you. Since he was in school. I knew his family from before the war.'

Phyllis yawned again. 'I have to interrogate him every morning,' she said. 'I know him pretty well. I know 'em all pretty well. Even the new ones.'

The Australians were mucking about on the hearth, building a castle with peat blocks. Phyllis pointed them out one by one.

'They all went to the same school and joined the air force together. None of 'em a day over eighteen, and you wouldn't believe they were that old if it wasn't on their papers. The ginger lad with the great mop of hair, that's Dougie Kerr, their wireless op and gunner. The one who looks like he's only about twelve, that's their navigator, Gavin Hamilton. Harry Morrow is their pilot – the scarecrow. Harry shouldn't really be a pilot – he's too tall, doesn't *fit*. He has to fly with his knees up around his ears. He's a terrible softy – he's got a photograph of his dogs back in

Sydney that he sticks on the dashboard when he flies!'

The peat block castle tower fell to pieces. Sparks flew in the hearth, and our Jamie pushed himself away from the counter and grumbled, 'Och, you can do better than that, surely, lads? Give it a bit of a base. Get the bricks interlocking as they go on up – come and lend a hand, Silver. These children don't know anything about construction.'

So Britain's finest set to work turning the Limehouse hearth into a building site.

'The third pilot's Polish,' Phyllis finished. 'Ignacy Mazur. He's the one with the grand moustache – don't you think it suits him? He *walked* across half of Europe to get here, after the Germans invaded Poland. Speaks pretty good English now, and a bit of Welsh, too, believe it or not. His navigator, Derfel Cledwyn, is Welsh. Derfel's the one with the squashed nose.'

Louisa said, 'What a funny name.'

'A Welsh name,' I said. 'But he gets called Taff. Also because he's Welsh. All Welshmen are Taff, just like all Scotsmen are Scotty, and the Texan is Tex.'

Phyllis laughed. 'But their gunner's just plain English, Bill Yorke – the other moustache, the thin one. He transferred from another squadron. I haven't worked out Bill yet: a bit quiet. Unhappy about something, I expect. Perhaps he's not quite used to Ignacy and Derfel shouting at each other in Polish and Welsh when they're dropping bombs. They're pretty tight, and he might feel left out.'

Jane laughed suddenly.

'It sounds to me,' she said, 'as if they are your babies as well as Nancy's.'

'They're not our babies at all,' said Phyllis warmly. 'They're our brothers.'

Jamie:

The lads counted down the seconds to half past eleven as if it were the New Year.

'*Seven! Six! Five—*'

They drummed on the brass countertop and stamped on the stone floor, chorusing, '*Four! Three! TWO! ONE!*'

Nancy slid a pint glass beneath a tap and began to fill it with ale that foamed like liquid carnelian.

'See, we can cooperate when there's a good reason for it,' Silver whispered, and I laughed.

'Who's first, lads?' Mrs Campbell called out.

I looked up at the black oak beam above the Limehouse bar. Gleaming silver, exactly where I left it, was the tanner I'd put there for luck six weeks ago. I swear, Nancy polished those coins while we were away. I reached up and twisted my shining sixpence out of the wood and slapped it down on the brass counter with a tinny clink.

'Make that one Silver's,' I said. 'I'm paying. Best observer in the RAF, he can see in the dark. Pull me a pint, too, while you're at it, Mrs C. I'm parched.'

'Right you are, Flight Lieutenant Beaufort-Stuart.'

She beamed at us over the taps, looking for faces she recognised. 'How about you, Sergeant Wingate?'

'Sure thing, Nancy,' said Chip, and pulled his own sixpence from the beam.

When he turned around, Bill Yorke and the young Aussies were watching with interest. The wishing coins were new to them.

'You put a tanner or a bob up there before an op,' explained Derfel. 'Then when you're safe home, you take it out and buy yourself a drink.'

Along with me and Silver, Chip and Derfel, Ignacy was the only one of us who had left a coin there. The rest were new to Windyedge, and had to dig into their pockets. Nancy began to hand round pints as fast as she could pull them.

Dougie started to take a sip.

'*Not yet*,' Ignacy warned. The Australians all looked at me, confused.

I shook my head. 'Wait for everybody.'

No one drank. Silver was right; they *could* cooperate.

When everyone held a brimming glass, I raised my own towards the untouched coins still shining in the ceiling. 'Absent friends.'

The murmur went around the room. *Absent friends.* The girls raised their teacups.

'Sergeant Colin Oldham,' Silver said quietly, holding up his pint to me.

'Cheers.'

We tapped each other's glasses, remembering. Only two weeks ago.

'Och, you'll soon learn our ways,' Nan told the new lads, her eyes wet and glinting. Then she went back to work, as she'd been doing for twenty-five years.

Everybody quieted down a bit now that there was something to drink. Nancy doled out tinned beef sandwiches. Bill Yorke pushed a chair across to sit next to the girls, and got out his cigarette papers. The first two he pulled out were torn, or wrinkled, or something, and instead of flattening them, he crumpled them up and dropped them in the ashtray. He rolled a cigarette for himself before offering them round.

Yorkie was nearly ten years older than the rest of us, a career RAF man, and his windburned face and thin moustache gave him a permanent cynical look. The West Indian lass edged away from him cautiously. I didn't think she'd had much experience with men.

Bother, I thought; I ought to keep an eye on him.

But I knew that Phyllis already thought so too, and Ellen wouldn't put up with any nonsense. And he wasn't doing anything forward or suggestive – just being very generous with his cigarettes.

Louisa:

It was Ellen who fished the cigarette paper out of the ashtray.

She smoked faster than everybody else, no-fuss efficient. Phyllis looked like she was joining in to be polite, and Jane was taking her time, enjoying it. Bill Yorke showed me how to put my cigarette together, but I let it go out almost the second after he lit it. I'd never smoked, and I could just imagine what Mummy would say if I started now, in the pub surrounded by sweaty airmen! So everybody else puffed away around me.

Meanwhile I perched on the edge of my seat, trying not to show how excited and anxious I was, while they described how the U-boat sank the British ship and how maddening it had been not to be able to do any damage to it. Oh God, I knew how that felt. I was torn between wanting to leap up and tell them so, and choking on fresh anger that maybe Daddy's ship went down because it wasn't equipped to defend itself. Also, oh, I was *jealous*. I wanted to be Jamie Beaufort-Stuart, pointing my guns at the deadly underwater shadow. I wanted to be David Silvermont, able to see in the dark, up in the nose of the Blenheim, spotting lifeboats. I even wanted to be Chip Wingate, rescuing survivors by radio. I *ached* with it.

And I wished I knew how to smoke, because it would have been something to do with my hands, a way to pretend I was calmer than I felt. I thought of Mummy sitting on the veranda by herself one evening in May of 1935, quietly guarding the house by the light of her cigarette. Daddy was away and I was only ten. There'd been strikes and riots in the northern ports off and on all that month, and then, in a protest march in Kingston that day, a woman was shot by the police. Mummy didn't seem scared; but she smoked and smoked all alone on the veranda long after she'd told me to go to bed.

I am pretty sure that Ellen picked up the crumpled cigarette paper just because she wanted another cigarette and didn't want to ask Bill Yorke for one. I wouldn't have either;

I didn't like him any more than I liked Chip. He leaned in too close to your face when he talked, and kept clasping your knee or shoulder when you weren't looking. I saw Ellen unfold the crumpled paper, frown faintly, and put it in her pocket. She reached for the other he'd tossed away and did the same thing.

I picked up my own unsmoked cigarette and handed it to her.

'Have this one!'

She gave me a cool nod. 'Ta, Louisa.' Then she got out her own box of matches to light it.

The young men from 648 Squadron stayed three hours, till afternoon closing. When it was time for Mrs Campbell to shoo them away, two of the Australians – Harry, the tall pilot, and Dougie, the gunner with the wild gingery hair – had both fallen asleep at the long table in the middle of the pub with their heads pillowed on their arms among the empty glasses.

'Flying all night will do that,' Phyllis told us.

Jane said it made her feel exhausted just thinking about it.

'I'd better go open up the Tilly,' said Ellen. 'They'll never make it back on foot.'

Bill Yorke, too, had fallen asleep, slumped in his chair in his flight suit by the fire with his legs spread and his elbows cocked on the wooden arm rests. Ignacy and Derfel, the Pole and the Welshman, were still awake, but they were slouching against each other's shoulders as if they couldn't sit without support. Pimms Section's commander, slender, sly-faced Jamie Beaufort-Stuart, looked relaxed now, but bone-tired.

He was deep in conversation with good-looking David Silvermont, and as I watched I saw them click their mostly empty glasses together again.

Ellen stood up and reached for her overcoat. Jane lifted one drooping hand, like a dying opera heroine, and asked her, 'You wouldn't happen to have another cigarette on you, would you, darling?'

'Aye, of course, Mrs Warner!'

Ellen rummaged in her pockets. She came up with a battered paper packet of Woodbines and gave one to Jane.

The cigarette paper she'd fished out of the ashtray fell out of her pocket.

I didn't see it till she'd gone, along with everybody else. By then, Jane had smoked her Woodbine and decided she needed to go upstairs to lie down and 'rest her eyes'. As I was getting up to help Jane with her sticks I noticed the crumpled piece of cigarette paper beneath the table.

I only picked it up because I thought Ellen might want it back. Wartime rationing makes everybody terribly thrifty. It was a piece of paper not much bigger than a few postage stamps! Isn't it strange how you follow along when somebody else does something?

In any case, I picked it up and was about to put it in my pocket when I realised why Ellen had saved it – and why Bill Yorke had tossed it away.

It was covered with blocks and blocks of letters, beginning with two meaningless groups of three letters apiece and the rest in rows of five, lines of nonsense marching down the thin sheet. I couldn't read it. I mean, I could read the *letters*; they were neat block capitals, evenly printed. But they didn't say anything – they didn't make words that meant anything.

Whatever it said, it was in code.

Back upstairs in Room Five, Jane lay on the bed and rested her eyes.

I sat down and opened a book. But I kept thinking about the cigarette paper with the rows of meaningless letters. I felt like it was burning an imaginary hole in my skirt pocket. Was it important? No, it couldn't be, or Bill Yorke wouldn't have tossed it in the ashtray. But what if he'd done that because he wanted to get rid of it? Had Ellen noticed the writing – did she wonder what it meant?

I pulled the paper out of my pocket and spread it flat on my open book, like a bookmark. The sheet was covered front and back with the rows of printed letters. Bill Yorke was the wireless operator for his flight crew as well as their gunner – he must have taken this down in the air not long ago. Maybe only last night.

Then I had a wild thought.

I had a coding machine and I had a coded message. Perhaps I could put the two together.

By now, Jane was snoring gently as she rested her eyes. I shut my book on the cigarette paper and went to the wardrobe. When I opened it and dug out the coding machine and the box of extra rotors, Jane didn't stir. So I picked everything up, and my book and a pencil too, and let myself out of the room.

I listened for anyone in the passage. But Phyllis had gone with Ellen to deliver the 648 Squadron airmen to their barracks, and Mrs Campbell was downstairs washing up. I made my way quietly down the passage and into the loo – the toilet was separate from the bathroom, right next to it in a little closet with a door and an arrow-slit window of its own.

I locked the door and sat down on the loo with the book on my knees and the coding machine at my feet. I felt like Pandora as I opened the beautiful wooden box.

Jane and I had left Felix Baer's leaflets lying beneath the lid on top of the keyboard. I opened the first booklet. I couldn't read the German headings, but Jane had explained to me how to match up the rotors and plugs. The two groups of three letters on Bill Yorke's cigarette paper told me where the message began. I knew from Felix Baer's instructions that when I keyed them in with today's settings, they'd give me the starting letters for the rotor dials. I took a deep breath and began to type. I didn't really believe it would work.

I couldn't decode it quickly. There weren't any proper words to look at or remember. I had to do it letter by letter, and pay attention to make sure I was hitting the right keys. I hadn't thought to bring extra paper, so as the decoded letters lit up in the upper keyboard, I wrote them down on the blank endpaper at the back of my book.

After five minutes of struggle and with my back starting to ache from leaning down to the floor to hit the keyboard, I sat up and read in my notebook what the lamplit letters had spelled out:

FEIND LICHE NSCHL ACHTS CHIFF E …

It didn't look like nonsense.

I tried rewriting it by putting spaces between some of those bunches of consonants, and got:

FEIND LICHENS CHLACHTS CHIFFE …

And *that* looked like *German.*

The hair stood up at the back of my neck.

I couldn't read this, either, but I could tell it was real words. Maybe I hadn't split them the right way. But those letters meant something.

And with the cipher machine, *I'd worked it out myself.*

For a moment I was so excited I thought I was going to be sick.

I thumped my fist on the floor. Then I regretted that in case anyone heard it. I was all cooped up in this tiny little room and I wanted to shout and jump up and down, but there wasn't room to do anything, and also I knew this was as secret as secret could be, and whatever I did, I mustn't shout.

I had to tell Jamie Beaufort-Stuart. I had to figure out the whole message, and then the next time his squadron of Blenheim bombers went flying out over the North Sea, they'd know ahead of time what they were going to run into.

So the only thing to do was to sit there and decode the rest of it.

I was about to explode with excitement when I finally went back to Room Number Five. I felt as if I were tumbling to earth in a bomb dropped from a plane, Luftwaffe or RAF, I couldn't quite work out which.

Jane was sitting in her armchair in the chilly room. The radio was switched off and she wasn't reading. Her face was blank, but her expression changed as I came in. She looked away from me quickly, the way you'd pretend to be innocent if you were caught on your way to scamper up a neighbour's tree after their tamarinds, but you weren't actually anywhere near the tree yet.

'I tried to light the fire and it wouldn't go on,' Jane said cautiously, still not meeting my eyes.

She hadn't had to do that on her own before. She couldn't kneel, though she was very good at leaning over, and could even touch her toes, to make up for her knees hardly bending at all. It was an awkward way to get at the fire.

Guilt tore through me. I put down the cipher machine carefully, and laid the book on top of it – excited as I was, *Jane* was my first responsibility, and I'd left her here alone in the cold for half an hour at least. I looked at the meter. There was no gas flowing.

'It needs another shilling,' I said. 'Oh, Jane, I'm so sorry! Why didn't you call me? I was just down the passage in the loo!' I reached for the shilling jar and dropped in a coin. There was a moment of very quiet stillness in which I could hear the meter start to whir. I bent down to turn on the gas tap so I could light the fire.

And then I realised that the gas was already on.

She'd turned on the gas tap and hadn't turned it off again. If she'd started the meter herself without lighting the fire, the gas could have run and run, and filled the room. Maybe she would have sat there in the cold until she fell asleep again. How long would it be before the gas killed you?

It looked like an accident. But even so, what if I'd come back into the room and found her stone dead? After the warning I'd been given – how could I *bear* it? Just the thought of it made my eyes prick with tears. Accident or on purpose – I didn't know which would be worse. And it would be my fault for leaving her alone if anything happened, my fault for not being there with her.

I could scarcely bear even to think about it.

I knelt to light the fire and turned it up. I wanted her to get warm.

'*Tell me* when you want the fire on,' I begged. 'Please just *tell me*. Don't try to do it yourself. Let me take care of it. I'm sorry I was away so long just now—'

I glanced over at the wooden box by the door, and my stomach jumped again. I looked back at Jane, and the excitement came flooding back.

Jane met my eyes at last.

'What have you been up to, Louisa?' she asked.

Jamie:

'Jamie! *Jamie Stuart!* Hold on a wee minute—'

Ellen leaned out of the Tilly, yelling, as I crossed to the Blenheims beneath the half-moon.

I'd been avoiding her, but I waited as the van pulled up. Ellen was an old friend, a *good* friend. And here was I, not daring to return a fond greeting in case someone threw it back at me as bad behaviour. I felt like a rotten coward.

'Hop in,' she said. 'Och, don't look like that, I'm not going to kiss you again.'

'I'm sorry!' I said. 'It's this bloody new commander. If he thinks I'm fooling around he'll rake me over the coals, and Dougie Kerr can't keep his gob shut.'

'Well, I've met Cromwell now and he doesn't like me either,' Ellen said with sympathy. 'Hop in, no one's looking. I'll take you across in a minute, but I want to talk to you ...'

I threw my parachute, helmet, and gauntlets in the back and climbed in next to her. I ought to be grateful for the short ride; I was geared up, and walking isn't easy in a flight suit full of Ever-Hot bags topped off with a Mae West.

Ellen put the van in neutral. She reached into a pocket of her ATS uniform and drew out a folded paper.

'Should I read this now?' I asked. The airfield was darkness and inky shadows. The lights would only be turned on for take-off. Anything that showed might attract German bombers.

'I'll tell you what it says.' She paused. 'It's a coded message.'

I didn't know what to think. I sat silent, waiting for her to go on.

'It's a bit of the message you overheard on the wireless yesterday,' she added in a low voice.

I turned sharply to look at her, but it was too dark to read her face. 'How do you know about that?'

'Your gabby new Australian sparks was blethering about it at Mrs Campbell's. His pilot shut him up. You were busy buying Tex another beer.'

'Oh, Lord!' Bloody Dougie Kerr. 'How did you get it on paper?'

'That was Bill Yorke, your other new sparks,' said Ellen.

I shook my head in despair, and she gave a low, dry chuckle. 'It's like being stuck with a bunch of schoolkids, aye?'

'Half of them *are* a bunch of schoolkids,' I pointed out. 'Is this the best time to tell me? I'm away on an op in ten minutes.'

'Don't be fashed. It's not what you think. And I'm not Cromwell.' She took a deep breath. 'I know what the message says.'

We sat in the van in the dark, and I stared at Ellen without being able to see her.

I unfolded the paper and flattened it against my leg. Ellen lit a match and held it over a page torn from an ordinary school jotter, just long enough for me to see the writing: printed lines of clear English, beneath recognisable German, beneath unrecognisable code.

I didn't have time to read anything before Ellen shook the match out.

She spoke quietly, hesitating. It was a long time since we'd seen each other, and she knew I'd lost most of my squadron a couple of weeks ago, and it made us awkward.

'Yorkie – is that what you call him?' she began. 'Bill Yorke, the English bloke with the moustache. He wrote the code on his cigarette papers. I saw it when he tossed them away at Mrs Campbell's before. And I picked 'em up—'

'Traveller habit,' I scolded. 'You'll get caught.'

'Shut yer gob, Jamie Stuart.' The familiar teasing made her less uneasy. 'Well, I didn't get a keek before I'd dropped one of the papers myself, and then Louisa, that West Indian lass who looks after Nan's old auntie, picked it up next.

She's that canny, Louisa is, sharpest eyes I've ever seen, and that's saying something.'

'Fair dos.'

We both know the Beaufort-Stuarts have a reputation that way.

'Louisa took it and worked out what it meant,' Ellen said.

'How the devil did she do that?'

'Och, well …' Ellen hesitated. 'This is the mad bit.'

'Hurry up!'

'Windyedge had an unexpected visitor …'

Ellen told me about the German pilot. She told me about 'Odysseus', and how Louisa discovered the gift he'd left.

I knew it was true, because it fit. Even without the code name Odysseus, which I'd overheard, the jigsaw pieces fit. Odysseus flew the missing Messerschmitt, the one we never saw. The other Messerschmitt, the one we tangled with, was trying to stop him from completing his mission.

And his mission was to deliver this cipher machine.

'So he hid the machine and Louisa found it, and she made it work,' Ellen finished. 'She couldn't have done it without his list of settings, but she found that too.'

'Does she read German?'

'No,' Ellen said softly. 'She got the old woman to translate. So they both know.'

I whistled.

Foes' gifts are no gifts, warned my classical education. The real Odysseus's gift had been a trap.

'Did he bring it for *us*?' I asked. 'For 648 Squadron?'

'I don't know. I never heard of anything like it.'

'Neither did I,' I breathed.

Ellen held another match over the page.

'See. It's an alert to their pilots about the U-boat you met, telling them where to find our ships. If you'd known that when the message came in, you could have warned the navy. Or done something about it.'

The match was burning low.

'There's more,' she said, and shook that flame out too. 'I'll tell you this but once. You can get Silver to read it properly after you've set off.' She lit a final match, but only used it to light a cigarette. She said in a low voice, 'The last part tells where the German submarines will be tonight.'

I sat agog, my mouth hanging open.

'Just off Bell Rock Light,' she added. 'It says. A "wolf pack", they call it, six of 'em hunting together. Their coordinates look like military mumbo-jumbo to me, but Bell Rock's clear enough.'

She laughed at me gaping, and held her cigarette to my lips. I took a long drag, but the faint red glow wasn't bright enough to light the miraculous sheet of paper lying in my lap.

What had I said to Phyllis, on the morning of 7 November, two weeks ago?

I want to know where their submarines are. Some wee thing. One surprising smack in their faces.

'Buckets of blood, I have to get going,' I said. 'Drive.'

I folded the page and tucked it into my thigh pocket, and pelted Ellen with questions as she drove.

'How can we trust the old woman? Maybe she's just having fun with the girl. And what about her – Louisa – you only met her this week! Isn't she terribly young? Is this cipher machine real, anyway? Have you seen it yourself?'

'I don't know. Maybe. Aye, she's young. And no, I have not. But I *can* tell you Louisa is as sound as you or me. Braver than me. You should have seen her stand up to that Jerry! I trust her, and she trusts Jane, and—'

'*And we've nothing to lose.*' I couldn't believe my luck. 'You know what? I'd rather go on a wild goose chase for Nan Campbell's old auntie than take another blind order from Wing Commander Talbot Cromwell.'

Ellen pulled up by my Blenheim and told me, 'Louisa says you were lucky. She only managed to work it out because it was a full transmission. If any bit's missing, the letters get in a guddle. So tell your sparks to take care what he copies down.'

The plane loomed above us, shadow on shadow; Chip was a stocky, smaller shadow heffalumping about against the sky as he climbed into the rear hatch. We were being sent on patrol again, bombed up this time, to escort navy ships heading into Edinburgh through the Firth of Forth.

Silver yanked open the door of the Tilly.

'Thank goodness you're here, I was worried I'd have to do the flying myself tonight,' he said. 'Then you really *would* be in trouble.'

'You have *no idea*.' I grabbed my gear and jumped out. I didn't think about whether what I'd do next would get me in trouble – I might never get a chance like this again. 'Have you plotted our course? I want to take us on a little detour.'

'Where'd you get this?' Silver asked. He sat at the navigator's chart table in the Blenheim's nose, juggling an electric torch and his wind-direction calculator. 'This is Tex's code! Translated! But—'

'You cracked the Kraut?' Chip called from the back. 'I thought special codebreakers had to do that.'

'Special codebreakers did do it,' I said evasively.

The intercom crackled as Silver started to talk but changed his mind. Finally he said, 'East of the Bell Rock Light! Twenty minutes down the Angus Coast. Well, it's not far off where we're meeting tonight's convoy …' Over the dashboard, I couldn't see what he was doing as he changed our route. 'Are Pimms and Madeira going together?'

'No, I'm going to send Madeira on to Edinburgh alone. Then no one can accuse B-Flight of being late.'

'Will this get you another reprimand?'

'Probably.'

'It's your funeral,' said Silver cheerfully.

Fifteen minutes after we took off Chip called out, 'I'm getting more of those danged coded signals.'

I shivered in the heavy flight suit, but kept my hands steady on the controls, followed my course, watched the quiet moon.

'Take down as much of it as you can,' I said to him. '*Get it all.*'

No one questioned me when I ordered Adam Stedman to keep Madeira Section on track for the convoy, and Bell Rock wasn't far out of our way. The lighthouse there got shot up by a swarm of German bombers not long ago, so it stayed dark unless British ships were about. Tonight it was lit. That was a good enough excuse for checking it out. I knew I could trust Silver with our secret; I could tell him later, and I wouldn't need to confess to Phyllis or Cromwell.

'We'll catch up to you in a jiffy,' I said to Adam. 'I want to sweep around the lighthouse.' To Pimms I said, 'Stay with me.'

I passed the light, and we kept going, following our strange instructions twenty miles further out to sea. We could still see Bell Rock gleaming. Silver peered through the observer's window up front, and I glided lower to get a better view.

Gunshot suddenly exploded around us.

I felt the shock as it hit, somewhere in the back of the plane. But the control surfaces held.

I called to Ignacy and Harry. '*Climb away, Pimms!*'

'*What the—*' yelled Chip – of course he couldn't see anything, sitting at the radio behind me. 'That went right past my ear!'

'You OK? Get in the turret—'

'Two German submarines,' Silver confirmed. 'Right next to each other. They've both come up for air; you'll see when we turn around. What do you think, Scotty? Apart from their guns they're sitting ducks.'

'Ouch!' I kicked at the rudder – it felt as if I'd been stung by a wasp, and instinctively I tried to shake it off. A wasp in the plane in November, what the devil? Must be a leg cramp. I flexed my calf and focused on keeping the wings level.

'They must know we've got ships passing,' I answered Silver. 'So we'd better try to take them out.'

It wasn't as if the hand we were playing was a sure bet. Most of the Blenheims that didn't make it home got shot down by anti-aircraft fire from the ground or from ships at sea.

But we'd surprised *them* this time – those U-boats were at their most vulnerable. They can't dive when they're taking on air.

Silver suddenly started to laugh.

'What? *What?*'

'*There's another* – it just came up! You wait and wait for one, and they all come along at once—'

'*Like London buses!*' we howled in chorus.

'Hey, pipe down, you two,' Tex complained. 'Are we going for them or not?'

'All Pimms aircraft, line up behind me,' I called to Ignacy Mazur and Harry Morrow. 'I'm on the near one, Mazur in the middle, Morrow last. Morrow! You know what you're doing? When your load's away, climb and head to meet Madeira.'

'Cheers to that, Pimms Leader!' yelled Harry Morrow. 'About time we saw some serious combat!'

We lined up for the bombing run.

I flew as low as I dared through a hail of anti-aircraft fire. My headset was full of Chip whooping it up in the rear turret as he fired back.

'*Great shot, boys!* Right between them – Mazur's load went down on the other side of that middle sub – there she blows! Aw, I can't tell what happened, it just looks like a giant geyser – no, wait, *the Morrow kid made a direct hit!*'

Mazur's victory yell came crackling over the radio.

'*All three, we got all three of the bastards*—'

I looked over my shoulder as I climbed away.

The side-by-side submarines stood nearly on end as the explosions lifted them out of the water, like great whales breaching in the dark. Their wet hulls gleamed silver in the moonlight and then sank again, going slowly straight down like ships that have struck an iceberg.

Ellen:

B-Flight came safe home next morning, but not completely sound, because all three of Pimms Section's Blenheims were full of holes. Jamie's one was like a sieve, and he got hit in the leg, just a tiny hole in his flight suit and a neat graze in the back of his calf. He wasn't a mite fashed. Proud of it, pleased it was him and not anyone else that got hurt. Silver made him strip off his boots and flight suit right there in the shade of their plane to make sure he wasn't bleeding to death. Jamie looked like a schoolboy sitting on the frosty grass in his rumpled blue uniform and socks, with Silver bent over his leg playing doctors and nurses.

'I'm hoping for a wound stripe,' Jamie told me, grinning. 'For my sleeve. A decoration will impress the lads.'

'All you're going to get is a dab of Dettol and some sticking plaster, mate,' Silver told him.

Jamie dragged on his boots and stood up.

'Go on and limp,' said Silver. 'Let's give Cromwell some drama. You've got some explaining to do.'

He took one of Jamie's arms over his shoulder.

'If you're a fighter pilot and you shoot down five planes, that makes you an ace,' Jamie told me, all full of himself. 'We can't battle Messerschmitts, so we're counting U-boats. *We've just bagged three.*'

'*You what!*' I cried.

Those clear hazel eyes were blazing. He looked tired. Excited. *Alive.*

I wondered if the wound hurt more than he was letting on.

He said breathlessly, 'Just two more, and then I reckon Pimms are all aces.'

'Well done Pimms!' I exclaimed. 'You heading to the Limehouse to celebrate?'

'We've got to go get debriefed just now,' Jamie said. 'After.'

Silver looked at the sky. 'Another winter storm tonight, and the last November moon tomorrow. With weather and luck, no more night flights until December. Plenty of time for the pub.'

'Aye, well, don't imagine you'll get a rest,' I told them. ''Specially not you, Flight Lieutenant Beaufort-Stuart.'

'Not for one single second do I imagine that.' Jamie gave a hop, trying to look at the back of his leg in step with Silver, who was four inches taller than him. 'I say, Volunteer McEwen, could you introduce me to Nan's old auntie? I need to learn a bit more German, and I want to chat to her about some lessons.'

'*Scotty!*' Silver scolded. 'Cromwell will have your head if he hears.'

'I'll hide in a tree, like Charles II. Silver, do stop fussing –

I'll let you in on things in a moment,' Jamie said. The grin was back. 'Oh, and Ellen? Here's that ten bob I owe your dad—'

'What ten bob?'

He rolled his eyes. 'Does *no one* trust me? Pass it along.'

In the Tilly on my own, I unfolded the banknote – very generous if he meant me to keep it. Just like a Beaufort-Stuart, throwing money about, even when they didn't have any. A pilot's salary is a deal higher than a driver's, but it was likely his only income.

Hidden inside the ten shillings was a sheet of notepaper from Jamie's wireless operator. It was covered with blether in Chip's sprawling American print. Rows and rows of five letters apiece, none of it anything like words.

Pass it along, Jamie had said.

I thought I might send the ten bob to my dad as he'd bid me. But I knew who the pencil scrawl was meant for, and it wasn't old Alan McEwen.

I had a guess what Jamie was up to. And I thought this would help him and I wanted to help him. So I did.

It should not have been the carry-on it was to get Louisa and Jane alone with me and Jamie for five minutes.

For several days of dreich misery, sleet whipped at RAF Windyedge, and you'd be surprised how busy our Jamie was kept when he wasn't in the air. I was kept busy too. Phyllis could write her reports sitting in Nan Campbell's office or in the bar at the Limehouse, but I had to be at the aerodrome to do my work. Each day I'd bicycle over (to save the Tilly's petrol), in a great big mackintosh through the wet, up the long lane to the airfield. Then I had to drive Wing Commander Cromwell over to Deeside to meet with 648 Squadron's A-Flight, or take a mechanic to Stonehaven to collect aeroplane parts from the rail station, or give Jamie and Adam Stedman a lift around the airfield to do inspections.

There wasn't room in the hangar for all B-Flight's aircraft, and icy spitters drove at the wings of the sad planes left outside. The sleet came down so hard that Adam and Jamie crawled up through the escape panels in the floor of each plane instead of opening the overhead hatches, while I sat in the Tilly, blowing on my fingers and watching through the streaming windows. One of the shot-up planes sat for nearly forty-eight hours before Jamie spied that water was seeping through the bullet holes. When he put his head up into the cabin he ducked back out sharpish. I could see him gagging.

'What is it?' I called, cranking the window down about an inch.

'The cabin's all full of mildew. Reeking with it! That's just happened in *two days*. Ugh. I'd better taxi her into the hangar or she'll be unflyable. Get someone out here with a starter for me, will you?'

And I left him and Adam peering up into the plane and holding their noses while I sped off on that errand.

Nobody wanted to walk to the pub through the mud and slush and falling sleet after a day like that, and I couldn't use the Tilly to drive them time and again.

Next day it was blowing a gale, though the sleet eased. Old Flash rang to say I wasn't needed at the aerodrome. I could have kissed him. At half past eleven on the button, Jamie's lot came singing past the limekilns.

'Jane, Jane, go upstairs,' Louisa urged.

'Won't you play the piano for them again?'

'I will, but let's go upstairs on our own just now,' Louisa said. She started from her chair beside the fire and snatched up Jane's sticks. 'For a bit of quiet before the party starts.'

The old woman caught on. For the first time since B-Flight's last mission, we four would be under the same roof. Jane took the sticks and hobbled out of the bar.

'What is it your old auntie drinks, Mrs C.?' Jamie asked, pulling his tanner from the black oak beam. 'Whisky and a drop of water? I'll treat.'

'Not for sixpence,' Nancy said firmly. 'Not even for you. That'll be two and six.'

'Highway robbery,' he complained. 'How does she afford it?'

'She doesn't. She had two the day she arrived, and that's that. Take her a pot of tea if you want to be nice.'

'Feels a bit mean, Nancy.'

'Oh!' I said, getting a dig in. 'Wasn't there something about ten bob you owed someone, Flight Lieutenant Beaufort-Stuart?'

He shrugged. 'I've not got it on me now.'

Nancy was not to be moved. So it was tea.

'Very proper, too,' Jamie said solemnly.

'Come on, Jamie Stuart, I'll help you through the doors with the tea tray,' I offered.

'I shouldn't allow Scotty around that fine woman without a chaperone,' Silver agreed.

Jamie gave him a half-hearted clout. 'Jealous.'

'Just wondering what you're up to!'

'I'll tell you when I find out,' Jamie said.

At last. Four days gone, and I hadn't once caught Jamie or Louisa alone without Phyllis or Silver tagging along. I held the hall door for Jamie, and led him upstairs and down the passage to Room Number Five.

Louisa let us in. Jane sat by the unlit fire wrapped in a woolly blanket – of course, it wasn't three o'clock yet. Some jazz singer was warbling on the wireless, sat like a queen on a doily taking up most of the dresser. Jamie perched the tea tray on a shaky table covered with another doily, and for a wee while we all looked at one another without saying anything.

Then Mrs Warner said, 'Show them, Louisa.'

Louisa leaped to the wardrobe and delved behind furs and a forest of skinkling, gauzy gowns that I could not see either of them ever wearing. She came up with the Jerry pilot's precious wooden box, and she set that on the bed and undid the lid. There was a school jotter laid over the keys. She picked that up and, solemn as a judge, passed it to Jamie.

He stood gawping at the thing in the box. It wasn't quite a radio and it wasn't quite a typewriter.

'What is it?' Jamie breathed.

'The cleaning instructions say it's a cipher machine,' said Louisa. 'And – well, I guess it is. You know about the German pilot who landed here, don't you? He left the machine, and he left lists of settings for it. We worked out the message that you picked up the other night – it's all in there.' She waved at the jotter. 'I did the decoding, and Jane did the translating. So we both know what it says.' She swallowed, with that worried frown puckering her schoolgirl face. 'I'm so afraid it will get Mrs Warner in trouble.'

'Not you?' said Jamie. He stepped closer, hesitated, and then pressed a key. A lamp came on in the top plate of letters.

'Well, me too, I suppose, but Mrs Warner—' She stole a keek at Jane.

What the old woman confessed then made my mouth drop open.

'I am German,' she explained softly. 'A registered alien.'

I'd never thought.

I'd never thought. Here was a body hiding the *exact* way I hid: behind an accent and a name and face and flesh like anybody's.

If people knew where she came from, what would they do? Who'd trust *her*?

But Louisa did trust her.

Mrs Warner held her head up. 'My stage name was Johanna von Arnim. I was *arrested* –' she sounded a mite proud of that – 'last summer. They said I was a category B detainee. After they arrested me, though, they demoted me to category C. I was in prison for three weeks and then interred in a camp for another four months.'

So that's what they did.

Nan must know. Mrs Warner was her aunt. Crabbit Nancy Campbell was paying a wage to look after an old German woman!

'Did you do anything?' Jamie asked. 'To make them arrest you.'

'If you mean, did I cause any risk to national security, I should say not,' said Jane. 'But I'm telling you so you know.'

He nodded. Then he glanced up at me.

For a moment I imagined it was a challenge, and he wanted me to give my own confession. But my secret didn't make me a war enemy. With his la-di-da private school and family castle it probably never crossed Jamie's mind that I was like Jane. He was just asking me if I trusted Mrs Warner.

I nodded back to him.

'Well,' said Flight Lieutenant Beaufort-Stuart of the Royal Air Force, and offered his hand to Jane to shake. 'You helped us sink three German U-boats the other night. And I'm telling you so *you* know.'

She beamed at him over their clasped hands like a shop girl making eyes at a film star.

'Aren't we lucky!' she exclaimed. 'Isn't Windyedge lucky!'

'Yes,' Jamie said, beaming right back at her. 'Yes, at last we're going to be the lucky ones.'

Louisa:

He opened the jotter and held it so Ellen could read over his shoulder.

SEA PATROL SHETLAND HOLD HALF MOON

ABERDEEN SECTOR CLEAR YEAR END

ABERDEEN SECTOR CLEAR START XII UNTIL FURTHER NOTICE

JU LXXXVIII SPECIAL DETAIL LISTA TO DEESIDE SOUTH GREEN LIGHT

ABERDEEN SECTOR AWAIT DS COMPLETION

I worried that it sounded so mysterious. I said quickly, 'We think the spacing's right, but we're not sure. There was a block of letter *X*s between each line, so that seemed like where the breaks ought to be.'

Jamie Beaufort-Stuart stood studying the page, his face torn between joy and disbelief.

Jane patted the tufty bedspread, letting him know it was all right for him to sit down.

'Thank you, Mrs Warner,' he said.

He sat carefully next to the coding machine and laid my exercise book open on the bed beside him. He wasn't a big man, but it was tight with four of us in the room, and it was hard for me not to be in awe. A real RAF pilot, in uniform, *sitting on my bed*! I never thought I'd get *so close*.

But then, I never dreamed I'd have a German coding machine to share with him, either.

'I wonder how many of these there are in Britain,' Jamie said softly, running his fingertips lightly over the keys. 'It must be jolly difficult getting them here. And jolly brave of the chap who brought it.'

'Yes,' I said, remembering the piano, the records, the gunshot in the van. Each bit had been awful, but it added up to bravery. 'He was.'

'Did he tell you how to use it?' Jamie asked.

Ellen and I shared a look and then we joined in a high chorus of a laugh, remembering that night.

'He didn't tell us a thing,' I said, when I got my breath back. 'But he left instructions. They're in the German leaflets. When he knew I was watching, he dropped a hint about where he'd hidden them. We'd never have managed without the leaflets – the settings change every day.'

Jamie frowned down at the puzzling English phrases in my jotter, narrowing his eyes at it.

'The bit about the half-moon makes sense,' he said at last. 'When the moon is dark, it's probably just as difficult for the Luftwaffe to find targets as it is for us. So this means something like "leave Shetland alone till the next half-moon".' He pointed further along my pencil jottings. 'And here it looks like they're going to lay off Aberdeen while this other thing is going on. The city took a pounding in October. Those Roman numerals must mean a Junkers 88 bomber, a Ju-88. I wonder what their special detail from Lista to Deeside is.'

'Where is Lista?' Ellen asked.

'Norway. Just about the closest point to Scotland – we think they're planning to build an aerodrome there, but it's not much more than some surveyors' stakes at the minute. We've taken pictures.'

'We ought to warn Deeside,' Ellen said. 'Else A-Flight might run into trouble.'

Jamie screwed up his mouth, staring at the machine. Suddenly he seemed less intimidating. He looked stubborn and baffled and not much older than me.

He nodded. 'I'll warn them,' he said. 'But I'm not telling Cromwell. I'm damned if I'm going to hand this over to Cromwell! Not when we've got an edge on the Luftwaffe *at last*. I know him, he'll send the machine off to Coastal

Command for fingerprint testing, or make us wait till he tries it himself, or refuse to let anyone else near it. He'll block us from using it because it's not in the rule books, *especially* if he thinks I have anything to do with it.'

Ellen hesitated, and then blurted out, 'But Jamie-lad, what if it was sent for someone else to use, and not for 648 Squadron? That Robert Ethan, that Intelligence toff, he isn't anything to do with you. The Jerry who brought it was supposed to meet him specially.'

Jamie narrowed his eyes again, thinking about it.

I shook my head. I didn't want to let the machine go, either. What Jamie had said – *Not when we've got an edge on the Luftwaffe at last*. Not when I was *finally* able to do something useful to fight back.

'Felix Baer left the settings for *me*,' I said. 'He said my name and looked straight at me, and stuck a key up in the bar like your airmen do with their sixpences. *For luck*, he said. In English. And he'd hidden a note in it.'

'Aye, he did that,' Ellen admitted.

I suppose it was odd Felix Baer would do that. Why had he chosen *me*? I wasn't even in uniform. Perhaps he guessed his contact would talk to me later, and I was the one who had seen the machine.

However, Robert Ethan hadn't asked about the machine, and I didn't find it till after he left.

Jamie reached out a fine, narrow finger and dialled back one of the rotors.

'You said the settings change every day,' he said. 'How many do we have?'

'We think until the end of January,' I told him.

Jamie said forcefully, 'So we have to use them *now*.'

Ellen gave Jamie a long look, took a deep breath, and nodded in agreement.

'I'll have to spin a tale,' Jamie said. 'I mean, a tale about where we got this gen.'

'Gen?' Jane asked. She hadn't said a word since he'd shaken hands with her, but she was leaning forward with her head cocked so she could hear everything, and I could tell she was just as excited as the rest of us.

'Information. Sorry.' He grinned over at her with bright eyes, amber-green flecked with brown, like dried palm fronds with the sun behind them. 'We all have our own mumbo-jumbo, and I don't get off base much.'

Ellen chewed at her lower lip, watching him like she was worried about him. I didn't think they were sweethearts, but I knew they'd been friends for a long time, since before the war. She wanted to help him.

I had an idea.

I leaned forward and picked up my *L* key. It came off the keyboard easily. Then I flipped to the back of my exercise book and found Felix Baer's strip of onionskin paper that had been rolled inside the key.

'November's almost finished anyway,' I said. 'If we just keep the November setting chart that has the instructions, I can copy out the December and January charts for us to use, and you can give the real ones to Intelligence. I bet they're what Robert Ethan was looking for anyway. You can pretend you found this key just now, in the bar downstairs with the other wishing coins, and that you found the leaflets where he hid them in the Django Reinhardt record album. And Jane can write this last message in German in the cover of one of the charts, as if the pilot left it there himself.'

'And when I "find" it, I'll have to pretend my German's better than it is. I'll see if I can borrow a dictionary off my wee sister.' Jamie stood up. 'Let me take your key and your note and do some sleight of hand with it downstairs. You'd better make those copies now, so I can take the charts with me today. Then I'll warn Deeside.'

'Ellen can get them to you,' I promised.

I didn't think I'd get my letter *L* back, once Wing Commander Talbot Cromwell got hold of it. But I passed it to Jamie.

'I'll see you again, ladies,' Jamie said, giving a gallant little bow.

Then he and Ellen went back downstairs.

Jane and I were alone again, me and my eighty-two-year-old operatic registered-alien German companion, involved in a wonderful small conspiracy that was going to help win the war.

I set to work copying German code settings.

When I'd finished, I folded the exercise book and the copied charts over the keyboard of the coding machine and closed the lid. I put it back in the wardrobe, where it was safe enough hidden beneath Johanna von Arnim's old evening clothes. Now all we had to do was wait for Ellen to come back to collect the leaflets for Jamie.

'Why don't you play your flute for me again?' Jane suggested.

A different idea came to me all of a sudden.

'Couldn't you teach me Morse code?' I asked.

She turned over her upside-down teacup and lifted the teapot to pour herself some stewed, cold tea. She was surprisingly unfussy about her tea.

'What makes you think I can teach you Morse code?' she asked.

'You were a telegraphist,' I said. 'And if I learned now, I could join the forces, perhaps, when I'm older. I only left school two months ago – I feel like I should still be learning things. And … it might be useful.'

'It might be,' Jane agreed.

I screwed the sections of my flute together.

'I thought I could learn it and practise at the same time,' I said, and held the flute to my lips. I drew in a deep breath, as if I were about to dive into cold water. Then I held down my thumb and opposite pinkie and the first two fingers of my left hand and played an A.

'Oh, of course!' said Jane.

She sang an A.

'Tra-*laaaa*.'

Dot-dash. Short-long.

I played another A, *tra-la*, quaver and crotchet, *tra-la, tra-la, tra-la*.

Jane's amazing near-contralto swooped up a step to a B. '*Traaaa-lalala*.'

I echoed her on the flute. AB, AB, *tra-lahh, tra-lalala, tra-lahh, tra-lalala*.

And on up the A-minor scale, getting quicker and surer all the time, until by G we were both breathless and had to stop because Jane started to mix up notes to test me, and I trilled them staccato back to her like sleet against window glass, and we laughed so hard we couldn't sing nor play.

And in one afternoon I learned almost a third of the alphabet in Morse code.

Phyllis wasn't in on it. We didn't dare tell her – she was under Cromwell's thumb. When Jamie had to give her his report after they blew up the U-boats, he used the Bell Rock Lighthouse being alight as an excuse for sweeping the area around it. I don't think he lied to her; I'm not sure anyone *could*. She talked to you like a primary school teacher, brisk and firm. She settled all of Ellen and Mrs Campbell's arguments (over Ellen's ration coupons, Ellen smoking in the bedroom, Ellen propping her bicycle against the shed door instead of properly putting it inside, Ellen hanging her wet mackintosh in the bathroom). Phyllis stuck to the rule book about *everything*. The Isle of Man butter ruffled her feathers something terrible.

'Oh, no, Mrs Campbell, don't butter my toast this morning, *please*. I don't want to know where it came from, and I shall have to report it if any more comes in!'

I didn't think she really *would* report Mrs Campbell for a pound of contraband butter; she was kind as kind. But she would have reported the Enigma machine.

So Ellen and I didn't have much chance to talk about it, because she and Phyllis shared a bedroom, and there was almost always someone else about when I saw Ellen. I was hardly ever on my own.

I had Jane to look after. She couldn't go far or fast, but she was determined to make the most of her freedom, and

I was constantly panicking that she'd go off without me and get herself into some difficulty. When the gales cleared off, she decided we should take the bus to Stonehaven to visit the library there. We timed it so Ellen could give us a lift to the bus stop (with Phyllis in the van too, on her way to the aerodrome; there was no escaping her).

A thing happened on the bus that scared me and Jane both.

We got on and I paid our fares, and we went and sat just across from a young mum with a wobbly baby on her lap and a little boy next to her. Jane, I discovered, could not resist a baby.

'Hello, little man!' She leaned forward, around me, to see him. She covered her eyes and uncovered them quickly. 'Peepo!'

The baby gave a gurgle of a laugh. His big brother, not yet old enough to be in school, stared.

'How old are your boys?' Jane asked in a friendly way.

'Bertie's four, and wee Angus is just nine months old today,' said the woman.

The four-year-old Bertie wasn't staring at Jane. He was staring at me, sitting right across the aisle from him.

Suddenly he buried his face in his mum's arm, clinging and fearful. His shoulders shook as he started to sob.

His mum leaned down to listen to him, then looked up and laughed.

'No, don't be a silly-willy!' she told the boy. 'Of course she isn't a German!'

Jane gasped and flinched. I heard and felt it. I'd only known her for a fortnight, but in that time we'd seen

Liverpool bombed and had faced down an enemy soldier with a gun, and delivered the code that sank three U-boats. I had never known her to be shaken by anything until this moment when she thought she'd been found out.

And she hadn't even done anything to give herself away; she'd just been caught off guard somehow by a small boy. She stiffened, and sat up straight so that my head blocked the people opposite from seeing her face, and her hands went tight where they were propped on the sticks that lay across our laps. I could feel the sticks pressing hard against the tops of my thighs as she pushed on them.

But I knew that the boy had been looking at me, not her.

He wouldn't raise his head. He muttered into his mum's arm.

'I shall ask her myself.' She leaned over her little boy and spoke to me directly. 'You're not from round about, are you? Where do you come from?'

Jane got it, then.

But she didn't relax; the sticks pressed down more fiercely into my legs.

'I grew up in Jamaica,' I said. I could feel the blood rising to burn in my cheeks, the familiar anger and the unfamiliar urge to fly into a fight, the way I'd felt when that horrid Chip Wingate called me a darkie. 'I'm British. My dad is—' I swallowed. 'My dad was a seaman in the merchant navy, but his ship was torpedoed. Hardly anyone was rescued.'

'Oh, darlin', how terrible!' The young mum's concern was warm and honest. 'My husband too, last spring. Just after Angus came along, as well. He never saw the wee 'un.' She bent her head so she could speak into the cowering boy's ear. 'You see, Bertie? Her daddy's been lost at sea just like yours. She wouldnae speak English if she was a German!'

Jane flinched again.

The woman looked back up at me and gave an apologetic little laugh. 'You must be the most northerly Jamaican in the kingdom! He's no' seen one before. Nor a German, for that matter. But he worries about Germans a great deal. Silly wee lad! There's no Germans here.'

I was the most foreign-looking person that boy had ever seen, so he thought I must be German.

And here all the while was this German woman sitting stiffly afraid beside me and hoping no one would notice. For once, Jane hadn't spoken up for me.

I tried to smile – that poor young widow was being nice, after all. But I couldn't manage it. People being nice to you after someone has made you feel like a criminal or an enemy is just like sticking cardboard in your window after a bomb has blasted all the glass out of it. The hole is stopped up, but the glass is still smashed and you can't see through the window any more. Everything in the room is uglier and darker.

Mummy would have poked fun at these people, helped me laugh it off, swept up the invisible broken glass, painted pretty patterns on the cardboard in the hole. Alone, I was helpless with anger. I didn't want to live in the ugly dark room with the smashed window.

'I'm sorry about your husband,' I murmured.

And that was that – nobody said anything else to one another throughout the whole eight-mile bus ride to Stonehaven.

But after we got off the bus, and Jane and I were by ourselves being scoured by the salt wind as we made our way very slowly down the High Street to the library, Jane asked me about my parents.

'Mummy was English,' I told her. 'She was born in London. Her father was in the Royal Navy, based in Jamaica, and directed a band for them. He died – both her parents died before she was married. But she was already grown-up then, teaching music at a secondary school for boys in Kingston. I look like her, except that she was blond! We have the same face, same shape of eyes and mouth. I can wear all her clothes now, well, if I take them in a bit at the top.'

It felt good to talk about her, I realised.

'She gave harp and piano lessons, and used to play at weddings and things like that. Sometimes I got to go along and sit in a corner guzzling wedding cake.'

'How did she meet your father?' Jane asked.

'They both sang. They were in the same operatic society. He was a seaman, too, like her father, but ...' My daddy, Lenford Adair, always bringing me presents from faraway places and shouting with laughter at my school stories. Arguing politics with our landladies in London in his sea-deep baritone voice. My very earliest memory is of him singing on the veranda, while I lay in my cot under the mosquito net in the dark warm night and lizards scratched on the screens and the window slats. *Come sit on my knee and sing, Carrie!* he'd call softly to Mummy. *I've missed you, girl.*

'Daddy's mother, Granny Adair, lives on the tiniest farm on the edge of Kingston, and Daddy ran away to sea when he was fifteen. He was in the merchant navy. So my mother was alone with me a lot. And when I was in primary school there were labour strikes and workers rioting all over the Caribbean, and Daddy's ship stopped more often in Southampton than it did in Kingston, so Mummy came back to London with me in 1937. She was glad she did it, too, because the very next year there was a big strikers' riot in Kingston and people got killed.'

And two years after *that*, the London bus she was riding on fell into a crater made by a German bomb and *she* got killed.

Suddenly I felt like I was going to choke on the unfairness of this stupid war. How did I get here, walking at a snail's pace down this windy cobbled street full of cold granite houses, carrying ration books and a forged passport for an ancient German opera singer, helping her find something to read while we waited for a winter evening bright enough to drop some bombs by moonlight?

'My father wasn't let in the Royal Navy because he wasn't born in Europe,' I added. 'He'd been a British seaman since he was *fifteen*, but that wasn't good enough for the Royal Navy. Even though he ended up dying like a navy man.'

My voice was getting shrill.

It still made me furious, and I dreaded that the same thing would happen to me when – if – I tried to enlist. I thought about the little boy on the bus, who'd taken one look at me and decided I must be the enemy, just because he'd never seen anyone who looked like me before.

But there was the Enigma machine. If I never got another chance to serve, at least I had the Enigma machine now.

I hated the bitterness I'd heard in my own voice. I took a deep breath.

'Sorry,' I said quietly. 'I'm sorry. It didn't seem to make him angry – he volunteered and they said no. They told him he was doing vital work that needed doing, and that made sense to him. And he *was*. But it made *me* angry. It still makes me angry.'

Jane didn't answer for a minute or so – just concentrated steadily on moving forward, tap-step-tap-step, with her feet and her sticks.

Then when we got to a corner where we had to cross the road, she stopped to rest a moment and straightened up.

'You have all your life ahead of you. You will have to start fighting,' Jane said, as if it were a straightforward and practical plan for me: destroy the British Empire's colour bar and save the world from fascism at the same time.

'I envy you, a little, my dear,' she went on. 'I'm doing it the other way round. I started out my life with all doors open to me, and the world's events of the past ten years have held nothing but sorrows and disappointments as those doors, and more, slammed closed. My nation has poisoned itself. I will never go home. I will never belong anywhere again. I have no people.'

My heart gave an anxious little skip that was becoming familiar. 'Oh, Jane,' I scolded. 'When the war ends—'

She cut me off. 'If the war ends tomorrow, I will already be eighty-two years old! My future is rather more predictable than yours.'

She started tottering across the road.

'But you, girl,' she added to me over her shoulder, with

the warmth coming back into her voice, 'you might be able to change things.'

Ellen:

I was the courier now.

It made me nervous. I admit it, I was scared of Cromwell finding out. I hadn't crossed paths with him much, except to drive him to Deeside. But I knew how Jamie hated him, and that made it worth the risk. Anything, now that Jamie had a whiff of his old self back. Pimms were the heroes of the day after that last op. The lads said Jamie never got so much as a *Well done* out of Cromwell, but that was his own fault for striding in for debriefing and boasting, '*Guess what happens when we're armed properly!*'

I stopped at the airfield gate on my way out to Stonehaven to collect a crate of administrative bumf from the rail station, and waited for Nobby Fergusson to raise the barrier. He sidled up to the Tilly looking important.

I cranked down the window. 'What now, Nobby?'

'Watch out for that bus stop when you get to the crossroads, Volunteer McEwen,' he said. 'We have reason to believe it's the centre of a dangerous spy network.'

My belly lurched. What had he seen? Had he noticed my back-and-forth carrying-on between Jamie and Louisa? But I'd not gone at all out of my way!

Nobby's mate Jack Hinton put in, 'I never liked that telephone box much, either.'

'What are you lads gassing about?' I said through my teeth.

'Didn't they tell you at operations?' asked Nobby, pleased to be the bearer of bad news. 'A German bomber flew over last night, dropped a load of TNT up on the main road, and scarpered off back to Norway. Flattened the bus shelter and knocked over the telephone kiosk!'

'They missed a very suspicious postbox,' Jack added with a wink. 'It sits all by itself in a field wall. Perfect place to get rid of a secret message. Maybe the Jerries know something we don't know!'

'I'm sure they know all sorts you don't know,' I told them as they raised the barrier.

That explosion hadn't even shaken me out of bed. Why would the Luftwaffe send one lonely bomber to an empty, wet bus stop guarded by drookit sheep?

It put out the telephone line into Windyedge village for a day or so. But we still had the radios at the aerodrome, so 648 Squadron was all right.

In daylight, plain daylight, the Luftwaffe was back the next afternoon with three Junkers Ju-88 bombers. They went skriking past the Kingsleap Light and swung north along the cliffs. Pimms Section got scrambled out to chase them; Old Flash radioed Deeside to beg help from the Spitfires. And Wing Commander Talbot Cromwell leaped into the Tilly with me as his driver.

'McEwen, is it?' he growled. 'Take me to the signal box just before the railway crosses the Clemency Bridge.'

I didn't have a clue where that was.

'I'm sorry, sir,' I said. 'I've not been along the railway before.'

'What the devil have you been doing these past six weeks? There's been no active squadron here since October. You could have been checking routes!'

'Petrol, sir.' I swallowed. 'I mean, I wasn't to waste petrol.'

'You have a bicycle, don't you? Where's your initiative? *Christ.*' He had a fight with a map and won. 'There,' he said, smacking the limp page as if he'd like to do the same to me. 'Get moving – there's a farm track above the village that'll take us there.'

It had long grass growing up the middle, being travelled only by tractors and horses, but that didn't stop Cromwell making me drive full skelter along the clifftops.

The Ju-88s had cleared off back to Norway when we arrived. But Jamie was up there flying in circles round the smoking holes in the railway line. I knew Silver must be on his belly in the Blenheim's nose, giving directions, and Tex would be on the floor in the back with the escape hatch open, snapping pictures in the icy wind.

That was the first bomb damage ever I saw. I couldn't make full sense of it. Where the explosion happened, the track looked like sheep's wool snarled on a wire fence. Cromwell strode around the wreckage and I trailed along after him with my mouth hanging open.

'Hah! Unlucky fellows,' he exclaimed at last, standing at the edge of the hole in the railway line. 'Poor show for the Jerries! They missed the Clemency Bridge. This'll take a week to mend, I shouldn't wonder. But if they'd hit the bridge, the line might have been out for months. Where's my clipboard, Volunteer McEwen?'

Of course I didn't have his clipboard.

'Good God, you're inefficient, girl! Go get it out of the Hillman. I'll ask for anti-aircraft defences to be installed on this stretch of the line. They won't surprise us here again.'

Was it my fault he'd left his flipping clipboard in the Tilly? No wonder Jamie couldn't stand him.

It was dark when I was let go that evening. All day folk ran about like mad things, railway officials came and went, and RAF officials blethered and shouted at one another. Someone else took the Tilly away overnight, full of iron-mongery, and I got sent home on my bicycle. Jamie dashed out as I was leaning over the front wheel to make sure the lamp was properly dimmed, as Phyllis had told me off more than once for riding home with a light showing, and I'd had enough telling off that day from Cromwell without Phyllis joining in. In any case after seeing that hole in the railway, I didn't want to let the Jerries know where I was.

'It's hard work catching you alone,' Jamie said breathlessly. 'Here – it's another German message. There's a sweet spot in the sky just east of Aberdeen where we seem to get signals straight from Norway. It's clearer at night, but we had an excuse for haring about this afternoon because of that raid. Wasn't it lucky! No one was hurt, and now we're on to the Jerries again! I say, Ellen, if Louisa works out this message, can you ask her to leave it somewhere I can collect it myself? She could hide it in the same record album, and pop a penny among the wishing coins to let me know it's there, and no one would notice. Just on the outside edge, where I put mine. I'll know to look for it.'

'You and all your folk are a clan of lying, crooked schemers,' I told him, straightening the front wheel of my bicycle. 'And to think the McEwens get called sleekit, just for being Travellers!'

He laughed. 'You're an angel. Listen, I've told Silver about this, so he could deliver the cipher machine key and the leaflets and tip-off message to Cromwell – it seemed easier to pretend Silver found it in the Limehouse bar than for me to get in another battle with the Old Roundhead. So Silver's safe if you need to pass anything on through him, but don't let Phyllis know what's going on. She's a lovely lass, but Cromwell's got her in his pocket.'

'I'd be mad,' I said, warmed to the heart by his laughter and his hope.

I so wanted another win for him.

I shot off into the dark on my bicycle with his scrap of paper in my breast pocket.

Louisa:

I *loved* the Enigma machine. It was such a *beautiful* thing, with its nickel-trimmed keyboard and polished wood case. Its steady lamps picked out letter after letter for me to transfer to my exercise book, and in the moment when the meaningless soup of code became German it always felt like a jolt of electricity was going through me. It was *magic.*

I made duplicates of the next translation, one to leave in the record album, and one to give Ellen, in case she got to

Jamie first. The message was complicated: something about a U-boat surfacing for urgent repairs between Scotland and Denmark, asking the Luftwaffe to protect the maintenance ship that was going to meet them. The coordinates were all in Roman numerals, as the cipher machine didn't have numbers on it. I worked through the code three times to be sure I'd got it right.

I was more anxious about hiding my penny above the bar than I'd been about anything since meeting Jane on the Isle of Man. I thought Nan would less likely notice something new up there than something old missing, but it was a risk. I didn't want her to catch me. Was I breaking the law? I didn't think so, I didn't think there *were* any laws about what I was doing, but if there were and I was, I couldn't imagine the consequences. I didn't want *anyone* to catch me.

'Rules are made to be broken,' I whispered aloud as I folded the copied messages.

We didn't use the thick paper in my exercise book to leave the message on. We didn't want anyone but Jamie noticing it behind the notes in the Django Reinhardt record. Jane cut a thin strip from a page of one of her own books, a beautiful edition of a fat novel called *Ulysses*, itself hidden in a paper dust jacket off a French/English dictionary.

'Why is your book in disguise?'

'They never would have let me take it to Rushen Camp if they knew what it was,' said Jane smugly. She could be quite smug for an old woman. 'Quite the filthiest piece of writing ever published. It would upset Nancy more than an enemy cipher machine if she found a copy of it under her roof!'

A racy book disguised as a stern old dictionary – it rather reminded me of Jane herself.

I wrote out Jamie's message in English. Jane guessed a little about how the German coordinates worked, and added a note for David Silvermont at the end. I added a warning on the back about keeping our new communications system secret – as if they needed to be told that!

I waited nervously until the middle of the night to hide it. I lay awake listening to the wind in the Scotch pines on the ridge above the house. Jane wasn't worried – her relaxed, gentle snore began almost as soon as I put out the light.

When the luminous dial of Mummy's little Bakelite alarm clock showed it was after midnight, I climbed out over the foot of the bed. It was freezing. I didn't put on my dressing gown or slippers, though. Cold would keep me alert and I still had enough of the Jamaica bush in me to feel more confident in bare feet.

'Louisa?' Jane whispered.

I'd woken her getting out of bed.

'I'll only be five minutes!'

I felt my way across the room and through the door, and padded down the passage. My jumping stomach made me incredibly sneaky.

I switched on the light in the loo that Jane and I shared with Ellen and Phyllis, and closed the door. Then I crept on down the passage. If anyone heard me and saw the light around the edges of the door, she would think I was using the toilet.

The cold stairs felt good against my soles. I kept to one side, holding the banister, feeling the smooth wooden treads beneath my feet at the edge of the woven coconut matting. By the time I reached the bottom, my heart was hammering as it had never done when the bombs were falling around me in the Blitz.

No one's on guard, I told myself. *Nobody's down there.*

There wasn't any light. I didn't want to switch one on. I felt my way across the cold flagstones, found the poker, and stirred up last night's fire. Old embers glowed red beneath the banked ash, and gave me the little bit of light I needed.

I still had enough of the Jamaica bush in me that I climbed up to sit on the bar to reach the ceiling instead of standing on a chair. Ellen had told me where to put my penny.

Then, quiet as could be, I crossed the room and slipped the message into the record that I'd left on top of the pile so I wouldn't have to hunt for it in the dark.

Afterwards, I crept upstairs, opened the door to the loo, and pulled the chain to flush. Then I switched out the light and went back to Room Number Five.

Jane was asleep again – her magical power, able to sleep under any circumstances. There wasn't a stutter in her even, purring snore as I climbed into bed beside her.

Of course I had to do it all again a few days later.

I was just as nervous sneaking around in the dark the second and third time I did it. But I learned which floorboards creaked, which stair rail rattled, how to stick to the wall so I didn't bump into furniture. The nerves didn't go away, but I got better at my job. I wondered if that was how the airmen felt about flying into battle.

The next message wasn't much use – and half of it was missing.

REPEAT SPECIAL APPROACH STORM FRONT IV XII

FIRST GREEN LIGHT BEFORE HALF MOON

Jamie:

Another German submarine! Coastal Command sent us on a not-too-risky mission to blast holes in Lista, the Luftwaffe aerodrome that didn't exist yet, as retaliation for the railway attack and to create a headache for the Nazi planners. We wouldn't have spotted that disabled U-boat if we hadn't known it was there, but it *wasn't even out of our way*. I let Adam Stedman in Madeira do the honours of sinking it. I didn't want to make Pimms look greedy … or to push our luck.

But our luck held, even though the incomplete message Louisa deciphered next wasn't as straightforward.

I tossed and turned on my narrow top bunk for three hours instead of sleeping, wondering what it meant.

REPEAT SPECIAL APPROACH STORM FRONT IV XII

FIRST GREEN LIGHT BEFORE HALF MOON

St Nicholas Day, 6 December, would be the half-moon. Christmas was coming. IV XII came before that,

4 December 1940 … And already it was past midnight on 2 December. The fourth was the day after tomorrow. What storm front was approaching on the fourth?

'Blimey, Jamie, give it a rest,' Silver hissed from the mattress below. 'When you turn over you shake the whole bunk.'

'Sorry.' I lay on my back like a block. Every inch of me felt uncomfortable.

'What's eating you?'

'Are we due some bad weather?' I asked. Silver always kept an eye on the met conditions.

'Just the usual overcast and wind,' he told me. 'Do you want an excuse to stay on the ground? "Lack of moral fibre, Flight Lieutenant Beaufort-Stuart!"'

I snorted. '*Now?* As if!'

'As a matter of fact it's going to be quite nice for a few days, which will give the ATA a chance to deliver those new Blenheims – well, old ones without holes. New for us.' Silver's voice dropped to a whisper. He asked almost inaudibly, 'What's really eating you?'

I leaned over the edge of the bed so my head hung closer to his, and he leaned on his elbows so his head was closer to mine, and we carried on whispering.

'I can't figure out the last message.'

'Maybe we need to pass it to a real codebreaker,' Silver suggested.

'Yes, I thought of that, but then we'd have to tell Cromwell. Even if we went straight to Intelligence he'd find out.'

'He'll find out eventually,' Silver warned. 'The lads are wondering what's going on. Sooner or later you'll run out of excuses for the good luck.'

'If we don't run out of rotor settings first,' I pointed out. 'It's the Lucky-Rotor Aero Race!'

I choked on laughter, smothering my face in my mattress for a moment.

'How long are the settings good for?' Silver hissed. 'Two months?'

'How long is a Blenheim crew good for?' I whispered back.

He didn't answer.

'Should I tell Cromwell?' I asked.

'No,' Silver said. 'The lads need this as much as you do. It would be nice to make it to 1941.'

Silver was right about the weather – we had two glorious days of low sun. It was the beginning of December, but it felt like spring. When our new planes turned up and we tested them over the moors on low-level flight manoeuvres, I half expected to see lambs and daffodils below us. Ellen went about without her mackintosh, whistling. The whole of B-Flight, Windyedge's ground crew, and the visiting ATA ferry pilots who'd delivered the fresh Blenheims all piled into the Limehouse on the evening of the third. The pub was so full that people spilt outside, as if it were summer.

I didn't see the old woman and the young girl, but I heard Louisa's flute and Jane's singing. They must have stayed in their room because it was so crowded downstairs; you couldn't get to the bar, and the lads passed their pint glasses back over one another's heads. But Louisa and Jane had their window open to the mild night, and outside you could hear them working through the *Oxford Book of Carols*, getting ready for Christmas. Every now and then the flute stuttered for a bit, as if Louisa were warming her fingers.

'Wow, I've got a headache,' Chip complained the next morning as we lined up to shave. 'Too much flute tootling over at Nancy's place.'

'The *flute music* gave you a headache?' Silver scoffed in disbelief. 'Yanks must be lightweights! Are you sure it wasn't the beer?'

'I'm not a Yankee,' Chip growled. 'I'm from Texas. You're the navigator – check a map! What do y'all think of a darkie learning Morse code, anyway?'

'Can you be more polite, and more specific?' I asked.

'The hired girl at Nan's. She was practising the Morse alphabet all evening.'

'What are you talking about?' Silver grumbled, muffled by foam and looking at himself in the mirror, not at Chip.

'She was tooting it on her flute. Took me back to when I was learning – it's not easy, you know, until you've got an ear for it. And once you know it's Morse you can't *stop* listening, so that's all I heard all evening – those durned ABCs up and down the scale, whistling up a storm!'

Silver laughed. 'Well, a flute's a wind instrument,' he said.

'There's no need to whistle up a wind *here*.' I laughed, too. 'It's always windy. They don't call it Windyedge for nothing.'

I bent over the basin to rinse my face. I'd only heard music, Louisa playing scales – but all Chip had heard was the letters she'd been rapping out. How differently you understand things when you start from a different place, I thought, the way my heart gave a jump of relief last night when I saw the Kingsleap Light flashing green as we walked back to the airfield. I was always so relieved to spot it in the air at the end of a hop, and it took me a second before I realised it didn't matter because I was already on the ground, and it was lit for the fishing trawlers and not for me.

Something clicked in my head.

Whistling up a storm – a wind instrument.

REPEAT SPECIALAPPROACH STORM FRONT IV XII

FIRST GREEN LIGHT BEFORE HALF MOON

Green light

They don't call it Windyedge for nothing.

A different starting point.

The fragments came together, and their meaning clicked into place. There wasn't any 'storm front'. It was a translation error.

It wasn't Jane Warner's error – we checked, later. 'Storm front' was how the German wireless operator understood 'windy edge'.

They were going to attack Windyedge on 4 December – in the dark, while the green light was lit. They must already be most of the way here.

'Silver, back me up,' I hissed.

I tossed aside my razor, wiped my face on my vest, and yelled, '*B-Flight! Pay attention!*'

Everyone stared.

I didn't have proof, and if I was wrong I'd probably be court-martialled. But I couldn't risk losing a whole fleet of freshly mended Blenheims to a Luftwaffe bombing raid.

'Ablutions postponed,' I told them. 'Drop everything and get out to the hangar. We need every single one of 648 Squadron's planes in the air *now*.'

'What, in my pants?'

'I'm cleaning my teeth!'

'Before breakfast?'

Harry Morrow, who was younger than me, said, 'Wake up, Scotty – you're still dreaming!'

'Or thinks he's still lord of the manor,' sneered Bill Yorke, who was ten years older, *damn him*.

'Or maybe I'm following orders,' I snarled, 'as *you're* meant to.'

Everyone else had protested or complained. But Bill Yorke was stirring up mutiny.

This time they didn't just stare: they held their breath. I don't think they were hoping for a fight, exactly; just wondering what would happen next.

Silver shrugged. 'A drill's a drill,' he told Harry, ignoring Bill Yorke. 'Get used to it.'

'*In my pants?*' Dougie Kerr repeated incredulously, and everyone laughed.

The tension eased. Once again, Silver had given me the edge I needed.

'A timed drill,' I improvised. 'No warning, *as if we're under attack*. We have ten minutes to get in the air for a rendezvous off Aberdeen. The past week's been wizard for B-Flight, don't bugger it up now; let's show the Old Roundhead what we can do. Kerr, get your trousers on! Tex, do a head count. We need every plane in the air, the trainer as well; we'll take the shot-up Blenheims and let the ferry pilots fly the ones they brought.

Stedman, you're mostly dressed, you go get them moving. Silver, you come with me and raise the ground crew.'

I knew I wouldn't have any trouble with the ground crew – they pre-dated Cromwell.

Silver and I met each other's eyes.

He moved his lips soundlessly. *Not a drill?*

I shook my head.

'I'm with you,' Silver said aloud.

Louisa:

We were still in bed that morning, 4 December, when we heard the Blenheims taking off.

I sat up and counted and got to ten.

'That doesn't make the least sense!' I exclaimed. 'I thought there were only six aeroplanes in B-Flight.'

'Perhaps they keep spares,' said Jane.

We heard footsteps running in the passage, and the bathroom and toilet doors slamming. Phyllis and Ellen had both leaped into action.

'The planes took off in the *dark*!' I said. 'The moon went down hours ago – I thought they couldn't fly without a moon!'

Jane squinted at my luminous alarm clock.

'I think they struggle to find targets without a moon. But they can fly, and it will get light in half an hour or so,' she said. 'It's a quarter past eight. You and I are slugabeds. Perhaps they've been posted elsewhere.'

Ellen and Phyllis clattered downstairs and the front door banged.

Jane went back to sleep.

I don't know how she *could*, except that she had the gift of instant sleep. I couldn't even make myself lie down again.

Five minutes later I recognised the *whomp-whomp* of German engines, like the bombers flying over London.

I catapulted out of bed and hauled the blackout curtains from the window facing south-east over the sea. The Kingsleap Light bloomed bright green in the dark, flashing as the lamp swung round. There must be British fishing boats about, or the lighthouse would be dark. I leaped across to the narrow north window that faced the airfield, but I couldn't see anything there. The terrible throbbing German engines were louder now – they sounded like they were right overhead.

Then the fins whistled as the bombs fell.

I couldn't see the airfield, but WOW did I see the explosions.

'Jane, Jane!' I screeched. 'The aerodrome's being bombed – come look!' The need to look was fiercer in me than the sensible need to dive for cover. If something was going to blow me up, I wanted to see it coming.

Or perhaps, like Jane, I just didn't want to miss anything. She was as silly as me about the fireworks. We crowded for the view at the narrow window.

'My word, that is a direct hit – something is on fire!' Jane exclaimed.

We heard distant sirens. We couldn't see anything on the

ground, only oily black smoke lit by the red glow of flames. A thick column rose in the sky, showing the German pilots exactly where to aim on their next pass.

They came back. We couldn't tell if they hit anything the second time. Then the Royal Air Force came roaring in to chase them off – not our Blenheims, but a swarm of Spitfires from Deeside. It was like watching the Battle of Britain all over again. I thought I'd never grow tired of it: the soaring dots against a bottle-blue predawn sky, the whine and roar of engines, the twisting loops of vapour trails as it started to get light – and in my stomach a knot of painful envy because I was not up there too, doing something useful, able to fight back.

It didn't last five minutes before the Luftwaffe planes turned tail. They didn't have a fighter escort to protect them.

'Hitler is a madman,' Jane pronounced. 'What a waste of fuel and effort, bombing an empty aerodrome! I suppose it is a miracle those boys managed to get all their planes off the ground before the bombs fell. Somebody must have seen the storm coming—'

'"*Seen the storm coming!*"' I cried. '*Storm front! Windyedge!*'

Jane grabbed my arm.

'Jamie got *all the planes* out in time,' I breathed.

'I hope the girls are all right,' said Jane.

Jane and I spent the afternoon by the peat fire in the public bar feeling nervous, while Nancy Campbell sullenly served and washed up after the villagers. She glanced at the wishing coins every now and then, muttering under her breath, as if she were praying to them. The Blenheims didn't come back.

Of course the aerodrome telephone was knocked out again, and they couldn't spare anyone to bring us news, so we had to wait. We played records on Jane's gramophone to count off the time. It took ten hours and twenty minutes to get to the bottom of the record pile, she said, but we'd only played three hours' worth (not counting while the pub was open) when the front door slammed in the vestibule.

Mrs Campbell practically fell over herself with anxiety. She threw open the wooden gate and leaped from behind the bar. '*Phyllis? Ellen?*'

It was Ellen on her own. She stood in the doorway.

'I won't come through just now,' she called across the room hoarsely. 'I'm all over soot. I had to help with the fire-fighting, and then I had to drive to Aberdeen and back twice.'

She was not joking – soot covered her from head to toe. Her eyes were red and swollen, and her hand on the doorknob was covered with blisters.

I gasped, 'Oh, Ellen, your poor hands!'

Mrs Campbell looked her up and down and said grudgingly, 'I'll light the boiler for the hot water before six p.m., just this once. Mind you don't fill the bath beyond the five-inch mark. There's a war on.'

'Aye, Nan Campbell, I might have some idea about there being a war on,' Ellen rasped.

Mrs Campbell dared to ask, 'Where's Phyllis?'

'She's still at the aerodrome, filling out forms. We lost a

big supply of tinned food, and she's trying to order more. She's all right. *Everyone's* all right. The Jerries missed the operations hut. But the hangar is burned to the ground.' Ellen sucked in a deep breath, and coughed. 'The lads are all right, too, Mrs C. They had to land at Deeside, because the surface at Windyedge is all over holes. Cromwell was there last night so I had to collect him and bring him here to look at the damage, and then I had to take him back to Deeside again.'

Nan Campbell clutched the brass counter of the bar and gasped with relief. She gave a quick glance at the wishing coins.

'The ground crew's filling in the holes, but we won't be able to bring the Blenheims back till next week at least.' Ellen coughed again. 'Phyllis will want a bath, too, when she gets here.'

'Och, no bother, I'll light the boiler the now and you get yourself cleaned up,' Nan said. 'And when you go back to the airfield, tell the lads working there that if they get hungry they can come here. I'll see if Morag can put in extra time behind the bar.'

Morag Torrie was the timid village girl who helped Mrs Campbell when it was busy.

'Ta for the hot water,' Ellen said, and turned around to stalk upstairs.

'Take her a cup of tea, will you, Louisa,' Mrs Campbell uttered. 'Oh, and there's some Germolene in the kitchen on the shelf above the sink. For the burns.'

It was as close as I had seen her come to anything like sympathy.

Ellen:

It took me a long time to get my uniform off, for my hands were so sore. Cromwell already had a go at me for wearing mittens knitted by one of my cousins, instead of my gauntlets, which would have protected them. *No one to blame but yourself, McEwen.* But how am I supposed to drive in those bloody great things? Like wearing wellington boots on your hands.

When I was quaking with chill in my underthings I realised the water in the boiler wouldn't be warm for another wee while. I'd been dreaming of that bath for the past half a day, I must be going soft, living under a roof with hot water out of a tap!

I hung up my clothes on the back of the bathroom door and wrapped myself in the shawl that Nan disliked because it wasn't a proper dressing gown. I ran cold water in the basin while I waited for the hot, pulling the stool up so I could sit and soak my hands.

A tap came at the door.

'Ellen? Shall I leave this outside?'

That was Louisa with a tea tray.

'Come along through,' I said, and she edged through the door. 'All right, Louisa?'

'I'm all right.' She gave me a smile and jerked her chin at my hands. 'What about you?'

'Aye, no bother. Ta very much for the tea, just set it on the floor there.'

'Mrs Campbell sent you up some burn ointment, too,' Louisa said.

'Och, she didn't! She's got a soft heart under that hard shell, hasn't she? Like an old pearl mussel stuck on a stone in a river bed.' A corner of the shawl was trailing in the basin and getting a good soak too. I sighed, and watched Louisa put down the tray and stand up again.

She didn't leave, though.

I gave a jerk of my own chin towards the bathtub, telling her to stay. She sat down on the edge, dark eyes eager, waiting for my news.

I wiggled my sore fingers, splashing water about in the basin. If Nan had a fit of kindness and decided to bring me some sticking plasters as an afterthought, I didn't want her to hear about our amateur codebreaking.

'Is the old woman behaving herself?' I asked. 'Mrs Warner – do you like working for her?'

'I love it,' Louisa said, and I saw that what she meant was that she loved *Jane*. But she wore a worried frown as she said it.

'Is it difficult?'

'It's the easiest work in the world. I do up her buttons and help with her stockings, and keep our room tidy. And I play my flute or piano duets with her, and we listen to records or the radio, and I read novels out loud. She's always interested and lets me read what I like. And with Mrs Campbell giving me room and board, I can save most of what she pays me. *But*—'

'But there's bombs,' I said.

Louisa shook her head. 'That's not it. There were more bombs in London. It's that I worry about *Jane*. She leaves the gas tap on without lighting the fire. She tries to go out on her own and she *says* it's because she doesn't want to wake me, but the cobbles are always black with ice first thing in the morning and you know how steep the lane is past the limekilns. If she falls or gets hurt or … or worse … well, even if it isn't my fault, the more I like her, the more I couldn't ever forgive myself if something happened and I wasn't there to help.'

She looked away. She gave a quick sniff, then turned about again.

'She's teaching me Morse code!' Louisa said shakily, as if she wanted to talk of something else. 'She could teach me to sing opera. I bet she'd teach me *German* if I really wanted to learn something useful.'

I stared at her. '*Useful! German!*'

'I want to do something to help with the war. I could translate for prisoners, perhaps, when I'm older. I don't know. Be a spy, like Mata Hari.' Louisa frowned again. 'Your poor hands! Do you need help?'

It was most unlikely anyone was listening.

But Louisa rabbiting on about bloody Mata Hari and learning to speak in Morse code like a Jerry made me not want to take any chances.

'I don't need help. I'm going to have a bath.' I stood up, shook my wet hands, and turned on the bath taps. The water roared, covering the sound of our voices beyond the bathroom door.

'I had a word with our Jamie, over at Aberdeen,' I told her. 'He worked out that message this morning, and ordered the planes away from Windyedge. In the dark – most of the lads took off in their vests and braces! Must have been *perishing* up there without flight suits.'

'But what did he tell the commander?' Louisa asked, wide-eyed. 'Where did he say he got the tip?'

'He put it back to the first message – remember that one about "Deeside south green light"? Jamie worked out it means *us.* We're south of Deeside, just off the green light at the Kingsleap Rocks. They tried to hit us in daylight last week and got the railway by accident, but when the light was lit for the fishing boats this morning, they tried again. They'd have surely got most of our planes on the ground if it hadn't been for Jamie. Even Old Cromwell saw that. And what do you think he said?'

I pulled Cromwellian eyebrows and put on my best posh English accent. '"Good thinking, Flight Lieutenant Beaufort-Stuart, but insubordination nonetheless. You didn't ask permission. Confined to barracks for a week except for operational flying."'

'Poor Jamie!' Louisa exclaimed.

'Bloody Cromwell,' I muttered.

The water was nearly to the five-inch line Nan had painted in the bathtub. I'd have to turn off the taps in a moment. I spoke in a rush.

'Old Cromwell thinks the Luftwaffe is using Windyedge for bombing practice,' I told Louisa. 'It's the shortest hop from Norway to Scotland. But you and I know there's a Jerry coding machine hidden in the wardrobe down the passage. And I think some Jerry knows it, too – not the one who brought it, but someone else, someone who doesn't want it here. And they're trying to destroy it. They'll keep at it until they think they've hit it, and as long as we keep using it they'll know they haven't got it.'

That angry little frown split Louisa's forehead again.

'No, that isn't at all sensible,' she said. 'The machine could be anywhere. We could have taken it to London by now, or Wales, and still be using it to decode messages for Windyedge. Perhaps they're trying to punish us because Felix Baer landed here.'

The bath was five inches deep.

'Or perhaps,' she added, 'they're trying to destroy the airfield so he can't come back.'

We couldn't talk any longer because I had to turn off the taps.

Jamie:

B-Flight flew out of Deeside along with A-Flight, on fishing-fleet and battleship escort duties for the whole December moon, getting in the way of the Spitfire fighter squadron based there. Meanwhile the holes in the runway at Windyedge were mended and a new hangar got thrown up next to the crater where the old one used to be.

ABERDEEN SECTOR CLEAR START XII UNTIL FURTHER NOTICE

Normally I'd have had my heart in my mouth worrying that we might run into Messerschmitt 110 night fighters on these ops. That message in Louisa's notebook reassured me. Aberdeen had been bombed pretty fiercely right through October; now the Luftwaffe seemed to be holding back.

Phyllis came to Deeside with us, but I only saw Ellen twice while we were there, taking Cromwell on some inspection errand. The second time I didn't even get to talk to her. She just gave me a look and shook her head ever so slightly.

I shrugged in reply, and went off whistling, to let her know everything was all right.

Actually, everything was *fine*.

I'd wanted an edge over the Germans and now that I had one, I felt like our luck had changed. Finding that coding machine, getting unexpected tip-offs that helped us sink four U-boats, saving all our planes from being turned into scrap metal on the ground when the aerodrome was bombed – being one step ahead of the enemy for a week or two – made us *lucky*.

We hadn't lost a man since 7 November. That was six weeks ago, and that was a record for 648 Squadron. It is true that one night on warship escort with A-Flight we got caught in the crossfire of a naval battle. One of my propellers was blown away by anti-aircraft fire from a German battleship, and they also smashed Dougie Kerr's gun turret. But the Royal Navy took care of the German battleship, and although it was no fun limping home on one prop, I managed to land upright. Dougie, whose head stuck up in the shattered turret of the Aussies' plane, came home with a bloody ear – he'd been clipped by a shard of flying Perspex. Not by a bullet. He'd ducked out of the way just in time.

Lucky!

The mechanics got to work on my plane and we were

back in the air two nights later. The turret was harder to fix than the propeller, but a ferry pilot brought in another new Blenheim and took the old one away. Dougie walked around with a plaster over his left ear for a few days.

Six weeks and nobody even had an *injury*, apart from my lucky bullet on the Bell Rock Light run, and Dougie's lucky clip on the ear. Dougie's grazed ear didn't qualify for a wound stripe any more than my grazed leg did, but in Aberdeen we all chipped in and bought him a gold hoop earring like a pirate.

Windyedge was ready for B-Flight to come back just in time for Christmas.

The moon was old on Christmas Eve when we walked to Nancy's place from the airfield, crunching ice in half-frozen puddles, howling our way through 'Deck the Halls'. Nobody knew all of it so there was a lot of fa-la-la-la-la-ing. The sixpences we'd left there the night before the aerodrome was bombed were waiting in the oak beam above the bar. And that Django Reinhardt record album was waiting also, waiting for me to leave Louisa another mysterious message, so she and Mrs Warner could magically translate German code into sensible King's English.

The war turned Christmas into hard work – London, Manchester and Liverpool were pummelled by the Luftwaffe bombers. The food rationing seemed endless; we were told to buy war bonds as presents. But Louisa looped paper chains made of old issues of the *Scotsman* from the ceiling of the Limehouse, and heaped pine branches twined with ivy over the mantel, and wound ivy around the tree trunk posts holding up the bar. There was a candle in a jam jar on every window ledge, even though you couldn't see them from outside because of the blackout curtains.

As we came marching in, Louisa started to pound out 'Deck the Halls' on the piano, picking up our song, and Mrs Warner's wonderful old contralto pulled our 'fa-la-las' into line.

Between carols, I pulled up a chair next to Louisa's piano stool.

'There's a sort of unofficial "no bombs" ban over Christmas,' I told her. 'Both sides do it. But of course Old Cromwell's being a Scrooge about making us fly on Christmas Day, since the ships don't get a holiday either, and we thought we'd have some fun behind his back. We're going to take Ellen and Phyllis along for the ride. What about it, Louisa?'

She turned to me staring.

'To the airfield? In the Tilly?'

I laughed. 'No, in a Bristol Blenheim,' I said. 'Out over the North Sea during the Christmas truce.'

Very softly and slowly, she played the opening bars of 'Joy to the World'.

Then she stopped. She glanced at me, biting her lower lip, and croaked, 'Yes, please.'

She was so eager it made her look like she was about ten years old. I laughed again.

'You'll get a ride in the Tilly as well, come to think of it, if Ellen brings you over tomorrow morning,' I said. 'Wear extra socks. Wool. Three pairs at least. It gets colder the higher you get.'

Louisa:

The sun on Christmas morning rose shining through clouds, bright red as a cherry-flavoured boiled sweet, a poinsettia in full bloom, a glowing punch bowl of holiday sorrel. I leaned into the window and pulled back the blackout curtains and thought, I will be *up there with it* today!

Jane was excited because I was excited. She came downstairs to see me off, wearing a beautiful short silver fox-fur cape. Mrs Campbell was slamming things around behind the bar. She couldn't keep public hours until the twenty-seventh of December, and fretted about not being able to work.

Phyllis scolded, 'Think of those young men in the air on Christmas Day! They're not complaining.'

'Why are you in and out the kitchen if you're not working?' Ellen provoked Nan.

'I've to fix Christmas dinner for you girls, haven't I?' Mrs Campbell grumbled. 'You'll be hungry when you're back from your flight. Morag's mother, Mrs Torrie, has sent a bit of venison.'

Most of Mrs Campbell's meals involved tinned beef, cabbage and turnips, so a morsel of fresh meat would be a proper treat.

Jane took off her cape, bundled it into a fluffy roll, and piled it on top of the counter.

'Happy Christmas, Nancy,' she said. 'I thought you might like to have a fur, as I've little reason now to wear them all.'

Nan Campbell went as pink as when 648 Squadron were chanting her name the day they got there.

'Why—' She spent so much of her life grizzling that she struggled when she was pleased. 'Why, Aunt Jane. That is— That is—' She looked at the lovely soft thing as if she expected it to come back to life as a dozen foxes and bite her to death. 'I couldn't!' She put out a hand as if she were going to push it away, and instead she patted it.

Then there was no going back.

'Well, if you're not wearing it, as you say,' she conceded. 'Thank you, Aunt Jane.'

Jane had given me one of her fur coats, too. I was stunned. I'd saved enough of my small salary to buy her a record album, as I hardly ever spent money on anything except the gas meter. I'd bought it in Stonehaven when I went by myself to return the library books: William Walton's Viola Concerto. I thought Jane might like some new English classical music. I was very glad I had something nice to give her.

Ellen gave me and Phyllis each a silver sixpence, because we were going flying with 648 Squadron.

With a dramatic flourish she pushed a silver coin of her own into the beam above the bar.

'Go on. You do yours now, Louisa.'

My heart seemed to turn somersaults. The ceiling was low enough I could touch the beam with my fingertips, but I wasn't tall enough to force the sixpence into a crack.

I couldn't climb on the counter with Nan watching.

I dragged a chair to the edge of the bar to stand on. I could see Jamie's sixpence, waiting for my penny to turn up beside it the next time another decoded instruction was ready for him. I didn't want to draw Nan's eyes over there.

I pushed my sixpence into a crack in the old wood right at the other end of the beam. I'd easily remember where it was – exactly opposite Jamie's.

My fluttering heart soared, plummeted in terror, and leaped into my throat.

Rules are made to be broken, Lula, Mummy's cheerful voice reminded me in my head.

If I died that afternoon it would be worth it to ride in an RAF Bristol Blenheim bomber.

I touched my sixpence with the tip of my finger. *Keep me safe.*

Jamie:

I found myself whistling 'The Wassail Song'. It was not regulation for Pimms Section to take three girls along on our Christmas mission, and Phyllis was so nervous it was hard not to tease her.

'No worries, this isn't a bombing run, we're just on patrol,' I told her cheerfully. Oh, it was like being in school, if school had included aeroplanes! It gave me the same feeling of truant joy, the heady satisfaction of undermining authority just for fun.

The ground crew helped the girls into flight suits, pleased as punch to be pulling a fast one on Wing Commander Cromwell.

'Helmets, good – don't worry about masks, they won't need mikes and we'll stay low enough they won't need oxygen,' I told the fitter who was equipping us. 'Can you get three more Mae Wests? Extra gauntlets and as many Ever-Hot bags as you can find! Don't tell ops.'

'As if I would! Whose head is on the block when someone twigs, anyway?'

'Mine, mine, always mine,' I assured him. 'Nobody's fighting today. There won't be a bit of trouble. It will all be *wizard*.'

In flight suits and life vests, the lasses walked to the waiting planes without attracting attention. Madeira Section had already taken off, and Old Flash had promised to make sure Cromwell didn't go near the hangars or the radio room. Phyllis and Ellen and Louisa stayed close together, a complicated collection of nerves.

Phyllis wasn't afraid of flying – she was just terrible at breaking rules, and she dithered with anxiety. 'Oh dear – oh dear, I shouldn't be doing this. It's so important I set a good example—'

I knew Ellen was scared. I'd taken her up before, and she hadn't liked it. But she wouldn't admit it. She steeled herself by looking angry and bored, and kept close to Louisa, the baby of the gang.

'Who do you want to fly with?' I heard Ellen whisper to her. 'Phyllis is going with the Aussies. You can choose.'

Louisa was the only one of the three who was visibly *sparkling* with excitement.

'You go with Jamie. He's your friend,' she said decisively. 'I'll go with Ignacy and Derfel.'

'All right, Ignacy and Derfel are safe as houses, but look out for that Yorkie,' Ellen told her. 'He's pinched my bum five times since they got back from Deeside, once a day, regular. If he does it again I might have to thump him in the teeth.'

Bloody Bill Yorke.

Nothing I could do about it now; he wouldn't be able to bother Louisa from the rear cabin.

But I made a note to keep a close eye on him back on the ground.

I wasn't going to let him ruin my day, nor anyone else's.

Louisa:

The only plane I'd been close to was Felix Baer's Messerschmitt 109. Now I was going to climb inside a Bristol Blenheim bomber. With an engine mounted in each wing and the glass turret riding on its back for the gunner, it seemed gigantic. Its tail rested on a tiny wheel against the ground and its nose pointed at the sky as if the silly tail wheel embarrassed it and it couldn't wait to take off.

Jamie hustled me on to the wing of Ignacy's plane, giving me a river of instructions.

'Walk up the wing along this rough bit; you won't slip. Sit on your parachute just in front of Taff's feet – you're only wee, you'll fit. Once we're in the air you can hop on to the observer's seat in front of him and you'll have a super view out the nose. Don't worry about Yorkie, I know what Ellen's been telling you, but he's stuck in the rear cabin minding the radio and the rear gun. Mazur and Taff are a sound pair – they'll take care of you. You won't be able to hear much, or talk to anyone, so thumbs up for everything bang on, and thumbs down if you need to be sick! Here you are – pop your foot into my hands and I'll boost you up. Climb in through the hatch—'

Squatting on the broad wing next to me, he locked gloved fingers together.

'Warm enough? All buttoned up? Mae West tight? Righto, we're off to the North Sea – just wait till you see the Scottish Highlands from the air!'

The front cabin of the Blenheim didn't feel gigantic, though. With three of us squeezed in together, it was like being a bit of saltfish in a tin. Ignacy and Derfel chattered to each other in Polish and Welsh as they checked the flight instruments. I wondered if they were doing it on purpose to wind up their new gunner. Or me – they must be used to Bill Yorke by now.

I thought of Phyllis squeezed in with tall Harry Morrow, the Aussie flying the third Pimms plane with his knees around his ears, and Gavin Hamilton, who still looked like he wasn't old enough to shave. I thought of Ellen squeezed in with easy-going, handsome David Silvermont and Flight Lieutenant Jamie Beaufort-Stuart. For a moment I felt a stab of envy.

But if I'd gone with Jamie and Silver, I'd have to go with Chip Wingate, the American from Texas.

My pilot, Ignacy, waved to get my attention.

'All right, little one?'

I gave him a thumbs up. He grinned. 'Engine start!' he yelled to the ground crew.

One propeller began to turn, then the other. Within

seconds they were both alive and it became wildly, deafeningly loud in the cockpit.

Through the clear panes in the canopy overhead, I saw clouds rushing by as we gained speed for the take-off. Then the tail of the plane lifted and I could see trees and moorland ahead of us. Finally, the way a ripe mango suddenly comes unstuck from its stem, we just lifted away from the ground. I could *feel* we were aloft.

I was in the sky.

Ignacy pushed levers and turned knobs, holding the control yoke lightly with one hand. He waved at me again, gesturing *Up, up!* He pointed into the Blenheim's nose. *Get up and look!*

I crawled forward to a swivelling stool in the nose of the plane. There were wide, clear Perspex panels in the front. I crouched on the metal seat in a cocoon of glass and I could see *everything* as we took off to the west, into the wind.

Jamie was right about the super view. The Highlands were magical ahead of us. We were still lower than their snow-covered heights, white and pink and gold in the elusive winter sun like a glittering Christmas card. We flew over the moors where the main road passed on its way to Aberdeen. Beneath my feet was a herd of red deer, dozens of them, leaping away as we skimmed overhead.

I hadn't realised how beautiful it would be. I forgot it was dangerous.

Derfel tapped me on the shoulder and beckoned. When I crawled back to him, he offered me his own leather helmet so I could hear the radio.

'Hallo, Louisa!' came Ellen's voice in my head, crackling over the static. 'Happy Christmas!'

Only Ignacy had a microphone that connected to Jamie's plane, so I couldn't answer her. All I could do was beam. It was smashing.

Ignacy's voice spoke clearly in my ear.

'You want to fly?'

He lifted his hand from the controls, and to my surprise the plane flew steadily on.

'The Blenheim flies herself,' he told me. 'Here, try, you will do it—'

He let me crouch next to him and hold the controls. He coaxed me to tilt the wings, following Jamie ahead of us.

Ellen:

Jamie had one extra leather helmet with a headset in it, and I was the lucky lass who got to wear it.

'All right?' he asked.

'Braw!' I said. I'd been up with him once before and never showed him how it frighted me the first time, and I wasn't going to now, either.

'Stand up and take a look out the back!'

'Stand up? Are you daft?'

'Maybe, but look at Ignacy waving to us!'

I was too tall to stand all the way straight, but I put my head up in the clear canopy for about three seconds, holding hard to Jamie's seat back and Silver's shoulder. I could see

Ignacy's Blenheim flying behind us away off to our left, with the Aussies lined up on our right. The wings of Ignacy's plane were rocking gently up and down.

After a moment Jamie dipped our own wings to wave back, and I tumbled over into Silver's lap.

'Jamie Stuart, you raging gumpus!'

Then Silver and I laughed so hard untangling ourselves that I feared it would make Jamie crash the plane.

But of course he did no such thing, and with the rest of Pimms Section close behind us, we all veered round together to head out over the North Sea.

Louisa:

Ignacy waved me away from the controls so he could turn, and Derfel plucked his helmet off my head and put it back on his own. I saw him talking. But over the roar of the Blenheim's twin engines I couldn't hear a thing he and Ignacy said.

They seemed tense and focused now.

I crawled back to the observer's seat to stay out of their way. Then through the panel in the clear nose of the plane, I saw why they were paying attention. We'd reached the navy ships we were looking for. From the air they seemed tiny, fragile things, black water bugs in an absolutely endless world of grey.

For a moment I thought, *It could be Daddy!*

Then I remembered it couldn't.

Not on a navy ship.

Nor on a merchant navy ship any more, either.

Oh, Daddy. How did I get here? I wondered again. *How did I get here?*

My pilot and navigator now seemed to forget I was there at all. That frightened me a little. I wondered if this was how they felt all the time they were flying: a little bit scared.

We followed Jamie's plane into the grey sky of fitful sun, and the other Pimms Section plane followed us. Somewhere ahead of us, I knew, Madeira Section was also on patrol. *Safety in numbers.*

We were faster than the ships below us, so we swooped around and back, sweeping the skies for enemy planes, who might have guns even if they'd agreed not to use them today.

Who made that agreement? How did they let each other know? A radio message? In code? In German? In English?

It was *impossible* not to feel uneasy.

Ellen:

'Aw, fer cryin' out loud,' said Chip in the back. 'The Luftwaffe is out here on Christmas Day after all. I can hear 'em jabbering away in Kraut. Tune in and listen, cap'n, they're not on the same frequency as us—'

Jamie twirled the dials, and then I heard it too, crackling in and out: men's voices barking orders in a tongue I could not understand.

I had a queer sense of the sky full of invisible young lads ready for a fight.

Jamie and Silver felt it too. They were pulling worried

faces at each other. It made my mouth go dry.

I swallowed and licked my lips. 'What's up, Jamie Stuart?' I challenged him.

'Ah, well, lassie,' Jamie said in a low voice, 'I might not have brought you along if I'd known there was going to be a surprise party. I suppose that's the nature of a surprise party, actually.'

Louisa:

Ignacy and Derfel burst out laughing.

Derfel handed me his flight helmet. We'd picked up the Luftwaffe radio signal too. They were probably patrolling their own shipping, like us. I couldn't hear much – mostly crackling static.

But now and then came a man's voice, singing in German.

It was a Christmas carol. I listened and listened.

Jamie:

'Bloody Jerries,' said Silver.

They were singing 'O Tannenbaum'.

'You hear that, Pimms Leader?' called Ignacy.

'It's the Christmas truce of 1940!' I exclaimed. 'But wasn't it "Silent Night" the Jerries sang with our lads in the trenches in the last lot?'

I gave the Germans a taste of their own medicine. '*Stille nacht, heilige nacht—*'

There was deafening stillness.

Then, in a burst of defiance, the German voice shouted: '*Deutschland, Deutschland über alles, über alles in der Welt!*'

All of B-Flight heard it.

'That's no Christmas truce, that's the Nazi national anthem!' yelled Harry Morrow. 'Can we go get 'em?'

Bloody hell, I thought, *not with the girls on board, you young tosser.*

'We don't know where they are,' I said. 'Let 'em sing.'

Louisa:

We didn't see any German planes.

But we heard the singing, off and on, the whole time we flew over the battleships. Derfel kept passing me his headset so I could listen.

We circled the ships for two hours, until Jamie said we'd passed the English border with Scotland. After that, another RAF squadron from further south came flying up to meet us. Everybody waved their wings at each other in a friendly way and shouted *Happy Christmas* over the radio. Then that lot took over our job and we could go home.

We'd passed the Firth of Forth and the Firth of Tay and were heading up the Angus Coast towards Stonehaven when we met the Luftwaffe bomber.

It was a Junkers 88, a Ju-88 – I recognised it as German the moment I saw it. To me it looked like the perfect match for the Blenheims we were flying, twin engines just like ours and about the same size, except the wingtips were sharply squared instead of rounded like ours. It was flying low along the sea cliffs, scouting, an ominous black shadow below us against the winter sea.

Ellen:

I haven't Louisa's eye for German planes. But I worked it out quick enough, because when Silver pointed, bloody Jamie stood the Blenheim practically on its wingtip in a turn that made my stomach tumble the wildcat. I held on to my porridge, and I got an eyeful of the Jerry bomber out the side of the canopy, with one of our own Blenheims diving after him.

Flight Lieutenant Beaufort-Stuart suddenly pushed the nose of his Blenheim forward, too, and we swooped in a swan dive towards the planes below us.

Jamie:

Those young Australian blockheads were going after that Ju-88 *with Phyllis on board*. I could see the tracers flaming from Harry Morrow's guns.

I dived after him. I couldn't *stop* Morrow, not once a fight started. But I had to be there if he needed me.

Ellen:

God help me, I prayed.

I sat on the floor with my eyes squeezed shut and teeth grating and my hands clutching the hard, cold edge of the seat on either side of me. I knew that if I came up alive without being sick it would be a flipping miracle.

'All right, lass?' came bloody Flight Lieutenant Beaufort-Stuart's voice in my head. Through the headset, I mean.

I winked an eye open to take a keek at my pilot. He was frowning. He was *listening*.

I squeezed my eyes closed again. But my ears were open. And then I heard it, too. Someone in the German plane was whistling.

Ignacy's Polish voice spoke into my open ears. 'The musical Jerries are out today,' he said. 'This fellow knows the classics.'

Jamie:

I may have a classical education but I don't have a musical one, and I didn't recognise the mournful tune over the crackling static.

Silver did. He agreed with Ignacy. 'That's Mendelssohn's *Hebrides Overture*. The tune's all right, but his rhythm is off.'

Louisa:

'Oh!' I cried. 'Don't shoot! *Tell Jamie not to shoot!*'

Ignacy glanced at me, startled. He couldn't hear me over the deafening engines.

I scrambled up beside him and peeled the leather helmet away from the side of his head so I could scream in his ear.

'It's Odysseus. *Odysseus! Tell Jamie not to shoot!*'

Ignacy's voice came calmly into my ears through the microphone in his mask.

'Tell him yourself. Don't yell like that.'

I could see the Pimms planes below us on the German bomber's tail.

The mournful whistle, only two bars, shrilled in my ears, then cut out as Ignacy held down a button on a handheld microphone that he raised to my mouth.

Ellen:

And the next thing I heard made me let out in a gasp of surprise the long breath I was trying to hold.

'Jamie, Jamie, it's me, Louisa! Don't shoot that plane! It's what the German courier played, Odysseus, you know who I mean! It's a message – it's an SOS—'

Then Jamie's voice, answering her. He said one word only.

'Mendelssohn?'

And finally Tex's drawl came in from the back, and he agreed with Louisa.

'It's literally an SOS,' Tex said. 'That Kraut is whistling SOS in Morse code.'

Jamie:

'*BREAK, MORROW*,' I yelled at Harry, still firing his guns below me. '*BREAK, YOU TOSSER, HOLD YOUR FIRE*.'

Louisa:

The silhouettes of the Blenheim and the Junkers 88 below us suddenly separated, curving in different directions, like a stalk of sugarcane split down the middle.

The German plane headed out to sea. The British planes made long, lazy curves up through the sky to join us, one after the other.

I gasped with relief, then was torn with doubt.

SOS?

That doesn't mean 'Don't shoot.' It means 'Send help.'

The plane was a distant speck heading east towards Norway, and the whistling pilot wasn't getting any help.

Jamie:

Ignacy was outraged. I'm pretty sure the only thing that stopped him going after that Ju-88 himself was Louisa sitting next to him.

'*What the hell, Scotty?*'

The German bomber was an ink splodge on the horizon.

'Mendelssohn's banned in Germany,' I told him. 'And it's bloody "Pimms Leader" to you.'

'*What the hell, Pimms Leader?*'

'We're supposed to be holding fire anyway, and I'm not shooting down a dissenter on Christmas Day.'

'That is not what I meant by what the hell!'

'Well, what did you mean then?'

'What is all this nonsense about Odysseus and a German courier?' Ignacy asked me.

The whole of B-Flight had heard us. All six of my flight crews had heard – eighteen men. Well, seventeen not counting myself.

Phyllis might have heard. And even if she hadn't, she was in the same plane as Dougie Kerr, who couldn't keep his mouth shut for five minutes. I'd have to collar her the second we were back at RAF Windyedge – but dammit, then she'd interrogate every one of us in debriefing. Someone was bound to sing.

Ellen, I could trust Ellen to deal with Phyllis. But I'd have to warn her before we landed—

'I'll tell you on the ground,' I said, trying to shut up Ignacy – and everybody else. '"*Careless talk costs lives.*"'

Louisa:

When we landed at RAF Windyedge, Ignacy climbed out first, so he could help me get through the hatch and on to the wing. Derfel came behind, guiding me.

I'd completely forgotten about Bill Yorke. He'd been in the back with the radio and the rear gun the whole time, not saying anything – or not saying anything I could hear, at any rate. He had his own hatch to climb out of and was waiting for me when my feet landed on the ground. He threw a careless arm over my shoulders.

I hadn't felt sick in the air. I'd been so worked up with excitement and awe and fear – I'd been wondering at the beauty of the sky and panicking at the possibility of being part of an air battle, and astonished that Felix Baer might be near me again in another German plane, and I had not devoted a moment to my stomach. But back on earth I suddenly felt sick.

I swallowed and swallowed, shrinking under the heavy arm of the strange gunner.

‘Where did you learn German code names, then?’ Bill Yorke asked casually. ‘Do we have a little Colonial spy in our midst?’

Ellen:

I had my own wee mission now – one desperate chance to catch Phyllis as she got out of the plane, before she was able to talk to the lads. The second my feet were on the ground I sprinted for Harry Morrow’s Blenheim, just pulling up behind us.

I had to pause for a moment because I couldn’t keep down the oatmeal any longer. But then I kept on running.

Louisa:

What that gunner said to me felt like a bomb going off in my head, and when Ellen stumbled and was sick, I lost everything too.

Jamie:

Yorkie leaped away from Louisa in horror, checking down his front to make sure she’d missed him.

I grabbed him by the wrist and shoulder of his leather jacket and shook him until I hoped his teeth were rattling in his hard head.

'*Stow it*, Yorke, you don't know what's going on because you're not supposed to! Are you going to accuse me of spying, too, for calling off the attack? And Tex, for recognising an SOS? Also *keep your mucky hands off the lasses*.'

Yorkie staggered back against the Blenheim's wing, trying to decide whether it was worth going for me. Ignacy and Derfel watched with intense interest – who'd win this time?

'I get that a jumped-up flyboy doesn't want to tell a lowly air gunner what's going on,' Yorkie snarled. 'But I don't get why the hired girl knows.'

Louisa was bent over on the grass beside the rear fuselage of the plane, the back of one hand up over her mouth. Silver dodged around us to kneel beside her with his handkerchief.

'Because she was here when the German agent dropped off the code strings we're using,' Silver said, looking up at us. 'The Windyedge-based ground crew was all here too. Only they've been told to shut up about it, *so they do*.'

Code strings! It sounded deadly important in its magnificent vagueness.

Oh God, Silver was the *best mate* a body could have. *The best*.

I took a step back so Yorkie couldn't use his height against me. 'Flying Officer Yorke, I said I'd brief everyone on the ground, and I will,' I said coldly. 'But call your commanding officer a "jumped-up flyboy" again and I'll see to it you're docked a month's pay.'

The lads all knew that wasn't an empty threat.

'Understood.' Yorkie straightened his collar and tie. Almost as an afterthought, he dropped me a contemptuous '*Sir*'.

Then he stormed off towards the operations hut.

'You handled that as well as could be expected,' Silver said, grinning.

Part Three

Calypso

-.-. .- .-.. -.-- .--. ... ---

Jamie:

Felix Baer. That was the German pilot's name.

He brought the Enigma machine to Windyedge. He flew the plane we *didn't* find when we tangled with the Messerschmitt 109 in November; I'd imagined him as a lost wingman, but he turned out to be a resistance agent who somehow eluded the fighter chasing him.

Can you hear me?

I hear nothing.

Was it also Felix Baer whistling an SOS in the Junkers 88 we let go on Christmas Day?

I wondered about him. I wondered what he'd risked to get that cipher machine over here.

I wondered if he guessed we were using it.

As our intelligence officer, Phyllis surely already knew a bit about 'Odysseus's' visit to Windyedge. Ellen softened her up between the Blenheims and the operations hut, confessing how the rogue German pilot held her hostage; how he spent the night at the Limehouse going through

Mrs Warner's record albums; how Louisa recognised the whistled tune during our North Sea Christmas party, the same music he played on the piano in the pub that night.

Incredibly, when we got to debriefing, Phyllis was as prim and neat in her uniform as if she'd never been off the ground.

'It feels terribly odd to ask you to tell me in the usual way what happened up there, when I saw it all myself,' she said apologetically. 'But what happened up there?'

B-Flight lined up on their folding chairs, except Dougie Kerr, who was still hovering hopefully over the tea trolley as if he expected more shortbread to magically appear.

Hiding in plain sight seemed safest. I'm a quick liar, but not always a consistent one. I wanted to tell everyone the same story, and keep it simple, so I took on Phyllis and B-Flight at the same time.

'We weren't ever going to be heroes during a Christmas day ceasefire,' I answered Phyllis. 'But there was a good reason not to go after that Luftwaffe bomber today.'

I turned around, leaning over the back of my chair, to include Pimms and Madeira.

'A German resistance team left Windyedge a list of upcoming U-boat manoeuvres last November – that's why we've had such good hunting this month. We know where a few of them are going to turn up. That whistler on board the Ju-88 is probably the man who left the tip-off.'

There was a murmur of comprehension as B-Flight fit this with what they already knew.

'So you lads keep quiet about what you heard today and don't second-guess the next mission, fair enough? We're *privileged* to have this information, thanks to a brave man from the other side. We're on our way to being aces.'

They straightened in their seats.

Beside me, Silver fiddled with his box of rosin, grinning down at it.

I didn't have to mention the coding machine.

I wondered how many others like it there were in Britain, and how I'd explain myself when I finally had to confess I had this one. I didn't wonder about it *much*, though, just the way I didn't wonder whether I'd still be alive in the spring. Nobody in a Blenheim aircrew wondered about such distant futures. The next singalong in the pub was as far as we got.

I knew our Enigma honeymoon was temporary. At the end of January we would have used up the rotor-dial settings Felix Baer had left behind. And if the Germans suddenly changed the rotor sequence at random, we'd be stuck. Intelligence would have to figure out how to get anything else out of the machine. Until then I had the most wonderful secret weapon in the world, and I didn't have a plan for what would happen to it when I couldn't use it any more.

That's perhaps not an easy thing for anyone else to understand. But you couldn't fly if you thought about being alive next spring.

We were bombed after Christmas and again in the first week of January. 'It's the Windyedge Blitz!' said the villagers in the pub, pleased to get attention that usually went to Aberdeen. One attack hit moorland, sending sheep and red deer running in terror, turning heather to confetti. The second attack blew up the three-hundred-year-old breakwater at the bottom of the cliffs in Windyedge village. No one was hurt, and it didn't make the national news.

The Germans used the Kingsleap Light for navigation. So did we. The lighthouse keeper was told to step up security and keep it dark unless he got a special release code from Cromwell himself.

JU LXXXVIII AND CX ESCORT DEESIDE S GREEN LIGHT XIV I

That was straightforward once you translated the Roman numerals: a Junkers bomber and Me-110 night fighters navigating via Kingsleap on 14 January 1941. We didn't take on the Me-110s, which would have made mincemeat of us. Silver pretended he'd spotted them in the air – just about plausible, coming from Silver, with his night vision under a full moon. He hadn't seen a thing, but Chip sent a warning home anyway. Cromwell called the fighters from Deeside to go after them and they never got near the coast.

U BOAT MANOEUVRES FRASERBURGH N XVIII I

That was a gift – like our Bell Rock adventure.

By the end of January, Madeira Section had sunk two submarines and Pimms was at four – one more, or a battleship, and I reckoned we in Pimms could call ourselves aces.

And when it happened at last we'd go to the Limehouse to celebrate, and Louisa would be at the piano, and Mrs Warner would choose records, and we'd sing and toast one another as if we'd never been in the sky three hours earlier with dry mouths and cold hands, dicing with death.

HOLD GREEN LIGHT AWAIT FOG

PREVENT HAPPY WAGON AND SO ON

What in blazes did that mean?

Happy wagon?

Pimms Section raced Madeira home beneath the February moon, beating up the German Navy halfway to Norway. We were out of settings for the cipher machine, but the last January messages we'd picked up were just beginning to play out. This was a fairly ordinary op and hadn't been mentioned in the code – we dropped a lot of high explosive on a lot of German ships – a Madeira flight crew actually hit one. The ones we didn't hit fired a lot of anti-aircraft guns back at us. We didn't hang about after our bombs were gone. It was a long flight, and the navigation was hard work – Chip didn't dare transmit for bearings because we were so close to Norway, so Silver had to stare at the stars. We were knackered by the time we made it safely back to Windyedge.

Wonderful to see the green glow of the Kingsleap Light guiding us in. I touched down ahead of the other planes, braked, adjusted the power, and turned to taxi back to the hangar. The weird Enigma message was still nagging at me.

PREVENT HAPPY WAGON AND SO ON

I wondered if it was another translation error, like *storm front* and *Windyedge*. What was *happy* in German? Dratted classical education – all I could think of was Latin.

In Latin, of course, it is *felix*.

*

I thumped one fist against the cockpit window, spluttering with the discovery, steering with my feet on the rudder pedals.

But if *felix* was the Latin translation of *happy*, what did *wagon* mean? The Latin translation of bear was *ursa – baer* in German – like Ursa Major, the Great Bear, the stars we'd been staring at all night. A fragment of *The Odyssey* came back to me: *the Bear, surnamed the Wain …*

Of course. The Great Bear. The Wain. If you know what a wain is.

It's a wagon, of course, and 'the Wagon' is what the Germans call the Great Bear.

PREVENT HAPPY WAGON

Wherever Felix Baer was now, the Nazis were on to him.

By mid-morning, when the order came to scramble back into our planes, we were every one of us dead asleep in our bunks.

The Pimms aircraft had been refuelled and rearmed. That meant we were the ones who got told to hop to it.

When I'd whipped us up to get the Blenheims out of the firing line the first time Windyedge came under attack, I'd been in my underwear. This time when I leaped out of bed to answer the telephone call from operations, at least I was in my pyjamas. I pulled on trousers and boots over the top and tripped over Silver pulling on *his* boots as I turned to haul the blankets off the slumbering Australians.

'What's going on?' Chip asked, throwing off his own blankets.

'One Ju-88 on its way to Windyedge,' I panted. 'All by itself. A fishing boat spotted it and then Coastal Defence picked it up on their screens. They're scrambling some Spitfires from Deeside, but it's coming from the south-east so we might get there first. Get moving, Pimms!'

High in the pearl-grey sky, with Scotland a smudge on the horizon behind us, we reached the lonely German bomber before the Spitfires. Ignacy and I went in first.

'Looks like they have a hit already,' Ignacy said. 'It is trailing smoke—'

'That's a banner,' came Chip's voice. 'Tied to their tail. Wonder what they're advertisin''!'

The Junkers had white sheets over its Luftwaffe and Nazi markings. There wasn't a banner, but a piece of loose webbing was trailing out behind the aircraft like a thin streamer of smoke.

Instead of shooting at us as we swooped towards them, their pilot flashed his lights and waggled his wings like billy-o.

'Hold your fire, Mazur,' I told Ignacy. 'This fellow's trying to surrender.'

I heard the Polish pilot's groan of disappointment.

'Oh, Scotty. Excuse me, I mean Pimms Leader – not this again!'

'Flashing lights and a white flag,' I said. 'You're absolutely forbidden to shoot at him. Don't worry, it'll still be jolly good fun, we'll bring him home with us! Anyone ever performed a formal interception?'

Of course no one had. I struggled to remember the international air law I'd learned in ground school.

We waggled our wings and flashed our lights back at the Jerries. Then we turned to slot into place around them, and nobody fired a shot.

'Ah, Pimms is magnificent,' Silver murmured. 'If only the Old Roundhead could see us in action. He'd be *proud*.'

'He'd give us a bollocking because nobody knows the rules for an interception,' I said.

Ignacy and Harry lined up on either side of the German plane, and I pulled ahead to lead it in.

'Keep an eye on that Junkers, Tex, would you?' I called to Chip, in the gun turret. 'It's making my skin crawl not being able to see what they're up to behind me.'

'I've got both my eyes on it,' Chip said. 'If those Krauts try anything they're going to get a faceful.'

At that point three Spitfires from Deeside found us, which made a grand total of six RAF aircraft escorting one solitary Junkers 88, so I felt a bit more secure.

We flew home the way we'd come, lining up over the Kingsleap Light.

I would have to land first. According to international protocol, the surrendering Luftwaffe bomber was supposed to follow me. The other Pimms planes would come in behind us, and the Spits probably wouldn't land at Windyedge at all, but hare off home to Deeside.

The Luftwaffe pilot followed me like a lamb to the end of the runway. I knew he was there, but I couldn't see him. Suddenly Chip yelled from the rear turret, 'He's making a run for it! No, he's *diving*—'

'He will hit the cliffs!' Ignacy yelled from behind the Luftwaffe plane, cutting off Chip's voice.

While these dramatics were unfolding, I clenched my jaw and focused on the runway. I was too close to the ground to do anything tricky.

'He straightened up, he's OK—' Chip let me know. 'He's lining up behind you again.'

Our undercarriage touched the earth and we bumped along the field. I braked, ready to get out of the way as quickly as possible so the planes behind me could land. Then Chip gave a wordless howl of terror, and all the sky in the clear canopy above my head was blotted out. I looked up and saw nothing but the hideous belly of the Junkers 88, *inches* away from my face.

If it landed on top of us we were dead.

Louisa:

Jane was good at keeping busy, but goodness, she hated being cooped up. Sometimes she decided she needed air at ten o'clock at night, and then we would spend a few hair-raising minutes feeling our way in the dark along the steep cobbles to the limekilns and back. Or just after dawn we'd stagger down the hill together to the harbour to watch the sun climb over the sea cliffs. We both longed to walk on the tiny beach, but it was full of the ruins of the exploded breakwater, not to mention mines and barbed wire and 'dragons' teeth' concrete blocks meant to keep out German landing craft.

So Jane jumped at the chance of an outing to choose her own library books and treat me to tea and buns in a cafe on the Stonehaven seafront. On that day in the first full week of February, Ellen had to go to the railway station to pick up a courier who was delivering new maps which needed a proper guardian on their journey to RAF Windyedge. The Tilly would be empty going to the station and again going home after Ellen took the courier back in the afternoon, so she gave me and Jane a lift. We sat three across the front as usual with me in the middle, and as we drove we sang something we all knew the words to because we heard it on the radio just about every day – the Joe Loss Orchestra's 'Spitfire Song'.

We were on the way home and turning off the main road by the rubble of the bus shelter when black dots began to dance on the horizon.

'Is 648 Squadron in the air?' asked Jane.

She saw them too. Not bugs; not birds. Aeroplanes.

'They were out last night,' said Ellen. 'They should be tucked up in bed.'

Four aeroplanes, about the same size, and three smaller ones above them. Ah, three fighters flying in formation, *beautiful* – my heart gave a leap as I tried to work out what they were.

'Whew, they're low,' Ellen added. 'They must be on a drill.'

'Blenheims?' asked Jane.

'Aye, those big ones,' said Ellen. 'But the others—'

'*Spitfires!*' I crowed. The thrill of recognising those neat tapered wings never wore off. I sang, '*The Deeside planes are here* …' and Jane reprised 'The Spitfire Song' and we laughed.

'Are they training with them?' Ellen wondered aloud. 'Or—'

She slowed the Tilly to a stop, right in the middle of the road, so we could watch.

The planes seemed to grow larger as they descended, and we watched as the first, one of the Blenheims, touched down at RAF Windyedge.

But the big second one, the odd one in the middle, flew so low over the landing Blenheim that we all gasped in horror.

For a moment we thought one plane would land on top of the other.

'God pity us, they'll be *killed*!' Ellen cried.

Then the one on top began to climb into the sky again.

The first stayed on the ground. All the rest, two Blenheims and three Spitfire fighters, followed the odd plane back up into the sky.

They roared towards us, black, throbbing machines growing swiftly larger, like genies coming out of bottles or balloons inflating. It was *just* like the day we arrived, only with more planes.

And the one that had nearly collided with the first was German.

I recognised its silhouette as it passed overhead. I'd seen a plane like it once before, black against a steel-grey sea instead of a dove-grey sky. It was a Junkers 88.

'They're chasing a Luftwaffe bomber,' I gasped. '*648 Squadron's chasing a Luftwaffe bomber!*'

One of the anti-aircraft batteries on the perimeter wall let out a drumroll of machine-gun fire as the Junkers passed it. But the guns stopped almost instantly – the Blenheims and Spitfires were too close to the Junkers to risk firing at it. Six planes rushed past in a deafening roar of engines and black shadow. In perfect unison, like a music hall act, Jane and Ellen and I craned our necks and whipped our heads around to watch the planes soar onward and upward. I got a flashing glimpse of a sinister black swastika painted on the tail of the German bomber, and something like white smoke flying from the tail and the cabin. Then the closed back of the Tilly hid everything.

Ellen reached behind her seat to grab a pair of field glasses, cranked down her window, and stuck half her body out, sitting on the window ledge and looking up.

'Is it our musical pilot come back again?' suggested Jane.

Again my heart turned over. Perhaps Felix Baer was bringing us a new set of code charts. I leaned on the dashboard, trying to see what was going on.

'How do I know?' said Ellen, staring at the sky through the glasses. 'Och, they're coming round again.'

She slid back abruptly into the driver's seat, shoved the Tilly into gear, and started it up.

She drove too quickly. A freezing wind howled through her open window, and I braced myself against the dashboard. Jane, beside me, clung to the window crank and the door handle. We rounded the bend in the lane, and instead of carrying on ahead into the village to drop off me and Jane at the Limehouse, Ellen swerved into the drive of RAF Windyedge.

I held my breath. Ellen screeched to a stop in front of the barrier at the guards' hut and waved.

One of the soldiers began to lift the barrier. The other came over to the van and glanced at the pass that Ellen held out. Then he stooped to peer in at her passengers – me and Jane.

'You have got to be joking,' he said.

'Oh, you know Louisa, Nobby,' Ellen exclaimed in irritation. 'And this is Mrs Campbell's old auntie, haven't you met her yet? She's been living at the Limehouse since November!'

Jane gazed out the window at the planes, which had finished a single loop out to sea and were now heading back to the airfield.

'I haven't the time now to drop these ladies off!' Ellen exclaimed. 'ID, Louisa?'

I dug in my school bag. Jane beat me to it, and did the magic trick with her dead husband's passport.

'Highly irregular,' grumbled Nobby. 'You know that—'

But the other guard had already raised the gate. Ellen cut off Nobby's protest by rolling up her window. The Tilly sailed past the barrier, spraying through icy puddles.

Ahead of us, the planes were roaring in for another go. One of the Blenheims had flown ahead of the Ju-88 to lead it. Another came behind the Luftwaffe plane, escorting it, and the Spitfires stayed above the others, guarding the Blenheims. Ellen guided the Tilly off the driveway and over the longer grass to the mowed runway's edge, where she threw open her door and leaped out to watch. I leaned out the open door behind her; Jane leaned over my shoulder.

The leading aircraft touched the ground and taxied out of the way.

'That's Ignacy,' Ellen said. 'It's Pimms Section in the air – most of 'em. Jamie must have been the first to land …'

The Luftwaffe bomber was coming in now, its wings rocking, its nose rising and dipping. It looked very unstable. Harry Morrow in the Blenheim behind it came down as calm and steady as anything. Something was wrong with the German plane, or with its pilot.

Meanwhile poor Jane was struggling to open the door on her side of the van.

'How does one release oneself from a utility vehicle?' she demanded.

I couldn't reach across her. I slid out past the steering wheel and ran around to haul open the passenger door from the outside. Jane lowered herself to the ground without waiting for me to help, letting gravity undo all the work it took to get her in there in the first place. But she needed my shoulder and an arm around her waist to help her stand, because her sticks were in the back of the van.

Now the third plane came down. The Spitfires circled above us, and the German plane taxied towards us from the far end of the runway, following Ignacy, growing closer. Airmen and ground crew were milling about everywhere, and Flight Lieutenant Jamie Beaufort-Stuart suddenly split away from the crowd and came over to where we were. He wore a life jacket and boots over what looked like a pyjama top and uniform trousers, but he didn't have on any other flight gear, and his fair hair was standing straight on end as if he'd grabbed it all by the roots and pulled.

'What's going on?' Ellen called to him. 'Was that you flying the lead plane?'

'D'you think I'd be out here in my jim-jams for fun?'

Ellen shrugged. '*You just might.*'

He ran one hand up over his face and through his hair, and I could see exactly how he'd got it to stick up in spikes. Then he waved at the German plane, which had trundled a lot closer. What I'd thought was smoke turned out to be a white towel or pillow slip fluttering from the cockpit window up front. Another long white streamer trailed behind the plane.

The Junkers was nearly twice as big as I'd thought it was in the air. It towered over the Blenheims. Its huge propellers clattered to a stop, and the white banners fell limp. The other planes switched off at the same time, and the stillness rang in my ears as if I'd gone deaf.

Then Ellen exclaimed in concern: 'Jamie!'

She reached into the breast pocket of her uniform for her Woodbines and a matchbook and gave Jamie a cigarette. He took it, but when she offered him the matches he shook his head, put the cigarette in his mouth, and held up his narrow hands briefly, to show her.

He was trembling so much he couldn't light a match. It was awful. I sucked in my breath between my teeth.

Ellen lit one for him. He leaned over her hand to dip the cigarette into the flame. She was taller than he was, but it didn't make him look like a schoolboy. He looked like a bent old man.

'Sorry.' He drew in a deep breath. 'That landing gave me the screaming abdabs. Apparently these chaps—'

He waved the cigarette at the Luftwaffe aircraft.

'They came over from Norway this morning. I don't

think they have enough fuel to get back. They seem to be unarmed – they want to surrender. Or to negotiate. See the white flag?'

Jamie took another long drag on the cigarette. 'I don't know what happened. Maybe they had a change of plan at the last second, or something – the pilot seemed to lose control completely. The plane just went berserk. I suppose the loose webbing might have tangled in the tail—'

He pulled in a long breath of air that had nothing to do with smoking, and said, 'I thought he was going to land on top of us.'

'So did we,' Ellen said soberly.

Jamie looked down at his shaking hands. 'And I guess this is what it feels like when you actually do lose your nerve! Thank God it didn't happen in the air.'

A section of the clear dome over the Junkers 88 cockpit slid open, and a hurricane of angry German shouts tore through the air. Jane, who always favoured her left ear over her right a little bit, stood listening with her head cocked on one side like a bird watching a worm.

Suddenly a man catapulted out of the plane as if he'd been shot from a cannon. He tried to catch himself on the way down, missed, and sprawled beneath the wing on the tawny winter grass. He was wearing a flight suit and leather jacket and helmet, which I couldn't have told apart from any of our British gear. A moment later another man climbed out after him.

The first scrambled to his feet and leaped at the other, pulling him to the ground. They rolled over and over beneath the wing of their plane, wrestling and throwing lightning-fast punches at each other. Then a third airman climbed out and joined the pile-up.

By now there was a big crowd watching. It was nothing like a secret operation – nothing like last November. Young men in hastily buttoned uniform jackets piled in to try to separate the fighting Luftwaffe airmen.

The first man, the one who'd been thrown out of the plane when the hatch opened, got the worst of it. He fought like a cornered mongoose, but he didn't stand a chance against so many, or even just against Chip Wingate. The American gunner, in pyjamas and a life jacket like Jamie, fought like a whole family of cornered mongooses, and he seemed to enjoy it, too. The others wrestled the flailing German airman to the ground, pinned him flat on his face, and wrenched his arms behind his back. Finally one of our ground crew pulled off his belt and used it to lash the German's arms together.

Even then he still kept struggling, like a red snapper reeled in from the green waves on a fishing line.

Someone snatched off the German's leather flight helmet and goggles.

I recognised Felix Baer.

Jamie:

Louisa lurched forward. Jane was hanging on her arm, and Ellen grabbed Louisa's other shoulder.

'Whisht. Take care,' Ellen said.

They both recognised that captured German.

I was looking at 'Odysseus'.

One of his fellow airmen bent to yell a single ferocious word at him, and Felix Baer spat in his face in reply.

The other man wiped his cheek, and I saw he held a Luger pistol in his gloved hand, which in another second he pressed against Baer's head.

Almost everybody froze.

Not Tex. Sergeant Chester Wingate took this opportunity to slam his fist into Baer's face and break his nose.

'*Stop it!*' Louisa screamed. '*What are you doing?*'

Ellen's arm was around her shoulder, but to be honest I think the only reason the kid didn't run forward to stop the fight herself was because of the old woman leaning on her.

I tried to wade in and stumbled. I was still shaking like a leaf. Silver hauled Chip off the German bloke by the back of his life jacket.

Felix Baer's face was awash with blood, one eye already beginning to swell shut. He spat again, but he might have been trying to clear his mouth. He said to the other German airman – my German is not fluent but I know what he said – 'You can't kill me, you blockhead.'

'No,' answered the other, and according to Jane, he added, 'But I'll blow your ear off if you don't stop fighting.'

Baer's teeth were chattering. I could see it – could see his jaw shaking as badly as my own hands. I had no doubt he was the pilot who'd been flying when his plane nearly collided with mine.

No one else noticed. Everybody was too busy starting a fresh brawl with the Luftwaffe airman holding a gun in the middle of an RAF aerodrome. There was another tussle, less dramatic than the first, as our lads took possession of the pistol, searched the enemy, and grabbed hold of the third German while they were at it.

Felix Baer sat sullenly on the frozen ground watching with his hands tied behind him and his nose dripping blood. He kept his mouth pressed tightly shut, trying to calm the shaking.

I stepped forward and held my cigarette to his lips.

'Hell of a landing,' I congratulated him, even though I knew he wouldn't understand it. 'Glad you missed me.'

Ellen:

I thought my heart would burst. I'd never seen Jamie Stuart so broken down he *couldn't light his own smoke*.

It made everybody quiet. Not a soul there but didn't see the trembling as his neat, slim fingers held out that cigarette to the enemy.

When Felix Baer lifted his head to take it, I saw that he was shaking too.

Then I knew why Jamie offered it. Death had missed them both by an inch, come close enough they saw what it looked like – now they were surprisingly alive after all and able to share a smoke.

Baer nodded and took a drag on Jamie's cigarette, sitting with his arms tied behind him, breathing hard and with a face like raw mince. Jamie stood there, helping him nurse the smoke as if the Jerry pilot were a burn victim on his back in hospital.

'Hey, anyone here speak Kraut?' Chip asked.

There was not one volunteer. Jamie gave a start, as if he were going to speak up for Mrs Warner, but he thought better and kept quiet.

Then 648 Squadron's Wing Commander Talbot Cromwell came striding out, all ruffled up with importance, his frowning eyebrows like hairy caterpillars having a battle. Phyllis trotted behind him, running like a terrier to keep up.

'Beaufort-Stuart, what's the matter with you, are you some kind of collaborator now?' Cromwell rumbled. 'Stand back. I want all three of these men under lock and key.'

'Shall I ring Coastal Command Headquarters and ask for a prisoner transfer?' Phyllis offered.

'Pennyworth, don't you dare.'

Phyllis looked startled. Jamie backed away from Baer and took a shaking, defiant pull on his Woodbine, watching our crabbit commander through narrowed eyes like hot coals.

Talbot Cromwell didn't want to let those Jerries out of his hands. He had a sack of excuses ready.

'This is an Intelligence issue uniquely connected to Windyedge,' he puffed. 'There's a designated agent to contact. I'll conduct the first interview myself.' He took a keek around him and asked the same question as Chip: 'Have we a German speaker here?'

Hanging on to Louisa with one arm, old Jane raised her other hand high. She stood straight as a spear, eyes snapping fire and ice, like a very ancient goddess. In her music hall trumpet of a voice, Jane volunteered, 'I speak a little German.'

Old Cromwell's hairy caterpillars tried to do backflips.

He growled, 'Volunteer McEwen, what in blazes are these civilians doing on this aerodrome?'

'I had to collect the map courier from Stonehaven,' I said. 'I gave Mrs Warner and her girl a lift from the library, as a favour to Mrs Campbell; no petrol wasted. But when the planes came in I didn't take the time to drop off the civilian passengers. Sergeant Fergusson let us through. Sir!'

Cromwell barked at me, 'Got an answer for everything, haven't you, McEwen?' Then he barked at Phyllis and Jamie. 'Flight Officer Pennyworth – incident report! Flight Lieutenant Beaufort-Stuart! Take your lads for debriefing. And get some clothes on, all of you.'

Cromwell turned to fire on someone else. 'Lock up those Jerries in the limekilns – I'm told that's a good, secure prison. The harbour master keeps the keys. Make sure they've got camp beds and blankets – oh, and paraffin heaters, it's a bit damp. Send four lads to keep an eye on 'em – no, make that six, two for each, and make sure they're armed.'

He paused to catch his breath. Then he lit his own cigarette and had a go at me again. 'You take the old lady and the girl back to their lodgings. Tell Mrs Campbell what's going on. See that the Limehouse is closed to the public so we can use the place as a meeting room. Then get back here to collect the rest of us. I'll question those Jerries myself, and I want Pimms there too.'

Jamie:

I rode to the Limehouse in the Tilly along with Cromwell, Chip, Silver and Phyllis. By the time we got there, the public bar already looked like a medieval courtroom. A fire roared in the hearth, winking orange light off the coins in the black oak beams. The long table was pulled out to the middle of the floor, with three chairs set up on one side of it, facing towards the door. The other furniture was shoved out of the way.

The Old Roundhead walked in as if he owned the place and sat in the middle chair. He spread one of the new maps across the table.

'Over here, Pennyworth.'

Phyllis sat down obediently and got out her cardboard notebook.

'Now you, Flying Officer Silvermont. Show me how that Ju-88 came in.'

Silver pointed and scribbled with a china pencil. Chip and I hadn't been told to do anything, so we stood stiffly at attention in front of the table.

Nancy Campbell had been told to clear off. She wasn't allowed to hear what was going on. Ellen wouldn't get a look-in, either. But in a minute Louisa nipped into the room and pressed herself against the wall next to the hall door, waiting for an appropriate gap to get Cromwell's attention.

A few seconds later, the vestibule filled with the noise of thumping boots and slamming doors, and the three German airmen came trooping in. They'd been allowed to have their hands free, but they were escorted by guards with pistols. Behind the guards and their prisoners came the rest of Pimms Section. I don't think I'd ever seen my lads so smart and polished, in smoke-blue RAF service dress uniforms, everybody's face freshly washed and shaved and everybody's hair slicked down with Brylcreem, even Dougie's.

They lined up alongside me and Chip in front of Cromwell, with Pimms at one end and the German prisoners at the other. Harry Morrow's head nearly brushed the low ceiling.

The Germans hadn't scrubbed up as well as us, even the two who hadn't taken a beating. They didn't have pressed uniforms to change into; they were wearing the flight suits they'd arrived in. I longed to get a good look at Baer, and turned my head ever so slightly to try to study him. His broken nose was taped with sticking plaster, while the rest of his swollen face was beginning to turn purple.

This was my *informer* – our *conspirator*.

Baer glanced around, too, and his eyes settled on the gramophone. Then he gazed at Louisa for exactly the same length of time.

Then he looked away. His battered face was absolutely blank.

They didn't let on that they recognised each other.

A thunderous, ringing silence seemed to fall, like the still moment when an aircraft's engine shuts down. Cromwell looked around impatiently.

'Where's the old girl?' he asked.

Louisa:

Jane took a long time in the bathroom and didn't want help. Waiting in our room, I heard the Tilly labouring up and down the hill as Ellen brought people over from the airfield. I opened one of the south-east windows, trying to eavesdrop. Doors slammed, and there was a hubbub of men's excited – maybe angry – voices. But they were muffled by the corner of the house and I couldn't understand a word.

I went to check on Jane. She'd been bolted in the bathroom for at least half an hour.

She opened the door when I knocked.

That old woman had transformed herself into a film star. I'm not sure what part she was playing – judge? Ambassador, perhaps? No – ambassador's wife? She'd changed into a long, tight-fitting black knit dress with a high neck and ruffles at the wrist and down the front. It was stylish and modern, though it couldn't be new. Her short silver bob was pulled back with glinting jet combs.

'Oh, Jane, you are *stunning*!' I exclaimed. 'No wonder people can't tell how old you are!'

Jane smiled modestly and turned around. 'Zip me up, please, darling. I simply cannot reach my own back any more.'

I zipped.

'Now then, these ridiculous *sticks*. How I detest them! It will take me forever to get down the stairs and I know the young men are here already. Run ahead and tell them I am on my way.'

Off I went back down, like a courier racing between army units.

The awful commander was busy looking at a map with David Silvermont when I came in, and I didn't like to interrupt. I stood against the wall waiting for a gap. Then I was glad I did, because it gave me a moment to set my face and not smile or frown or anything when Felix Baer looked me straight in the eye.

Did he *know*? Did he know it was me who'd figured out his codes, who was using them?

Almost instantly he turned away. I swallowed. Wing Commander Cromwell glanced up.

'Well, girl! Is the old woman ready yet?'

'She's coming down now,' I said. How was I supposed to address him? I didn't have any idea. I added, 'Sir. The stair takes her a while. She ought to have a comfortable place to sit.'

'Indeed. Kerr, Yorke, get moving,' Cromwell snapped, looking back down.

The wireless operators scrambled to rearrange the furniture, pulling Jane's chair up to the table next to Cromwell. By the time they finished, Jane had arrived. I hovered at her elbow as she came in, wondering if Cromwell would kick me out when she was seated. Her sticks tapped against the stone floor, and for a moment the only sounds were that tapping and the crackle and hiss of burning peat.

Jane reached her chair and I took the sticks. She braced herself against the armrests and made her terrifying backwards plunge into the seat. Jamie and Silver and even one of the German airmen threw themselves forward in alarm to try to support her.

Jane looked up and smiled.

'I am perfectly all right.'

'Pimms Section, *attention*,' ordered Wing Commander Cromwell, and they all leaped into their stiff line-up in front of the table.

I laid Jane's sticks on the floor and purposefully planted myself behind her chair, holding my breath. Jane reached for my hand, anchoring me. 'I need Louisa here, please,' she said. She raised her arm a little, and our hands stayed firmly clasped over her frail shoulder.

Cromwell looked at Jane, frowning. He looked up at me.

'You were here in November, weren't you, Miss Adair?' he asked. 'One of the hostages?'

I was astonished. I thought he had no idea who I was.

I'd known he was pig-headed and stuck on following rules, but I'd mistakenly also thought he was stupid. I realised now I might be jumping to conclusions, just like *everybody* did about me.

'Yes, sir,' I said politely.

'All right, I'll allow it. Make a note, Flight Officer Pennyworth; the girl can take an oath of secrecy along with the rest.'

I was in.

He moved on as if he'd never noticed me in the first place.

'Find out why they're here,' he said to Jane, and waved his hand at the German prisoners.

Jane leaned forward. She spoke German hesitatingly, as if she were choosing her words with care. She was *good* at pretending to be English speaking German. An old actress! She tilted her head, favouring her left ear, and waited for a response.

Felix Baer and one of the other Germans both spoke at the same time, and in a minute they were shouting at each other. Baer backed down first – he threw his hands up in frustration and waved the other man ahead.

'Eberhard Moritz,' the airman introduced himself, laying one hand on his heart. He stepped forward and held the hand towards Jane. When she took it, he bowed his head and gave her hand a formal kiss. Then he stepped back and answered her.

I listened and listened, trying to understand anything. But I couldn't – not one word. It made me wild with frustration, even when Jane relayed his message. I hated being so ignorant.

'This man, this Eberhard Moritz, says he and his companions want to defect.'

'Defect!' echoed Cromwell in amazement.

Jane nodded. 'He said they want to renounce Germany. Their connection to British Intelligence has been discovered and the Gestapo secret police are hunting for them – this flight was a perilous chance, and they had no choice but to take it. They dropped their life rafts in the North Sea to make it look as though they'd crashed on their way here! Moritz is their gunner, but he also leads their resistance cell. He apologises for his companion's behaviour – that's Felix Baer, the pilot.' She nodded towards him. 'Moritz says that

Baer tried to shoot their navigator, Dietrich Althammer, just before they landed, and Moritz had to wrestle the gun away from him.'

Jane paused, frowning. 'They haven't stopped arguing about Althammer,' she added. 'That's what you heard before Moritz spoke to me. They disagree as to whether he can be trusted.'

'Go on,' Wing Commander Cromwell said quietly.

'Moritz asks for amnesty for all three of them. But Baer says that Althammer is a double agent and is here on some dubious mission of his own. They went back and forth, you heard – arguing. Moritz accused Baer of carelessness on an earlier mission, and Baer denied it.' Jane added smugly, 'They used stronger language, of course!'

Cromwell growled, 'Ask Althammer for his side of the story.'

Jane turned to the third German and murmured, 'Dietrich Althammer?'

He bowed his head to her. When he saw how she tilted her left ear in his direction, he leaned closer so she could hear him. It reminded me of the way Jamie talked to her, patient and interested, as if the German navigator were used to speaking to old women. I suppose even Luftwaffe airmen must sometimes have grannies who are hard of hearing.

'Althammer says that Baer's distrust is egotistic nonsense,' Jane said finally. 'He thinks it is a war of protocol – Baer, the pilot, should naturally be the commanding officer of their aircrew. But in their resistance cell, Moritz, the lowly gunner, is the designated leader. So they argue over matters of authority.'

'*Matters of authority!*' Wing Commander Cromwell gave a grunt of disgust.

It sounded a lot like Jamie's struggle with Cromwell, and I knew the commander would be puzzled – should he believe the German flight crew's commanding officer or the resistance cell's designated leader? Directly across from me, Jamie was lined up standing at attention at the end of the row beside Silver, and our eyes met. I thought they were both struggling not to laugh. I had to look away so they wouldn't infect me with it.

Wing Commander Cromwell rumbled, 'If they can't agree on their story we can't get sense out of any one of them.' Without warning he told the guard at the door, 'Call Mrs Campbell back out here. We all want tea.'

Nan crept through and let herself behind the bar, where she put the kettle on to boil and tiptoed about rattling teacups. Jane and Eberhard Moritz started talking to each other again while Phyllis scribbled frantically in her cardboard notebook, trying to record everything properly.

It was hard not to fidget. Jamie's rigid Pimms Section crews stood lined up like statues. *Put your shoulders back, Lula*, Mummy always told me as I stood up to play the flute. *Make your daddy proud*. If Pimms could do it, so could I.

'Moritz says none of them will speak in confidence here,' Jane relayed finally. 'He objects to a civilian translator – that's me, you know – and requests a translator aligned with the services, and also reminds us that according to the Geneva Convention of 1929, he and his companions are not required to tell you anything more than their name and rank.'

I thought that all sounded quite stuffed up, even if it was true. I looked over at Felix Baer. His face was turned away as if he couldn't stand to watch. He was seething with fury.

Eberhard Moritz added something else, less stiffly.

'He's just apologising for being rude about me doing the translation,' Jane explained. 'He credits my German as being very good.'

Baer tried once more. Pale beneath the bruises, he faced Cromwell directly. He reined in his anger, but I was sure he was *desperate* to make himself understood.

Jane was cool as she translated.

'He insists that Althammer is lying. He says that he and Moritz have risked their lives to deliver concealed information which, they hope, will be of mutual benefit to Britain and Germany. Baer believes Althammer is trying to prevent them from delivering it.'

Jamie:

Nancy's clattering fell silent; she froze in the act of holding up her teapot. Cromwell sat with his mouth open and his fists clenched on the table in stark bafflement, waiting for an answer.

I stared at the floor. I didn't dare catch Louisa's eye again.

Moritz and Baer uttered another duelling fugue of frustration and defiance.

I was torn over which of them to believe. I thought I knew what it was like to be Felix Baer, struggling with an unruly flight crew, utterly unable to sacrifice himself to authority because of his own experience and knowledge. But I also sympathised with Eberhard Moritz, trying to command someone who was uncooperative and had his own plans.

Is that how Cromwell felt about me? The same way I felt about my lads?

Mrs Warner repeated in English, 'Moritz says this place is informal and insecure. Baer says he won't share War Office information with anyone but his contact. A man called – Mr Nestor?'

'"*Nestor!*"' exclaimed Wing Commander Cromwell.

My classical education wasn't going to waste after all. I knew who Nestor was: Odysseus's faithful adviser in *The Odyssey*.

Cromwell worked it out too.

'"Nestor" indeed,' Cromwell repeated. Then he sighed. 'Our man with Intelligence, Robert Ethan, is in Abyssinia. What *damnably* poor timing. It will be at least a week before he can get here – if we can reach him.'

He paused to think. Phyllis looked as if she were holding her breath.

'Pennyworth, make a call to Coastal Command Headquarters to send us a translator. One of their German-speaking wireless operators.'

'Yes, sir. Now, sir? On the Limehouse telephone? It's a public line, sir.'

'Ask for a Y girl. Mention Nestor and Odysseus. They'll know what to do.'

Phyllis scurried off to the hall telephone.

Chip took two long steps forward and confronted Felix Baer. They glared at each other coldly. 'I'll take over if you want,' Chip said assuredly. 'I'll make him talk.'

He was going to get me another reprimand if he didn't settle down. I clamped a hand hard on his shoulder and pitched my voice low.

'Back off, Tex.'

'C'mon, it won't take long.'

Then I got insurrection from the Polish and Welsh contingent as well.

'If the Yankee breaks a few more filthy Nazi noses, no one will cry,' Ignacy said. 'Or let Taff at them. He is good at throwing punches.'

Derfel nodded enthusiastically.

'Your U-boat score is thanks to these so-called Nazis,' I reminded them.

'Back in line, all of you,' barked Cromwell. 'You're a disgrace to enlisted men.'

Everybody snapped to attention again.

Cromwell spoke directly to the prisoners, cold and formal.

'This base is not equipped for a tribunal. As military men you will appreciate we have made hasty accommodation here, but I will postpone our discussion until an appropriate translator is summoned. I will not release you to a higher command until I have been ordered to do so by the contact you yourselves have named.'

After Mrs Warner translated this, Cromwell pushed back his chair and stood.

'Every person here, subject to the King of England, is bound in the strictest confidence to anything witnessed here today.' He singled out the civilians. 'Mrs Campbell and Miss Adair – do you understand how weighty this matter is? If you ever speak of anything you have heard here, under the Official Secrets Act you will be considered accountable for treason.'

Louisa nodded seriously and whispered, 'Yes, sir.'

Nancy Campbell just nodded.

Even I knew that wasn't going to be good enough for Cromwell.

'Pennyworth!' he bawled. 'Get back in here. I want you to make a list of all those present and get them to sign it.'

While Phyllis got to work, the Old Roundhead allowed Nancy to tiptoe about the room serving cups of tea, which we all very much needed. She wouldn't go near the Germans, though.

'Louisa,' she whispered, 'would you offer this to *them*, please.'

Their navigator, Althammer, stubbornly waved the tea aside. The gunner, Moritz, stared at Louisa curiously – the first Jamaican girl he'd ever seen? – and accepted his with a nod.

But that girl stood one second too long in front of Felix Baer as she held out the tea tray, and he stood one second too long searching her face before he picked up his cup.

Not staring, like Moritz. Communicating. Looking for the answer to a wordless question in a mutual language.

Louisa:

It was a crazy thing to do. But I wanted him to *know* we had the Enigma machine.

Face to face with him, I thought of a way to do it.

I lowered my head over the teapot and cup as I held out the tray. He could see my eyes, but I wasn't looking straight at him, so maybe no one else would notice. While his hand trembled faintly over the cup, I blinked my eyelids in Morse code.

I spelled out the only German word I knew: *danke.* Thank you.

I wasn't even sure he noticed.

Jamie:

'Danke,' he said to her, lifting the teacup, and she turned away quickly.

For such a quiet wee thing she seemed to have nerves of steel. She didn't spill a drop.

Louisa:

Jane created a distraction of her own.

She stood up. She never stood as dramatically as she sat, so long as she had something to push against, and just now she leaned on the table. 'Sticks, Louisa,' she demanded. I gathered them up and gave them to her, and she toddled over to the piano.

Wing Commander Cromwell watched her, gaping a

little comically – he hadn't told her she might stand, but he couldn't scold her the way he would have scolded Jamie.

'Louisa!' Jane called. 'Wind the gramophone, please. There's something I'd like us all to hear. An Italian version of a German composer recorded in London by a Polish pianist—'

She held up the record sleeve so everyone could see. It was a blocky modern painting of a dove and candle floating among blue musical notes.

Wing Commander Cromwell recognised it.

'Johanna von Arnim's first record!' he exclaimed. 'Great Scott, that goes back a bit! I heard her sing in the flesh, Béatrice in Berlioz's *Béatrice et Bénédict*. She must have been over fifty then. But still a sensational performer!'

Jane blessed him with a saintly smile.

'You're a fellow opera lover!'

'It's my opinion that Von Arnim must have been the greatest mezzo-soprano of the last century. I greatly regret I was too young to hear her Carmen.'

Jane stood for a moment staring down at the record balanced in her hands, glowing.

But she didn't say anything else. She just placed the record on the turntable and moved the needle into the outer groove.

The record spun, and the room flooded with the waterfall ripple of Bach's Prelude in C, which I know perfectly well because it is the easiest thing he ever wrote for the keyboard and the only Bach that I can play; and over the top of it, in slow, ringing tones of strength and beauty, came a woman's voice like a bell, singing *Ave Maria, gratia plena.*

Everyone turned towards the sound – all the young British airmen and soldiers and the German prisoners too.

*

I have lived with music all my life. I grew up with it – an ordinary thing, a way to earn a living, always there to be shared. Granny Adair plaiting my hair and carolling hymns on a Sunday morning. Hearing Daddy's strong, deep voice coming up the dusty road singing 'Good Evening Caroline' – Mummy and I both giving a scream of excitement, then racing to meet him. Falling asleep in a strange garden under coloured paper lanterns in the dark, listening to Mummy playing the harp at some navy officer's wedding party. Turning pages for her at school-hall concerts, in Kingston and in London. Christmas songs at the piano and playing records for 648 Squadron's B-Flight on sunny afternoons and stormy nights.

Ordinary.

But this was something else.

This music – this music was *outside time.*

It was just a recording, a sound coaxed from shellac through a thorn needle. But while the music played, we were not doing anything but listening. We were not at war. We were not enemies. We weren't anybody special or different from each other – just people listening.

People listening to music together.

Jamie:

When the record ended I could hear the needle scratching in circles. We stood hushed.

The war had to begin again; the Germans were led to their prison, and the rest of us got ferried back to the airfield in the Tilly. Sitting on the floor in the back of the van, leaning against Silver's shoulder, the Bach was still with me like a lullaby, and I was asleep in the five minutes it took to ride to our barracks.

I dreamed I was leading Pimms Section over a shining sunlit sea hunting for U-boats. But there were no ships and no submarines, nothing but the shadows of coral reefs below clear turquoise waves all the way to the horizon, and dolphins leaping. When I tried to make a radio call to the other planes nobody answered. The only thing I could hear on my headset was the high, haunting trill of a flute. It wasn't Bach, though. I didn't recognise the music, but I knew it was Mendelssohn.

Ellen:

Och, it didn't fash me I missed the interview with the German prisoners. I had my own fun. I drove Phyllis to Stonehaven to collect the German translator who came on the train the next day.

We'd been told her name, Sergeant Elisabeth Lind. *She'd* been told to look for the Tilly, I suppose. At the rail station I got out of the van first, and the translator made straight for me as she came through the barriers.

She wore a smart grey Parisian suit – though it must have been a mite outdated – beneath a sealskin coat as sleek as slate and soft as silk. Her hair the colour of ripe straw was done in a tight plait around her head, like a picture postcard of a German milkmaid, if milkmaids went about in fur coats and matching pillbox hats. Her face was made up like a film star's, with long thick eyelashes and red lips.

I didn't recognise her straightaway because of the hair and make-up, but the moment I saw her eyes, clear bright hazel in her bonny vixen's face, I knew who she was – Jamie Stuart's wee German-speaking sister. The pair of them at Windyedge together!

I must have gawped, because she gave her lips a quick tap with a finger gloved in soft grey chinchilla, telling me to hush, and I remembered that she was using someone else's name.

A cloud of soldiers and railwaymen buzzed about her like eager bees. She'd shared out her things amongst them – a small case, an even smaller overnight case, a handbag, and a gas mask. *God pity us*, I thought, swallowing a laugh and thinking of the 648 Squadron lads.

She minced up to me like a fairy in furs. I felt tall and awkward as she held out her small hand for me to shake as if we'd never met. She said, 'Volunteer McEwen? I'm Sergeant Elisabeth Lind.'

'Whisht, *Elisabeth*?' I repeated. 'Just like the Queen!'

That was the name I'd given her myself – *Queenie*.

'*Sergeant Lind*, if you don't mind,' she said quietly.

I'd seen her play-acting a thousand times before, and I wasn't going to give away her secrets any more than she'd give away mine. I didn't know what her game was, but if she'd found a way to play-act and win the war – well, I was glad to see her having a good time. I liked my job, too, or at least as long as Cromwell wasn't poking his neb in.

I said, 'Sergeant Lind it is, then.'

She took her overnight case from the lad at her shoulder and unlatched it and tipped every single thing in it over the kerb next to the Tilly. She made it look like an accident.

Shaness! I didn't know whether to laugh or to howl.

It was all lipsticks and face creams and kohl pots and unmentionable other female items, and the young men all scooted back in horror as if they'd tumbled into a snake pit.

'Don't worry, Volunteer McEwen will help me,' she called over her shoulder to the lads, and most of them slunk away whilst only a couple of the hardiest, the ones holding her things, kept an eye on the queen bee from a safe distance.

We knelt on the cobbles with our heads together, and in a flash she muttered at my ear, 'Please warn Jamie – I'm sorry about the surprise! My commanding officer feels that German prisoners are more at ease with a native speaker translating, and as he isn't here and I am good at being Swiss, they simply *wouldn't* send anyone else—'

'You do it very well and all,' I whispered.

'Don't speak as if you know me,' she warned.

Phyllis got herself out of the Tilly and now came bounding over to help pick things up.

'I'm Flight Officer Pennyworth,' she said breathlessly, sweeping bits and pieces back into the case. 'Or Phyllis, when we're off duty. Hello and welcome! How very embarrassing – we'll have this tidied in no time—'

Phyllis shooed away the last of the admirers. 'Is this her handbag? Follow Volunteer McEwen with the other case, thank you – Ellen, open the back, I'll finish here.'

In no time the show was over and I'd not said anything I shouldn't have.

'Sergeant Lind' sat herself in the passenger seat of the Tilly. Phyllis climbed in back so that we shouldn't have to squeeze up together in the front. But as I headed out to the Aberdeen road, even from the back Phyllis managed to keep the chit-chat going.

'We'll let you settle in at the Limehouse, Sergeant Lind, and then Ellen can drive us to the aerodrome for three o'clock. I've got a pile of gen to prep you on – information, I mean, background and such. I do apologise, you're not English, are you? I'll try to simplify the lingo. We've arranged a bicycle for you, as it's not far and it saves on petrol – oh dear, you are able to ride a bicycle?'

Sergeant Lind laughed. 'I'm pretty fluent in English and I do know how to ride a bicycle. Don't worry, it will be easier in uniform than in this coat.'

She was play-acting even with her own posh accent, speaking English like royalty, as if she had a mouth full of river pebbles and could neither swallow them nor spit them out. I thought I'd strangle with laughter – I wished I had a smoke, just to think about something else.

'Thank goodness it isn't snowing,' Phyllis said anxiously. 'They have been walloped with it west of here. Perhaps we can arrange for boots if you haven't brought any.'

'Thank you, I should love for boots to be arranged!'

I am not ashamed to say I gave thanks to God that I didn't have to speak to her myself. I didn't trust myself to speak a *word*.

As Sergeant Elisabeth Lind swept into the Limehouse,

Phyllis was too busy trying to make her feel at home to notice my face doing acrobatics. Mrs Warner was in her chair by the fire and Louisa on the piano stool where she often perched, and they both watched the queen bee with interest.

'Mrs Campbell?' called Phyllis. 'Mrs Campbell, could you come through? Sergeant Elisabeth Lind is here – the German translator.'

Nan planted herself behind the bar with her hands on her hips. 'Not another one!' she exclaimed.

'You already have a translator?' asked Sergeant Lind.

'I meant—' Poor Nan went red.

'Not another German?' guessed Elisabeth Lind. 'No. I am Swiss. I am from Bienne, and my first language is French, but I speak German, too.' She laughed. 'And English, of course!'

She unpinned her sealskin hat and laid it on the brass counter, and unbuttoned her soft gloves. She was no taller than Louisa and had to stand on her toes to lean across the bar. She said, 'I am at the disposal of Wing Commander Cromwell. I am to stay here at the Limehouse, and Flight Officer Pennyworth will brief me on what's happened at the aerodrome.'

Nan gave a wabble of her head with her mouth open as if she had forgotten how to speak.

Elisabeth Lind filled in the gap. 'You needn't call me Sergeant unless I'm in uniform – as your guest, Miss Lind will do nicely. I would like to go to my room now, if I may, and freshen up before I visit the aerodrome. I never do sleep on the train …'

She leaned in closer to Nan and added in a low voice, 'And if you could make me a cup of coffee it would be the best present I have ever been given.'

'There's only ersatz coffee,' Nan said sulkily. 'Chicory syrup. I daresay it's not what you're used to.'

'Indeed I am,' the translator said triumphantly. 'It's the same in every RAF canteen since the war started. I would be delighted to receive a cup of ersatz coffee.'

She dropped back down on her heels and took a keek at her surroundings: wishing coins, piano, gramophone, stone floor, fireplace, white-haired old woman, brown-skinned Louisa.

'Hello.' She gave Louisa that crooked smile of hers, friendly.

'Miss Lind,' Louisa answered politely like a good wee Colonial. 'I'm Louisa Adair. I look after Mrs Campbell's aunt Jane.'

Mrs Warner waved hello from her chair by the fire.

'Oh.' Elisabeth Lind laughed again. 'A house full of women! I am glad. I was worried they would make me stay at the air base.'

I did not dare catch anyone's eye. I could not imagine the fireworks when she came up against Wing Commander Cromwell.

But I knew she was a canny and a clever lass, good at getting her own way, and perhaps she'd be better able to manage him than Jamie or I.

'I'll show Miss Lind to her room,' said Nan. 'She can have Number Four. The best double. Louisa, bring her up a cup of coffee, would you?'

'Please don't be long,' Phyllis said anxiously. 'Wing Commander Cromwell is expecting us.'

'I won't be two ticks,' said Sergeant Lind. 'Just the time it takes to finish my coffee and change!'

I felt limp with relief when she left the room.

Jamie:

Cromwell brought her into the officers' lounge to introduce her.

'Sergeant Elisabeth Lind will be with us for a week or so as a German translator.'

Elisabeth Lind? Well, it wasn't the first time she'd made me call her by some made-up name.

Every young man in that room catapulted to his feet. Ignacy bowed. She was wearing an air-force blue WAAF uniform exactly like Phyllis's, but we didn't meet many new girls, and this one, as I knew well, lapped up attention. People leaped to pull out a chair for her, light her cigarette, get her a tea. Gavin Hamilton and Dougie Kerr squabbled over who'd hold her gas-mask bag. When Dougie lost, she made it up to him by listening attentively to his life's story.

I had enough trouble with my lads. I didn't need this.

She met my eyes briefly, and I could tell she was very worried I was going to blow her cover.

She tried carefully to stay away from me. Fair enough. She'd gone to a lot of trouble with her make-up so the Stuart family resemblance wouldn't be obvious.

Derfel and Ignacy were the only ones who sat down again besides me. We let the others get on with it.

'Scotty, you look like you have got a headache,' Ignacy said.

I was leaning on one elbow, shading my eyes with my hand. I lifted my face in an effort to appear more sociable.

'I was expecting a Teutonic battleaxe, not a flipping Rhine maiden,' I said.

'What do you not like about Rhine maidens?' he joked.

'God, look at Yorkie,' I complained. 'He's got his arm around her waist already. In the officers' lounge! I'd better break it up.'

I heaved myself out of my chair again. I wasn't sure if I was protecting my baby sister from my squadron or protecting my squadron from my baby sister.

But by the time I'd crossed the room she'd managed perfectly well to protect herself, skilfully extracting her slender waist from Bill Yorke's grip all on her own. She cosied up to Phyllis, making it harder for the lads to get near her. Now she was chatting to Chip, and didn't look at me until Phyllis tugged her arm and said, 'This is Flight Lieutenant Beaufort-Stuart. He's in charge of B-Flight and flies with Pimms. They're the ones who picked up all the German messages.'

'Oh yes, I've heard about you from your wireless operators.' She still didn't look at me as she spoke. 'You're on the list to be interviewed.'

'Whenever you like,' I said, trying not to provoke her.

'I hope there's not much more opening ceremony,' she added. 'I'm here to talk to the prisoners, and I would quite like to get on with it.'

Once the shock began to wear off, I realised how hard it was going to be to ever get to talk to her alone – even harder than trying to talk to Ellen. 'Happy to have a chat with you now in the debriefing room, Flight Officer Lind,' I said through my teeth.

She pealed with laughter. 'Whatever would the rest of your squadron think if we two had a private tête-à-tête? Your interview is with your wing commander, not with *me.* And it's *Sergeant* Lind.' She turned aside to show me her stripes. 'I'm a translator – not in charge of anything!'

I didn't answer. I could do without her laughing at me in front of B-Flight, and she'd been bloody cheeky about questioning them already. God knew what she'd pulled out of Dougie. My sullen silence made her throw me a curious glance. Then she looked away quickly, puffing on her cigarette.

'I'd love to get a chance to chat to the old woman at the inn, though,' she said thoughtfully. 'Jane Warner, is that her name? I wonder what she thought of the Germans when she spoke to them. It might be useful.'

'Buy her a drink,' I suggested. 'She likes whisky and water. It'll cost you two and six.'

Louisa:

Mrs Campbell hated having the Germans around.

She also hated Elisabeth Lind, who felt like a sort of German. She hated waiting on her and cooking for her, and

Mrs Campbell hated having to feed the real Germans, too. She made them corned beef sandwiches and porridge and sent them flasks of tea or pretend coffee. But she wouldn't take the food to them. She tried to get Morag to do it, but after the first day Morag carried on so much, crying real tears because she was so afraid of Nazis, that Nan asked me to take over. And I was glad to.

Those limekilns! I couldn't shake that haunting 'lion kill' shiver just at the thought of them, only these ones *really did* hold brave and terrible people locked inside.

The limekilns were like honeycomb cells in the hillside, and each German airman was shut in his own cold cavern prison behind a huge oak door like the entrance to a dungeon. When the guards let me through with the tea and sandwiches, the makeshift cells were every bit as chilling in real life as in my head. The walls were mildewed whitewash over bare stone, with old lime ovens bricked up in the back. One electric light bulb hung from the ceiling in each cell, and the only furniture was portable camp beds, wooden folding chairs and paraffin heaters.

Eberhard Moritz and Dietrich Althammer nodded thanks to me when I came in, but otherwise I might as well have been invisible. I bet they were just as aloof when Morag brought them food the day before, with too many important things on their minds to be curious about timid teenage serving girls. They were perfectly polite, even to their guards, so I don't know why she was so wet about it. All I had to do was put dishes on a packing crate and move on to the next cell. But Felix Baer …

When I came in with his porridge and coffee, two days

after he got there, he was lying on his back staring up at the whitewashed ceiling. His face was a mess of black bruising, but he turned his head as the door opened.

He sat up slowly when he saw me, swung his legs over the side of the bed, and got to his feet. He strode to the bricked-up kiln and stood with his back to me and the two soldier boys who were on guard. Then, as if he wanted to show how much he disdained us, he began to whistle.

My heart fell. What did I expect – a big welcoming smile? For him to hand over more cipher machine settings, with a flourish? For him to kiss my hand, like Eberhard Moritz did to Jane? Felix Baer wasn't that stupid, anyway. He knew I wasn't supposed to have anything to do with him.

Maybe I just wanted to hear another *danke*. I never imagined he'd turn his back on me on purpose – even the other two German prisoners hadn't been *rude*.

Then I realised he was whistling the opening bars to the *Hebrides Overture*.

But no – as he went on I recognised that it wasn't the beginning. It was a similar eight bars from somewhere in the middle. He didn't go on – he just repeated those eight bars. And the rhythm was off. It was off in odd places – sometimes it seemed right, other times he seemed to stutter.

Oh, crumbs, was it Morse code?

My heart lurched. I balanced the edge of the tray on the packing crate with one hand, and with the other I slowly lifted the coffee flask and put it down on the crate.

I'd showed him I understood Morse. Was he doing it on purpose – for *me*?

My whole body gave a shudder.

He *was*. I knew he was.

But I'd only just learned Morse, and when I practised with Jane I was much slower listening to it – 'receiving' – than I was at transmitting. He repeated the same passage three times, and I still didn't catch most of the letters. I heard *A*s and *M*s and an *I*.

I wasn't fast enough. I was going to miss it because I wasn't fast enough.

I picked up the china cup Mrs Campbell had sent, and instead of putting it next to the coffee flask, I gave it a whack against the edge of the tray and let it slip from my fingers and smash on the dirt floor.

'*Bother!*' I exclaimed loudly.

Baer stopped whistling. He spun around to look.

'Oh dear, what a mess—' I apologised to the guards, and mimed sweeping. 'Let me run and get the dustpan and another cup.'

'Need a hand?' one of them asked.

I put the whole tray down on the packing crate next to the thermos flask. 'No, I'm fine, but it was clumsy of me! I'll be back in a jiffy – is that all right?'

'Jerry's not going anywhere,' said the guard.

When I came back five minutes later Baer was pacing. He didn't look at me. But he kept whistling the whole time I was sweeping up the broken crockery, and eventually I got it – there wasn't much to get, only twelve letters, over and over, fitted carefully into eight bars of Mendelssohn.

FA
LLE
FA
LLE
ENIGM
ENIGM
A
X

I'd nearly finished clearing up when Wing Commander Cromwell came in, steering Sergeant Elisabeth Lind ahead of him with a big hand on her shoulder. For a moment, Baer didn't stop pacing, or whistling. But he stopped whistling in Morse. He finished the music naturally, in its proper rhythm. Then he gave a little bow to Cromwell and the translator.

One of the soldiers pulled up a folding chair next to the portable heater for Miss Lind. She sat down primly with her hands in her lap.

'Sorry, sir, I've just finished tidying this,' I said.

'On you go then,' Cromwell rumbled. He opened a tin of cigarettes and offered one to Baer.

Miss Lind sat waiting for her translation duties to begin. I thought she looked angry; her narrow-eyed glare reminded me of something. A cornered rat? Something else, too. It was hard to tell what she really looked like behind the big fake eyelashes.

I picked up the tray and the broken bits and pieces, leaving a poor cold breakfast for Felix Baer.

I was bursting to find out what *FA LLE ENIGMA* meant.

Jamie:

The weather got worse as the day wore on. Evening brought a storm of howling sleet, impossible to fly in. I probably couldn't have stopped anyone from slogging to the Limehouse through the gale if I'd tried, and I didn't want to test my strength on something so harmless. There was a stack of jazz records, and now there were *four* females worth dancing with, not counting Nancy, who could probably be persuaded if you were feeling generous. Sergeant Elisabeth Lind was at the bar when we got there, leaning in on her elbows to talk to Mrs Campbell. She wore civilian clothes: a tight-fitting grey skirt and a just-as-tight black pullover with a high neck. She turned when we came in and pressed her shoulder blades against the bar, facing the room. It would be hard for any of the lads to get his arm around her.

The other lasses, Phyllis and Ellen and Louisa, huddled at the table by the fire with Mrs Warner. They looked as if they were waiting for a show to start.

That's exactly what they got as B-Flight sailed in, all eighteen airmen from Pimms and Madeira. Elisabeth Lind smiled at Yorkie, who reached her ahead of the pack, and then at Chip, who was about one second behind him. They whipped their sixpences from the beam above her head, slapped them down on the brass counter at exactly the same time, and chorused, 'Can I buy you a drink?'

They couldn't have been more in unison if they were on stage performing Gilbert and Sullivan. Everybody laughed.

'I need to pull Yorke in line,' I murmured to Silver.

'Give him something to do, maybe.'

The lads gathered around Sergeant Lind like bees around a blooming rose. They lit pipes and cigarettes and grabbed for their wishing coins to buy drinks.

'I don't like these thick walls,' Elisabeth Lind said, ducking out of the way as Harry Morrow reached over her head to pull his sixpence from the ceiling.

'Why?' asked Chip. 'Because the house is so old?'

'No, because ghosts live in thick walls. They live in the walls like damp. If you want to get rid of them, you have to light the place up. Then they come out to get warm. They dry up when they get warm enough, also like damp, and then you don't have to worry about them any more.' She took a sip of a discreet wee sherry that was all she'd settled on. 'What this place needs is a good blaze.'

'We can fix that!' said Gavin Hamilton, the Australian navigator, and stirred the fire.

'That's a jolly daft theory.' Adam Stedman laughed. He hailed the landlady. 'Mrs Campbell!'

There wasn't room for all of us at the bar. I stood by the ladies' table with my hands in my pockets. 'All right, Jamie Stuart?' Ellen asked, grinning.

'Aye, no bother, lass,' I answered.

Elisabeth Lind was going after Ignacy now, either because he was safe or because he was more of a challenge, being joined at the hip with Derfel. 'Where were you when Hitler chopped Poland in half and threw the bones to Stalin?' she asked him. 'How did you get out?'

'On foot and by ship, through Istanbul and Casablanca,' Ignacy answered. I knew for a fact that it had taken him most of a year to get here, and he was proud of it. He threw the question right back at her. 'You are Swiss,' he said. 'Your country is neutral. Why do you put on a British uniform every morning?'

She shrugged.

'My school chums are all French and English. I came with them, when the war started. Also –' she laughed – 'I love to dance.'

The moment everyone was waiting for! Silver extracted himself from the pile-up around the bar and made for the gramophone. 'May I, Mrs Warner?'

'Go right ahead!' said the old woman with a benevolent wave to the local population, like Queen Victoria on her tour of Scotland.

Silver put on a record. It was a popular song from five or so years ago – about a third of Mrs Warner's records were banned in Germany. 'Ah, American jazz!' Sergeant Lind exclaimed, tugging Ignacy by the hand. 'Cab Calloway playing "Moonglow"! I couldn't stay neutral when dance music is at stake. Just by *listening* to it you're undermining Hitler. Come along, I *know* you're a good dancer.'

Holding Ignacy's hand, she coaxed him into a small space between tables, raised her other hand so he could put his arm around her waist, and let him lead. They glided over the flagstone floor in a seamless foxtrot. Ignacy *was* a good dancer, formal and light-footed. She picked the right bloke to show off with.

When the record ended, Ignacy thanked her in French. They chattered to each other in French for a minute, nothing of any substance – Ignacy knew I was listening, and thanks to my French grandmother my French is as good as my English. No doubt Mrs Warner knew what was going on, too. The rest of Madeira and Pimms flew into a competition over who would get the next dance, clearing floor space and arguing over records.

'I love a good hop!' exclaimed Phyllis, jumping to her feet. 'I'm in!'

She held out a hand, and Harry Morrow grabbed it first. Silver went for tall Ellen.

Louisa looked directly at me.

She gave a quick, bright-eyed nod, pushed back her chair, and stood up.

In two steps I was by her side with my hand out.

'Like to dance, Louisa?'

Louisa:

I knew I only had about three minutes.

He was taller than me, but he didn't tower over me like the others. His eyes were the clear green-yellow-brown of sunlight through palm fronds, and his hands holding mine were cool and fine-boned. He bent his head and we were face to face, closer than I'd ever been to any boy. I'd never even *danced* with a boy before – at school there were only girls, and we danced with each other.

Silver set the needle on the record. It was another Cab Calloway tune, 'Jitterbug', fast and light-hearted. Harry and Phyllis were laughing together. I fixed a smile on my face – it was easy to smile at Jamie, but not so easy to pretend we were making small talk about jazz or Jamaica.

'We can't use anything we learned from the coding machine any more,' I told him. 'Odysseus. He warned me.'

He didn't miss a step.

'How?'

'Morse code. No accident.'

FALLE. ENIGMA.

'The Nazis are on to him, and they're on to us, too, I think,' I rushed on. 'Jane translated. He said "trap, trap; Enigma, Enigma".'

'Yes, I think they've been on to him for a while,' Jamie breathed. '*Buckets of blood.*'

We were both a little breathless now. He guided our steps towards Jane, on the edge of the dancers, and spun me to face away so the others couldn't see me speaking.

'Jane and I talked about it,' I told him. 'I haven't had a chance to tell Ellen. The Germans must know we're breaking their codes. Now they're trying to catch us.'

He nodded in understanding.

'Trying to catch *you*,' I corrected, because it wasn't me flying out over the North Sea hunting for submarines.

'That last message –' he spoke close to my ear, almost in a whisper, hurrying – 'the last one you passed to me after the weird "happy wagon" message. *U BOAT OPERATIONS UTSIRA XIV II*. I wondered if the date was wrong. February fourteenth gives us two weeks' more lead time than most of the other messages. Utsira's an island off the coast of Norway. You think that's a set-up?'

'*I don't know*,' I said. 'It could be. They could lure you there and send in night fighters and you'd all be dead.'

His hands tightened around mine.

'When did you see Baer?' he asked.

'I take him his meals. And the others, too.'

'Louisa, you'll get in trouble.'

'Won't we all?' The phoney smile felt like it was going to crack my face. 'Aren't we *already* in trouble?'

The record was coming to an end.

'Don't go to Utsira on the fourteenth!' I begged. 'You don't *need* to go hunting for U-boats.'

'We've got to go where they send us,' he pointed out. 'Even on Valentine's Day!' He laughed, pretending it was nothing. Dancers talking about Valentine's Day!

'Tell Ellen,' I said.

'I will.' His smile was phoney too.

We were out of time.

Mrs Campbell cleared everybody out at ten, so it was late when I heard tapping at the door of Room Number Five, where I was already in my nightdress. I opened the door expecting Ellen.

But it was Elisabeth Lind.

She looked ready for bed, except her face still glowed with perfect paint. Her fairytale-gold hair was unpinned in one long plait, bound with a black silk ribbon. She wore a quilted grey silk dressing gown that made her look like she was snuggled into a cloud. I couldn't see much of what was underneath, but black silk printed with silver peonies clung to her ankles.

Her elegant clothes weren't new. The dressing gown was fraying, its sleeve ends whipped with thread that didn't quite match. There was a hole in the quilting somewhere, because now and then she shed a down feather or two, like a moulting chicken. It wasn't just thrifty wartime mending – her clothes had been *made over*. I did the same thing to Mummy's clothes to make them fit me, which is why I noticed. Elisabeth Lind's expensive dressing gown was hemmed and tucked because it used to belong to a taller woman – to *someone else*.

She wasn't as wealthy as she seemed. I felt like I'd won a round of poker. I knew more about her than she knew about me.

'Ah, Louisa, I'm sorry to disturb you so late! Could you help me? I can't make my gas fire come on.'

'Oh—' I glanced at Jane, already in bed.

Jane put her book aside and pulled herself up in curiosity. 'What's the matter, darling?'

'I'm going to light the fire for Miss Lind,' I told her.

'Of course,' Jane agreed. 'It's very cold tonight.'

I snatched up my own silk dressing gown – Mummy's, that is, also not new – and followed Miss Lind down the dark passage.

No one had stayed in Room Number Four since Felix Baer, though Robert Ethan had poked about in it. There was plenty of credit on the meter. Miss Lind watched politely while I showed her how to turn on the gas.

'You're a keen reader,' she said irrelevantly.

I drew in a sharp breath and stared at her, startled. She'd been noticing things about me, too.

'Well, I am,' I said. 'How do you know?'

She laughed at my expression. 'I saw the books in your room.'

'Jane has books,' I said warily.

'*Swallows and Amazons*? *National Velvet*? Those aren't hers. She's over eighty. You're in your teens.'

'You're Swiss,' I said. 'Those are English books.'

She shrugged. 'I went to school with English girls. We swapped. Reading English books is how I learned English. And listening to the BBC, of course!'

She did sound like she'd learned English by listening to the BBC, posh as posh.

She knelt beside me on the hearth. 'Let me try the fire now,' she said. She turned off the gas tap and the fire went out. She turned it back on, struck a match carefully, and lit it again.

'Have you read any Greek myths?' she asked. 'Bulfinch's *The Age of Fable*? Or Lamb's version of Homer's *Odyssey*, perhaps?'

How much did she know about our 'Odysseus' – and was she wondering the same thing about me? If so, she was being cautious about it.

I thought I should be cautious too. She could go straight to Cromwell with anything I said.

'No,' I said. 'No, I haven't, but we read *The Children's Homer* in school.' I stood up. 'I have to help Jane get ready for bed.'

'Isn't she in bed already?' Miss Lind tilted her head to look up at me with her crooked smile.

'Yes, but – I have to turn out the fire. And the standing lamp. You're all right now, aren't you? You did that perfectly.'

Beneath the powder and lipstick her face nagged at me, familiar – until all I could think was that she reminded me a bit of Felix Baer himself. With his bruised eyes and swollen nose I couldn't tell what he really looked like, either.

Miss Lind stood up now too, in a swish of grey-and-black silk. She snatched my hand and squeezed it as if we'd known each other for years.

'I won't keep you,' she said. 'But I don't know if I shall get you to myself again. I can't ask you about Odysseus when anyone's listening.'

I stood still, my hand in hers.

'I don't know what you mean,' I said carefully. 'I thought you were here to help Wing Commander Cromwell while he's questioning the Germans.'

'Let's not play this stupid game,' she said. 'I know you've heard the name Odysseus because I've been briefed about everything that's happened here. I know he's one of the Germans locked up in those awful pits below the hill; he's Felix Baer, the pilot. He's supposed to talk to me. They're all supposed to talk to me; I'm standing in for their British contact. I even have a code name from *The Odyssey*, which Eberhard Moritz made up himself just in case this happened, so they can identify me and trust me.'

It took every ounce of strength in my body not to pull my hand away. My skin crawled with suspicion, as if I'd bathed in syrup and woken up covered with ants. I said quietly, 'What do you need me for, then?'

'My code name is *Calypso*.' Miss Lind let go of my hand. 'Do you remember who Calypso is, from your *Children's Homer*? She's a goddess who lures Odysseus to her lonely island by singing to him. Then she won't let him leave for seven years.' She hugged the grey silk around her. 'Calypso is also a type of music in the West Indies. Perhaps you know that.'

'Yes, in Trinidad,' I said.

'Where are you from?' she asked me. 'Jamaica, isn't that right? An island in the Caribbean Sea, like Trinidad. Even the British tried to ban Calypso music, and I'm sure most Germans don't bother to distinguish where it comes from, if they've even heard of it. Just another type of forbidden music from a West Indian island full of British subjects of the Crown.'

She'd lost me completely now. I shook my head, wondering if she was a little mad. 'I don't know what you're talking about.'

'I need your help,' said Elisabeth Lind. 'None of the Germans believe I've been sent by their British contact. They won't tell me *anything*, and I know why. Felix Baer thinks *you're* Calypso.'

How was I supposed to know it was a code name?

'I didn't do it on purpose—' I gasped. 'I didn't know!'

The *disappointment* was almost as great as the shock.

Of course Felix Baer hadn't thought there was anything special about *me*. He hadn't left me his message or singled me out because he thought I was clever or brave or connected to the aerodrome. He knew only that his contact was called Calypso, and here was I, fresh out of the Caribbean Sea and able to recognise Mendelssohn.

But I'd still helped, hadn't I? Without me, B-Flight would never have found those U-boats. I'd helped a *little*, even if it was unofficial and over now.

'How can I fix it?' I asked. 'How can I tell him?'

She shook her head, looking into the fire.

'I don't honestly know,' she said. '648 Squadron's dragon of a wing commander is always breathing down my neck whenever I see any of the German prisoners. I have my own commanding officer who's supposed to cope with this, but he's in *Africa*, and I can't even speak to him. I'm just a deputy – I'm still in training and I feel rather out of my depth. None of those Germans want to talk to me *anyway*, not with Cromwell there, even if they believed I'm their contact.'

She turned to look at me searchingly. Her expression was softer now, and for a split second I nearly caught why she looked so maddeningly familiar, and then it was gone.

'*You* believe me, don't you?' she asked uncertainly, and it was like seeing a big crack opening up in a suit of armour.

I nodded. 'You couldn't know about Calypso otherwise. He called me that the first time he was here.'

'Let me think about what we can do,' she said. 'You think about it too. I wish Cromwell wasn't involved. I wish *you* weren't involved—'

That's when Nancy Campbell barged in without even knocking.

'Aunt Jane's just gone downstairs on her own without her sticks, hanging on the banister and hunting for hot-water bottles,' Nancy said shortly. 'So I've made one up for her and helped her back to bed. Heavens, Louisa, I don't pay you to sit about blethering! I shall cut your week's wages if I have to see to Jane again!'

I opened my mouth to make excuses, and shut it without a word.

Jane going down those stairs in the inky dark, on her own, without her sticks!

'I'm so sorry, Mrs Campbell!' I gasped, leaping to my feet. 'It won't happen again.'

But as I rushed from the room I realised how hard it would be to catch Miss Lind alone another time.

Ellen:

The moon was nearly full, but it was pig-awful dreich flying weather. At Windyedge we had sheets of sleety rain; five miles inland, higher up, the moors got a blanket of snow. Three Blenheim ops got cancelled. The lads slept all afternoon in case of a night-time clear-up, and Phyllis and I stayed at the Limehouse making toast over the fire while Louisa and Jane pounded out piano duets.

Louisa was tense as a fiddle string. Whenever they finished a tune and Jane turned pages, Louisa leaped up to peep through the rain-flecked front window.

The only folk who came in were Wing Commander Cromwell and Elisabeth Lind, after their afternoon with the Jerry prisoners.

'Sergeant Lind, you're dismissed. Volunteer McEwen, take me to the aerodrome,' Cromwell demanded. 'Come along, Flight Officer Pennyworth, you're needed to write up my report. Toss your cycles in the Hillman, and you can ride back later and save the van making another trip.'

Oh, ta very much, Wing Commander Cromwell. Flight Officer Pennyworth and I were looking forward to a push-bike ride through a sleet storm!

While Phyllis and I pulled on our overcoats, Sergeant Lind stirred up the fire and then threw herself down in Jane's comfortable chair. But she didn't call for Nan to get her tea or coffee or sandwiches. As we filed out after Cromwell, I stole a keek in her direction, and, oh, was I going to have to worry about her and Jamie both now? She was that tightly wound she couldn't relax. She sat stiff and straight, gripping the arms of that chair like she wanted to break them off, staring at Louisa's piano-playing back as if she were trying to lay a curse.

I dropped off Cromwell and Phyllis and slogged back on my push-bike, dodging icy raindrops and spraying slush up my shins. I was away about twenty minutes. When I came into the dry at the Limehouse again, the musicians were still tinkling away at the piano, and Sergeant Lind was asleep with her head on the table.

Jane turned to smile at me.

I raised one finger to my lips and pointed. '*Whisht.*'

Jane didn't lift her hands from the piano keys – just let them fall still. She sat with her head atilt, favouring her left ear. After a few more notes Louisa stopped playing, too, and listened.

The big room was mostly empty, but it was full of soft wee noises: the sound of the low peat fire burning, the Scotch pine boughs swishing outside in the wind, sleet tapping against the window glass.

And Elisabeth Lind was talking quietly to herself in German. In her sleep.

'She's counting,' Jane told us. 'Up to thirty. She's done it three times.'

'It is German, isn't it?' Louisa asked softly, with her worried frown.

'It's Swiss German,' Jane said. 'She's just counting.'

We held still, listening to the wind and rain and fire, and to that slurry voice murmuring in German.

'*What is she doing?*' Louisa hissed.

'I think she's practising,' the old woman said. 'So she doesn't blow her cover story. Her standard German is excellent and she has a lovely regional Helvetian accent. French may well be her first language. But she didn't learn it in Switzerland, and she certainly isn't Swiss.'

'Don't let Nan hear you,' Louisa begged.

Eins, zwei, drei … achtezwanzig, nünezwanzig, dreissig. Eins, zwei, drei …

I went to give flipping Mata Hari a gentle tap on the shoulder to wake her up and shut her up. I wondered what Cromwell had said to those Jerries, and what Felix Baer had said to her. I was glad I didn't have her job.

Louisa came into the bathroom to brush her teeth while I brushed my hair. We ran the taps like spring torrents to cover our whispered secrets.

'That German pilot – Odysseus, Felix Baer—' She was so quiet I had to lean in to hear her. 'He won't talk to Miss Lind. *He thinks I'm his contact.*'

I dropped the hairbrush.

Over the noise of the water the clatter wasn't anything. Louisa stayed bent over the basin.

'You don't even speak German!' I exclaimed.

'Remember he talked about Calypso when he was here the first time? That's her code name. He thought it was me – that I'd been sent to meet him. And when I gave him that tea, in the pub after Chip punched him up, I thanked him by blinking at him in Morse code! *So stupid of me!* I just – I just wanted to talk to him, somehow. And when he warned me about the trap, I messed about to give us time! Now I don't know how to fix things. I tried to talk to him today and I couldn't, not with the guards listening! I don't know what to do.'

I picked up the brush and weighed it in my hand.

I took a deep breath.

Finally I whispered, 'You should give the cipher machine to Sergeant Lind.'

'What about Jamie?' Louisa objected.

'Even if we had the new settings for it, we daren't use it now, not if they're trying to catch him. Give the machine to Sergeant Lind,' I said again. 'She's the one your Jerry meant it for; she'll know what to do with it.'

'How can we trust her?' Louisa gasped.

I put down the hairbrush and wound my shawl tight about my shoulders. Queenie, that canny, bonny lass, my old friend, was putting on her nightdress in the next room, and I had to pretend I didn't know who she was! It was hard.

But Louisa needed to know.

'She's our Jamie's sister,' I whispered over the rushing water. 'You can trust her because she's Jamie's sister.'

'*Oh!*'

Louisa laughed wildly.

'*Of course she is!*'

She leaned over the basin with her toothbrush, which had not come near her teeth for at least five minutes.

'Whisht. Don't tell,' I hurried to add. 'She wants the Germans to think she's Swiss.'

'*Jamie's sister!* Their eyes are exactly the same! No wonder she hides behind those stick-on lashes! But,' Louisa asked breathlessly, 'won't she tell Cromwell? Isn't she supposed to?'

'I don't think so,' I said. 'I don't think he's meant to know a thing about it. She might report it to her own commanding officer. But she'd have a long jaw with Jamie before she did that. If she ever catches him alone.'

'How am I going to catch *her* alone?' Louisa wailed.

That was the hard part. Sharing a room with Phyllis. Always carrying some gadgy in the van. Cromwell breathing down your neck. Worrying Nan would hear you.

'Do *you* talk in your sleep?' Louisa asked suddenly, reading my mind. 'What if Phyllis heard? Do you think *Jamie* talks in his sleep?'

'Silver will shut him up if he does,' I said, hoping so, as I turned off the taps.

Jamie:

I tossed and turned in my bunk again, but tonight everyone was restless.

Derfel was singing under his breath in Welsh. The Australians chattered quietly. 'Tomorrow at Mrs C.'s?' I heard one of them say. I didn't know any of them well enough to tell apart their accented voices in the dark.

'Too right,' another answered. 'My turn to dance with Sergeant Lind.'

'She's talking to the Jerries in the afternoon and we're flying tomorrow night. We won't even see her.'

'I can dream, can't I?'

'Go ahead and dream,' said the first – probably Harry. 'Flight Officer Pennyworth is mine.'

Meanwhile, Chip and Yorkie argued softly on the other side of the room. I couldn't hear most of it, but it was about the German prisoners. If Cromwell was getting information out of them, he wasn't sharing it. Our ground crew had gone over every inch of the captured German bomber and we'd all had a nosy inside the cockpit, but no one found any hidden secret messages or classified Luftwaffe radar gear. Or fresh code settings for a German cipher machine.

I needed another meeting with Ellen and Louisa and Mrs Warner all together. Passing messages down the line while dancing in the pub or racing to climb into a Blenheim before an op was doing my head in.

Also, I was dogged by dread of Felix Baer's warning.

Trap. Enigma.

A snare for B-Flight – not just me. Eighteen of us that I was responsible for.

Bill Yorke raised his voice. 'If you ask me, the coloured girl knew they were coming.'

'She knows how to transmit Morse,' Chip agreed. 'And

the old lady speaks German. They could have a radio hidden up there. They could be sending messages in German to the bombers.'

'*Come bomb us, please*,' Ignacy put in sarcastically, and Derfel laughed.

I sat up in alarm. I had to nip this in the bud.

'Flying Officer Yorke, if anyone's accused of careless talk, you're going to be first in the queue for court martial,' I growled. 'You're the one who left German code transmissions on cigarette papers in the public bar.'

'*I did what?*' Bill Yorke cried. 'I copied out the transmissions and turned them in to Intelligence, like I always do! Tex told me to get rid of the scribbling papers!'

'I said to burn 'em,' Chip protested. 'Not leave them in an ashtray.'

Everybody went quiet. I couldn't keep throwing threats at Yorkie, hoping one would make him start playing cricket with the rest of the side.

Give him something to do, Silver had said. He hadn't said what.

Before I lost most of my old B-Flight in that November op, I'd never had trouble with my aircrews. But had I *always* leaned on my navigator to point me in the right direction as much as I did now? Was my civil war with Cromwell keeping me from solving my own command problems?

For a start, I could put an end to this stupid scrapping.

'Stow this nonsense about old women and kids being Nazi spies and go to sleep,' I said. 'Nothing happened. Volunteer McEwen found those codes and turned them in. She keeps mum about it, and if she can do it, so can we.'

As I said it, I suddenly knew how to take some of the edge off Bill Yorke.

I could put him in charge of Dougie – get him to keep Dougie's chattering tongue in line. I'd have a quiet word in the morning. The wireless ops hung around together anyway; Chip and Yorkie were already wingers. Yorkie must have felt like I was nothing but a brand-new sprog bossing him about. It would do him good to earn the respect of the *real* sprogs.

It would take some of the pressure off me, too.

Ellen:

As long as they were chasing U-boats, Jamie's lads pulled together. Shut them up for a week of bad weather and they became a cloud of biting midgies.

B-Flight was scheduled for its first night-time op since the Jerries landed. But they stopped by the Limehouse before their afternoon kip, no doubt hoping for a keek at so-called Sergeant Lind. She was away translating German that day, so they'd have to wait. The wireless ops all ganged together, chatting up Nan's mousy village lass Morag behind the bar, until she was blushing and getting orders wrong.

I saw Bill Yorke give Dougie Kerr a warning thump in the shoulder, and Dougie went red. Yorkie gave him a wee lecture.

It looked more like a superior officer dressing down a sprog than Yorkie's usual stirring up mutiny. I caught Jamie's eye, and he raised his glass ever so slightly. He was watching the wireless ops too. He still looked knackered. But not so *old* these days.

I wished I could take over his job for a day and have a go at whipping his lads into shape.

The wireless ops took their drinks and left the bar, crowding on stools among the rest of us lasses. Yorkie sat himself between Louisa and Phyllis, with his thigh pressed against Louisa and his arm over Phyllis's shoulder. Phyllis was such a flipping good girl she put up with it, but Louisa scooted her chair to get away from him.

'Coloured gal's playin' hard to get,' Chip Wingate drawled.

'Coloured gal prefers Germans,' said Bill Yorke. 'Bats her eyelashes at 'em like she wants to get paid.'

'Oi, set an example, Flying Officer Yorke,' Jamie warned. 'I'm counting on you.'

Louisa stood, her hand quivering on her chair back.

She'd told me she'd blinked Morse code at Felix Baer. Yorkie was a wireless operator – she must be feared he'd noticed. She couldn't risk getting angry.

She moved to put Jane and the table between herself and Yorke.

'I prefer musicians,' she said.

That fetched a good laugh from the lads. I stood up to join her so she'd know I had her back. But Yorkie didn't move aside for me to pass.

'Gadgy pillock,' I muttered, going round the table the other way.

Shaness. I'd used a Traveller word.

Nobody noticed. Or if they did, they didn't wonder why

I'd used it. Ignacy Mazur, the Polish bloke, told Yorkie, 'You will never win a lady by questioning her character.'

Dougie Kerr laughed. Then he opened his flapping gob and said, 'Mazur, mate, you're not qualified to give advice about girls.'

They were all ready for a fight.

'Shut it, you blabbermouthed Australian git!' snarled Derfel. 'You blab about every flight, you blab about every transmission – you blabbed to Morag that you've taken an oath under the Official Secrets Act, what kind of a chat-up line is *that*?'

'I didn't *tell* her anything!' Dougie said, hurt. 'I said I *couldn't* tell her anything. Anyway, leave it out, Yorkie already had a go at me earlier. *Careless talk costs lives* – I'm not daft!'

Chip said, 'Taff's not sore about careless talk. He's sore because you're blabbing about him and Ignacy.'

Silver said, 'Aw, keep quiet, you stupid Yank.'

'I'm *not a Yank*, you stupid Jew!'

Jamie swore – '*Break it up! Silver! TEX!*' – and Nan cried, '*Lads, lads!*' but Dougie blethered cheerfully: 'A Scot's a Scot, a Pole's a Pole, a Taff's a Taff. So why isn't a Yank—'

Derfel growled, 'I said *shut your gob, you Aussie prick*.'

Chip and Bill swapped glances, then both turned back to look at Derfel.

Chip said, 'A pansy—'

And Pimms all lost their heads.

'*Oik!*'

'*Pom!*'

'*Sheep-shagger!*'

'*Yid!*'

'Bloody *ENGLISH*!' Jamie roared at his best mate, and Chip and Derfel tumbled over the flagstones trying to beat each other's brains out.

Jamie and Silver dived after Chip. Ignacy went for Derfel. A tableful of glasses crashed to the floor. Phyllis shrieked and jumped up, knocking over her chair; Jane knocked over her sticks. Louisa and I stared. It was like we'd chucked a match into a tank of petrol.

Ignacy pulled Derfel off by the back of his collar. They fell into a guddle of broken glass and spilt beer, cursing in Welsh and Polish.

That wildcat Chip Wingate wouldn't stop. Jamie and Silver sat on him, but he kept fighting, and Adam Stedman piled in. They pinned him until he lay completely squashed, heaving angry breaths.

What a way to win a war, aye?

Poor Jamie looked up at us shocked women, me and Louisa and Jane and Phyllis by the fire, Nancy and Morag behind the bar. He glowed red to the tips of his ears.

'I'm— I—'

Nan Campbell stood agape with her hair bunching out of its grips. Never had I seen her so close to weeping.

Then Morag babbled the most gobsmacking propaganda-poster display of British bulldog spirit: 'Och, it's to be expected. Boys will be boys.'

God pity us, isn't that the exact blether of Dougie's that started off the stramash?

I'd suddenly had enough.

'*To be expected!* Tear up the place like a pack of wild dogs – it's to be *expected*?' I cried. 'Shaness, *nothing's* to be expected! I didn't expect Louisa to talk so posh! We didn't expect the Luftwaffe to fly in waving white flags! No one expected we'd win the Battle of Britain! If everybody went on doing what people expected, I'd be selling pins and willow baskets door to door instead of hauling this lot about between their battles! And you, Miss Morag Torrie, you'd be looking down your neb at me for being a Traveller lass, instead of mooning over my ATS driver's badge and wishing you were old enough to join up! Everybody shoves their sixpences into that bar *expecting* to come back for another drink and *look at how many of them never come back*!'

I saw the shiver go through them all.

Morag's mouth hung open. Nancy Campbell pushed hair out of her eyes and whispered, 'Whisht, Ellen, lass, don't say such things.'

'Every other body says whatever they think!'

'And you're no' a tinker.'

'Aye, so I am,' I said. 'Your bonny English WAAF shares her room with a filthy tinker.'

Phyllis grabbed my hand and squeezed. 'She's very clean, Mrs Campbell,' she said.

I pulled away from her in fury. '*Nan knows that.*'

Nancy turned about and armed herself with a heather broom, probably made and sold to her by a relative of mine, and a pan and a cardboard box.

'I hope you lads are all *ashamed of yourselves*,' she said bitterly.

They looked as if they mostly were.

Jamie croaked, 'Pass those here, Mrs Campbell, and we'll tidy up for you.'

He got to his feet and gave an order in a low voice. 'Sort the mess and get back to base. The moon is full and we're flying tonight. None of you will drink another drop the day, and you'll not set foot in this place again until I've worked out how we'll make it up to Mrs C. You're all banned.'

Derfel helped Ignacy to his feet. 'I'll manage him,' he said to Jamie.

Suddenly B-Flight were working together again. I suppose that wasn't to be expected, either.

Harry Morrow and Gavin Hamilton set to with the broom and the dustpan. David Silvermont and Adam Stedman picked up the table; Dougie Kerr and Bill Yorke squatted collecting broken glass. Now and then the English lads threw me curious glances, looking at me in a new way.

Chip Wingate got stiffly to his feet. He put a chair right and sat on it.

'Tex, get a move on. Help out or get out,' Jamie barked.

Chip leaned over his knees in silence.

'Come back for him later,' suggested Silver.

'Volunteer McEwen will drive you if you're too puffed to walk,' said Jamie.

Everybody looked at me all at once for a moment.

Then they went back to work.

Louisa:

It was late when the Tilly pulled up at the Limehouse again with its gears screaming, and a few minutes later Ellen pounded up the stairs. She saw our light on under the door and didn't knock.

'Louisa, come and give us a hand. Oh – you're in your night things!' She looked me up and down. 'We need another bod and you might have to go outside. Do you have boots? I'll get you Nan's wellies.'

I pulled on a sweater and tucked my nightgown into a skirt. If 648 Squadron could do it, so could I. I already had on wool stockings because my legs were always cold, but thinking of Nan Campbell's wellies, which she kept in the lean-to outside the kitchen door, I pulled on another pair of socks.

'Windyedge is the most exciting place I have ever lived, which is saying something,' Jane said, watching me jealously.

'Please, *please* don't go downstairs till I come back. *Please.* Here's the torch, make sure you take it if you need the loo.' I kissed the top of her head.

'Take care,' Jane called after me.

'You take care!'

Morag was washing up, her head lowered over the glasses.

Chip Wingate was *still there*.

He was snoring by the dead fire in Jane's comfortable chair. Nan stood there, nervously holding a jug of water in one hand and twisting her pinny with the other. Jamie Beaufort-Stuart, dressed for flying, slapped his rear gunner back and forth across the face with a wet dishcloth.

'Come *on*, mate – *come on*—'

Chip shifted in Jane's chair, trying to dodge the wet smacks.

'You're going to get the full jug in a moment,' Jamie growled.

'Aw, take a hike, Scotty, lemme alone!' moaned his gunner.

Jamie looked up at me and Ellen. 'He's still blind drunk and we're flying *in an hour*.'

'Where's Silver?' I asked, pulling on Nan's boots.

'Doing his job putting together tonight's flight plan, and doing mine and checking out the kite, and making sure nobody notices Tex isn't around to do his. If we get him on his feet maybe we can shoogle him out to the Tilly with me on one side and you two on the other—'

Chip roused himself and said, 'The gorgeous redhead's gonna give me a hand? Miracles do happen! An' the cute li'l darkie?'

Did either of us need to help this good-for-nothing?

Of course we needed to help *Jamie*.

'One more wisecrack and I'm pinning today's punch-up on you, Sergeant Chester Wingate,' Jamie threatened.

He got Chip's arm over his shoulder. Bracing himself against the table, Jamie managed to get them both to their feet. They were about the same height, but Chip was heavyset. Ellen slipped herself beneath Chip's other arm and he laughed.

'Oh, I like this—'

'Stow it, you clot,' barked Jamie.

Ellen said grimly, 'Louisa, you'll have to help.'

I took a deep breath.

But I did it. I slid in next to her, my arm around her waist, and hung on to Chip's wrist where it dangled over my shoulder.

'Get the door, Mrs C.,' Jamie grunted. 'What were you thinking, to let him get shot up like this!'

'You left him here! You should have carried him out before, when the lads could have helped!' Nan Campbell gasped. 'He's never flying in this state!'

'If I don't get him in the air tonight he'll be court-martialled! And probably so will I, come to think of it.'

'Don't you fret, Tex is much less likely to cause trouble this way,' Ellen told Nan. 'He can sleep in the air.'

I saw Jamie glance at the coins in the ceiling. Nan followed his gaze, her face pale.

'In my pocket—' Chip tilted his head. 'Go on, Scotty, give her some of the funny money. Sixpence, a tanner, is that what you call it? A tanner for my next pint—'

With a heavy sigh, balanced beneath Chip's arm and not daring to tempt fate, Jamie managed to reach into Chip's trouser pocket and somehow came up with a sixpence. He gave it to Mrs Campbell.

'You keep that safe for him.'

Ellen:

Nan held the doors, and the rest of us heaved Chip through and slung him in the back of the Tilly. He was away with the fairies as he hit the floor.

'You'd better come,' I told Louisa.

'Ride up front with Ellen,' Jamie added. 'I'll keep an eye on Texas Sunshine.'

'What about Jane!' Louisa objected.

'I'll look in on her,' said Nancy quickly. 'Just this once. Of course I will.'

Under the bright full moon I didn't need headlamps – not that they're worth much in wartime, narrowed to slits with black paint. Louisa offered her passport at the barrier, but Nobby saw her too often to care; he rolled his eyes and waved us through.

Jamie coaxed and scolded his rat-arsed gunner all the way, but Louisa cracked away with me just as she'd done when Felix Baer took us for hostages.

'What are tinkers?' Louisa asked. 'Is it like being a Gypsy?'

'Aye, a mite like that. My folk are Travellers,' I said shortly. '"Tinker" is what the gadgies call us. That would be like folk calling you a darkie – you wouldn't call yourself that, would you? *Filthy tinker.*'

'You must have stories!' Louisa said.

'But no address. No home to go to. People don't like that – they think it makes you shifty. Lazy. Outsiders, not to be trusted.'

'We were outsiders too,' Louisa agreed. 'Me and my English mum and Jamaican dad. We didn't fit anyone's rules, and it was hard being out and about together. But we *loved* being together. You have family to go to, as well, don't you? Doesn't that count?'

We'd reached the barracks. I pulled up and jumped out. Louisa was close behind me as I opened the back of the van, and David Silvermont pounded across the moonlit airfield to join us.

'Got him?' Silver demanded.

Best Jamie could do was make Chip sit up, but he wouldn't get out of the Tilly.

'Goddam it, Jamie!' Silver exclaimed. 'He isn't suited up!'

'I know it,' Jamie said grimly. He sounded done in. 'Get his gear and we'll drive him to the plane.'

We couldn't get Chip into his flight suit, either. No amount of bawling in his earhole could stir him. Silver looked at the luminous dial of his watch.

'Jamie, we take off in ten minutes. For God's sake. Leave him. It's not your fault. We're on fishing-fleet escort; we won't be taking headings and we can manage without a gunner. You can work the radio from the pilot's seat.'

'The start-up crew will notice if only two of us get in. And if my gunner gets court-martialled, I'll be in for it too. If we could just get him into the plane!'

Louisa knelt on the floor of the Tilly by the slumbering Texan, holding his flight suit.

'Hey,' she said slowly.

She sat and hauled Nan Campbell's boots off her feet. A moment later she began to climb into Chip Wingate's flight suit. By the time she'd got her legs in and struggled to pull it up over her shoulders, I jumped up to help. In another second Silver was giving us a hand too.

Every one of us wanted to save Jamie's skin. We didn't give a toss about Chip Wingate.

'No, no, *no*,' Jamie objected. 'Not *Louisa*.'

'Why not Louisa!' I said. 'We'll leave Tex to sleep it off! He'll be all right under blankets and canvas.'

'No!'

'We'll have to swap her back the second we're on the ground,' said Silver.

'I'll wait here,' I said. 'I'll drive up to the plane when you land and she can hop back in the van, and we'll unload Texas Sunshine at the barracks door. No one will notice it wasn't him with you the whole time.'

'Tomorrow you can pretend he fainted on the flight back and had to be carried to bed,' said Louisa, and Silver and I burst out laughing.

Jamie:

Were they all absolutely bonkers?

Louisa thought we were likely to fly straight into a German deathtrap sometime in the coming day or two, and here she was trying to stow away on our next op?

I took her by the hands as we crouched on the van's wooden floor next to my snoring wireless operator/rear gunner. We knelt facing each other; I hadn't put on my gauntlets, and her grip was firm.

'Louisa, you can't come,' I said. 'I've got enough on my plate, and I'm not going to let you risk your life for this tosser.' I nodded over my shoulder towards Chip. 'He's not worth it. Don't be a martyr.'

'Why in the world would I do it for *him*!' she exclaimed hotly. 'Are you mad? *I want* to do it. I want to *so much*. I want to fly. I loved it before. And—'

She spat the words under her breath. 'And no one will let

me fly like you, because I am a girl and what they told my dad – "*not of pure European descent*".'

Before I could protest again, she added quickly, 'Well, also, I want to help you.' She sucked in a breath. 'I can practise receiving Morse code! I can listen to the radio for you!'

I gave a gasp of a laugh. She wouldn't even know how to turn the radio on. But she was *so keen*.

'You could take me instead of Louisa,' Ellen put in persuasively. 'Only I'd be sick again, and I couldn't receive Morse code. You'd let me come, aye? You'd let *me*.'

'Yes, but – that's not fair. You've left home. You're responsible for yourself.'

'So have I,' said Louisa. 'So am I.'

As long as we didn't get shot at, she'd be fine, and no one would know Chip hadn't gone with us. Still – I shook my head. 'You don't need to be involved.'

'I'm already involved. You know how much.' She laughed.

If anyone found out, I'd be in bigger trouble than she would.

'Oh, let her come if she wants to that badly,' said Silver. 'It's not a bombing run.'

I sat back on my heels, throwing my hands in the air in surrender. If Silver was going to side with the girls, I was doomed.

'Cheer up!' he said as he climbed in next to us. 'Think how much trouble she'll save, not how much she'll make! Louisa never makes any trouble.'

Ellen shut us all in the back of the van.

'You'd better have another pair of socks,' I told Louisa.

'Or two. Silver, can you spare some socks? If we each give her a layer, no one will end up with frostbite.'

Louisa laughed nervously as we dragged off our boots and passed her our socks in the dark.

'What—'

'You'll get Tex's chocolate ration, too!' Silver exclaimed. 'Make sure you eat it before you take off, so it doesn't go to waste if we—'

'Shut up, mate,' I interrupted. 'We won't. Not this time.'

Ellen gave Louisa her pullover. Outside it was colder than it had been on Christmas Day. The poor wee lass could hardly move by the time we'd packed her in woollens and stuffed a dozen Ever-Hot bags between the layers, but it helped bulk out Chip's flight suit. With the legs and sleeves rolled up, it wasn't too bad – he wasn't any taller than me.

Then we helped Louisa into his padded gauntlets and life vest, and finished off the disguise with his helmet and mask. She had her own oxygen and a microphone this time. You couldn't see anything of her face but her eyes.

So when Ellen pulled up by Pimms Section's lead Blenheim, where the ground crew were still refuelling, three suited airmen climbed from the back of the Tilly.

Standing next to the plane I knew we never had a chance of getting Chip into it. There was no way we could have lifted him on to the wing and through the rear hatch. We struggled enough getting Louisa up there, in Chip's flight suit and Nan Campbell's wellie boots, and she was lighter and more cooperative than Chip. I leaned over to cram my top half through the hatch behind her so I could show her where to stow her parachute and plug in her oxygen.

'The rear gunner's also the wireless operator,' I told her. 'Sit at the radio for take-off – once we're in the air, hop into the gun turret if you want to see out. When I get the hydraulics switched on, you can make the gunner's chair go up and down by twisting the handles.' I pointed. 'It'll move the gun, too; careful you don't hit the firing button by accident. You're connected to the intercom so you can talk to me and Silver, and you'll be able to hear the radio, but you can't transmit to the other planes. Let me know if anything bothers you!'

'Do I have to do something?' She waggled her fingers. She could hardly bend them in Chip's gauntlets.

I laughed. 'Don't worry – you're just here to be a third bod. But if we come under fire, *get out of the turret*. The rear gunner sticks out like a sore thumb, and you'll be a sitting duck. Silver's having a quiet word about you with Ignacy. He and Derfel will be flying right behind us, and they'll cover you. I've got a gun of my own up front. You make sure you keep your head down.'

I'd just have to stay high if we ran into anti-aircraft fire – or low if we met an enemy plane. I couldn't risk getting shot up with Louisa in the back.

I think she knew that.

'You can still change your mind,' I said quietly. 'It's five minutes till engine start.'

'Rules are made to be broken,' she said. 'I'm not going to change my mind.'

Part Four

Aces

.- -.-. . ...

Louisa:

This time I hadn't put a sixpence in the ceiling – or even my secret penny. I didn't let myself think about it. I was not a fool-fool country gal.

The engines roared and the Blenheim bumped over the airfield. I couldn't see the take-off, but I knew when we left the ground because the jouncing stopped. I wrestled myself up into the clear Perspex gunner's turret. There wasn't any point worrying about *anything* for the next few hours, and the beauty of the sea and sky in silver moonlight and blue clouds was like a fairy world, a dream world. I was amazed by the cold night sky, the clouds filled with luminous light and shadow as we rose through them, the full moon dipping in and out of view, stars frozen still overhead. I wasn't afraid of anything.

Jamie's laughing voice came over the intercom.

'Rear gunner, you're making a lot of noise. Keep it down.'

I was humming *Rhapsody in Blue*. Just the way Mummy used to hum without thinking about it! The sky was *wonderful*.

And the cold – the *cold*! It was *unreal*. Even after three years in England, I was not ready for this kind of cold. After ten minutes I had to grip the sides of the turret to stop my body from shuddering. My toes and fingers began to ache. Frost began to fur the inside of the plane – all the struts and rivets and wires grew velvety white coats. When I breathed, the inside of my mask was slick with a thin layer of ice. The Perspex near my head became foggy, froze, and fogged again.

I kicked my feet and clapped my gauntleted hands to warm them up. Jamie and Silver had both given me their extra socks. I was bundled up with heated Ever-Hot bags. What could anyone do if I complained? I *couldn't* complain. We were in the sky over the North Sea.

Now and then Silver gave Jamie a heading or a height. Through the crackle and fuzz of the headset I could hear people talking in the other B-Flight planes. Nobody was singing in German or sending coded messages. The cold, beautiful sky was quiet in its garment of clouds and moonlight.

I don't know how long we'd been flying, but after a bit I wasn't getting moments of moonlight any more, and I could only see a star if I looked straight up. Then there were no stars, either. Clouds rose all around, blue and black and mysterious, more shadow than light.

Then there wasn't any light. It was all the close darkness of fog.

'All B-Flight aircraft, this is Pimms Leader,' Jamie called. 'Better turn back, lads. I don't like this cloud.'

I heard protests from the other airmen. Ignacy's Polish accent stood out. 'A good cloud is the Blenheim bomber's best friend!'

'You're not hedge-hopping over the Netherlands any more, and it isn't summer. Remember A-Flight in the fog in Shetland? We've got too many sprogs flying tonight – no offence, Stedman, but most of your lads are just as fresh as mine. North Sea ice and fog are no conditions for new pilots.'

'Righto, Pimms Leader,' called Adam Stedman, Madeira's leader, in agreement. 'But I'm not a sprog. I'm on instruments.'

'So am I. You and I can complete the op ourselves,' said Jamie. 'The rest of you head back now. Get beneath the cloud if you can; watch out for engine and airframe ice. And spread out. Don't try to stay together. I don't want any collisions.'

I couldn't see any horizon – it was all murk.

Jamie had said to let him know if anything bothered me, and something did.

'If you can fly on instruments, can't the Luftwaffe also?' I asked.

'Someone in a crate like ours could, yes,' he answered lightly. 'A bomber could. But they're unlikely to send any Messers out into this soup. Fighters have to see you to shoot at you. Don't worry.'

I tried not to worry. It was smooth flying. But if a mountain or another plane suddenly loomed in front of us, we'd never see it.

Jamie:

'Just checking we're on parallel headings,' Adam Stedman came in over the static. 'And that you're above me. I can't see you.'

'Affirm to both. And I can't see you either.'

'Give that de-icer another pump, would you?' Silver said. 'Those engines sound rough.'

'Aye. Wish we could get out of this muck.'

'Shall we try a different heading?'

'I don't want to run into Stedman,' I said. 'I'll go higher and see if we can clear the cloud. We'll give it fifteen minutes and reassess. I can't believe any Jerry pilot's out here in this frozen cotton wool trying to bomb a fishing boat. They can't see what's down there any more than we can.'

Ugh, Louisa could hear everything we said. She wasn't a worrier, but I was pretty sure she was worried.

'You all right back there, rear gunner?' I said over the intercom.

'A bit cold,' she admitted.

'Can you feel your toes?'

'Yes, and I wish I couldn't!'

Brave lass! 'No you don't. If they hurt they'll be all right.' I felt I owed her more of an apology. 'I'm sorry about the clouds. I wouldn't have invited you if I'd known you wouldn't see anything.'

'It was lovely before,' she said staunchly.

We flew on. The seconds crept by. It felt like an hour by the time fifteen minutes had ticked off. Well, we'd given it our best shot; we'd never find anything out here tonight, and neither would anyone else.

'That's it, Stedman, let's go,' I said. 'This is a washout. Hold your height. And take care.'

'See you back in Scotland,' crackled Stedman's voice.

'Heading two-zero-five,' said Silver.

I began to turn, eyes glued to the instrument panel. Poor Louisa probably couldn't tell which way was up. Outside was nothing but suffocating cloud and the faint, pale glow of the frosted airframe.

The flight home seemed longer than it should have been. It wasn't; I could tell by the clock. But I began to feel I was flying in circles, even though I *knew* I was holding a steady course.

'Aren't we there yet?' I asked Silver.

'Give it another minute on this heading,' he answered, and there was strain in his voice, too.

Time crawled on. The luminous clock dial told me so.

Louisa dared to ask, 'Are we lost?'

'No, we're not lost,' I assured her. 'But it's not fun to fly in.'

'Oh,' Louisa said. She didn't sound reassured.

'Heading one-nine-zero,' said Silver.

Louisa didn't say anything else. There wasn't anything she could do to help.

'Can't you give me a direct course?' I asked.

'No, in case we overshoot and fly into a mountain,' Silver answered. 'We don't want to descend below safety height. Not in cloud like this – one-nine-zero—'

I banked slowly to port.

Louisa's voice yelled in my ears.

'*Kingsleap Light!*'

I saw it too, far below, a brilliant green ray piercing the clouds for one second. I spiralled down over the lighthouse, knowing I wouldn't hit anything out at sea. The cloud was so low it sent fingers wreathing around the lighthouse tower. But we could see white foam against the black waves below, crashing on the Kingsleap Rocks.

Louisa's voice came urgently in my headset.

'"*Hold green light await fog!*"'

'What?' I asked automatically. '"Hold green light"?'

A second later I realized why the words were familiar.

HOLD GREEN LIGHT AWAIT FOG

'"Await fog"! It's an instruction!' Louisa cried. 'They always say "green light" when they mean Kingsleap – it means wait for a fog and then have another go at Windyedge!'

She'd cracked it.

'What the—?' Silver asked.

We were so close to Windyedge we ought to have seen the flashing beacon at the end of the runway. It wasn't on, because I hadn't called in yet. Presumably it was on earlier, when the rest of B-Flight came back. I couldn't see the sea cliffs. If I left the lighthouse I would have to climb into fog to be sure I didn't hit them.

But an enemy bomber wouldn't have to worry about hitting the cliffs if he oriented himself by the lighthouse and stayed high as he came in over the airfield.

'There may be a Luftwaffe bandit heading this way,' I said to Silver. 'We'd better do a bit of a patrol. There's plenty of fuel left. If anyone asks, we'll give credit to our ace wireless operator overhearing enemy transmissions.'

I called Adam Stedman to join me, and I called to the radio room on the ground and told them not to light up, and to man the anti-aircraft guns. Finally, for Louisa's benefit, I said, 'Hold on back there. Could be a false alarm …'

Adam came rumbling out of the clouds and flew right round the base of the lighthouse, making sure we could see each other. Then we both flew in long ellipses, one of us on each end of the curve, out to sea and back, peering into nothing.

It felt as though time had stopped still. Maybe we were already dead and this was purgatory, circling in the frozen dark forever, adjusting the angle of bank on the long turns, looking for an enemy that might not exist.

'*There!*'

Silver and Louisa yelled together.

It was a Junkers 88 Luftwaffe bomber, a hulking black shape caught in the green loom of the lighthouse beam.

'*Get out of that turret!*' I yelled at Louisa.

Louisa:

But I didn't – if I was going to die in an air battle I wanted to see it.

The Luftwaffe plane came out of the fog below us, a black shadow bathed in green light. I couldn't hear the German engines' tell-tale throb because of my headset and our own engines.

'I'm going in,' called Adam Stedman, and I saw sizzling red tracks through the air made by his firing guns.

The lighthouse beam turned. I couldn't see Adam's Blenheim or the German plane.

'Are you out?' Jamie called.

'Yes, on you go—'

We dived. *I* couldn't tell where the target was, but Silver barked directions to Jamie as if he could see in the dark.

The Blenheims took turns heckling the Luftwaffe bomber. When Jamie swooped down, all I could see was the frosted Perspex of the turret, glowing red as the inside of a pomegranate. I felt the dive and heard the guns in my stomach.

We swooped back up, avoiding the swinging lighthouse beam. Below us, red and blue light flickered as the Madeira Blenheim and the Ju-88 fired at each other. I saw a burst of orange flame, but it instantly went dark again.

'He's away!' came Adam Stedman's triumphant yell. 'I think I got an engine. He wasn't expecting an attack, was he!'

'Think he'll risk climbing into the cloud and bombing Windyedge on one engine?' Jamie asked sharply.

'Don't know – hope not – well, *I* bloody well wouldn't if it was me. It's a long way back to Norway on one iced-up engine.'

Over the sea cliffs I saw a warm yellow glow like a great big firefly in the dark. It was a window in the Limehouse whose blackout curtains were pulled back. The light blazed boldly into the war-torn night at two o'clock in the morning.

'*Bloody hell*,' cursed Adam Stedman. 'That'll tell them where to aim, if they're still flying.'

'Someone's scared of the dark,' Jamie muttered. 'I bet I know who.'

He radioed Windyedge and told them to ring the Limehouse and get Mrs Campbell to 'close her bloody curtains'.

Only the double bedrooms faced south-east. Mrs Campbell would be the first to get in trouble, but it wasn't her bedroom showing light. Miss Lind's room had the big bay window.

Jamie:

Stedman and I patrolled for another twenty minutes before we landed. But the bomber didn't come back, and finally I got Windyedge to light the beacon for us. There wasn't much gap between cloud and land, but we could see the flashing red light at the end of the runway.

It wasn't my best landing. But we'd done a hell of a night's work.

'I hope you haven't turned into a block of ice,' I called to Louisa as we bounced over the frozen field.

'I'm warm as toast!' she lied through chattering teeth.

Wonderful Louisa!

HOLD GREEN LIGHT AWAIT FOG

What if she hadn't been along, putting the puzzle pieces together?

We'd have landed, and the Ju-88 would have seen the beacon and followed us in.

All the B-Flight Blenheims would have been lined up on the ground beneath the bombs.

Ellen:

I spent most of the night worrying that Texas Sunshine would freeze to death in the back of the Tilly, so I sat freezing with him to make sure he didn't.

It was fearsome to watch the haar sea mist roll in and the moonlight disappear, and after the first planes came back, to spend a terrible hour waiting for the section leaders – and, *God pity her*, for Louisa. I heard the engines, Adam and Jamie flying round and round above us out at sea, as if it were too foggy for them to land. They circled most of another hour. No one outside the radio room knew what was happening. The beacon stayed dark, and Adam and Jamie stayed in the air.

Then came the battle over the lighthouse. You couldn't see anything but flashes in the cloud, like distant lightning.

And then, hurrah, *hurrah*, the beacon winking on, and the planes roaring in with their landing lights shining, safe as houses.

I fired up the Tilly and raced to meet Jamie's Blenheim trundling over the frozen grass. I got there before any other body and was halfway up the wing myself when the crew tumbled out. I hugged that rear gunner as tight as I could hug, and felt wee arms in deep padding hugging me back. *God be thanked*.

‘All right, lads?’ I asked, when we all had our feet on the ground.

‘Not dead yet,’ Jamie answered cheerfully. ‘Give us a smoke, lass.’

‘Got the shakes again?’

‘Don’t be silly. Takes more than a mite of cloud and a few squirts of machine-gun fire to make me lose my nerve.’

I lit him a cigarette anyway, and he gave it to Louisa, who I’m guessing had never smoked in her life. Clever lass passed it to Silver straightaway – she knew she’d blow her cover if she started choking and spluttering over her first cigarette. Silver took a drag, handed it back to Jamie, and went to open the van.

‘We’d better get this gunner to bed, don’t you think?’ he said. ‘His toes might be a bit cold, and he’s in no state for debriefing.’

‘Right you are!’ said Jamie.

Chip was still snoring as Jamie and Silver carried him into their barracks. Louisa stayed out of the way and rode home with me on the back of my bike as Jamie and Silver headed to ops to be grilled about their flight.

‘Give that Swiss milkmaid a bollocking for leaving her light on,’ was the last thing Jamie told us.

Louisa:

Scolding Elisabeth Lind for her blackout violation wasn’t the first thing on my mind as I limped up through the inky stairwell in the Limehouse. My feet had never been so cold in my entire life.

I stayed in the bathroom for nearly two hours, sitting on the chilly linoleum in the dark, rubbing my feet with a towel and crying as quietly as I could. The bathroom was safe; no one would come in during the night. The hot water was off till 7 a.m., and the loo was in its own closet next door. If I made no noise, no one would notice me.

I kept an ear out for Jane in case she got up, but by four o'clock in the morning I was so tired I thought I might be able to go to bed and sleep off the rest of the pain. I dragged myself out of the bathroom and started down the passage to Room Number Five.

As I crossed the landing at the top of the stairwell, I heard a noise in the hall below me like a trapdoor closing.

I panicked.

How had that woman got herself downstairs without me noticing? Not again!

The rest of the house was silent, still and dark. I knew for a fact Nancy Campbell finished counting in the landing Blenheims over three hours ago.

I put one burning foot down on the top step, then hesitated as I realised what the sound downstairs had been. There was a big medieval wooden bench in the hall with storage under the seat. The sound I'd heard was the lid closing. I didn't think Jane could stand and lift that lid herself.

Then I heard the door of the telephone cupboard open, and I could tell that someone was sweeping the beam of an electric torch about inside it. I waited, listening. The torch went dark; I couldn't hear footsteps, but a minute later the door of Mrs Campbell's office snicked open.

Whoever was down there was moving so furtively that I wondered if we were being burgled.

But the creeper seemed too familiar with the place to be a sneak thief – perhaps it was Nan checking windows after the blackout violation. The office door closed again. There wasn't any more light. The person was being very cautious.

Footsteps came treading deliberately up the staircase.

I took another step down and grabbed the rail, gasping with the shock of the sudden weight on my feet.

Whoever it was must have known now that I was there. If I tried to run back to the bathroom or my room, it would just look suspicious. Even ridiculous. So I sat down at the top of the stairs and waited.

Three-quarters of the way up, the stalker stopped and lit a match.

'Oh,' said Miss Lind when she saw me.

For a moment our eyes were level.

Hers were clear amber, like dark honey, in the match-light. She shook the match to put it out before it burned her fingers.

'Hello,' Miss Lind said softly.

'What are you looking for?' I asked.

'What are you doing up?' she fired back.

Her pretty vixen's face lit again as she struck another match and touched the flame to a cigarette. She vanished into the dark once more as the match went out. She took a quiet drag on her cigarette; the red glow of its burning tip wasn't enough to light her face.

'I was in the bathroom, not sneaking around in the dark!' I objected. 'And you had your light on before, which anyone could see from ten miles away,' I added in accusation. 'There was a Luftwaffe bomber out there!'

She made an alarmed noise like a cat's hiss.

'I heard the engines,' she whispered. 'I thought it was our own planes coming back! I knew the Blenheims were circling, and I thought they couldn't land because of the fog! I put on the light for *them*, not for the Luftwaffe – it's *terrible*, waiting on the ground and not being able to help!'

'It was jolly careless of you if you're working for Intelligence!'

'I know it. Cromwell chewed me out on the telephone and said he'd report me.' I heard her give a sharp, snorting sigh through her nose. '*I'm sorry.* But I thought if they could see my light, they'd know which way to come in. I *had* to do it.'

'I know,' I said. I understood why. 'You're Jamie's sister.'

She was silent for a moment.

I added quickly, 'Don't tell me your real name. I don't want to use it by accident.'

'I wasn't going to.' She drew on her cigarette. It glowed red and faded again before she asked, 'What gave me away?'

'Ellen told me.'

'Thank heavens you didn't work it out yourself,' she said. 'It's *hell* not being able to speak to Jamie in case someone notices the family resemblance. It's such a stupid charade, trying to keep the Germans happy, when they won't tell me anything anyway. Although I suppose it is good practice.'

Miss Lind lit another match. She cupped it in her hands, holding the cigarette between her fingers, and came the rest of the way up the stairs. She sat down beside me on the top step before the match went out. I felt her shuffling about in the dark as she reached into the pocket of her silk dressing gown. 'Would you like a cigarette?'

'No, thank you,' I said. 'What were you hunting for downstairs?'

She returned fire just the way she did earlier. 'How do you know my light was on?'

Oh, *bother.* If I'd been in bed when I was supposed to, with our own blackout curtains properly drawn, I shouldn't have been able to see her window.

'I'll tell you if you tell me,' I offered.

'You first, then,' she said.

'I went flying with Jamie.'

She took a deep breath.

'All right.'

She spoke practically in a whisper. I could feel her close beside me, a warm bundle of rustling inky silk in the inky dark.

'I told you Felix Baer doesn't trust me. I know you haven't been able to do anything about it – how could you, really? But I can't just come clean with Cromwell, either. I also have to answer to my department in Intelligence, and the German navigator – Dietrich Althammer – told me the most extraordinary thing today. He accused Cromwell of using a coding machine that Baer brought here in November. He says Baer had no authorisation to give it to Cromwell, and Althammer and Moritz want to convince Cromwell to turn it over to the correct authorities. My department. *Except* …'

She paused. I didn't say anything.

'Except Cromwell hasn't got it. Cromwell doesn't know anything about it. Yet the Germans think someone's using it.'

I kept my lips pressed together.

'The thing is, my department has been *expecting* this particular machine. The German Navy and Luftwaffe have used these things since the beginning of the war, since *before* the war, to generate code for the messages they send each other about their attack plans. Intelligence has an entire operation trying to crack the codes these machines generate, and they can't do it. Coastal Defence hears German wireless communications flying about *all the time*, but no one can decode any of it. We already know how their machines work. But if we could capture one and get the settings to go along with it, we'd have a chance of cracking their code. Not just in the North Sea. All over the Atlantic. One machine, and a few pages of paper.

'And Odysseus was supposed to bring us both,' she finished. 'But the paperwork was destroyed when the airfield here was bombed, and the machine never turned up.'

The paperwork was destroyed when Windyedge was bombed!

'Oh, crumbs,' I breathed. 'I didn't know – none of us knew.'

'Didn't know what?' Miss Lind asked carefully.

'That it was the only one!'

None of us realised how special it was. Not *really*.

'Does that mean—' She caught her breath.

'Cromwell doesn't have it,' she said. 'You have it. *You have it!*'

Her excited voice didn't get louder – it dwindled to a sharp, hissed whisper. '*Who's "us", anyway?*'

'Jamie and Ellen. And Jane.' I rushed to get the confession over with. 'Jamie picks up the code and Ellen drops it off here. I decode it with the settings Felix Baer left. Jane translates the German. Then we know where the U-boats will be.'

'*Settings!*' She laughed wildly. '*You have the settings!*'

'We copied the leaflets,' I whispered. 'I made copies before Jamie turned them in.'

'Proper little secret society!' she gasped. 'My God! Do you know how many scores of codebreakers are frantically trying to crack this technology?'

'No,' I answered, still whispering. 'How could we?'

Elisabeth Lind drew a shaky breath on her cigarette, tapped off the ash, and brushed it beneath the coconut matting on the stairs.

'Ellen said to give you the machine,' I admitted. 'It's – it's *contaminated*. We've run out of settings, and the Germans know we have it and they're laying a trap for our planes.'

'How in *blazes* do you know that?' she exclaimed.

'Felix Baer told me.'

'Of course he did.' She was breathless with excitement. 'I am most impressed.'

'I wanted to help,' I said, feeling idiotic.

'You did. You have.' She laughed again. '*You have. You are.* How were you to know there wasn't a stolen Enigma machine in every RAF base in Britain? *Jamie* might have guessed, but *you* weren't to know. At any rate—' Her cigarette glowed. 'At any rate, now we have one!'

'Shall I fetch it for you?' I asked. 'It's in Jane's wardrobe.'

'*Ah—!*' She hesitated. Then she said reluctantly, 'No. No, not just now, not at four in the morning. It's as safe there as anyplace, for the moment. It will take a bit of work to ship it to the proper Intelligence boffins. It would be jolly bad luck if another bomb dropped on it.' Her voice fell to a whisper again. 'But I would love to *see* it.'

'Come visit us tomorrow,' I invited.

Never had I been so glad to climb in over the foot of the bed in Room Number Five and curl up next to the old woman I was here to look after. Jane's soft, purring snore seemed like the quietest sound I'd ever heard. I was still cold and my feet still hurt, and my confession to Sergeant Elisabeth Lind hadn't untangled the knots in my stomach. I didn't know what *Falle Enigma* was going to be; the German prisoners were still locked in the limekilns; the Luftwaffe bombers would come back.

But as I lay in the dark next to Jane I still felt sure I was in the safest place in the house.

I slept nearly till permitted hours the next day, and woke to find Jane pottering about in one of her fur coats. I sat up in bed. It was just gone eleven o'clock in the morning; the gas fire glowed warmly, and the windows gleamed with a dull, pale light I'd never seen before.

'It's snowing,' Jane said. 'It has been coming down all morning. Nancy lit our fire early, entirely for your benefit, I believe, and she has even brought up a pot of tea. She says the snow is halfway to her knees already! When did you come in?'

'Snowing!' I exclaimed, scrambling for the window. '*Snowing!*'

I'd never seen proper snow. In London we got sleet or sometimes sooty slush. The high moors around Windyedge had been white all winter, but this was the first picture-postcard snow I'd ever seen up close. I threw the window open and leaned into the sill over the books.

'It *smells* different!'

I scooped snow off the sill and licked it. A flurry of wet flakes gusted into my face and the Scotch pines sighed.

'It *sounds* different!'

Jane laughed at me. 'Shut the window,' she said. 'The fire is on.'

'Can the Blenheims fly in snow?' I exclaimed.

'I shouldn't think so,' said Jane.

'I told Miss Lind about the Enigma machine,' I confessed.

Elisabeth Lind came in for five minutes, carefully avoiding Nancy Campbell. She was so excited it made her *weep*. She gave a little sob as she opened the shining wooden lid of the cipher machine, and another as she pressed a key and a lamp came on.

'I've never touched one,' she whispered. 'Show me how the code works.'

I opened my exercise book to the first message I'd decoded, and showed her.

'It's so *beautiful*,' she said. 'Don't call it contaminated just because they want to trick you. It's the purest piece of machinery I've ever seen. It has to do what it's told.'

I know it sounds mad, but I knew what she meant.

'When the snow is gone I shall have to send it away,' she said wistfully. 'I'm a bit envious of you getting to *really use* it.'

The 648 Squadron airmen spent the day digging out Blenheims and clearing the runway, and the ground crew paraded up the lane to clear it as far as the main road. Ellen was busy hauling spades and soldiers; the Tilly rattled on tyres wound up in chains. I kept running to the window to try to see what was going on, and just before it got dark Jane insisted I run outside. She sat in the bar where Mrs Campbell could keep an eye on her, while I borrowed Mrs Campbell's boots again and went down to the harbour to look at the snow falling on the cliffs and in the sea. My feet seemed back to normal, thank goodness.

Low gold winter sunlight streamed through the south-east windows when I woke up the next morning, lighting corners of the room and casting shadows behind the furniture. The radio played while Jane poked about in the top dresser drawers, hunting for something. I jumped up to help.

'Oh, just a clean handkerchief!' she told me. 'I can't find a single one.'

'I washed them all yesterday. They're on the drying rack by the bathtub. I'll fetch one – but it won't be ironed yet, you know! Do sit down – I don't like to leave you on your feet.'

'I can manage being on my feet in this room by myself perfectly well, as you know.'

'All the same!'

I made her sit. I darted down the passage, stepped into the bathroom, and switched on the light.

The whole world seemed to explode.

It was a roar louder than being inside a Blenheim in the air, louder than standing next to a Messerschmitt 109 starting its engines. It was an explosion of thunder so suffocating I couldn't hear my own shriek. The light overhead flickered out. The house shook. The floor beneath my feet shook. All I could think was that it was an earthquake, as once happened when Mummy and I were hanging out washing in our Kingston garden and we were both knocked off our feet – nothing else I ever felt could make a house tremble. I pressed my back against the bathroom wall, waiting for the earth to stop moving.

When the world set itself aright, I tore back to Room Five where I'd left Jane sitting in her nightgown listening to *Music While You Work* on the wireless.

The radio was dead and she was lying on the floor.

She had jumped up when the thundering started. The shaking hadn't knocked her over – it just startled her so much she lost her balance.

She was doubled over between the armchair and the bed, whimpering. She had taken all her weight on her right hand as she threw it out ahead of her to break her fall.

It was as if she'd stepped into a time machine and come out twenty years older.

She cried and sobbed. She didn't cooperate when I tried to help her sit up. I coaxed and pleaded and finally scolded. That made her whimper in a new and different way, whiny and snivelling, which shocked me. Finally I managed to make her roll on to her side – and gaped in horror when I saw that the last three fingers of her right hand were bent sideways.

But it was her wrist, not her fingers, that she grabbed at

with her other hand. She cradled the hurt hand against her chest, moaning. I thought she'd broken her arm.

I was either going to have to leave her to get help, or yell my lungs out to make someone hear me.

'Help! *Help! Ellen! Phyllis! Nan!*'

I'd left our door open, and Elisabeth Lind came flying into the dusty sunlight of our room wearing nothing but a fancy French silk bra and knickers, and one very ordinary darned wool stocking that was part of her WAAF uniform. She'd been getting dressed. She was not the least bit embarrassed. She knew what to do.

'Stop moving her about,' she told me sharply. 'Mrs Warner, can you hear me? Did you hit your head? No? Ah, thank goodness—'

'My wrist – *mein Ärm ist gebrochen* – ah—'

'Shh – no German.'

With Miss Lind on one side and me on the other, we helped Jane to sit. She moaned again as Miss Lind examined her hand. Her twisted fingers were horrible.

'I don't think these are broken,' Miss Lind said cheerfully. 'The same thing happened to one of my brothers, well very nearly, and when we rushed him to the doctor's it turned out they were only dislocated. May I?'

I could not look. I held Jane tightly, and Sergeant Elisabeth Lind straightened those fingers out all by herself.

'Can you bend them?' she asked kindly, and Jane could, a little. 'Good. And the wrist – can you move it?'

Miss Lind held her own hand palm to palm against Jane's, their fingers interlocked. She rocked Jane's hand gently back and forth and side to side.

'I don't think you've broken a thing, Mrs Warner,' said Miss Lind. 'I think the wrist is just a sprain. But it will all hurt a good deal while everything mends. We ought to bind these fingers together and wrap up your wrist.'

'But I won't be able—' Jane sobbed.

And I thought of a hundred things she would not be able to do, just without those three fingers, never mind her wrist. Playing piano duets was the least of it. She wouldn't be able to dress herself; go to the toilet; put on shoes; *use her sticks*. She wouldn't be able to walk independently, or sit down on her own, or stand up again.

'How shall we get you off the floor?' Miss Lind mused. 'I don't think we can lift you.'

'If I put this arm around Louisa's shoulder and you help on the other side, I think we can manage,' Jane whispered.

I was so relieved to hear her speaking sensible English without tears that I kissed her. She was still in pain, unsteady, but no longer a defeated, whimpering old woman.

'What happened?' I asked Miss Lind. 'I thought it was an earthquake!'

'It was a bomb,' said Elisabeth Lind in a low voice. 'They very nearly got us that time.'

'Yes they did,' I answered accusingly. 'They know just where we are. Maybe they will stop if they think it was a direct hit.'

She flushed and changed the subject. 'Last time I was caught in an air raid I had my clothes on! This is most embarrassing.' She snapped the top of her one stocking against her thigh.

'On the contrary,' whispered Jane. 'You always look lovely.'

It was true, Miss Lind was *annoyingly* lovely, even wearing nothing but underthings and one darned stocking, her hair flying out of its plait like an untidy cloud of corn-coloured candy floss. Her make-up never seemed to smear – I wondered if she slept in it. She didn't even look *cold*. She jumped up and began scavenging for something to wrap up Jane's fingers and wrist.

I kissed Jane's silver-white hair again. She was recovered enough to be herself – I could tell. Fighting. Thinking.

But my job had just become a hundred times more difficult.

Ellen:

I was downstairs in uniform and eating porridge when the bomb hit. The glasses rattled. My bowl slid and smashed on the flagstones. Nancy gave a wail and disappeared for a moment below the counter on the other side of the bar.

By the time the roaring stopped and I'd dived behind the bar to haul Nan to her feet and try to shut her skriking, Nobby Fergusson was pounding on the door – he'd seen the bomb fall and thought it hit the Limehouse. I left him with Nan and ran upstairs to Jane and Louisa.

There stood Sergeant Lind in her naughty French underthings and one stocking. I let out a howl of laughter and choked on it one second later when I spied Louisa on the floor with Jane.

'That was a Luftwaffe Junkers 88 with a fighter escort of Me-110s,' I told them, passing on what Nobby told me. 'They came straight here and scarpered off again, whilst our lot are stuck on the ground clearing snow, and *one* of our lads, not saying *who*, never made it out of bed yesterday. And Deeside is snowed in too. Not a single RAF plane in the sky to chase off the Jerries, and they *still missed the airfield*!'

'They might be aiming for something else,' Louisa said quietly.

'Mrs Warner needs a bandage,' Sergeant Lind said. 'She's twisted her wrist and dislocated her fingers.'

'I'll fetch Nan's first-aid kit. Are you hurt, Louisa?'

Louisa shook her head.

'They got the hill above the limekilns,' I went on. 'If they'd waited a tenth of a second longer it would have hit this house.'

Elisabeth Lind went to get dressed, but Louisa didn't want to leave Jane. We bound up the old woman's wrist and fingers, and pulled her off the floor and pushed her into the big stuffed armchair. But we couldn't put clothes on her and there was no way to get her downstairs unless someone carried her.

The bomb that missed the Limehouse did not fall harmlessly. You could tell that by leaning from Louisa's window. There were sirens and shouts, and a scraping and pounding noise of men using spades and pickaxes against rock. The trees on the hill were aflame, and there came a delicious smell of burning pine, even through the window glass.

'Louisa, you *must* go find out what's happening!' Jane told her.

'But you can't get up! Supposing the house is on fire!'

Jane snapped at her, 'Goodness, girl, you'd better find out if it is, hadn't you!'

Louisa and I both jumped. We'd neither one of us ever heard her speak so sharply.

'You can get about and I can't,' Jane scolded. 'Stop dithering and earn your keep.'

Louisa looked as if she'd laugh and cry all at once.

'Bring me some coffee if the house isn't on fire,' Jane added in a gentler voice. 'I will hold the fort, as they say.'

In the public bar, soldiers and firemen and the village Home Guard were running in and out and shouting to one another. The house did not look as if it were on the brink of falling down or burning up, but it was dark as a well because of the electricity being out. Nan rushed about boiling kettles and supplying folk with towels and blankets through the back door.

'What's happened?' I exclaimed.

'The limekilns have collapsed,' Nan answered grimly. 'Those Jerry prisoners are trapped. Maybe worse.'

'Oh *no*!' Louisa cried.

Nan gave her a strange look.

'RAF Windyedge sent their fire crew across. They'll dig 'em out,' Nan said. 'The snow's melting fast, and if they clear the runway I think the lads will be flying tonight.'

'I ken, I've got to hike back to the airfield in case they need me in the Tilly,' I said. 'Phyllis went before the bomb fell. Where's Sergeant Lind?'

Nan shrugged. 'Wing Commander Cromwell popped in and nabbed her so she can translate when they dig out the Jerries. There's that much going on, I'm as glad not to have the house full of guests the day. Louisa, could you take this can of porridge out—'

'I'll do it, Mrs Campbell,' I interrupted. 'Louisa has to stay with Mrs Warner. She tumbled over when the bomb hit and she's hurt her arm. She can't use her sticks.'

Nan pushed her wispy black hair away from her face and rubbed her eyes.

'Whisht, I never believed I'd see this day,' she muttered, and slammed a full kettle on the hob. The blue flame of the gas burner gave a merry glow – God be thanked, the gas mains weren't damaged. 'Is she all right?' Nan asked. 'Does she need the doctor?'

As a Traveller I don't believe I ever wanted a doctor in all my years, but after I'd seen one or two airmen fly in with punctured lungs after an op, I respected medical folk more than I did as a wee lassie. Aye, Jane ought to see a doctor – but it could probably wait until the blaze in the nearby trees had been put out, and the trapped men rescued.

Louisa thought the same. 'She'll do for the moment,' she said. 'I'll look after her just now.'

Louisa:

Jane said she wanted coffee.

I tiptoed around the kitchen, trying not to get in Mrs Campbell's way as I put together a tray. I couldn't bear to think of what was happening in the limekilns; it took every bit of sense I had in me not to pull on Mrs Campbell's wellie boots again and rush outside. I carried Jane's tray upstairs. We couldn't listen to the radio, but we heard the men digging.

Early in the afternoon, the emergency workers uncovered Eberhard Moritz, and he was all right. They moved him to the aerodrome and kept digging. At the same time, men were also mending the underground electric cables that powered the Limehouse. I found this out from Morag Torrie, who brought us tea and sandwiches and some arnica tincture to rub on Jane's hurt hand.

'Mrs Campbell's popped down to the village,' Morag said. 'There were so many folk in this morning, with the rescue, that she's out of milk and tea and cheese. I don't think she'll get any at the shop – she's not got the extra ration tickets and is cross about it. You've got the last of the bread. I'm off work now so I'll lock up, as the other girls are at the air base and you're alone here. Is Mrs Warner warm enough? Oh, the fire's on and it's not three o'clock yet. Does Mrs Campbell know?'

We both looked at the fire. I noticed that the meter had about an hour to go before it would need another shilling.

'She said to put it on for Mrs Warner, as she's hurt and can't come downstairs,' I said.

'Mrs Campbell is a very generous woman underneath,' said Morag stoutly. 'She'll let herself in, but don't open up to that emergency crew, because there isn't anything else to feed them!'

'You can count on us to hold the fort,' Jane repeated, as if it hadn't taken her twenty minutes to get to the toilet and back, hobbling with me for support and hanging on me with her bad arm over my shoulder while she wiped with her good one.

So Morag went and we held the fort.

Holding the fort meant trying to read aloud to Jane and stopping every ten minutes to stick my head out the window and try to work out if anything new had happened. We were both wildly restless. After an hour Jane exclaimed, 'This will never do! Louisa, why don't you bring up the gramophone? We can have a concert.'

So I went to get it.

Downstairs was dark. Even in daytime the unlit hall was gloomy, because it faced north-west and had only the one tall, narrow window letting in light opposite the landing at the top of the stairs. The public bar was gloomy too just now, without the fire burning or the lamp lit. I felt like an intruder. I hadn't ever been there during the day without people about.

I chose a stack of five record albums and laid them on an empty table to come back for. I took the gramophone up to Jane, set it on the floor between her and the bed where she could reach it, and came back down for the records.

As I returned to the shadowy front hall with my arms full, I heard footsteps above me shuffling along the passage from the back of the house.

My heart did its too-familiar somersault of guilt and fear. Had Jane managed to get to her feet and tried to reach the loo without my help? If she was using just one stick and fell again, wouldn't she likely try to catch herself with her empty hand – the hurt one?

I'd only been gone a *minute*!

I put down the records to free my arms so I could hold up Jane if she needed it.

Just as I started to climb the stairs, a young man in a flight suit crossed the landing above me and vanished down the dim passage.

I didn't see who it was, though I didn't think it was Jamie; it looked like a bigger man. But I wasn't afraid – there were airmen all over Windyedge. How had he got in, whoever he was? Morag had locked the door behind her. Had he been here *all afternoon*, since before Nan Campbell left the house?

I went up the stairs after him.

By the time I got to the landing, he'd reached Room Five. I'd left the door open, to make the return trip easier, expecting my arms to be full of records. I heard the airman gently close the door behind him.

I followed him down the passage and stood outside my own shut door, listening.

Jane was speaking calm, matter-of-fact German.

She didn't sound frightened. She sounded perfectly at ease – interested. Pleasant. *Amused*.

The man answered her in German.

His voice was hoarse and ragged, a person at the end of his strength and patience. The polite way he spoke to Jane was familiar, and I remembered how the navigator Dietrich Althammer had bent towards her so she could hear him, as if she were his own granny.

Althammer was the one Felix Baer didn't trust, the one he'd tried to *kill*, just as they were coming in to land, when Althammer had least expected it.

I heard him say a word I understood, and Jane repeated it.

Enigma.

He was looking for the coding machine.

I didn't know what to do. If I went in, wouldn't Jane and I both be trapped? One smallish fifteen-year-old girl and one tottering eighty-two-year-old woman with a sprained wrist were not going to overpower a strong young airman, even if he had been locked up underground for a week.

His footsteps crossed the room as he made for the door.

I fled down the passage and through the first doorway I came to that was standing open – the loo.

I darted behind the open door. *Better not to try to close it …* Was I breathing too loudly, and why was he taking so long?

I *forced* myself to take slow, deep breaths. He might hear me if I panted, and I wouldn't be able to hear him. I listened, trying to think of a sensible thing to do—

And I heard one of Jane's sticks tapping.

The German airman was escorting her down the passage. She must have asked for help to reach the toilet. And, since she seemed to be a friendly, cooperative, ancient German native, he offered his strong arm for support. He coaxed her in German, and I heard her grateful response. She struggled through the doorway into the loo on her own.

Jane closed the door and saw me standing in the dim light cast through the arrow-slit window below the high-up water tank. She raised her bandaged hand to her lips to warn me to be quiet.

We heard the airman go downstairs. I slipped my arm around Jane's waist so she didn't have to put all her weight on one stick.

'How did he get in?' Jane whispered.

'It must have been the kitchen door!' Morag said she would lock up, but she might have only done the front. He could have come in any time that day. No one would have questioned anybody in a flight suit, even if they'd noticed him. 'He must have used the service stairs at the back. Is it Althammer – the navigator? What does he want?'

'He's looking for the coding machine. I played dumb, but he'll try to find it now.'

'Perhaps *that's* what Baer meant by a trap,' I gasped. 'A trap for the machine itself! If the Luftwaffe bombers can't destroy it from the air, perhaps they sent Althammer to try to destroy it on the ground!'

My voice had risen.

'Shhh,' Jane hushed. 'I thought of that.'

'*What should I do?*'

'Wait,' said Jane. 'Just wait. Let him hunt. He might not find it. He's bound to start with our room when he returns upstairs, but he'll rush, because he knows I'm going back there.' She paused, tilting her head to favour her left ear, listening. 'I pushed the gramophone under the bed. He's likely to look there first, and as it's in its case, he might think it's the cipher machine and just grab it and run.'

The house was silent around us. The only noise came from outside.

'Hush,' Jane repeated. 'All we need do is wait.'

Once more, I had that false and foolish feeling that with her I was in the safest place in the house.

Suddenly, and irrelevantly, I remembered that the meter had run out and our gas fire must have cut off by now.

★

We heard the German airman come upstairs, and Jane was right – he went straight back to Room Number Five. We heard him close the door. But there was still so much muffled banging and shouting outside that we couldn't tell what he was doing.

Jane whispered urgently, 'I must sit. I suppose there's only the throne. Help me—' It was easier lowering her than before, and we didn't have to fuss with her clothes. 'Do you think you could open the window, Louisa?'

The narrow glass in the arrow slit was solid – there wasn't any latch. 'It doesn't open,' I said.

'You'd better break it, then.'

I stared at her.

'Why?'

'I think we should have some fresh air.'

'But!'

'Use my stick,' she told me.

'*Whatever will Mrs Campbell say!*'

'We need fresh air,' Jane insisted, and then confessed softly, 'I forgot to turn off the gas tap when the fire went out.'

'The gas doesn't come back on until you put in another shilling,' I told her.

'But I did,' she admitted. 'I put in a shilling just before I asked that young man to help me out here.'

'Did you light the fire again?'

'No,' she whispered. 'I couldn't reach. I didn't want to ask him to do it …'

'But that means he's been in there with the gas leaking full on for half an hour!'

We stared at each other.

'Break the window,' Jane told me.

And I did.

I took long breaths of fresh air before I set out to do the awful things that only I could do.

You have to breathe quite a bit of coal gas before it kills you. It makes you sleepy – people who die of it usually die in their sleep. I didn't *feel* like I was going to fall over in a dead faint, but I didn't know how much gas was in the passage, or how much I'd already breathed, or how much more I might have to breathe before I managed to open the window in our room, turn off the gas tap, and get out again. Or what I would do if Dietrich Althammer was perfectly all right and ready for a battle.

The only thing I was sure of was that I had to stop any more gas leaking into the Limehouse.

I crept to the closed door of Room Number Five and listened to the terrible stillness on the other side. I thought of my gas mask, chucked under the bed out of the way after the journey from Liverpool. It couldn't help me now, and the German navigator would not have known it was there.

I went in.

He'd worked hard before the fumes overcame him. He'd tipped the mattress off the bed and up against the wall, and threw aside Jane's chair and the lamp and table to get to the gramophone in its shining wooden case.

He didn't even open it. He used my flute case to pound the gramophone into a mangled wreck of beaten metal and splintered wood. I couldn't tell if he'd done it out of fury, just because it wasn't what he was looking for, or if Dietrich Althammer really thought, at least before he started, that its polished lid hid the stolen Enigma machine.

Dietrich Althammer also lay in a crumpled heap next to the hearth, his mouth open and his eyelids half shut. I didn't think he was breathing, but I didn't want to get close enough to make sure.

I had to step over his body to reach the gas tap.

Biting back sobs, I climbed over the fallen standard lamp to throw open a window. The radio sprang suddenly into life, right in the middle of a tune, as the electricity came back on.

It was 'The Spitfire Song' again.

I wrenched open the wardrobe. The other glowing box sat there nestled safe and sound among the furs and tropical silks. I grabbed the rotors and snatched up the wooden case in both arms as if I were rescuing a baby from a burning building, and fled from the room.

Elisabeth Lind volunteered to move into a smaller room and give Mrs Campbell's best double to me and Jane, so we didn't have to sleep in Room Five that night.

This makes no sense at all, but after I crawled into bed next to Jane as usual, I no longer felt safe.

She was an eighty-two-year-old woman with a sprained wrist and knees that did not bend, and she had, in cold blood and full awareness, killed a young man ten hours earlier.

I know she did it to protect me. I *think* she did it to

protect me. I don't know if she could have done anything else. Dietrich Althammer was an enemy soldier. He was violent and frightening and dangerous – there wasn't any question about that now. But no matter how I danced around the facts and made excuses for her, a man who was alive that morning was dead that night, and Jane had done it.

I wondered if she had done it before.

I lay awake beside this familiar stranger, wondering, and counted the Blenheim bombers as they roared out to sea under the waning moon, all six of B-Flight's aircraft, one after another.

It was just after midnight on Valentine's Day. *XIV II*.

I must have fallen asleep at last, because I didn't hear any of them come back.

Jamie:

The joke was, as the Valentine's Day moon came round, that of course we weren't sent to Utsira. No one was sent there – no one but me had seen that baited message about mythical U-boats.

'This'll remind you of last year's Norwegian Campaign, if any of you were around for that,' Cromwell told us. All of us except Bill Yorke shook our heads; none of the rest of us had been operational a year ago. Ignacy and Derfel and Silver and I had fought in the Battle of Britain last summer, but we'd only been flying in combat for seven months. Wing Commander Cromwell sighed and cleared his throat.

'You're being sent on another retribution mission. You'll be targeting Stavanger, the Norwegian aerodrome they're using to get at Windyedge, and Coastal Command would like you to take flash-bomb photographs of the new field at Lista while you're at it. A-Flight will attack Stavanger, and B-Flight will move on Lista again. We want to do damage on the ground – exactly what they're doing here. Get in and out quick as you can and keep away from the anti-aircraft artillery.'

It was a routine op. It wouldn't be safe. But it wasn't unreasonable.

Cromwell hadn't asked us to do anything unreasonable since – since mid-December? Since he confined me to barracks for getting the planes out of Windyedge when it first got bombed. And he'd complimented me at the same time for doing a good job. He sighed and barked and grumbled at me, and I argued with him. But now he *listened*.

For a few seconds I was light-headed with relief that I wasn't leading anyone to Utsira – and a moment later my stomach was in knots with a new anxiety.

I couldn't let A-Flight take the op to Stavanger. That part of Norway is all peninsulas and islands and inlets, and Stavanger to Utsira is less than forty miles in a straight line, about ten minutes in a Blenheim flying at cruise speed.

'Permission to speak, sir?'

Cromwell sighed again.

'What is it this time, Beaufort-Stuart?'

'They'll expect a raid, after so many attacks here, won't they? Stavanger's a huge operation,' I pointed out. 'They'll be ready. But Lista will be a piece of cake – it's still under construction. And who has more combat experience, A-Flight or B-Flight?'

I knew that just by our U-boat score, B-Flight would win that contest hands down. For all our scrapping on the ground, we flew together confidently now.

'Let me guess what you're trying to say, Beaufort-Stuart,' Cromwell rumbled. 'You're suggesting that B-Flight make the Stavanger run, while A-Flight takes on Lista?'

Then my lads astounded me.

They backed me up.

'I'm in,' said Adam Stedman. 'Madeira Section is ready for a fight. Stavanger will be a tougher op than Lista, but Beaufort-Stuart's always one step ahead of the Jerries.'

'Yes, he has a nose for them,' Derfel Cledwyn said.

'Scotty is careful, too,' put in Ignacy Mazur. 'Though we do not always agree!'

'He's usually right, though,' said Chip.

Bill Yorke snorted. But he said, 'I'm in.'

'I didn't think I'd last a week when I joined 648 Squadron,' said Harry Morrow. 'At least now I know what we're up against. Scotty's a jolly good flight leader. I'm in.'

Up and down the operations room, Pimms and Madeira claimed the Stavanger assignment for B-Flight.

I was a bit stunned.

Silver nudged me in the ribs. 'You're a jolly good flight leader.'

'Stow it, mate,' I muttered. 'Behind every good flight leader …'

He held up his hands: still in one piece.

We knew that every single op might end in nothing but death. But this time I felt sure no one was going into it blindly. We were doing it together.

'No heroics with Messerschmitts,' I reminded them.

'Keep us well south of Utsira,' I told Silver.

We flew north along the Scottish coast, past Aberdeen and RAF Deeside, on past Peterhead and Fraserburgh. Out to port, looking over my gauntleted left hand on the control yoke, I could see moorland blanketed with snow, gleaming like icing sugar beneath the rising moon. Scotland lay quiet and still and dangerously cold. I wished Louisa could see it, and then I was glad she couldn't, was glad she wasn't there.

Off Fraserburgh we headed north-east out to sea. We flew at fifteen thousand feet to make the most of our speed, then came down to low level to avoid being tracked. Somewhere in the sky, A-Flight's leader, Rob Lucknow, called over the radio on his way to Lista. 'Hullo, Flight Lieutenant Beaufort-Stuart!'

'It's a beautiful night for flying!' I told him, as if we were larking about.

'Enjoy it while you have the chance!'

We were over Norway in a little more than an hour.

Norway was as bright with snow and moonlight as Scotland, the rocky islets spread out in black and silver. It felt strangely still, nothing moving anywhere, no anti-aircraft guns firing. We passed low over the aerodrome at Stavanger and dumped our bombs on their runway and hangars. No one fired a single shot at us. There was nothing to hear but the hum of our own engines, and the explosions beneath us in the dark.

'Circle over the docks and dump whatever's left, and let's get out of here,' I said.

'Too right,' called Adam Stedman. 'This place is giving me the heebie-jeebies.'

We knew there was only one reason they weren't firing.

There must be Luftwaffe night fighters patrolling – probably not more than ten minutes away, waiting for us to turn up at Utsira hoping to bag another submarine. The gunners on the ground didn't want to hit their own planes, so they couldn't fire at us, either.

We detonated another load over the shipyard.

I climbed away, scanning the moonlit sky for dark wings, holding my breath. We were high now – we'd just about got away with it.

'Cup of tea, Jamie?' said Silver, handing me the steaming cap of the thermos flask. I took it and raised it to my mouth.

I'd been expecting an attack for the last half an hour; we all expected it, but none of us saw it coming. The first I knew there were Me-110s in the sky with us was when I saw one of Adam Stedman's engines explode into flame beyond our starboard wingtip.

I banked automatically away and got a faceful of hot tea at the same time. Silver caught the cup as I dropped it, spluttering and cursing, and a bloody good thing he did, or it would have been rolling around jamming the rudder pedals. I saw Stedman's Blenheim screaming downhill as he dived in a desperate attempt to put the fire out, and I saw the black shape of the Messerschmitt 110 dive after him, then nothing but flames below.

The sky was suddenly full of the black wings of night fighters. Someone must have called them home. And of course they hadn't had far to go.

When you're there, fighting, it's hard to keep track of anyone but your own crew. People hare off out to sea to get away, or inland to make a crash landing, or down to treetop level to try to hide, or up to the heavens to get a better shot. And when a plane is in a spiral dive engulfed in flames, you often can't tell if it's one of your own or the enemy's. So a lot of my impression of that battle is based on what my crew was yelling into my earphones at the time. Silver had his head in the freezing gale out the open starboard window panel, barking instructions about which way I should turn; Chip gave us an irrepressible non-stop narrative from the gunner's turret like an auctioneer or a horse-race announcer.

'There goes another Messer, *hot damn*! Doesn't that make us official aces? I don't know who got that one – we're definitely down two Blenheims but I can't tell who's still flying. Pull her up five degrees, would you, cap'n, I don't want to shoot our tail off! Thank you – just a mo—' That was followed by the rattle of his gun. 'Aw, missed. Turn right, *turn right*—'

'STARBOARD!' roared Silver, and I threw the Blenheim into such a steep turn that the whole machine shuddered, and I dived to avoid tumbling into a stall. Another plane screamed past my left ear and soared away before I'd straightened the wings.

'Gonna try again,' Chip blethered on. 'Here he comes, a little higher—' Another rattle of gunfire and a whoop of triumph. He yelled, 'GOT YOU, TAKE THAT, YOU SON OF A—'

Something hit the turret so hard it knocked my head forward into the controls. I swam in sparkling blackness for a moment and when I came to, Silver was on his feet leaning over my shoulder desperately hanging on to the control yoke. An icy wind howled through the broken turret.

'I've got her,' I gasped.

'You're getting bloody low,' Silver gasped back. 'Never thought I'd try to fly a plane again—'

'Nice work, mate,' I croaked, levelling out.

'Cheers.'

We didn't say anything about Chip. There wasn't anything to say.

Silver pointed ahead of us, northward.

A flotilla of German battleships were cruising full tilt along the craggy coast, black against the silver sea. They wouldn't reach us for another ten minutes, but they were trying their damnedest not to miss out on the action.

That's what we would have found waiting for us if we'd gone to Utsira – a squadron of Messerschmitts above and a load of anti-aircraft fire below.

In the end, it was swings and roundabouts, really.

Suddenly Ignacy's voice crackled into life through my headset.

'I'm on one engine and Taff is bleeding all over the cockpit. Cover me, Pimms Leader, I'm going to get those German bastards if it kills me. Keep the Messers off my tail. I'm going to sink a couple of those ships.'

'There he is,' Silver said, pointing. 'Two o'clock high. Get behind him so nobody can sneak up on him, and I'll climb back and see if the rear gun will still fire in case someone comes after us.'

Everything else still worked. I had both my engines and all my control surfaces – only the rear turret dome had been shattered. I tore my mind away from Silver in the back, and what he'd have to deal with before he could climb into the rear gunner's seat. I focused on Ignacy and Derfel and Bill Yorke in the plane ahead of me.

We sped to meet the battleships. Silver and I had dropped our bombs over Stavanger a lifetime ago. I wondered, briefly and uneasily, why Ignacy hadn't already got rid of his. Or if he had, how he was planning to get through the flak and sink a battleship with the slow-firing guns in the nose of the Blenheim.

'Pimms and Madeira aircraft,' I called. 'Anyone about?'

Silence.

I hadn't even noticed the Australian schoolboys going down.

'Just us,' Ignacy answered. 'Thank you for the cover, Scotty, I am going in now – sorry, Yorkie, but I must take you with us.'

Then he said something in Welsh to Derfel in a low voice.

That's when I realised what he meant to do.

'*We're aces now, Mazur,*' I yelled at him. '*Taff, Yorkie! We're all aces!*'

He chose the two ships that were closest together. He calculated the dive so he hit them both, the Blenheim cartwheeling across the deck of one and slamming into the other.

I climbed away through a trail of flame and shrapnel and a hailstorm of anti-aircraft fire. No one came after us.

Silver tossed the bundled-up dinghy over the back of his seat and climbed into the front cockpit after it. He sat down next to me again.

'Tex won't mind if we ditch him. Thought you and I might need this, though,' he said.

'You are showing lack of moral fibre,' I answered hollowly.

We limped a hundred miles back west across the open water, leaking fuel through the bullet holes, and when the fuel ran out I made a Mayday call over the radio, because that's what I'd been trained to do. If there was anyone out there to hear it, the chances of them being friendly were remote; we were still closer to Norway than to Scotland. Silver opened the hatch above us before I levelled the Blenheim to plough on its belly into the black-and-silver swell of the North Sea.

'My hands are both still in one piece,' Silver said.

Then the Perspex in the nose gave way, letting in a waterfall of icy black salt water.

Silver grabbed the strap of the dinghy out of the deluge and shoved the whole bundle up through the hatch ahead of him. We were both in water to our waists in the dark and it was impossible to get a firm foothold. I managed to push Silver out after the dinghy, one of his feet in the palm of my hand and the other on my shoulder – I don't think he even realised he was standing on me. The Blenheim's wings kept her from going straight to the bottom of the sea, but they were full of holes like the rest of her and filling up fast.

Somehow I hauled myself through the hatch after Silver, and we knelt clinging to each other on the starboard wing, slippery with seawater as the swell washed gently over it and back. Silver got the cover off the dinghy, but he couldn't get the inflating valve unscrewed, which we'd only ever seen demoed once, and the distance between pretending you're doing something in a drill and actually doing it in the dark in the middle of the North Sea is like the distance between yourself and the shores of Scotland while you're floating there on your sinking plane.

'Let me do it,' I said, thinking of his chilblained fiddler's fingers. 'Keep your gloves on.'

I had to take off my gauntlets to release the valve. They were both instantly lost. Seconds before the Blenheim submerged beneath us, I finally got the dinghy to inflate. We didn't have time to climb into it. All we could do was to hang on as the plane went down.

Our flight suits were full of icy water now, and it was like wearing armour made of lead. Neither one of us had the superhuman strength it would take to lift ourselves up over the side of the dinghy and into it. In five minutes I couldn't feel my hands at all.

So that was us, hanging on to a life raft we couldn't get into, up to our necks in water so cold it made every breath painful, under the most spectacular moon and starry sky I have ever seen.

'Sod this,' said Silver through chattering teeth.

'Aye.' It was too hard to breathe to try to talk.

'No, I mean sod this. Sod moral fibre. I can't do it. I'm d-d-d – I'm done. Thanks for b-being my pilot, Jamie. And my f-f-friend. If you make it b-b-back to Nancy's, take my tanner out of the ceiling and b-b-buy yourself a drink on me.'

And then the bastard *just let go*.

Ellen:

When Louisa came down for Jane's breakfast tray on Friday morning, there was me standing at the bar picking at a bowl of porridge I would never eat if it were the last bowl of porridge on this earth. There was Nancy, banging cups about as usual, but not so usual was that she hadn't combed her hair – the hairgrips she fixed in it yesterday were sliding out and she'd not noticed. Elisabeth Lind sat at the table by the fire with her neb in a newspaper, studying the personal notices as if she were swotting for an examination. She turned the page and it covered her own untouched porridge, the paper making a wee camp tent over the spoon stuck out of the bowl. When Louisa came in, Sergeant Lind looked to see who it was and then looked straight back at her newspaper as if she were clockwork instead of flesh and blood.

I knew she must be dying inside. But we couldn't weep in each other's arms as we'd have done in peacetime. We had to play her stupid game of pretend.

'What's going on?' Louisa asked.

'Policemen, firemen, Germans, whatnot, I don't know,' said Nan, sounding angrier than usual.

That was yesterday's news and we all knew it. Dietrich Althammer had been carried away last night, but the room he'd died in was still a dog's breakfast. They'd found how he escaped: when the rescue crew broke into his prison from the front, the old chimney was open to the sky above a heap of earth and broken stone and bricks and snow. The bomb debris had not hurt him, nor trapped him, and he'd scarpered up the chimney and lain hidden among the ruined pine trees on the ridge before creeping into the Limehouse.

Nancy didn't answer Louisa, and I couldn't speak, so that left Elisabeth Lind to tell her.

'The young men from 648 Squadron ran into trouble last night,' Sergeant Lind said carefully, not looking up, turning another page. 'Two planes confirmed down in B-Flight, and the rest are missing. "Failed to return" is how they report it.'

Louisa met my eyes. I shook my head.

She put her face in her hands. I saw her swallow, but she couldn't speak. I knew what she wanted to ask.

'Jamie made a radio call to Rob Lucknow in A-Flight while the party was going on,' I told her, though I felt like my own voice would choke me. 'He told Rob that Madeira was two down and that A-Flight should clear off before the Messers got wind there were more Blenheims about. A-Flight got back all right, but that was the last we heard from any of the others.'

'What do you mean, *any of the others*?' Louisa croaked. 'Pimms and Madeira *both*? But it's broad daylight!'

Nan turned her back, not even able to take a keek at us while we talked.

'Phyllis said she'd ring if she gets news,' I said. 'They might have landed away like they did the first time Windyedge got bombed. Sometimes if they're shot up they'll land at the nearest base, any old base, instead of coming home.'

'Oh.'

Poor disguised Elisabeth Lind stared at her newspaper. Anybody could tell she wasn't reading it.

One of the firemen came in through the front door. We spun around.

'We've just got the last Jerry out,' he said. 'Do you mind if we bring him in to warm him up? Not sure where Old Cromwell wants him, but he's had a pretty rough time and he's not in any shape to march to the aerodrome – he's been fair buried alive for a solid day.'

Nancy faced the fireman with empty eyes and shrugged. 'Do what you like,' she said.

And they brought in our old friend, that Jerry pilot Felix Baer.

He was all over dust. His hair and face were all one colour, grey as grey. His eyes were black pools in the grey dust.

Elisabeth Lind jumped to her feet, but Louisa was there first. She leaped forward and snatched at his hand.

The grey dust cracked around his lips as he smiled at her faintly.

Louisa:

He took my other hand too. I thought of piano keys beneath those bony, nimble fingers; I could feel his ring with the engraved bear cool against my palm. They were things that made him whole before the war and were still part of him.

He leaned down quickly and I stood on my toes and we kissed each other's faces.

I felt the grey dust come off on my cheek. He let go of one hand to brush it off me; he didn't let go of the other.

I pointed to Elisabeth Lind. 'That is Calypso. *Not me.*'

She nodded in agreement, looking as if she were about to cry. 'It's true,' she said. 'I *am* Calypso.'

I didn't dare say anything else; the room was full of guards and firemen.

Miss Lind pulled Jane's comfortable chair close to the fire. The men from the aerodrome covered it with a blanket to protect it, and they let Felix Baer sit and lean forward with his hands close to the flames.

He spoke haltingly, trying to explain himself.

'He wishes he had stayed here in November,' Miss Lind translated softly. 'But he didn't want to break the link in his resistance network. After his first trip they began to watch him. They must have known what he'd done – what he left here. They sent him to bomb Windyedge himself – on Christmas Day, can you believe? But he didn't. Althammer was his navigator on that flight, and when Althammer didn't report his failure, Baer and Moritz disagreed about *why*. Moritz thought it was because he was sympathetic. But Baer suspected it was because he wanted to string them along and trap them both later.'

Miss Lind continued, listening to what Baer said and then going on again. 'Baer turned out to be right, but Moritz was in charge, so when they were forced into a corner and cooked up the idea of defecting, Moritz brought Althammer along. And that's exactly what Althammer wanted: a chance to destroy their secret on the ground.'

She and Felix Baer spoke together in quick, fluent German, nodding in agreement, comparing notes. She reached into her uniform pocket, fished out a handkerchief, and gave it to him so he could wipe his face.

I didn't know what the German meant, but I knew what she was telling him.

Althammer failed. He's dead. Your boss, Eberhard Moritz, isn't hurt. My commanding officer is on his way back from Africa. Felix Baer straightened up a little. *I have the Enigma machine, and copies of the documents you brought, and they are safe.* Beneath the bruising and the grime, his face was alight with hope. He glanced at me.

'I'm sorry it took me so long to understand,' I said. I meant it for both of them.

He said something else. Elisabeth Lind's mouth twisted into a crooked little smile as she translated. 'He asks if you would play some music.'

The gramophone was gone. If I started at the piano – Jane was upstairs waiting for breakfast, and she wouldn't stay put if she caught wind of music down here without her. To be honest, why should she? I knew how she hated to miss anything. But she couldn't come down the stairs.

'I want Jane to be able to hear,' I said. 'I'll get my flute and play it in the hall.'

The tea on Jane's breakfast tray had cooled. I knew she wouldn't care, and took it up with me.

She sat gazing out the big bay window in Room Number Four, staring far away over the rooftops of the village and the wide sea beyond.

But she turned her head as I came in and gave me a small half-smile.

'I was wondering where you'd got to!' she said.

'Felix Baer is here,' I told her. 'He asked for music.' I screwed the pieces of the flute together. The case was cracked and battered, but my flute was all right. Like me: jarred but undamaged. I stood up, took a deep breath, and played an F-scale. Still warming up, I started 'Jane and Louisa'.

Jane hadn't forgotten the words. She sang in harmony with the flute, a third below the melody. '*Jane and Louisa will soon come home ...*'

She broke off.

'Are they going to arrest me again?' she asked.

A chatty police inspector had come round in the afternoon yesterday, and he hadn't said anything about arresting her. But he hadn't let her off, either. *Sorry about your fall, I expect you are quite dazed – you must have a doctor in to look at your arm! Don't be careless with the gas fire.*

I wondered if she was hoping that they *would* arrest her.

'I don't know,' I admitted.

I stood halfway down the stairs, exactly between Felix Baer in the public bar and Jane Warner in the best double room. *What can I play for them both?* I wondered, feeling self-conscious and awkward.

Put your shoulders back, Lula, I imagined Mummy saying. *Make your Daddy proud.*

Mendelssohn.

But I couldn't remember the intricacies of the middle part of the *Hebrides Overture*. *Rhapsody in Blue*? I wouldn't make it the whole way through that, either; not without reading music.

And then I remembered the Bach 'Ave Maria', whose glorious long slow tones were easier to pick out and linger over: Johanna von Arnim's first record.

And as I played, I wondered if there had been music on Daddy's sinking ship, a bugle playing 'Reveille' or 'The Last Post'. Or had he sung hymns in his deep, rolling voice, the way we'd sung in the storm-tossed rowboat at Lime Cay? I wondered if Mummy had been humming to herself when the bomb fell, one of her students' exam pieces, or a hymn for someone's wedding. *Music*, right till the end.

I'd never know. I hadn't been with them.

I thought of Jamie in the moonlight over the North Sea last night, with Silver next to him and Chip Wingate alone in the back.

I didn't finish the Bach. In the hall below me, the telephone rang, and Ellen ran to answer it.

Ellen:

'The Limehouse, Volunteer McEwen speaking,' I croaked into the receiver.

'Hello, Ellen, pet, it's Phyllis.' She was hoarse too. 'I thought Mrs C. should know the latest.'

Dread clung like a strangling rope around my throat and I didn't ask her to go on. But she did anyway.

'Harry Morrow landed at Deeside five hours ago. Textbook landing. He didn't taxi, though, just shut down the engines on the runway, so the ground crew ran out to see what was going on. And when they opened up the hatch they found all three of those Australian boys were already dead.'

'All three of them!' I gasped.

She'd told it without a sob, but now she began to weep.

'However did they get home if they were *already dead*?' I cried.

'Dougie and Gavin had been dead for hours. But Harry, that lovely boy, I was dancing with him only *last week*—' She sobbed. 'He hung on and hung on until he made it home. One lung and his stomach *full* of holes and somehow he just kept flying until he was home, and he even managed to land safely, and – what was he thinking all that time that he managed to hang on so long? How he tried to kiss me in the porch of the Limehouse that warm night last December? Or just staring desperately at that stupid picture of his dogs taped to his instrument panel and longing to see them again? And then—'

I sat bent over myself on the stool in the telephone cupboard under the stairs, listening to her keening, and I felt as if those bullets were in my own lungs and stomach.

'The rest of Pimms?' I choked.

'Failed to return.' Phyllis took a breath. 'They might have got away, though. You know what Scotty and Ignacy are like, flying foxes. They'll hide in cloud, hedge-hop at sea level, whatever it takes. If they had to ditch in the water or make a crash landing in the middle of the Highlands, it might be days before we hear from them ...'

Phyllis's blethering trailed off. If they ditched in the North Sea or crashed on some mountaintop they'd likely just drown or freeze to death.

'I'm glad Rob's lads in A-Flight made it,' I breathed. 'Give him our best.'

'I will,' said Phyllis.

'And ring us again when you hear anything else.'

My throat closed up, thinking about those three young lads bringing themselves home on luck and hope, dead men even before they landed.

'I will,' Phyllis repeated. 'Tell Mrs Campbell.'

Louisa:

I couldn't believe they were all gone.

I just *couldn't believe it.*

But the day crawled by, and Phyllis didn't ring back. Next morning Elisabeth Lind went with Felix Baer and Eberhard

Moritz in a transport plane to deliver the Enigma machine to Intelligence. She caught hold of me before she left, smart and official in her uniform with her peaked cap fixed neatly over her braided hair. But she was pale and pink-eyed beneath the perfect make-up, as if she'd spent the night crying.

'Louisa, can I borrow you downstairs?' she said. 'I've only ever flown once before, so—'

She held up a sixpence.

'I wish you'd tell me which wishing coins are Pimms's ones. I want to put mine with them.'

'They don't do a thing,' I said hollowly. 'They're superstitious *nonsense. They*—'

My voice rose to a sob. Couldn't I have done anything else – convinced Jamie not to fly that way, that night? What if I'd got Felix Baer and Elisabeth Lind together earlier? What if I'd gone straight to Wing Commander Cromwell?

None of it seemed possible, but the what-ifs kept spinning in my head like a gramophone turntable that wouldn't stop.

Miss Lind reached up and caressed my cheek with soft fingertips.

'I know,' she said quietly. '*I know*.'

I couldn't imagine what it was like having to pretend your brother hadn't just been lost at sea. Or wherever he was lost.

'I want my sixpence to be there too,' she said. 'And I'm never coming back for it. I want it to be up there forever with the rest of them.'

I swallowed and nodded. 'I'll show you which is Jamie's,' I told her softly.

*

The moon was waning and the freezing fog returned and Windyedge was quiet.

Phyllis wrote her horrid reports by the fire in the Limehouse. The ground crew helped with the heavy work as we tidied up Room Five. I did not believe anyone could ever sleep in it again, but we put it back to being Mrs Campbell's second-best double room. Everything in it still worked.

The policemen didn't come back straightaway, but a doctor looked at Jane's wrist, and said it would be fine and gave her strengthening exercises. After a few days, Ellen helped me bring her downstairs. Nobody fooled about on the piano. We couldn't play records, though we read some of the album notes out loud. We swapped newspapers, doing the crosswords and fine-combing the casualty lists. The telephone never rang, and there were no planes to count in.

Exactly one week after the limekilns were bombed, as permitted hours began at half past five, I unlocked the front door for Mrs Campbell. Standing in the vestibule, I heard tyre chains and an unfamiliar engine labouring up the lane. I opened the door to look, just as a low-slung red motor car coughed to a stalled halt in front of the Limehouse.

Flight Lieutenant James Gordon Erskine Murray Beaufort-Stuart climbed out.

He didn't bother to open the car door. He crouched on the seat and swung his legs over the edge of the open top as if it were a hatch on a Blenheim bomber.

For a moment I thought he was a ghost.

Never mind all my modern education and not being a

fool-fool country gal. I actually thought he must be a dead man walking. I thought it must be a ghost-car driven by a ghost.

He was wearing the same flight suit and sheepskin-lined leather jacket he'd taken off in a week ago. They were stiff with water damage and crusted with salt. The thin, fair beginnings of a beard stubbled his filthy face. His eyes were unchanged, clear, bright hazel with a touch of madness in them.

'Hello, Louisa,' he rasped, and I held the front door open for him.

I was too shocked to touch him. I didn't dare. I didn't – he'd suffered something I didn't understand, and it scared me like nothing had ever scared me before. *What if it was my fault?* Had I helped send him into that hell?

I couldn't do anything but follow him into the house.

He limped to the bar.

Nancy Campbell looked up and dropped a glass. It smashed into a thousand pieces on the cold stone floor.

'*Oh, sweet Jesus,*' she sobbed.

'Jamie Stuart,' Ellen whispered. 'God be thanked.'

He didn't look at any of us. He raised his head and scanned the oak beam above the bar, all shiny with shillings and sixpences and threepenny bits. He reached up and twitched out one coin.

'Silver promised to buy me a pint,' he said hoarsely. His voice grated as if he hadn't used it since the last time we saw him.

The thin sixpence clinked on the brass top of the bar as Jamie slapped it down. For a few seconds he held his hand spread out there over the coin, staring at his fingers in fascination and disgust. Ellen and Phyllis and Jane were all sitting and couldn't see his hand. But Mrs Campbell could see it from where she faced him over the bar, and I was standing just one step behind him and I saw it too.

His little finger and ring finger were black as tar, black as bitumen, as if he had dipped them in ink to the second knuckles. The skin faded through grey and blue and green and purple back to where his fingers joined his hand. The rest of the hand was pale and filthy and covered with angry red blisters. But it was alive. The black fingers were dead.

Mrs Campbell let out another sob. '*What—?*'

Jamie shook his head. 'The others are the same,' he said. He laid his left hand on the bar lined up with his right hand, all ten fingers spread flat. The last two fingers of his left hand were mostly as blackened and dead as the ones on the right.

'Frostbite,' he said. 'It happened on the boat that picked me up. I was all right in the water – it was warmer than the air.' He rubbed his knuckles into his eyes. 'I got lucky. It was a fishing boat working with the Norwegian resistance – they had machine guns hidden in oil barrels. They heard my Mayday on their radio and came looking for us. But it took two more days to make landfall in Shetland, and it was bloody cold sitting on the deck.'

'*Us?*' whispered Mrs Campbell.

'Give us a drink and I'll tell you what happened,' Jamie said, rapping the sixpence on the countertop. 'I'm parched.'

Ellen:

He told his dreadful tale in a dull voice. We listened without daring to speak, though Nancy sobbed quietly all through the last bit. When he'd finished he wrapped both hands around his heavy ale as if it could warm them, and raised his glass.

'Flying Officer David Silvermont,' he said hoarsely. 'Absent friends. Madeira and Pimms. Now we're official aces.'

He drank slowly, and that's when I saw his blackened fingers.

'Och, Jamie-lad!' I exclaimed in alarm. 'Why aren't you *in hospital*?'

'I had to come here. Silver told me to buy myself a drink with his tanner at Nancy's, and I'm doing it.'

I wanted to shake him. Here he was alive, his two hands ripe with gangrene, and he'd nothing better to do than toss back a pint in the pub?

'You know my own twin brother nearly lost a leg with blood poisoning after Dunkirk last spring!' I said furiously. 'If you don't get those fingers off they will *kill you*.'

He shrugged. 'Can't feel 'em. Stopped worrying about 'em when they stopped hurting. Can't feel my toes, either, but I haven't looked. I can drive. I bet I can fly, too.'

He sighed, and put his head down on his arms on the bar.

'I went home first,' Jamie mumbled, his head sticking out of the wool collar of his leather jacket like a tortoise. 'One boat to Orkney and another to the mainland, and then I got a ride with a forestry crew. But I should have come straight here. The moment I got down from the lorry I wanted to be here. So I took the car and drove myself. It's not far.'

'Did you come in your mother's car? Does she know you took it? Where did you get the petrol? Is there enough left to get to Aberdeen?'

'Yes, no, don't know,' he answered wearily. 'Probably.'

'*Hospital*,' I ordered. '*Now.* I'll drive.'

Louisa:

We heard the car motor start, stop, start again. Then it roared away down the hill with its tyre chains clattering.

Jane bent at the waist, leaned over, and toppled a stack of peat bricks with one hand. She shoved them into the fire with her foot.

'Louisa is shivering,' she said. 'Louisa is always cold.'

'Well goodness, let's build the fire up at once,' Phyllis exclaimed. 'This place is never properly warm. What did Sergeant Lind say – the ghosts will leave if they get warm enough!'

Practical, well-behaved Phyllis suddenly leaped to her feet and slammed peat bricks into the fire. She grabbed the bellows and fanned the flames. Jane tried to reach around her with the poker and banged it on the hearth, not doing much but making a great noise. Phyllis shoved more peats on. Flames licked around the corners of the blocks and grew taller.

It was *wonderful.*

In a minute it became the biggest, brightest blaze we ever had in that house. It filled the room with rosy light and threw streamers of gold up the chimney. As it burned higher, light caught on the rows of copper and silver pressed into the wood, dull and burnished and shining.

'Build it up—'

I couldn't in a million years work out who to blame for what happened next.

It was Jane urging us on. She is the one who kept saying, 'More fuel! Another log!' But it was me who took the poker from Jane's frail grasp and stirred up the embers and turned over the flaming blocks of peat. Phyllis is the one who kept putting more of them in the fire. And Nan Campbell didn't ever tell us to stop.

In the blazing heat, something fell gleaming like a raindrop full of sunlight and hit the stone hearth with a *clink.*

Then there was another. *Clink. Clink* – another. Then half a dozen all at once, *clinkclinkclinketyclinketyclink* – as if someone had thrown a handful of coins into the fireplace.

We all fell still, listening and staring.

The heat of our inferno was sucking moisture out of the mantel, shrinking it as it dried, and the old wood was letting go of its wishing coins.

One by one they popped out of the black oak beam and plinked on the hearth, pennies and tuppences and silver threepenny bits put there by generations of fishermen and crofters, and by the young men who died in the first Great War.

Alan Anderson. Ben Knox. Cammy McBride.

The fire was warming them up, and the coins and the ghosts were leaping from the thick walls.

Duncan Campbell.

With a great sob, Mrs Campbell grabbed her heather broom and tried to sweep the coins from the hearth into the fire. But they fell out of the mantel faster than she could sweep.

Clinkclinkclinkety clink-clink-clink

It was like Morse code spelling the names of dead men.

In a frenzy, Nan accidentally swept the bundle of dried heather into the fire too. The broom flared up in her hands like an incendiary bomb.

She yelped and dropped it. Her apron was on fire as well. She ripped it off, threw it into the blaze, and leaped away from the hearth.

Then the mantel caught fire.

It went up all at once – the old wood just reached its flash point, and a curtain of flame stretched across the whole length of the hearth and up to the ceiling. For a few seconds, every one of us was too stunned to do anything – we just stared.

Then Mrs Campbell screamed, '*The ceiling!* Phyllis! There's a bucket behind the bar – fill it and help me!'

She became suddenly modern and efficient, wielding a proper soda-acid fire extinguisher in both hands, fearlessly aiming it overhead and sending a jet into the flames licking at the oak beam over the bar. 'Louisa, get Aunt Jane outside! Then come back and try to ring for the firemen at Windyedge! Get Jane a chair if you can—'

Phyllis ran to fill the bucket. I hauled Jane over my shoulder by her good arm.

I left her shivering against the stone wall out front, between the scorched pines on the ridge and the dancing orange light behind the deep windows of the Limehouse. I had time to dash in to make the Mayday call. But I didn't have time to get a chair. Nan and Phyllis turned me out as I tried to step into the bar.

Jane wasn't where I'd left her.

She lay on the gravel in front of the Limehouse. She'd tried to come back in by herself. What for? The records, her wonderful jazz collection and the Johanna von Arnim recordings – her faked British passport?

I think she came back for me.

It was much worse than her first fall. It was hard to tell what was wrong.

'Oh, oh, oh, oh, oh,' she moaned quietly, over and over.

'Louisa, run down to the Torries' and get a blanket and some brandy,' said Mrs Campbell. 'We can't move her without help.'

'Oh no!' I cried. 'I left her alone a minute ago and *look*! I'm not going *now*—'

'I'll go,' said Phyllis.

I knelt beside that wonderful old woman on the icy gravel with my arms around her, trying to keep her warm with my own warmth. The stones drove through my stockings into my knees like shards of frozen glass.

Couldn't I have stopped *this*, this one thing?

But I'd *had* to ring for the firemen!

'They won't arrest me now,' Jane whispered.

'Nobody's going to arrest you! Ever!'

She clutched my sweater. 'Louisa? Don't go, my lovely Louisa.'

'I'm not going anywhere,' I said.

Oh no, sang a panicked fugue in the back of my head, *don't do this to me, Jane Warner! Don't leave me alone again, I like it here, I like it with you, this hasn't been long enough, who will play duets with me? We haven't finished the last lot of library books, we need to buy you a new gramophone, there's no one else! Oh God, did Jamie feel like this,* like this, *when his best friend let go and sank in the icy black water? How did he bear it, how did he not let go himself?*

But he was there. *He was there* for Silver. And I was here for Jane.

I didn't let her know how I was panicking.

'I'm not going anywhere,' I repeated. 'You're not alone.'

I held her, while we waited for what would happen next, and I sang softly.

'Jane and Louisa will soon come home,
They will soon come home,
They will soon come home;
Jane and Louisa will soon come home,
Into this beautiful garden.'

Music. Right till the end.

So proud of my girl, said my daddy's voice in my head. *A real voyager.*

Ellen:

'Are you all right, Louisa?' I whispered.

We lay together one night later inside the dark-as-dark of an old-fashioned box bed, a thing like a huge cupboard in the big room of Morag Torrie's cottage. It had a heather mattress such as I slept on all my life until I joined up, piled with quilts and blankets. Another box bed beside ours held Morag and her parents – Phyllis and Nan were in a different cottage.

'I think I'm all right,' she whispered back. 'What about you?'

'Och, no bother.'

We lay among the lumps of dry heather staring into blackness.

'You always say that. Really, "no bother"?' Louisa asked.

'Well, a mite done in.'

I came back to Windyedge the day after the fire. I sat in the hospital in Aberdeen all night while Jamie had his fingers and toes chopped off, and then I stayed to comfort his mam the next morning while he slept off the sedatives and the morphine before the doctors let anybody see him.

'I'm awfully glad you're here,' Louisa said. 'I was by myself last night, and it was dreadful. Nan didn't want to share with me and I was so worn out and miserable after the firemen left, I just gave in for once and let Phyllis sort things. But I *hated* being alone.'

Morag's parents hadn't wanted me under their roof, either, after she told them I was a Traveller. But Phyllis sorted that, too. *Of course you must put Ellen up, she is a servicewoman! Louisa won't mind sharing.* Aye, throw the two outcasts together.

Neither of us minded sharing, but it is not nice to feel unwelcome.

'Morag said you walked the last ten miles to Windyedge from the rail station!' Louisa said.

'I like walking.' It seemed a long time since I'd walked anywhere, really *walked*. 'I like walking more than driving. It gives you time to think. My family walked all over Scotland when I was wee, following the work. It's hard with the war on. The young people have all gone for soldiers or are in factories, and most of us hate it – so many flipping rules and regulations, and the same routines day after day, and having to kill. My brother hates it. I'm lucky at Windyedge … except when the planes go down. It's like raising pet lambs, you give them daft names and watch them grow, and then when you send them to the butcher, you wish you hadn't bothered.'

Louisa sighed. 'Yes, it's *awful*. It's awful.'

'At the Limehouse I've been under one roof, the same roof, for longer than I've ever stayed in one place ever,' I confessed. 'Ten times as long. Fifty. I don't know.'

Louisa was quiet for a moment, and then launched one of her familiar well-aimed torpedoes at me. 'That old man was quite rude to you when you were having your sandwich in the pub the other day, I thought.'

'They're always like that to Traveller folk, unless we're digging their garden or mending their pots,' I told her. 'And of course Morag blethered about me to the whole village, so now everybody knows.'

'But her parents weren't so rude,' Louisa said. 'They were just … a bit like Nancy. They expected one thing, but they also knew you were the driver for RAF Windyedge and Phyllis's friend, and they had to – open up their heads a bit to take it in. I suppose I do, too.'

I was surprised to realise I knew just what she meant.

'That is how I feel thinking about Jamaica!' I exclaimed. 'It seems a fairytale, not a place where ordinary people live and buy stamps and make whooping-cough mixture and burn the cooking when they're weary. I wish I could see it.'

'Well, you say you are a Traveller – it's a good long journey!'

She made me laugh.

'You are so brave to have told everyone about yourself,' Louisa murmured. 'You *knew* the trouble it would make you.'

'I couldn't hide forever,' I said. 'But you can't *ever* hide.'

'No, but in Scotland I'm just *one*. People are often more curious than horrid if there's just one of you. The villagers stare at me, but they're not nasty.'

I laughed again, more bitterly. 'Would you listen to the pair of us – as if it's easier or harder for one or the other! It's *different*, but mostly it's just *hard*.'

'Jane said I had to fight,' Louisa said. 'She said the world was poisoning itself, and I was young, so it was up to me to make it better.'

I heard her sniff. She loved that old woman.

After a bit I asked her quietly, 'What will you do now?'

She sighed. 'Mrs Campbell asked me to stay and help her put the Limehouse right, and work for her when the damage is mended, at the same wages I had for looking after Jane. So I will be all right for a bit.'

'Can the Limehouse be mended?'

It looked like a great old smoking ruin when I saw it earlier the day.

'There was a fire inspector round this morning. He says the building's sound. The damage was mostly to the bar, and only Room One had smoke in it. They let us in to collect clothes and things! My flute and my passport and wages, and Mummy's album of Jamaica photographs – all fine. Mrs Campbell is Jane's next of kin, so she'll have a little extra to pay for the repairs.'

'I wish I'd seen the blaze,' I said. 'Poor old Nan. Poor old *Jane*.'

'It wasn't sad,' Louisa said. 'Or – I was sad, but Jane – she seemed *ready*. She *was* ready. And I was – I was so lucky to be there. I wasn't there for either of my parents. I was—' She grasped for the right word. 'It was a blessing to be there with her. I was *blessed*.'

'I'm glad,' I said, and twined my fingers through hers to squeeze them tight.

'How is Jamie?' Louisa whispered.

My turn to grasp at words, though I'd known she'd get round to asking when she was good and ready.

Truthfully, I didn't know how he was. I'd seen him for five minutes when his mam went in, and he was barely awake, dazed and mazy. I'd felt like an intruder on his mammy's grief, so I'd left them to it.

'Not very well,' I said at last. 'In pain. Missing half his fingers and all his toes. Out of work. And blaming himself for seventeen young men dead. Which isn't his fault at all, at all.'

In the black quiet of the box bed, Louisa cried so silently I didn't hear until she gasped for air.

'Oh God,' she said. 'Oh God, I think it's my fault.'

'*Your fault?*' The words burst out of me as a sob. 'It's not *your* flipping fault, Louisa! What about those Messerschmitt 110 night fighters?'

'I translated all that code.'

'He *gave* you all that code to translate! Nor did I have to pass it on, which I did willingly! We did it *together*.'

'But if he hadn't flown to Norway—'

'Och, you're just as bad as he is!' I exclaimed. 'He *had* to fly to Norway. That's what they *do*. It's their war work. Sometimes they don't make it back.'

I tossed off the covers and scrambled to my knees in the inky black. '*All right*, I can prove to both you gumpuses it was an op just like any other.'

Louisa:

Ellen threw open the door at the end of the bed. The room beyond held a faint memory of light, red in the hearth, paler black around the curtained windows. Ellen climbed out of the box bed, felt her way to the door where her satchel hung on a peg, and brought the bag back.

Back inside the closed box bed, she lit an electric torch. She gave me a square blue notebook, like a clothbound exercise jotter. She held her torch so I could look at the cover.

Printed on the blue cloth in black ink it said *Royal Air Force: Pilot's Flying Logbook.*

Beneath that was a space for the owner's name. In looping script like a schoolboy's was written *James G. Beaufort-Stuart.*

'He asked me to fetch it,' Ellen said.

I let the notebook fall open. It was a list of all the flights Jamie ever made with the Royal Air Force, right back to his first training flight, not much more than a year ago. I turned the pages carefully. His early operational entries, last summer as the Battle of Britain began, were like the casualty lists. He was supposed to log how long each flight took and where he'd gone, but he also noted every time anyone in 648 Squadron was shot down. Then there wasn't room for that. So sometime in September he limited it to just his mates in Pimms Section.

Then there was the entry for 7 November 1940.

That night, men had died in A-Flight as well as B-Flight. Jamie had listed the names of six men in Pimms and added a note that said, '*Also* five lost in Madeira and thirteen in A-Flight.' His pen nib had torn the page where he'd drawn a line under *also* for emphasis.

Twenty-four men died that night – two-thirds of 648 Squadron, more even than last week.

They'd died on a routine mission.

And I knew then that Ellen was right. The Valentine's mission had also been routine. The deaths that night didn't have anything to do with me.

But I also knew that I'd feel like they were my responsibility forever, all of us would feel responsible forever, even if there wasn't anything Jamie or I or Ellen or Felix Baer or anyone could have ever done to prevent those deaths.

I closed the book with a sob.

Ellen dropped the torch. She rocked me like a baby, dropping little kisses on my head and crooning in a language I didn't understand. She was crying too.

Jamie:

I fought my way up from the bottom of an endless cold black sea where the whole of me was frozen except my hands and feet, and they were on fire.

After a bit I remembered where I was, and how I'd got here, and I opened my eyes.

I didn't recognise the room. I remembered vaguely that Mother had been there, though, and it was pretty obvious she had, because I was surrounded by snowdrops and daffodils. There was a colony of jam jars full of dainty white drooping blossoms on the stand beside my bed, and a forest of white and yellow flowers in jugs and medical beakers on a wheeled steel trolley at my feet, and tall spears of unopened green buds were stood in buckets on the floor all around the walls. There must have been a thousand of them.

And my wee German-speaking sister was there, at work filling the window sill with more daffodil-stuffed jam jars, wearing her blue WAAF uniform and looking like herself again. She'd got rid of the operatic plaited crown of hair and the ridiculous fake eyelashes. Bit of lipstick, hair done up in that French-style twist our grandmother liked, still elegant. But more ordinary. Without the mask.

'Oi, Sergeant *Lind*,' I croaked. 'People will recognise you.'

She let go a handful of two dozen half-opened daffs, scattering bright yellow flowers all over the floor around her feet, and raised her head. She looked as if she'd been awake all night crying.

'Jamie-lad,' she breathed. 'How are you?'

'Och, no bother.'

'*Liar*.'

She dragged the one chair over by me and rested her chin on her folded hands on the bed next to my head. My own hands lay swaddled in bandages so that nobody including me could see what had happened to them, and my feet were under a little tent to keep the bedclothes off them. She was careful not to touch me.

'Who's the bloody liar?' I accused. '"*Sergeant Elisabeth Lind!*"'

'Lind *is* part of my name. And I borrowed Elisabeth from the Queen. Lots of people call me Queenie.'

'Only Ellen does that,' I disagreed hoarsely. 'Why did you have to get assigned to Windyedge, of all places?'

'I was supposed to collect a German coding machine for Intelligence,' she hissed in my ear, 'only some bugger from the RAF had stolen it and set up his own private special operations ring so he could go on submarine hunts.'

God, my hands and feet hurt – that wasn't a dream. I

didn't dare to move, and I didn't want to think back to that last flight.

'I thought you'd *help* me,' she added petulantly.

'We damn well did help you. It wasn't easy, though, with you being in disguise as a Swiss milkmaid. Ellen and I had a job not to fall about laughing and blow your cover.'

'I *had* to. I was *told*. That was for the Germans. So they'd take me seriously.'

'They took Louisa jolly seriously, and she just goes about as her proud wee self.'

'They're coming to see you,' said my sister. 'Louisa and Ellen, I mean, not the Germans. They said they'd wait until you were more likely to be awake.' She raised her head to plant a quick kiss on my cheek. 'I couldn't wait, though.'

It was nice to be able to talk to her properly, like coming up for air after thinking you were going to drown. A better painkiller than the morphine.

'I'm glad you didn't,' I said.

Louisa:

Jamie was sitting up when Ellen and I got there in the afternoon. His pale skin was covered with scabs beneath the scraggly week-old beard, and his bandaged hands lay in his lap. The clear hazel eyes, unfocused in his narrow fox's face, went bright and excited when he saw us.

His sister was perched on the edge of his bed, and she also looked up as we came in. Without her painted face and plaited crown of hair, sitting next to Jamie and wearing the same expression of welcome and relief, I couldn't believe I hadn't seen right away how alike they were.

I had to admire her for pulling it off.

Ellen strode across the hospital room full of spring flowers, leaned down, and kissed Jamie on the mouth.

'There you are, Jamie Stuart. You owe me that one from before.'

Then she turned to the girl who wasn't Miss Lind and they held each other so close and tight that the copper and gold hair tangled together at the sides of their heads.

At last they all stopped cuddling. I felt like a bit of a gooseberry. I wouldn't have dared to kiss Jamie, even on the cheek; I was still a bit in awe of him.

Ellen saw, and reached one hand to pull me closer.

'Show him the box of chocolates Nan sent,' she said. 'That's good for a laugh.'

I got them out of my school bag. 'She's been saving them since last year, and they've already survived a German bombing and a house fire, so watch out.'

'Ta, Louisa,' Jamie rasped. 'Put them in the drawer as there are no surfaces left. Ruddy female relatives and their ruddy floral tributes.'

'Here's your logbook,' said Ellen. 'Which bit did you want to torture yourself with?'

She sat in the chair beside him, holding it where he could see it, like a young mum reading a storybook to a small child.

'I just want to make sure the Stavanger op gets filled in properly,' he said. 'Get Louisa to do it – her writing's always tidy. See how I've done the other Enigma ops, look – I put a Morse *E* at the start, just a dot, to remind me which flights were connected with the coding machine. Don't want it to be too obvious.'

I knelt beside Ellen with the book against the bed as I wrote out the details, at his instruction, determined I wasn't going to weep. Miss Lind watched over my shoulder. When I'd done, and blown on the ink to dry it off, I shut the book.

It felt very final. We all knew he wouldn't write in it again.

For a moment we were quiet about that.

Then Elisabeth Lind, looking down, smiled her crooked little half-smile at me kneeling by the side of the bed.

'I'm Julie,' she said.

'Ellen told me. After you left Windyedge.' I simply couldn't think of her as anything other than Miss Lind.

'Ellen told *me* that you seem to think you're responsible for Pimms Section's flight leader being a headstrong Scots lunatic.'

'I wanted so badly to help!' I wailed. 'I wanted to *do* something!'

'Buckets of blood!' She sounded exactly like her brother. 'You did do something, Louisa Adair! You gave us our *only captured Enigma machine*!'

'I could have given it to you as soon as I found it. We could have contacted your commanding officer somehow. And then maybe everything would have worked out differently, and—' I glanced at Jamie. I wasn't going to be the first to mention *again* that not a single crew in Pimms or Madeira had survived their last mission.

Miss Lind looked thoughtful. 'But you know, if you *hadn't* used it, perhaps it would have been destroyed in one of those early bombing raids, just as the papers were. Or, if you hadn't ever found it, it would have still been in the Limehouse, but you wouldn't have guessed when the Luftwaffe was coming. And instead, you were always one step ahead of them. Remember the bomber you turned away in the air, that awful night of freezing fog? Maybe that bomber would have killed all of us *and* destroyed the machine at the same time, if the coded message hadn't warned you. And B-Flight would have still gone down in flames. Maybe if you hadn't done anything it would have turned out *worse*.'

'If you hadn't recognised Felix Baer whistling his SOS, we might have shot down his plane on Christmas day,' Jamie put in hoarsely. 'If he hadn't thought you were Calypso, and even if they hadn't bombed Windyedge, perhaps no one would have ever discovered where he hid the machine.'

I opened my mouth to protest, and realised they were right.

Not so much in that other, different, terrible things might have happened without my interference, but in that we just wouldn't ever know the millions upon millions of combinations that fate's rotor dials could have lined up.

Jamie's sister gave me that crooked smile again. I liked her much more without the disguise.

'Anyway this is how it's turned out,' she said. 'And I shall make sure the full story doesn't go beyond my commanding officer. The official version is that the machine was hidden behind the gas fire in Mrs Campbell's best double room until I found it there just before B-Flight went to

Stavanger.' She paused, and made a point of looking at us one by one until we each met her eyes. She did Jamie last, as if she thought he needed an extra dose of telling-off. 'You're all accountable for treason against the British Crown under the Official Secrets Act if you reveal a word about any of it for the next fifty years.'

'I'm not a child,' muttered Jamie. 'Nor are Ellen and Louisa. You needn't keep up your Intelligence officer act now that you've taken off your false eyelashes.'

'Well, I have to warn you about the Official Secrets Act, I've been *told* to, and I'm doing it now as I've got all three of you in one place and there's no one else listening,' she said crossly. 'And there's a difference between being held accountable for treason and actually being guilty of it. Accountable means you have to be able to justify your actions. I don't know how you'd justify *revealing* any of what you've been doing for the past three months, but you could probably justify *doing* it.'

'I bloody well *could* justify doing it,' said Jamie. 'I'd do it again.'

'Someone *will* do it again,' I said. 'Now that we've shared it.'

Jamie:

Louisa was going to be wasted staying at Nan's, with her head full of Morse code and her backbone of steel and her hunger for action.

I shifted my legs. It was practically impossible to sit up

straighter without putting pressure on my hands. I tried not to flail; they'd all go soft on me if they thought I was in pain.

'What are you going to do next to help win the war, Louisa?' I said. 'You should join the WAAF.'

Louisa shook her head and gave a terrifically prim response, sounding like Phyllis.

'I'm fifteen. They'd never let me in.'

I couldn't believe she'd let a little thing like that stop her.

'When's your birthday?' I persisted. 'You'll have to get an adult National Registration card when you turn sixteen. Sergeant Lind here fibbed about her age when she took her driving test, and if you need anybody to pull strings for you at the recruitment office, I'd say she owes you a big favour anyway.'

I couldn't understand why Louisa looked so *angry*.

And then I realised she thought I'd pushed her into a corner. She wasn't 'of pure European descent'. She thought the Women's Auxiliary Air Force would turn her away, the way the navy turned away her father.

'The air force lifted the colour bar in 1939,' I said. 'I guess it wasn't done with a big welcome or a lot of fanfare, but there are a few West Indians in the RAF. I met one myself last autumn, George Archer, gunner in a Wellington bomber. Family man, lovely chap. I think the WAAF would take you.'

As I watched the familiar excitement creep back into her heart-shaped face, I secretly thought that giving Louisa the tip-off that would get her into the services was perhaps my finest hour: the best thing I'd done for Britain since the war started. A bomber pilot sent night after night on missions of destruction doesn't get much opportunity to be creative.

Buckets of blood – what was *I* going to do next?

Weren't there a couple of one-armed ferry pilots in the Air Transport Auxiliary? I knew my wee sister had a friend who flew for them. Maybe she could introduce me.

It would be a while yet before the damaged bits of me healed, but the war wasn't over.

Ellen:

Louisa as a WAAF! I tried to imagine her in air-force blue and a peaked cap. I wanted to see it. I wanted to see her as an officer, bossing folk about.

I needed to shift gears, too. Under Nan Campbell's roof for fifty times as long as any other? *Shaness* – much too long.

I thought I'd apply for a bit of training. Gunnery – or those teams that raised the barrage balloons, protecting cities from enemy aircraft. Maybe even become an officer myself. I'd learned a lot watching Jamie.

The next few months wouldn't be easy, living with the Torries in Windyedge and waiting for a transfer.

But Louisa and I would have each other while we waited.

Louisa:

I remembered what Jane Warner had said about a razor and ink being all it took to fix her passport.

Rules are made to be broken, Lula.

When my sixteenth birthday comes around in the spring, I thought, and I get my new National Registration card, I have only to get rid of one stroke off the *6* and add another loop to make it an *8*.

You, Jane said to me, with warmth in her wonderful rich voice, *you might be able to change things.*

I'd have to fight. I knew I'd have to fight.

But I was ready for that.

A real voyager.

We'd all have to fight. I wouldn't be alone.

Author's Declaration of Accountability

When I started thinking about what I'd say here, I tried to remember the first spark for this story. And when I dug beyond the obvious – the Enigma machine, the defecting Germans landing in Scotland, the Blenheim crew, the coins in the pub ceiling – what I came back to was the old woman.

Believe it or not, that's what I started with. I wanted to write a story about a mysterious old woman.

Originally I just wanted to create a bond between a young person and an old person. It is mostly because I am losing, and miss deeply, my wonderful grandmother Betty Flocken and her generation – she was born in 1916 and died in 2015. In the back of my mind I was thinking of Margaret Mahy's *Memory*, which is about a troubled teen who ends up caring for a stranger with Alzheimer's disease, and Penelope Lively's *The House in Norham Gardens*, about a younger teen who has to care for her elderly aunts. But my stock in trade is World War II thrillers. How was I going to include a mysterious old person in my adventure story?

In the summer of 2014, the same summer that Betty Flocken suffered the fall that foreshadowed her decline and death six months later, I had one of the most wonderful experiences of my life: I took a flight in a World War II-era Avro Lancaster bomber. It, too, is among the last of its age, one of only two in the world that still fly, and I had a view from the gun turret as we circled over Niagara Falls. Afterwards, I chatted with the pilot, Dave Rohrer, who has spent more time at the controls of a Lancaster than any wartime pilot ever did. He told me about a pub he'd visited in England near a former World War II airfield, where a wooden beam over the bar was full of coins placed there by airmen who never came back from their missions. *Dead men's money*, the bartender called it, telling Dave not to touch.

From that moment, I knew I had to write a story about those wishing coins and the bomber squadron who left them there.

When I finally got to work on the idea, I thought I could set up my young heroine and her ageing companion in a pub like the one Dave visited, near a wartime airfield. The local Royal Air Force bomber squadron could somehow get involved with the viewpoint character. I thought it would be fun (*fun* as in *I will enjoy writing this*, not as in *this story will be light-hearted*) if I explored Jamie Beaufort-Stuart's background as a bomber pilot, which is only mentioned in passing in *Code Name Verity*.

In June 2018, I received a letter from an Australian reader who reminded me that it wasn't just British and American men and women who flew in World War II, and requested that if I ever wrote a 'Bomber Story', would I please remember the Australians. As it happened, I was in the midst of writing a Bomber Story. So at my correspondent's request I included Harry, Gavin and Dougie as one of 648 Squadron's aircrews. In fact, the RAF bases in wartime Scotland consisted of very few Scots, and the rest of Scotland was full of foreigners too. There were Polish, French and Norwegian naval units in Glasgow; Polish, French and Canadian troops were based throughout the country; there were civilians from Belgium, the Netherlands, Czechoslovakia, Poland, Norway and Spain; there were prisoner of war camps in Scotland holding both Germans and Italians. Later in the war, US military troops were also based in Scotland, of which about ten per cent were black. One wartime logging unit was made up of 900 men from British Honduras (now Belize).

I lived in Jamaica as a child and completed my first three years of school there, and over the past ten years I've become fascinated by the role of Caribbean men and women serving in Britain in World War II. I first became aware of them when I was writing *Code Name Verity*. I'd wanted to include a black airman at the end of that novel (and I did), because I hoped to paint in a little diversity among the mostly European and white cast of characters. My original plan was to make that airman American. But when I started digging, of course I discovered that the only black Americans to fly in World War II were the Tuskegee Airmen. They didn't fly in France and they didn't fly in bombers and they didn't fly in integrated crews, and I needed my airman to do all those things, so I made him Jamaican instead of

American. Out of some sixteen thousand men and women from the Caribbean serving in the military in World War II, about five hundred were enlisted in the Royal Air Force. The United States segregated their armed forces back then: the British, however reluctantly, did not. (When the US entered the war, the British bent over backwards to accommodate American Jim Crow regulations, resulting in frustration and resentment from servicemen and local populations all over the United Kingdom.)

It wasn't just Caribbean men who volunteered to join the war effort. Considering themselves to be British subjects and motivated by patriotism, about six hundred Caribbean women joined the Auxiliary Territorial Service to support their 'mother country' in World War II. Another eighty served in the Women's Auxiliary Air Force. They felt that they were fighting against the more ferocious institutionalised prejudices of Nazism – despite the ironic and infuriating prejudices they faced from their own governing bodies. For example, when the British sent two hundred Caribbean servicewomen to work in Washington, DC, only white women were eligible for the assignment, so as to avoid offending the Americans.

Louisa Adair is not really based on anyone but herself, but a starting point was Lilian Bader. Bader was born in 1918, in Liverpool, England, to a West Indian father and an English mother. After both her parents died she was raised in a convent school where she stayed until the age of twenty – it took her longer than most of her peers to find work because of her colour. When Britain entered World War II she joined the NAAFI (which ran military canteens), and early in 1941 she entered the Women's Auxiliary Air Force, where she was trained as an aircraft-instrument repairer, achieving the rank of acting corporal – and she even got taken up in a Royal Air Force plane so she could see flight instruments in action. Her experience of being taunted as a Nazi by a group of evacuee children who had never seen a German, or a black person, inspired Louisa's unsettling experience on the bus to Stonehaven.

Only one Jamaican (a white man) flew in the Battle of Britain, possibly the only Caribbean man to do so, though several others, some of them black, flew British fighter aircraft later in the war. The Jamaican who fought in the Battle of Britain was Pilot Officer Herbert Capstick, nineteen years old in the summer of 1940. He was the navigator in a Bristol Blenheim aircraft. After changing squadrons later in the war, he was part of a crew who sank a U-boat in 1942.

I might not have ever paid much attention to the type of plane Herbert Capstick flew, except that a chance remark of Jamie's in *Code Name Verity* forced me to create a Blenheim squadron for *The Enigma Game*. I must have done a quick search, ten years ago, to see what kind of bombers were being flown early in the war, and assigned Jamie to Blenheims. When I began writing this book, after only a little research I soon became obsessed with these overlooked Royal Air Force light bombers.

Thousands of Bristol Blenheims were in service at the beginning of the war, fighting in both the Battle of France and the Battle of Britain; the first bombing raid against Germany was made in a Blenheim. Blenheims were the most plentiful of the RAF's aircraft as the war began, and more aircrews were lost flying them than any other type of RAF plane. As Jamie mentions, only one Blenheim pilot, Flying Officer Reginald Peacock, became an official ace by shooting down five German aircraft during the fierce air wars of 1940. I didn't make up the story of the Blenheim crew who flew all the way back to their own base after a mission, shut down the engines, and died on the runway before they were able to climb out.

There is only one Blenheim flying today, rebuilt from parts, and based at the Imperial War Museum in Duxford, England. A Canadian version of the Blenheim known as the Bolingbroke is currently being restored to 'ground-running condition' at the Canadian Warplane Heritage Museum in Hamilton, Ontario, and a few other examples survive in static museum exhibits. I spent a day checking out the Blenheim on permanent display in the RAF Museum at Hendon, London, where the docent was kind enough to remove the front cockpit escape hatch so I could stick my head up into the nose of the plane (as Jamie does when he's inspecting 648 Squadron's aircraft in the rain) and try to imagine what it might be like to fly in it. Standing next to this Blenheim's wing, with my head level with the rear gunner's turret, I found my heart aching at how *small* the plane is. It is *much* smaller than other twin-engined bombers. It is two feet shorter than a Spitfire fighter plane and only a foot taller than a Messerschmitt 109 fighter. Its crew of three must have been tightly packed. And as one Blenheim pilot put it, if you met German fighter aircraft while you were flying, you didn't come home.

But the RAF continued to use these planes well into the war, in Africa and the Far East as well as at home. As the war progressed, the armour and armament improved, and the Blenheims were often equipped with early and experimental radar. Jamie's fictional 648 Squadron is most closely based on the real 248 Squadron, who also flew out of Scotland over the North Sea in the winter of 1940–1941. In real life, 248 Squadron did indeed pick up foreign language radio transmissions which they believed to be German.

The idea of overhearing German radio transmissions leads me to 'Odysseus' and his mission. Felix Baer's landings in Scotland were inspired by two unrelated wartime incidents: the flight of Rudolf Hess made on 10/11 May 1941, and the interception of a German bomber whose crew defected to the United Kingdom on 9 May 1943. Rudolf Hess was, believe it or not, Hitler's Deputy Führer when he flew to Scotland in a Messerschmitt 110 Luftwaffe night fighter fitted with long-range fuel tanks. Hess had consulted the aircraft designer himself, Willy Messerschmitt, about modifications and training on the aircraft to enable him to make the flight. To this day, no one is really sure what Hess hoped to achieve. Theories are that he might have had key information to deliver about Germany's imminent invasion of the Soviet Union in June 1941; or he may have been invited by British Intelligence; or he may have acted as an emissary on behalf of someone else.

Whatever his motive, his aircraft was spotted by a British detection station as he approached the north-east coast of England. Spitfire fighter planes were scrambled to go after him, but no one found him in the air. Hess apparently ran out of fuel and parachuted out of his Messerschmitt, which crashed south-east of Glasgow in Scotland (the remains of his plane are on display in the Imperial War Museum in London). He was found on the ground by a local farmer, given a cup of tea, and made a prisoner by the Home Guard. He insisted he wanted to talk to the Duke of Hamilton, saying that he hoped to negotiate a peace treaty between Britain and Germany. That didn't happen. Hess doesn't seem to have acted under anyone's orders but his own; the result of his failed mission was that he spent the rest of his life in prison, successfully taking his own life in 1987 at the age of ninety-three – not his first attempt.

Obviously Felix Baer is not based on Rudolf Hess himself, although Hess's flight made me feel that Baer's was plausible. But the real inspiration for 'Odysseus' and his collaboration with British Intelligence came from an 'Individual History' report describing a German bomber, a Junkers 88, now in the Royal Air Force Museum Cosford, in England. I've known about the events leading to the capture of this aircraft for some time – at least ten years – because I used the description of the RAF interception of this Ju-88 as source material for an interception scene in *Rose Under Fire*. On 9 May 1943, this Luftwaffe plane, with its crew of three, flew from Denmark via Norway and was then escorted by a group of Spitfires into Dyce near Aberdeen (the location of my fictional Deeside). One of the German airmen in the Ju-88 had been brought along at gunpoint, unwillingly; the other two may well have been working for British Intelligence since 1940. Intriguingly, it has been suggested that the pilot, Heinrich (or Herbert) Schmitt, may have landed in the UK twice before, in February and May 1941, both times on clandestine intelligence missions.

The RAF continued to fly this captured Junkers 88 on experimental operations throughout the war, and it was a *gift* for the British and the other Allied forces because it contained an up-to-the-minute German radar set which allowed the RAF to make some key adjustments to the existing technology that hid their own bomber aircraft from enemy detection. Despite the importance of this discovery, the details of the tech are so stunningly obscure and complex that I knew I couldn't possibly use them to create a gripping read. I asked my husband to brainstorm ideas about an alternative secret for my German resistance pilot to sneak into Britain, something which could be considered equally game-changing for the war effort but a bit more exciting. He immediately suggested an Enigma machine.

I'm grateful to Mark Baldwin for his energetic and enlightening lecture on the use of the Enigma machine, and for the brief opportunity to touch those keys myself and see how the rotors work. The first Enigma machine to come into the possession of British Intelligence in wartime was captured in May 1941, not February 1941 as in this novel. I hope readers will give me a little poetic licence over this slight anachronism. The timing of *The Enigma Game* was dictated very strictly by some of the less sensational events of *Code Name Verity*; when I sat down to write, it was already 'canon' that Jamie had lost his fingers and toes to frostbite after ditching a Blenheim in the North Sea some time before March 1941. Perhaps Felix Baer's Enigma machine was kept especially secret, or got snarled in administrative red tape, as Jamie worried it might. British Intelligence did make some shocking blunders; it's not impossible.

It's increasingly the case that my novels feel collaborative rather than an individual effort, and I owe a debt of gratitude to my international team of editors: Hannah Allaman, Emily Meehan, Lynne Missen, Ellen Holgate and Lucy Mackay-Sim, particularly Hannah and Lucy, who whipped this book into shape over three intense drafts. I'm also grateful to the talented writer Catherine Johnson, who graciously made time at short notice to give a careful reading of my manuscript and share her experiences as the daughter of Jamaican and British parents. And of course I would not be the writer I am today without the continued support of my agent and dear friend Ginger Clark. The same is true of my husband, Tim Gatland, who pointed out that I needed to run the Aberdeen rail line inland around my fictional RAF Windyedge, and who accompanied me on more than one reconnaissance flight along the North Sea coast of Aberdeenshire, even indulging me in a landing at 'Deeside'.

And I want to acknowledge and remember the Blenheim airmen who inspired me and for whom my heart is eternally sore, in particular the young crew of 21 Squadron's Blenheim R3914: pilot Harry Collinge, observer Douglas Osborne and wireless operator/air gunner Albert Moore. They were all between twenty and twenty-three years of age when they lost their lives on the night of 26/27

November 1940, crashing into a hillside in the north of England on their way home from an attack on a power station in Cologne, Germany. They were off course and didn't have a working radio. Their plane was seen in flames before it hit the ground, but since they made it back to Britain they may well have been shot down by British anti-aircraft gunners, mistaking them for the enemy in the dark.

LEST WE FORGET.

Elizabeth Wein
Mt Gretna, Pennsylvania
July 2019

Further Reading

Bourne, Stephen. *The Motherland Calls: Britain's Black Servicemen & Women 1939–45*. Stroud, Gloucestershire: The History Press, 2012. It's difficult to find accessible studies on this subject, but Bourne's book contains interesting personal accounts as well as a good list of films and television documentaries about black servicemen in Britain (see pages 134–135).

Chappell, Connery. *Island of Barbed Wire: The Remarkable Story of World War Two Internment on the Isle of Man*. London: Robert Hale, 1984. This book gives a good overview of the British internment of aliens during the war.

Nesbit, Roy Conyers and Georges van Acker. *The Flight of Rudolf Hess: Myths and Reality.* Stroud, Gloucestershire: Sutton Publishing Ltd, 1999. Hess was an enigmatic character who tried, and failed, to change the course of the war in an attempt to personally broker a peace between Britain and Germany.

Panton, Alastair and Victoria Panton Bacon. *Six Weeks of Blenheim Summer: One Pilot's Extraordinary Account of the Battle of France.* London: Penguin Books, 2018 (2014). This autobiographical account of flying Bristol Blenheims in wartime is fabulously readable and very moving.

Interesting Links

'Caribbean Aircrew in the RAF during WW2' contains a record of West Indians who joined the Royal Air Force during World War II, with photographs and lists of documentaries and news stories: www.caribbeanaircrew-ww2.com

'Was the RAF Especially Receptive to Black Servicemen in World War Two?' is an edited transcript of a podcast on *Dan Snow's History Hit* entitled 'Pilots of the Caribbean with Peter Devitt,' first broadcast on 24 June 2018: https://www.historyhit.com/was-the-raf-especially-receptive-to-black-servicemen-in-world-war-two/

Stephen Bourne has written a detailed obituary for Lilian Bader (1918–2015), one of the first black women to serve in Britain's armed forces: www.voice-online.co.uk/article/obituary-war-hero-lilian-bader-1918-2015

This web page from the Battle of Britain London Monument is a tribute to Herbert Capstick, the only Jamaican to fly in the Battle of Britain: http://www.bbm.org.uk/airmen/Capstick.htm

'Disaster at Balham Tube Station' is an account of the bombing raid that flooded the London Underground on 14 October 1940, with iconic photographs of the London bus that fell into the bomb crater: http://ww2today.com/14th-october-1940-disaster-at-balham-tube-station

The Library and Archive Service on the Isle of Man provides an online guide to their collection concerning the island's role in the internment of aliens during World War II: https://manxnationalheritage.im/wp-content/uploads/2018/10/WWII-Internment-Sheet-Library-and-Archive-Service-Digital.pdf

This 'Individual History' written by Andrew Simpson is a Royal Air Force Museum document describing the interception of a Luftwaffe Junkers 88 bomber in May 1943. The aircraft described has been in the collection of the RAF Museum in Cosford since 2017 (A/C Serial No. W/NR. 360043, Section 2B): https://www.rafmuseum.org.uk/documents/collections/78-AF-953-Junkers-Ju88-R1.pdf

The Aircrew Remembered website contains an account of Heinrich (Herbert) Schmitt's defection to the UK with his Junkers 88 aircrew: http://www.aircrewremembered.com/schmid-herbert-defection.html

The only Bristol Blenheim flying today was restored by the Aircraft Restoration Company. The aircraft is currently based at the Imperial War Museum in Duxford, England: https://www.aircraftrestorationcompany.com/blenheim

The Blenheim Society website: http://blenheimsociety.com/

All links were current in September 2019.

About the Author

Elizabeth Wein was born in New York, and grew up in England, Jamaica and Pennsylvania. She is married with two children and lives in Perth, Scotland. Elizabeth is a member of the Ninety-Nines, the International Organization of Women Pilots. She was awarded the Scottish Aero Club's Watson Cup for best student pilot in 2003 and it was her love of flying that partly inspired the idea for her internationally acclaimed novel *Code Name Verity*.

Old grudges, buried secrets and rare, glimmering river pearls …
Another exciting adventure awaits!

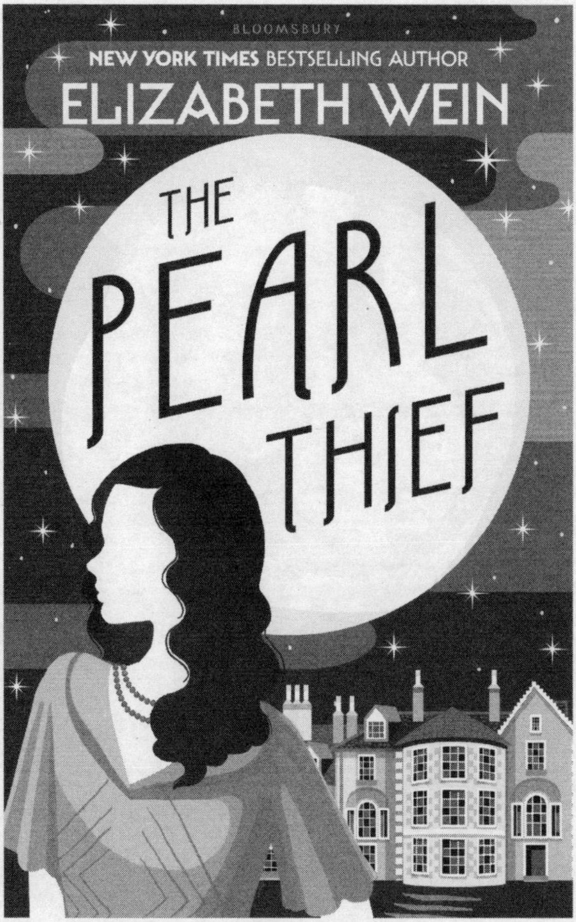

Read on for a glimpse of chapter one

AVAILABLE NOW

1

AN ASSORTMENT OF THINGS GONE MISSING

'You're a brave lassie.'

That's what my grandfather told me as he gave me his shotgun.

'Stand fast and guard me,' he instructed. 'If this fellow tries to fight, you give him another dose.'

Grandad turned back to the moaning man he'd just wounded. The villain was lying half-sunk in the mud on the edge of the riverbank, clutching his leg where a cartridgeful of lead pellets had emptied into his thigh. It was a late summer evening, my last with Grandad before I went off to boarding school for the first time, and we'd not expected to shoot anything bigger than a rabbit. But here I was aiming a shotgun at a living man while Grandad waded into the burn, which is what we called the River Fearn where it flowed through his estate, so he could tie the evildoer's hands behind his back with the strap of his shotgun.

'Rape a burn, would you!' Grandad railed at him while he worked. 'I've never seen the like! You've destroyed that shell bed completely. Two hundred river mussels round about, piled there like a midden heap! And you've not found a single pearl, have you? Because you don't know a pearl mussel from your own backside! You're like a bank robber that's never cracked a safe or seen a banknote!'

It was true – the man had torn through dozens of river mussels, methodically splitting the shells open one by one in the hope of finding a rare and beautiful Scottish river pearl. The flat rock at the edge of the riverbank was littered with the broken and dying remains.

Grandad's shotgun was almost too heavy for me to hold steady. I kept it jammed against my shoulder with increasingly aching arms. I swear by my glorious ancestors, that man was twice Grandad's size. Of course Grandad was not a very big man – none of us Murrays is very big. And he was in his seventies, even though he wasn't yet ill. The villain had a pistol – he'd dropped it when he'd been hurt, but it wasn't out of reach. Without me there to guard Grandad as he bound the other man, they might have ended up in a duel. *Brave!* I felt like William Wallace, Guardian of Scotland.

The wounded man was both pathetic and vengeful. 'I'll see you in Sheriff Court,' he told my grandfather, whining and groaning. 'I'm not after salmon and there's no law against pearl fishing, but it's illegal to shoot a man.'

Grandad wasn't scared. 'This is a private river.'

'Those tinker folk take pearls here all the time. They come in their tents and bide a week like gypsies, and go away with their pockets full!'

'No tinker I know would ever rape a burn like this! And they've the decency to ask permission on my private land! There's laws and laws. Respect for a river and its creatures goes unwritten. And the written law says that I can haul you in for poaching on my beat, whether it's salmon or pearls or anything else.'

'I didn't – I wasnae –'

'Whisht. Never mind what you were doing in the water: you pointed your own gun at my wee granddaughter.' Grandad now confiscated the pistol that was lying in the mud, and tucked it into his willow-weave fisherman's creel. 'That's excuse enough for me. I'm the Earl of Strathfearn. Whose word will the law take, laddie, yours or mine?'

Grandad owned all of Strathfearn then, and the salmon and trout fishing rights that went with it. It was a perfect little Scottish estate, with a ruined castle and a baronial manor, nestled in woodland just where the River Fearn meets the River Tay. It's true it's not illegal for anyone to fish for pearls there, but it's still private land. You can't just wade in and destroy someone else's river. I remember how shocking Grandad's accusation sounded: *Rape a burn, would you!*

Was that only three years ago? It feels like Grandad was ill for twice that long. And now he's been dead for months. And the estate was sold and changed hands even while my poor grandmother was still living in it. Grandad was so *alive* then. We'd worked together.

'Steady, lass,' he'd said, seeing my arms trembling. I held on while Grandad dragged the unfortunate mussel-bed destroyer to his feet and helped him out of the burn and on to the riverbank, trailing forget-me-nots and muck and blood. I flinched out of his way in distaste.

He'd aimed a pistol at me earlier. I'd been ahead of Grandad on the river path and the strange man had snarled at me, '*One step closer and you're asking for trouble.*' I'd hesitated, not wanting to turn my back on his gun. But Grandad had taken the law into his own hands and fired first.

Now, as the bound, bleeding prisoner struggled past me so he could pull himself over to the flat rock and rest amid the broken mussel shells, our eyes met for a moment in mutual hatred. I wondered if he really would have shot at me.

'Now see here,' Grandad lectured him, getting out his hip flask and allowing the wounded man to take a taste of the Water of Life. 'See the chimneys rising above the birches at the river's bend? That's the County Council's old library on Inverfearnie Island, and there's a telephone there. You and I are going to wait here while the lassie goes to ring the police.' He turned to me. 'Julie, tell them to send the Water Bailiff out here. He's the one to deal with a poacher. And then I want you to stay there with the librarian until I come and fetch you. Her name is Mary Kinnaird.'

I gave an internal sigh of relief – not a visible one, because being called 'brave' by my grandad was the highest praise I'd ever aspired to, but relief nevertheless. Ringing the police from the Inverfearnie Library was a mission I felt much more capable of completing than shooting a trespasser. I gave Grandad back his shotgun ceremoniously. Then I sprinted for the library, stung by nettles on the river path and streaking my shins with mud. I skidded over the mossy stones on the humpbacked bridge that connects Inverfearnie Island to the east bank of the Fearn, and came to a breathless halt before the stout oak door of the seventeenth-century library building, churning up the gravel of the drive with my canvas shoes as if I were the messenger at the Battle of Marathon.

It was past six and the library was closed. I knew that Mary Kinnaird, the new librarian and custodian who lived there all alone, had only just finished university, but I'd never met her, and it certainly never occurred to me that she wouldn't be able to hear the bell. When nobody came, not even after I gave a series of pounding kicks to the door, I decided the situation was desperate enough to warrant breaking in and climbing through a window. They were casement windows that opened outward – if I broke a pane near a latch it would be easy to get in. I snatched up a handful of stones from the gravel drive and hurled them hard at one of the leaded windowpanes nearest the ground. The glass smashed explosively, and I could hear the rocks hitting the floor inside like hailstones.

That brought the young librarian running with a shotgun of her own. She threw open the door.

She was bold as a crow. I stared at her openly, not because of the flat, skewed features of her face, but because she was aiming at my head. The library window I'd smashed was public property.

Nothing for it but to plunge in. 'Miss Kinnaird?' I panted, out of breath after my marathon. 'My grandad has caught a poacher and I – I need to use your telephone – to ring the police.'

Her smooth, broad brow crinkled into the tiniest of irritated frowns. She'd sensed the importance of what I'd said, but she hadn't heard all of it. Now she lowered her gun and I could see that around her neck hung two items essential to her work: a gold mechanical pencil on a slender rope of braided silk, and a peculiar curled brass horn, about the size of a fist, on a thick gold chain. She'd lowered the gun so she could hold the beautiful horn to her ear.

'Your grandad needs help?' she said tartly. 'Speak up, please.'

'STRATHFEARN HAS CAUGHT A THIEF AND I NEED TO USE YOUR TELEPHONE,' I bellowed into the ear trumpet.

The poor astonished young woman gasped. 'Oh! Strathfearn is your grandfather?'

'Aye, Sandy Murray, Earl of Strathfearn,' I said with pride.

'Well, you'd better come in,' she told me briskly. 'I'll ring the police for you.'

I wondered how she managed the telephone if she couldn't hear, but I didn't dare to ask.

'Grandad said to send Sergeant Angus Henderson,' I said. 'He's the Water Bailiff for the Strathfearn Estate. He polices the riverbank.'

'Oh, aye, I know Angus Henderson.'

She shepherded me past the wood and glass display cases on the ground floor and into her study. But I poked my head around the door to watch her sitting at the telephone in its dark little nook of a cupboard under the winding stairs. I listened as she asked the switchboard operator to put her through to the police station in the village at Brig O'Fearn. There was a sort of Bakelite ear trumpet attached to the telephone receiver. So that answered my question.

I went and sat down in the big red leather reading chair in Mary Kinnaird's study, feeling rather stunned and exhausted, and after a few minutes she came in with a tray of tea and shortbread.

'I expect Grandad will pay for your window,' I told her straight away. I assumed his wealth was limitless, three years ago. I hoped he wouldn't be angry, and I wondered how he was getting on, waiting alone with the vicious and miserable prisoner. 'I'm very sorry I had to break the glass.'

'And I am very sorry I pointed my gun at you.' Mary knelt on the floor beside me, there being no other chair but the one behind her desk.

She offered the shortbread. I found I was ravenous.

'Oh, I knew you wouldn't hurt me,' I told her. 'You are too bonny.'

'You wee sook!' she scolded. 'Bonny?'

'Not beautiful,' I told her truthfully. 'Your face is kind. You're sort of fluttery and quiet, like a pigeon.'

She threw her head back and laughed.

'*Prrrrt*,' she said in pigeon-talk, and this made me laugh too. Suddenly I liked her very much.

'What's your name?' she asked me.

'Lady Julia Lindsay MacKenzie Wallace Beaufort-Stuart,' I reeled off glibly.

'Oh my, that is quite a name. Must I call you Lady Julia?'

'Grandad calls me Julie.'

'I will compromise with Julia. Beaufort and Stuart are both the names of Scottish queens; I can't quite lower myself to Julie.' She smiled serenely. 'Not Murray? Isn't that your grandfather's name?'

'Some of my brothers have Murray as a family name.'

'You know the Murrays were in favour with Mary Stuart. There's a bracelet on display in the library that belonged to her when she was a child. She gave it to your grandfather's people because she was their patron, four hundred years ago.'

'Scottish river pearls – I know! Grandad showed me when I was little. They're the only thing I remember about the display cases. All those dull old books along with this beautiful wee bracelet that belonged to Mary Queen of Scots! And I'm related to her on the Stuart side.'

Mary laughed. 'Those books are first editions of Robert Burns's poems! I don't find them dull. But the pearls are everybody's favourite.'

My hidden criminal inner self noted what an idiot the wounded trespasser was, stripping young mussels from the river when this perfect treasure lay in plain sight of the general public every day.

But perhaps the river seemed easier prey than Mary Kinnaird.

She said to me then, 'So I'm a Mary and you're a Stuart. And I have the keys to the case. Would you like to try on Mary Queen of Scots' pearl bracelet while you wait for your grandad to come back for you?'

Mary Kinnaird suddenly became my favourite person in the entire world.

I noticed something. 'How can you hear me without your trumpet?'

'I'm watching your mouth move. It helps a great deal to see your mouth straight on. I don't like the trumpet much.'

'The trumpet is *splendid*.'

She twisted her mouth again. It wasn't a smile. 'But the trumpet makes me different from everyone else. And I am already a bit different.'

'No one's *exactly* alike,' I said blithely. 'I can find my mother in a candlelit hall full of dancers by the scent she wears. Everybody's different.'

It was very easy for me to say, flush with the fear and triumph of my last summer afternoon with my grandfather, the Earl of Strathfearn. I was safe now, eating shortbread in the Inverfearnie Library, and looking forward to trying on pearls that had once been worn by Mary Queen of Scots. *Everybody's different*: it was easy for me to say.